gardens 16.95/1131

D0438321

F LOF
Lofts, Norah
Pargeters

16.95

DATE DUE		
FE 13 '86		
FE 24 '86		
MR 6 '86		
MR 27 '86		
AP 21 '86		
SE 26 '89		
OC 14 '89		
JAN 1 9 1990		

PARGETERS

By the same author:

PARGETERS
NORAH LOFTS

DOUBLEDAY & COMPANY, INC.
GARDEN CITY, NEW YORK
1986

Library of Congress Cataloging in Publication Data
Lofts, Norah, 1904–
    Pargeters.
      1. Great Britain—History—Civil War, 1642–1649—
Fiction. I. Title.
PR6023.O35P37 1986   823'.912   85-12904
ISBN 0-385-19400-5

First published 1984 by Hodder & Stoughton,
London, Sydney, Auckland, Toronto
Printed in the United States of America

First American Edition

PART ONE

Narrated by Adam Woodley

Pargeting is hard work, very different from just slapping on plaster; and my own, self-chosen method made it harder still. However, though I might sweat even on a coolish day and cursed more often than I whistled I loved my work and wouldn't have changed jobs with any man in the world.

On this day of Michaelmas in the year 1624 I was about to begin a special task for which I had been preparing for some time.

It was already warm when I reared my ladder over the front door of John Mercer's new house. It was an ordinary ladder, except that it had hooks protruding from its sides near the top. In an outhouse I had a barrel of plaster well mixed and well ripened. It was the very best plaster – made by me. There was the basic ground limestone and for colouring I had not relied upon a vegetable dye which might fade. The pinkness of my plaster came from finely pounded bricks. For stiffening I had used the very best oxhair. There are substitutes: many plasterers use horsehair but it does not weather so well. John Mercer had not grudged expense and I had spared no labour.

When I began my work on this house the barrel had been full, now it was seven-eighths empty and I had to lean low to scoop out what I needed. I carried that bucket and one of water from the well and taking them up, one at a time, hooked them into place on the ladder. I then went down and opened my tool bag which contained the mould which I intended to use that morning. I knew it so well, having made it myself, putting into it an infinite amount of care and all the skill I possessed, yet I stood there in the early light and stared with as much enchantment as though I were seeing it for the first time. It was beautiful; and I had made it. At such moments I always thought I understood how God felt when He looked upon what He had created and saw that it was good.

Such a thought may smack of blasphemy; but there is so

7

much about the Bible which is mysterious and contradictory that to find something so easily understood is a pleasure.

I took out the flask of oil and a tiny brush and applied a light coating of oil to the whole inner surface, missing not the most minute crevice. I then replaced the mould in my basket and with it mounted the ladder again.

The space of wall left to cover this morning was not extensive, just a square immediately above the door. The walls of the new house had been plastered some time ago in the ordinary way and before I could begin applying my layer I had to use my knife to score the surface to give a better hold. I brushed the area with water. Then I took a handful of the pink, stodgy stuff and applied it roughly before working it well on with the small, flattish trowel. This process had to be repeated again and again, because I took care always to make my layers overlap, for even a hair line weakness can render a whole section vulnerable to frost and rain.

When the whole surface was covered, smooth as satin to the eye, I took out my mould and pressed it home.

The ancient man to whom I had been apprenticed had once told me that in the old days – by which he meant in the reign of Queen Mary – it was the custom to hold a mould in place while one said five Paternosters without haste. He had said, rather regretfully, "Now all is done by numbers," adding hastily, "Better so." It would never do to be suspected of hankering back to Tudor times, or of harbouring Catholic sympathies. Someone had worked out that a Paternoster said without haste was the equivalent of a count of thirty; so now I held the square of oak in place and counted a hundred and fifty. Then I prised it off.

It would be wrong to say that I had rendered Anne Borley immortal, but well-made plaster, properly applied, is pretty durable stuff and as long as John Mercer's house stood, there she would be, lovely and young. She and I would both age, and one day die; we should be forgotten. Or at least . . . Well, I did entertain the thought that perhaps when my son was old enough to understand I'd bring him

8

here and say: Look, that is your mother as she was when I first knew her. And perhaps he would tell his son.

I was rather old for such sweetheart thoughts; old indeed for first love, being a full thirty. I'd always felt a rather contemptuous pity for fellows who fell in love, saved their pennies, got married and ended up with a woman, too fat or too thin, and a houseful of hungry children.

I'd thoroughly enjoyed my bachelor life. Because I was so sound a craftsman and had acquired a reputation, I earned good money. While my mother lived I'd kept her in comfort. Since her death I'd been a lodger, sometimes in private houses, sometimes in inns. I could afford good clothes. I was singularly free to move about, for the Poor Law rules which nail men, especially married men with children, down to a certain parish, did not apply to a man alone with a well-paying craft in his hand.

Then I'd come to Minsham, seen Anne Borley and lost both my heart and my head. Maybe love, like measles, hits harder at the not-so-young.

I slid the mould back into my tool basket. That was too large to allow both handles to be grasped, so it sagged. I was descending the ladder when John Mercer rode up on his fine grey horse.

He was not a Suffolk man – he didn't even look like one. He was a Londoner who'd made his money dealing in woollen cloth and silk. He was already an Alderman and bade fair to be Lord Mayor but one of his daughters had married a Fennel of Ockley and he had come to visit her and fallen in love with the whole countryside. Since no suitable house was for sale at the time, he decided to build.

"Morning, Adam," he called. "How's the work?"

"I've just finished, sir."

I slithered down the last rungs and moved the ladder to give him a clear view.

"It's different," he said at last. "But I like it. In fact it's beautiful. Has it any significance?"

Even to his kindly eye I did not intend to expose my partiality. I had set Anne's head in an oval wreath of flowers and leaves.

"More mythical," I said. "You could call it the Spirit of Spring. But after all, sir, you did ask for the signs of the Zodiac."

"Ah. Virgo." He gave me a sharp look. "Well-disguised, I'm thankful to say. I'm glad you didn't give her a halo."

"Difficult to carve, sir. In relief, and in the one colour, a halo would look just like a hoop."

"You look warm, my boy. Come in and take a mug of ale."

He dismounted, nimble despite his bulk, and opened the front door. I had been in the house before and had drunk ale with him on previous occasions, but I had never before seen the interior of the front of the house. I liked it; spacious without being overwhelming, grand enough but with an eye to comfort. The square hall was well lighted, a window on each side of the door, a solid staircase rising on the opposite side, turning at a half landing and rising again. In the time that I was working on the real signs of the Zodiac I'd seen wagons arrive, laden with boxes and bundles and furniture muffled in sacking. Now I could see, through an open door to the left, things standing in disorder on the dark rich carpet.

"My other daughter and the servants will be here next week. Women prefer to do their own arranging."

He led the way to a corridor beyond the stairs, past other doors and into the kitchen with which I was familiar, for it was here, using a carpenter's bench as table, that I had made the preliminary sketches to his dictation after he had rejected all the moulds I had in stock, saying that he wanted something completely original.

He now bounced into the buttery and came back with two brimming mugs. He handed one to me and sat on a settle to one side of the hearth. I stood. He was invariably informal to the point of friendliness, but I was careful never to put a foot over the line.

"Sit, man. I shall get a crick in my neck trying to talk to you. How tall *are* you?"

"Exactly six foot, sir." I took the opposite settle.

"How enviable! Clothes, especially robes, look so much

better on a tall man. Well, have you another job in mind?"

"Two, sir. One I start tomorrow."

"Mark this," he said, with a change of manner. "You're not to use my moulds on another house. I wanted something unique and that is how I wish it to be. In fact I want those moulds destroyed."

I privately decided that nothing, nothing would make me destroy that of Anne.

I said, "You are well within your rights. You paid for the oak, and for my time. But, sir, suppose some other employer hit upon the same notion and asked for the Zodiac signs."

"Then you say they are outside your range." To that I did not reply, except to raise my eyebrows. "Well then, give them what they ask for, but do it *differently*. I want my house . . . And that reminds me. You're local aren't you?"

"I was born in Clevely, went to school in Baildon, served my apprenticeship in Nettleton. I've worked further afield, of course. But yes, sir, I think I am local."

"Then would you know anything about this land I've bought? Something, a story, a legend. Something I could use as a name for a house. I don't want Hall. Or Manor. Or Grange – too many of them around here. There again, I want something different."

I could think of nothing. The land he had acquired, roughly three hundred acres, lying half in Minsham St Mary and half in Muchanger, was not very profitable; it had frequently changed owners or tenants, and had been farmed off. Once it had been a sheep-run. I had a feeling that Sheep Run House or Sheep House wouldn't please him much. I couldn't see why he couldn't call it Hall; Minsham, unlike most villages, didn't have one. I wished I could suggest something apt and pleasing, for I liked him, he'd been easy to work for, appreciative, and the fact that he sat there opposite me, drinking, proved that he himself was different. Most employers – except the known mean ones – would give a man a drink at the end of a job, but no other I had ever encountered would sit in a kitchen and drink with him.

At last I said, "All I can think of, sir, is that your land embraces bits of two parishes, and boundaries used to be marked by a stone. Boundary House? Stone House?"

"Stone would be misleading. Boundary I don't much like. Too impersonal."

I had finished my beer. I had interests elsewhere. I must be on the move. I said rashly, "Zodiac House would be quite unusual. And very personal."

"Zodiac. Yes I like that. Zodiac House." He tasted it and brooded and then said, "No! Difficult to spell! But you had the right idea. Parget House. Better still, just Pargeters – like Mortiboys. That's it. Couldn't be better. Pargeters. How does that sound to you?"

"Very well indeed, sir." Inside myself I felt flattered. And I could imagine myself telling Anne that her portrait in plaster had so impressed Mr Mercer that he'd named his house Pargeters. How she would laugh. For if ever a woman held the gift of beauty lightly it was Anne Borley.

I'd lodged with the Borleys at Crowswood Farm ever since I started working on John Mercer's house. I'd thought myself very lucky, for the food on farms where it is produced is generally good or at least better than in places where it has to be bought. And the meal-times fitted working hours.

That morning Arthur and Mary Borley, their son Will, Anne and I had sat down to a sustaining meal of eggs and bacon and ale, with Mrs Borley's incomparable bread, and the supper dish, steak and kidney pudding, was already simmering in the black pot hooked over the fire.

Now, coming back soon after midday, I expected to see Arthur and Will at work in the field known as Twelveacre; one ploughing, one broadcasting the seed of winter wheat and kicking the ridges down.

There was no sign of such activity. Work had, I saw, stopped in mid-furrow; the horse had simply dragged the plough over the surface until he could reach the grass at the verge and stood there, placidly munching.

I thought: Arthur Borley has had his often predicted fit.

He was a choleric man. He did not get along with his son. He was fond of saying that this or that would give him a fit. Also he was a man of habit, donning his thick flannel shirt on the first of September however hot and taking to his linen one on the first of June, however cold. This was a very warm day. I thought I could see it all; father chiding son, son giving a saucy answer and – the fit.

Nonetheless, I began to run.

The house was very quiet. Nobody in the kitchen and the fire dead. Unprecedented. So was the table, the breakfast things still uncleared.

I wanted to shout, but something restrained me. I even found myself moving more quietly than usual as I went through the parlour and up the stairs. At the top I was separated from Anne's door only by the width of the small landing, and the door stood open. I could see the foot of the bed and Mr Borley standing there with tears on his furrowed brown face.

Two strides took me into the room. Anne lay on the bed, her face whiter than the pillow, for that was dark with spilled water. Her eyes were closed and she looked dead. Mrs Borley perched on the side of the bed, grey-faced but calm. In one hand she held a wet cloth, in the other a flask of grated hartshorn; a bucket of well-water stood beside her and on the floor lay a bunch of half-burnt feathers.

Something had a stranglehold on my throat; it took a great effort to croak, "What happened?" Mrs Borley didn't even look in my direction. Anne's father said, "The cow. The bloody, bloody cow."

"Is she – dead?"

This time Mrs Borley answered. "Still breathing. And Will's gone for the doctor." She then put her face close to Anne's and said, "Dearie. Wake up. Answer me. Answer me!" There was no response and after a bit she looked at me and said, "You try."

I went down on my knees, took one limp hand and spoke with urgency, calling her name; saying Sweetheart, saying Darling, saying my own name. Nothing, not even the flutter of an eyelid, answered me.

Mr Borley said suddenly, quite loudly, "I did warn her. More'n once. I said a cow with a new calf could be bad as a bull." He leaned against the bedpost and shed some more silent tears.

"And not a mark on her," Mrs Borley said. "Just knocked flat."

"Her head?" I asked, thinking of the thickness of the bright hair.

"Not even the smallest bump."

I remembered, against my will, a mason who had fallen from a roof. Of him it might have been said that he had no visible injury, but he was soon dead of some inward hurt.

"When did it happen?"

"You'd only just gone," Mr Borley said. "Will and me'd done one furrow. Then as we turned at the headland I see it happen. I bellowed. Will jumped the fence and drove the beast off afore it could do more damage . . . And later we didn't waste time neither. When she didn't come to in the kitchen I knew 'twarn't jest a faint. I sent Will off . . . And Jamie's a good horse. He went through Layer. He should be back."

Almost immediately there came the clatter of hooves in the cobbled yard; then feet on the stairs. Will Borley, flushed and sweaty with hard riding, came up the stairs alone. Before he could speak his father said with a ghost of the animosity he often showed towards his son, "And where's the doctor? I towd you to bring . . ."

"He's dead. They've got the plague in Baildon."

"The midwife'd hev been better than nothing."

"I thought of that! She'd got a case. Baby half born."

"Then one of *us*," Mr Borley said; and even before he took out his knife I knew what he meant and felt sick. Failing the doctor and the midwife who knew about such things, one of us must try what a little blood-letting would do.

I'd seen it work when heavy, full-blooded men suffered the kind of fit Mr Borley so often predicted for himself. I had also seen a leech – which operates on the same principle – suck away a raging headache. But would it work on a girl, so delicate? A girl who already looked so drained, as though her blood had all seeped away from some invisible wound.

We stood like people in a trance until Mr Borley moved to breathe on his knife and rub it on his shirt sleeve. Having done that he extended the thing to me, handle first.

"Thass for you to do. You're betrothed. In two months' time you'd have been one flesh."

On the fringe of my mind I remembered how bitterly he had opposed me as a suitor, deriding me as a man without money, or house, or acre. But at the centre of my mind flared the knowledge that I couldn't do it. Gladly, oh how gladly I would have plunged the knife into my own flesh if it would have restored her, brought her sitting up in bed and laughing at our grave faces.

"I can't," I said.

Mr Borley made a noise expressive of total disgust. "I always knew you were a gutless fool!"

I tried to defend myself. "I don't know where the incision should be made. I should do more harm than good."

"When my father took his fit he was bled from the heel."

"And died," Mrs Borley said. Her husband glared at her. His tears had ceased.

I said, "And Anne is not an angry old man in a fit. She's a girl who has had an accident."

Opposition merely strengthened his purpose. He shifted his hold on the knife and said, "You two get out. Mother, uncover her feet."

I was glad to go. It was not an operation I wished to watch. But I should have stayed within reach, hoping to be told that it was successful, had not a voice said to me as I followed Will down the stairs: Mother Nelly. And quick! I accepted the order with relief.

Will Borley said, "The other cow ain't even been milked yet. I better see to her." He half turned to me. "Dad did warn Anne, you know. Don't go in the pasture, he said: open the gate and call Daisy, he said, and milk her in the byre. If she'd done as she was told . . ." I did not think that he was heartless. I realised that he was trying to ease his own hurt. I muttered something about needing air and wrenched open the seldom used front door. Then I began to run towards Layer Wood.

About Mother Nelly people whispered, saying that she was a witch. But they say that of almost any woman who has outlived her family and her own generation and seeks the company of animals rather than people. Nobody had ever, so far as I knew, had a cast-iron story about any harm Mother Nelly had done to anyone. Had they done she would have had short shrift, for the laws against witches and warlocks had been greatly strengthened since James Stuart came to the throne. To the contrary, Mother Nelly was credited with some marvellous cures – all, she said, worked by herbal remedies. I knew her only by repute, but I knew where she lived.

We tend to associate witchcraft with darkness and a certain amount of squalor, but Mother Nelly's little house was neat, even pretty; freshly whitewashed, trimly thatched. It stood in a clearing, part of which was a garden, gay still with marigolds and a blue flower which I did not recognise. I had time to take note of such things because I had run so hard that I was out of breath and paused at the edge of the clearing to recover enough to make speech possible. At this time of day the sun poured into the clearing; a yellow cat lay basking on the windowsill and from somewhere behind the cottage I could hear the contented clucking of hens. People who spoke badly of her often asked what she lived on if the Devil didn't support her. One visit would have informed them. Behind the flowers which bordered the path stood rows of vegetables, cabbages, onions, beans – the pods yellowing, almost ready for winter storage. An apple tree, laden with scarlet fruit, stood to one side, and there were other trees.

I had my hand raised to knock when a voice, not that of an old woman, called, "Come in." I pressed the latch and opened the door and had a first small jolt. Mother Nelly said, "Ah. Adam Woodley."

"You know me?"

"As you know me."

"I want you to come. To Crowswood in Muchanger. There's been an accident."

"I know."

"How could you? It only happened this morning. Oh, never mind that. Just come. Please come."

"My going there would do no good. You yourself could carry a cure."

Yet I was sure that in the tales I had heard of her cures, she'd been there, smuggled in, smuggled out, but *there*. Oh yes, I recalled one. She'd cured a child dying of croup by scattering a potion into a saucepan of water and setting it to boil.

All this time without really looking, I had been noticing. She was very small, shrivelled with age. Much wrinkled, yet her skin looked soft, softly pink. Eyes the colour of a flax flower. For the rest, a dark gown, white apron, little white cap with some lace about it, set on tidy silvery hair. Anybody's great-grandmother. Yet there was something not pleasant, despite the delicate pink skin and the blue eyes. A mockery.

I said, "Of course I could carry . . . carry you if you don't feel up to walking. Will you come?" Suddenly I understood. Money! "Look, I haven't much. Only two weeks' pay, but I'll pay forever if you'll only . . ."

"And Arthur Borley is rich, is he not? Also he dotes on the girl. But I have never yet taken money." She actually laughed a little. "Besides, were I willing, I *dare* not. Somebody always talks and I am already maligned enough. Things have reached such a pitch that people can no longer distinguish good from evil. I have retired."

"We're wasting time," I said. "Wrap yourself in a shawl and I'll carry you as though you were a baby. And I vow nobody will talk."

In my desperation I seized her arm, thin as a stick, and heaved her to her feet. "Come, you must come. You shall."

Now that she was standing I observed that her right foot was bandaged. "I'll carry you," I repeated, and looked about for something in which to wrap her. It was there to hand, a grey shawl, neatly folded on top of a chest. Without releasing my hold on her arm, I reached out and grabbed it, shook it out, one-handedly, and draped it over her head. She made no resistance and said nothing even when I lifted her. She must have weighed under five stone; no burden for a man like me. I fumbled the door open and was out on the step. Then suddenly she stiffened in my arms and tried to push me away with surprising force.

"It would be a wasted errand. The girl is dead."

I lost all strength. My grip went slack and I let her fall on to the stone slab that made the doorstep. She did not cry out or give any sign of being hurt. Had she done so, I *hope* that I should have mustered decency enough to help her back into the house. The yellow cat jumped down and began to rub against its mistress. She fondled it and spoke softly to it. I just stood, absorbing the shock of the blow. I never doubted the truth of the dreadful words. Then Mother Nelly looked from the cat to me and said, with the utmost venom: "You will regret this." I turned and stumbled away.

Dwelling on grief does no good. Death had taken the only woman I had ever loved – or was likely to love; and there was no more to be said.

Work helped, so did brandy and I made free with both. I was spared well-meaning words and looks of sympathy, for outside Crowswood nobody knew that Anne and I were betrothed. Mr Borley had said, "Time enough to spread news when the banns are asked." He was then stubbornly hoping that she would change her mind.

Presently there was one last thing I could do for my love and that was to make her headstone unique. It would ordinarily have been of the same stone as Mother Nelly's doorstep, and carved by a mason. I offered to make it beautiful and Mr Borley, still broken by his loss, agreed. In fact, now that he need no longer accept me as a son-in-law, his attitude towards me had changed completely. He tended to cling; but I remembered how he had derided me and made meetings difficult in the early days, how gladly he would have booted me out except for the fact that he was avaricious and liked the money I paid for bed and board. So I was brusque with him. I was sorry for Mrs Borley – but she had her son, always her favourite, and Will had found a sweetheart.

When I left Muchanger on the day of the catastrophe I had left behind all the Zodiac moulds but that of Anne I carried with me and kept though I looked at it seldom for to look hurt, by reminding me, and I wished beyond all things to forget. I had yet to learn that there is no forgetting this side of the grave.

Now, on a fair April day, in Muchanger churchyard, I was using that mould again. This time the plaster was white, even the ox-hairs which bound it were white. I intended to work in two stages and when the upper half was well coated I pressed home the mould, counted and withdrew it. I looked once to see that the impression was good and then no more. It was too painful.

The second part of the work called for speed, since plaster does not remain workable long once it is spread. Just her name, the year of her birth, the year of her death and the Latin for Rest in Peace. Using Latin again made me think of a past with which Anne had nothing to do. My mother had gone to extraordinary pains to ensure that I had rather more than the minimum of education, but by the time I was fourteen I realised what a burden she was bearing and had gone out into the world ready to apprentice myself to anybody who did not demand a premium. The only man willing to accept me for nothing was the old pargeter at Nettleton. And so I had eventually gone to work on Mr Mercer's house at Minsham, and lodged at Crowswood, and met Anne . . .

In such circles the mind runs in times of distress.

I rose, gathered my tools and went away, leaving behind me a tombstone that gleamed white like marble. And my love under it.

The biggest and most prosperous hostelry in Baildon was The Hawk in Hand about which people said jokingly that whoever or whatever you were looking for you had only to sit on a bench in its forecourt and wait. It was a remarkable place because it catered for all conditions of men, despising none. Its forepart was rather grand, with parlours, some for private hire, a dining-room for gentlefolk, a larger one for farmers and the better class of trade and craftsmen. Then, towards the rear it declined, though never into actual squalor. There was accommodation for servants, grooms, coachmen, drovers. There was even a loft where a man without money could lie warm in the straw without paying anything. But to do that he must pass the scrutiny of the yard overseer, in my time a man called Job Handy, who must be satisfied that the penniless one was employable, not a regular beggar. Such a policy paid off, for an employer, finding what he wanted amongst Job's Jobless as they were called, would be pleased, go in and buy himself wine, or a meal, see that his new servant had ale and bread and cheese. The service went even further. Job might say: "Sir, your new man is ill-shod. I happen to have . . ." and from a secret repository bring out a pair of shoes or half-boots, never new, but soundly cobbled and roughly the right size. Cheap, of course.

Some men remembered such favours. I knew at least three men of substance in Baildon who boasted that they had slept in the straw at The Hawk and were now amongst its most regular customers.

I had slept at the inn when I left Crowswood in the autumn. Not, of course, in the straw but in a long, low room not unlike a school dormitory. After that I had worked on winter, indoor jobs as far afield as Colchester and Bywater. I had come back to do Anne the last service in my power, and in the morning I was setting out for Diss where a job awaited me.

That evening I went round to the rear and into the snug little taproom. I saw and spoke to Job who had the ability to be in three places at the same time, and who never forgot a face. In the taproom beer was served, but when, almost in a whisper, I asked for brandy, The Hawk lived up to its reputation and the barman simply nodded. "In a mug," I said.

"You mean a mugful?"

"Not quite. Half will do." Like so many things in this place, it came from a hidden source; pipes, however, were openly displayed, cheap white clay ones, a halfpenny each. A fill of tobacco cost twopence. Our King, James Stuart loathed tobacco, had even written a tract against smoking, but more and more people were falling into the habit. It was said to be soothing. I decided to try it. With a Lethe-like drink in one hand, a soothing pipe in the other, I went and sat on a bench near a table around which several men were gathered. Almost at once my attention was arrested. Somebody said, "What about Old Mother Nelly?"

He and those in agreement with him were accusing her – in retrospect – not merely of witchcraft, but of being a were-fox. I listened to the story . . .

It had all happened last autumn. A man out Minsham way had on several occasions been robbed of a hen. So he'd made a shed, with a roost inside it and a bolt on its door. Into this he coaxed his fowls at sun-down. He had, however, had further losses and had ceased to blame foxes, for what fox ever born could draw a bolt, or would close and re-bolt the door? So on the next night of full moon he'd sat up, fowling-piece in hand. And sure enough a fox appeared and sniffed around. The man had fired and caught the animal fair and square in the hind leg. It had let out a howl and limped away.

Three or four days later another man, walking a couple of hounds in Layer Wood, noticed the dogs, not at heel but chasing off on some errand of their own. And so he'd come upon Mother Nelly, dead on her own doorstep with her right leg bandaged. Didn't that just go to prove?

So far he had held his audience spell-bound. Ale had remained in mugs, pipes had gone dead. These things were now attended to and then the dissenter, of whom there is always one in any company, said:

"Well, what do it prove? I mean I can't see the *connection*."

"Plain as the nose on your face. She could change herself; woman into fox, fox into woman."

"Now that I might believe," said the dissenter, "if he

21

hadn't bin so hasty and let fly. I mean if he'd *seen* the change. But he never. So I still don't see."

"Me neither. Lotsa old women hev bad feet or bad legs. Lotsa old women die sudden. And bear in mind what the Coroner said. Natural causes."

"No he never. Starved to death he said. You can't call starving a natural cause."

Up popped the inevitable jokester,

"Things go on like this, taxes and all, we'll soon all be dead of that same natural cause."

There was some wry laughter and the talk digressed.

To the inexperienced it may sound strange but Mother Nelly had played no part in my memory. I'd gone blundering back to Crowswood and after that there'd been the blur of sheer misery.

Now I thought.

The old woman had greeted me by my name.

She'd known about Anne's accident.

She'd refused to come with me, saying she dare not, she was maligned enough already and had retired.

Then I'd picked her up and dropped her.

Had she huddled there, unable to get up? And starved and died?

Was I responsible for her death?

Then, with a jerk, I remembered how she had said something I had totally forgotten until now. "You will regret this." Perhaps such words spoken by that old woman might be regarded as a curse, but the thought raised no quiver in me. What could happen worse than had already happened? All the same, I knew that what with the tombstone and now this conversation, I was in for a sleepless night, unless I took action. I took it and climbed the stairs to the dormitory room with another good half-mug of brandy. As a result, for the first time in my life I overslept. Not that that worried me. When you can do something better than most others can, you can choose your time and people will wait.

I rose, a trifle shakily, went down to the yard and held my head under the pump. Back in the communal room I shaved before a slip of looking glass the size of a book page and was not pleased with what I saw. I made, not for the first time, some resolutions about moderating my drinking. A swift plunge into dreamless sleep was greatly to be desired, but it had to be paid for. Unless I were careful that slight morning shakiness could become permanent, and then how should I carve my moulds?

I was not the only one critical of my appearance. Job Handy's hooded eyes missed little. He must have been lying in wait for me, for when I stepped into the yard again, ready to go, he said, "I don't think much of that shirt."

"Nor do I, to be honest." It was the best of my three, but greyish from slovenly washing and clumsily mended. Hands as skilful as mine were at carving should have managed a needle well, but did not.

"I got a better one. Cost you sixpence." Justifying the price of a secondhand garment, he added, "Silk, with frills."

I waited while he produced it. Not a working man's garment at all. Job, mistaking my admiration for hesitancy, said in a coaxing voice, "Like to try it on?" I stepped back into the lobby and made the change. My old shirt looked even worse by comparison so I discarded it completely, giving it to Job with the sixpence. Some man with no shirt at all would give a halfpenny for it.

I bade Job goodbye and he said, "I expect you'll be back."

No need to explain that I intended never to return. Diss was on the border of Norfolk, from there I intended to go to Norwich, a great and growing city. And there was Lynn, a flourishing port.

I'd reached the forecourt when two riders turned in. Mr Mercer, more rotund than ever, and a young lady in a russet velvet riding-habit.

He recognised me, checked his horse and greeted me with great friendliness. "Adam Woodley! And how fares the world with you?"

"Very well, sir," I said, thinking how badly it had gone since I saw him last.

"Good. Good. Penelope, my dear, this is Adam Woodley,

who did the pargeting which is so much admired. And incidentally helped me to name the house."

She acknowledged me with a slight inclination of the head, and I bowed.

Education at the Baildon Grammar School was truly comprehensive, aimed at making young hobbledehoys mannerly enough to be at ease in almost any situation that might arise. I took it that Mistress Penelope was the daughter to whom Mr Mercer had sometimes referred, but in no way did she resemble him. He was plump, rubicund, cheerful; she was pale, thin and discontented-looking. Also I guessed that when they stood on the level she topped him by at least a head.

"You're on the move?" Mr Mercer said.

"About to go to Diss, sir."

"To my friend Mallory?"

"That is the name, sir."

He leaned forward a little, squeezing his paunch. "You mind what I said about the Zodiac signs."

"The moulds are all burned now – probably used to smoke bacon." That made me think of the one which had not been burned. It was in my reed basket where it now fitted, for in order to use it on the tombstone I had been obliged to reduce its size. Of the brave floral garland little remained now but a kind of scallopped edging.

Mr Mercer said, "Good. Good. Sir Joseph greatly admired your work, but I told him his designs must be different. What did he decide upon?"

"That, sir, I cannot say. Sir Joseph and I met only once, very briefly and we did not discuss details."

"Well, remember me to him."

It was dismissal. I bowed again, picked up my two reed baskets – one for tools, one for clothes – and set out for Diss.

The rest of April slid away; it was May, it was June. I had been very busy, for although Sir Joseph's requirements sounded simple enough, he seemed incapable of staying in one mind about anything for twenty-four hours at a stretch.

24

Even about the colour he was indecisive. He'd have pink, like Mr Mercer's. "That might look like slavish imitation," he said when the pink was prepared and ripening. "I think white." Finally he decided upon grey, a colour achieved by the addition of most finely pounded charcoal.

Like many men of his kind he had been much enriched by sheep and he wanted them given their due; at least three plaques: a ewe – perhaps feeding a lamb, a ram, with horns, a lamb frisking. "And yet that seems unfair to the other activities. Wool is exported by ships. Could you manage a ship?" I said I thought so. "Perhaps we should include a plough . . ." And so on and on. I often wondered how a man of such a vacillating mind had stayed on one course long enough to amass a fortune, so that he could buy not merely a knighthood but a baronetcy.

I did not mind the delay and the changes, for I was most comfortably housed. The Manor was large enough to allow me a room to myself. There I slept and worked, pecking away at the things which remained constant, the three sheep, the ship. It sometimes helped to be able to say, with mock dismay, "As you wish, Sir Joseph, but I have already begun . . ."

I took my meals with the steward, the housekeeper and the butler. The food was the best I had ever encountered and I was constantly being urged to eat more. All three were hearty to the point of gourmandising and seemed to feel that my lack of appetite was a reproach to them. To me it was proof that I had not put the past behind me as completely as I should have wished. I could seldom make much headway with food which had been served at Crowswood. Beef roused no memory, farmers seldom have it on their tables except after the autumn dispersal of livestock. At the Manor we also had fresh fish, hurried up from the coast. "You see, he can eat when he sets his mind to it," the housekeeper would say with her fat woman's laugh. Sweetmeats were safe, too. The elegant concoctions devised by the Manor cooks twanged no chord of memory.

I invented and held to a reason for my abstention: "You forget," I said, "that any minute now I shall be clambering up and down a ladder. Weight would be a burden."

The same excuse served me in my choice of liquor. "I'll not gainsay," said the steward, patting his paunch complacently, "that this is what is called a beer barrel belly, and that you don't want."

"Brandy can be provided," the butler said, "but only with Sir Joseph's permission."

I could wait for that to be given, for, not expecting such a concession, I had laid in my own supply as soon as I reached Diss. And I was trying to use it more sparingly – for the sake of my craft.

On that June day which my old master had still called St Peter's and St Paul's Day I was actually ready to start. Sir Joseph had run out of suggestions and counter suggestions and was enormously pleased with his decisions. "Anybody can see by one glance at my house that I am not like some people, ashamed of how I made my money."

The weather was perfect for my purpose, indeed so bright that I was glad to be working on the subdued grey rather than white. White!

I said to myself for perhaps the ten thousandth time: Pull yourself together, Adam Woodley. Keep your mind on the work in hand.

Being watched was no new thing to me. Everybody likes to watch somebody else at work. Take a shovel and dig a hole in the road and all with time to waste will stop and stare. But on the afternoon when I was making ready to apply the ship mould I was aware that I was being watched in a different way. From inside the house; from the oriel window which jutted out above the wide front door. Somebody watching – not the work, whoever it was could only have seen that by opening the window and leaning out. Watching *me*.

I pressed home the ship mould. Counted, withdrew it, inspected the result. Perfect, and so it should be, for I'd gone to the bother of riding into Yarmouth and making rough sketches of a sailing ship. Satisfied, I let the mould fall to the ground, then, rather covertly, I turned my head and looked at the window. I caught only a glimpse of a face, pale

26

between two areas of darkness. For no known reason one streak of sweat between my shoulder-blades ran suddenly cold. There had been something, the pallor, the intensity of the expression, the sudden withdrawal . . .

I worked on, plastering the section around the ship plaque, tidied up, made everything ready for tomorrow, went indoors and washed and redressed myself. After that I walked in the garden, enjoying the mingled scents of full-blown roses and honeysuckle and flexing my arm and shoulder muscles. The front of the Manor was wider than that of most houses, and the moulds had to be bigger and therefore heavier, and although I was work-hardened, I was not inexhaustible.

The first stars were pricking through when I went into the house to get a bit of supper. This meal I usually took by myself, or with the housekeeper – the steward and butler being on duty at the front of the house. Supper in the steward's room was always cold, but very substantial. I ate cold beef and salad stuff and some custard pie. Then I drew a measure of brandy from the small keg which stood on the side-table. The housekeeper had suggested that I take it to my room, but I knew the danger of waking in the night and seeking solace from the sadness that would flood in.

The steward came hurrying. "Sir Joseph wants you. In the library. You know the way." I did, for it was in that room that we had held what Sir Joseph called discussions. I thought, with weary patience, that he had changed his mind yet again. I knew from talk in the steward's room that there were guests in the house. Quite possibly one of them had suggested something new. Or worse perhaps he had taken a dislike to the ship now that it was done. It really is heartbreaking to be ordered to chip away something one has made with care, almost with love. In ten years it had happened to me only twice, but that was enough.

Sir Joseph was not alone. He had one of his guests with him and that guest was – no, it couldn't be, but it was – Mr Mercer. Aged, reduced and bleached as by an illness or a

27

grave misfortune. And not only in appearance had he changed, he had always been so friendly, so amiable; I'd liked him better than any man I had ever worked for. Now he was looking at me with marked disfavour, with definite distaste. I wondered what on earth I had done. He couldn't have looked more displeased if I'd flagrantly cheated and used his Zodiac signs on Sir Joseph's house.

From Mr Mercer I glanced at Sir Joseph and I didn't much relish his expression either; it was remote, faintly amused, faintly malicious. A spectator at some sort of contest, avid for the fun to begin.

Suddenly I was mightily glad that I was wearing my best clothes.

"Come in, Woodley," Sir Joseph said. "Come to the light." I went towards the long table where they sat, not quite together, but on the same side. Candles in seven-branched sticks burned at either end. Within reach of both men stood a container of brandy, very elegant, made of glass. Matching glasses, stemmed and shaped like the calyx of a flower, stood by each man.

Standing there, alone on my side of the table I had a feeling of being inspected and judged. For what? I was an honest man, plying an honest trade; I was law-abiding. I'd never done anyone any harm, I owed no man a penny.

Mother Nelly? That simply could not be. True, I had consulted her and I had dropped her into a position from which perhaps she had failed to struggle up. But only I knew that. And since the Coroner, whose word was law, had returned that bland verdict, she'd been buried eight months ago.

Sir Joseph said, "My friend, Mr Mercer, wants to know a little about you, Woodley."

"Mr Mercer knows what there is to know, Sir Joseph. He once asked me if I were local and I told him, born in Clevely, educated at Baildon and apprenticed at Nettleton."

Mr Mercer said, "Of course I remember that. What does it tell me? Are you married?"

"No sir."

"Betrothed?"

"Yes. She died."

"What was your father?"

"A farmer."

"Tenant or freehold?" Really, this was puerile. It was exactly like the inquisition which new boys at school were forced to undergo.

"My father," I said, addressing a space between the two men, "owned his fifty acres, as did his father before him and so for generations back. To the Middle Ages, when a venturesome man could hack himself a place out of the forest. It was called intake land. And the farm is there, still called by its name."

For two pins I'd have said: And where were the Mercers and the Mallorys when a Woodley carried his bow to Crecy?

"Your mother," Mr Mercer said in the nasty way which suited his new, grim expression, "took in washing and scrubbed bakehouses."

That angered me. "What if she did? All honour to her. I was four when my father fell ill. He lingered for five years. She could not tend him and the farm. It was ruined, no stock, no crops. So when my father . . . when he died, she wanted an education for me and moved into Baildon, tackling any job that offered. Boys resident in Baildon paid less fees. I'm not ashamed of my mother. And now that I have answered you, be so good as to answer me. *What is all this about?*"

They made no answer. There was silence. Then Sir Joseph rose to his feet. "I'll leave you," he said. "And I thank God I have only sons."

"And well you may! Now man, sit down."

I dragged up a stool and sat opposite him.

Mr Mercer had difficulty in beginning his explanation and then plunged into it somewhat incoherently.

"It sounds crazy. So it is! And I've had enough to drive a man mad! Tears. Ill-temper. Wouldn't eat. Couldn't sleep. Threatened to kill . . . I curse the day I ever heard your name. And I blame the damned books for putting ideas . . .

29

You don't know what I've been through. No peace day or night."

I had not forgotten how he had spoken of my mother. I said in a disrespectful way, "I wish you could tell me what this is all about. And how it concerns me. In straight terms."

"My daughter. Saw you once. Love at first sight. Love at first sight!" His voice rose, shrill as a woman's.

"Am I to understand that your daughter imagines herself to be in love with me?"

"That's just it. And imagines is right. Love at first sight. All damned nonsense."

But I knew it could happen. It had happened to me.

I said, "I feel sorry for her."

He bounced in his chair. "Sorry for her. Sorry? In God's name why?"

"Because I haven't the slightest intention of marrying her − or anyone else."

"Don't say that. Don't say that. I've done my best to dissuade her. Given her things. Taken her back to London to distract her mind. Nothing worked. I brought her here, thinking a closer look might undo the damage. It's ten times worse. I'm at my wits' end." And in that uncomfortable position he must stay so far as I was concerned.

I said, "I am sorry. Further talk will get us nowhere." I pushed back my stool a little and half rose.

"Sit down," he shouted, master to man; and then more placatingly, "Please sit down. There is more to it. Much more. Have some brandy."

"Thank you, no." A third glass stood there, speaking volumes.

"I was told that you had a taste for the stuff. Oh, I've been sniffing round and the only thing I could hear against you . . . Well, not exactly against. Nobody ever saw you drunk."

"Nobody ever saw me fall down in the gutter. Or pick a fight. But I do drink; often to excess. Perhaps if you tell Mistress Penelope that . . ."

"Man, if I told her you ate new-born babies for breakfast

30

it'd make no difference. No difference at all. She's besotted. You should be flattered. She's not uncomely, you know. I don't suppose you had a good look at her that morning. Not uncomely. Not without wit either. Nor without suitors. And she will be well-endowed. I settled money on Lydia – that's my other daughter. What I own now, what I hope to make in the future will be Penelope's."

I felt a kind of amusement bubble within me. Not of the right kind: rather sour and twisted; for it did seem ironic that when Arthur Borley finally gave way he had driven home the point that Anne would have nothing, since custom demanded that Crowswood, that two-horse farm, should pass to Will. Now here was another father in a somewhat similar position, practically prepared to bribe.

He had a certain wiliness. He said, "It did not escape me that when I spoke of your mother I gave offence. I apologise. You see I was looking for something, anything which would disillusion . . . Make you seem less romantic."

"And you found it, didn't you? You said: Do you wish to marry the son of a washerwoman?"

"That is precisely what I did say. And what answer did I get? Penelope said I should think shame to myself. She said she wanted to spit in my face. Since when, she shouted, had honest labour been a disgrace and how long was it since my grandmother sewed woolsacks? In a temper she is just like her mother. Yet a sweeter woman never wore shoes."

"Given her own way?"

"Given her own way," he repeated with a sick look. Then he returned to the attack. "Will you think about it? See her, talk to her, and think?"

Anxious to end this awkward interview, I promised to think.

I thought before I slept, and when I woke and while I had breakfast. I was neither blind nor stupid nor unworldly. I think that no one who has experienced grinding poverty in youth can ever be quite oblivious to the advantages of having money. And I remembered that Mr Mercer's attitude had changed and softened as soon as Sir Joseph had taken himself away. Without the support of a fellow rich man, he had weakened and practically pleaded with me. That meant that I could dictate my own terms – and they would be strict – a handsome sum downright for me. If I decided to marry Penelope Mercer, there was going to be none of this poor man, rich heiress situation, with her money tied up in settlements.

Inevitably Anne came into my thoughts. Suppose such a proposition had been made to me before I ever went to lodge at Crowswood, when I was heart-whole and fancy free. How far was my present reluctance to commit myself due to a lingering sentiment?

On and on, round and round.

I had intended that day to do the plain plastering between the ship and the ram, but as I swallowed the last of my breakfast I decided otherwise. I needed a more absorbing job, repetition being a wearisome business.

My ram was a fine animal – and quite different from the Zodiac ram which decorated Mr Mercer's house. That was a representative animal, well portrayed but still. In order to make this one different I had carved him in action, horned head lowered, ready to fight. When I had counted and withdrawn the mould, I realised that this was the best thing I had ever done – or seen done. I was usually pleased with my work, in fact I was always ready to discard a mould that didn't please me – but this was something special, action and movement in every line. I thought to myself, smugly: I was always good, and now I am getting better.

"It is indeed beautiful," a voice said. Startled, I looked down and there, near the foot of the ladder, she stood.

For a man with some claim to being an artist I had always experienced a difficulty in remembering how Anne looked at the moment when I fell in love. How she appeared to me later I could recall, and how she looked on her deathbed was painfully clear, but the first moment, the moment of revelation was irretrievably lost.

By contrast, I remember everything about Penelope Mercer.

Not uncomely, her father had said. She was not un-

32

comely. Not pretty either. Her face was triangular, rather like a cat's, and pale. Her hair was black and she wore it, as unmarried girls still did, drawn back from her face and flowing down her back, a silky, rippling mane. Eyes unusual, very large and green – like gooseberries. Below the prominent cheekbones her face was delicately hollowed, falling away to a narrow chin. Her lips were thin but sharply carved.

"Good morning, Adam Woodley."

I bowed, suddenly self-conscious and awkward.

"I hold," she said, "that no one should be asked to bid for a pig in a poke. You should have a chance to look me over. Before you complete your thinking."

She moved away from me, half a dozen steps, turned, dropped me a curtsey and came back. She was very graceful. Rather tall for a woman, and seeming taller because she was so slight.

I was deeply embarrassed. No blush could show on my sun-tanned face, but it burned. By the emphasis that she put on the word *thinking* I knew that her father had told her what I had said. I thought, angrily, that he might have waited until I had said yea or nay.

Yet surely, she was the one who should have been ill at ease. Mr Mercer's proposal to me was most unusual, and it had been provoked by her unprecedented behaviour. It was possible perhaps that a dairymaid might make an advance to the ploughboy she favoured, but above that level a female was expected to wait for at least a hint.

"If you could spare a few minutes," she said, "I would like to make my position clear. Shall we walk?"

I suppose I could have said No. The truth is that complete singlemindedness is a rare thing and confers upon its owner a kind of power.

She turned and went down the few steps which led to the garden, and I followed, my face still hot, my hands and feet three times their usual size. This particular garden path ended with a stone seat overlooking a little stream. Penelope Mercer seated herself at the extreme end and indicated that I should sit also.

"Have you ever been in love?" She had a low yet strong voice, almost gruff.

"Yes. Once."

"What happened?"

"There was an accident – and she died."

"I do not wish to stir memories painful to you; but I must ask. Did your love grow, little by little, or strike like lightning."

"Like lightning." And the painful memory did stir. My first visit to Crowswood, seeking a lodging; Anne opening the door and the absolute certainty that of all women this was the one, the only one.

"So it was with me," said the girl at the far end of the seat. "That morning. I could not even speak. And since then, day and night, night and day . . . Have I shocked you? I am only too well aware that my behaviour has been unmaidenly. Undignified. But . . . I am fighting for my life, for if you reject me I shall most surely die."

She spoke with a kind of ferocity. I thought of what her father had said: not eating, not sleeping, trying to kill . . . Of the sleeplessness and lack of food her pallor and thinness bore witness. And when I ventured to look at her the green blaze in her eyes struck a chill. It occurred to me that she might be demented.

I said, feebly defensive, "One cannot love to order."

"I am not asking you to love me. Especially now when I know that I must compete with a dead woman! I ask only leave to love you, to be with you, to look after you, see your smile, hear your voice."

This was precisely how I had felt about Anne. But it had seemed right, suitable for me to say such things. Now it was somehow wrong.

"You know nothing about me," I said. "I am a selfish fellow. Since my mother died I have lived without a thought for another's comfort or convenience. I drink too much. When I have my mind on a job I am surly."

"Decry yourself how you will. It makes no difference to me. I know in my heart."

So much that she was saying brought my own love to

34

mind that I did feel sorry for her – as I had told her father. I stole another look at her and tried to imagine us in bed. Something in me shied away, crying, No, impossible! My sensible part demanded, Why? You have paid women in your time.

So I had – but not since Anne. It was as though when she died she had taken not only my love and my happiness, but my manhood as well.

We sat there in the sun and in a silence which became momentarily more and more uncomfortable. Then she stirred and said, "I have no more words," and rose and went swiftly away.

The rest of the day was uneventful. I plain-plastered all the afternoon; then, anxious to tire myself out, I took a long walk, ate bread and cheese and drank brandy in an inn full of haymakers, all very happy because the weather had favoured them and there'd been a blood-red sunset – promise of a similar day tomorrow.

Back at the Manor I drank some more brandy and, still fearful of wakefulness, carried some up with me.

Last night's conversation and the encounter this morning had scraped off the thin skin which nine months had grown over my wound. All the old misery and desolation welled up again – now with a new thought to embitter it further. Somewhere in the front of the house did a gïrl lie, longing for me, as I longed for Anne?

Finally I fell into the sleep of tipsiness. My last thought was severely practical – shaky hands in the morning.

I dreamed of Anne as I had often done, happily while she was alive, and miserably since her death. The dream had come less frequently in the last few months and I took that as a sign that my mind was mending. It had a kind of set pattern. I was always in some ordinary, familiar place and suddenly she'd be there, coming from the trees in the orchard, emerging from a crowd of people on Baildon market-place, or just entering a room where I sat alone.

Never once had I dreamed of our being in bed together. Now I did. And the lust which I had restrained out of respect for her person while she lived, and for her memory

35

after her death, simply swamped me. I possessed her utterly, and she possessed me. I was, inside my dream, somewhat surprised by the passion of her response, infinitely more than a paid woman is paid to pretend. I had sometimes told myself that when the moment came I must be gentle, undemanding, unhurting. I had been quite wrong.

When it was over she cradled my head on her bosom, stroked my hair and said, "Sleep now."

I slept and woke to the dawn chorus of birds in the orchard trees under my window.

And I was sharing my bed, not with a memory or a ghost, but with Penelope Mercer . . .

My future father-in-law said, "You would have done well in business. You drive a hard bargain." There was not the animosity that could have been expected. Almost admiration. A lurking gratitude.

"It was an unequal contest," I said, feeling sorry for him and thinking that no child of mine should ever so dominate me.

I now owned the house called Pargeters and the three hundred acres that went with it. Of the business in London which he still controlled, a third was mine. Properly conveyed, too; I was not accepting verbal agreements.

I made concessions which to me seemed trivial. I said that of course he could live with us, entertain whom and how he would. And I agreed to add his name to mine. I recognised the whim of a sonless man visualising grandsons. We discussed quite amiably whether the name should be Woodley-Mercer or Mercer-Woodley. To me both sounded clumsy and slightly pretentious. He favoured Woodley-Mercer. I agreed. Such people as had known me before still called me Woodley; I thought of myself as Adam Woodley and to the end of my days, reserved the pompous hyphen for use on official documents.

PART TWO

Narrated by Sarah Woodley-Mercer

My grandfather was having one of his lucid spells. They came less and less frequently, but when they did it was always amazing to see that some part of his mind remembered things done and said when he was so astray in his wits as not to know what day of the week it was.

"I don't like the look of things at all," he said. "Heading straight for war."

Father said, "So it would seem."

Mother said, "I pray God not."

Grandfather said, "You've no cause to worry. I'm too old, Adam's too old and John's too young to fight. And here there's no question about how the cat will jump Puritans to a man. It's London I'm worried about."

Father said, "London is solid behind Parliament."

"I know. I know. I also know that my business is with silks and velvets and fine leather. All things much disliked by the Puritans. And the merest little squabble can lead to looting. How much more so a war?"

Father said, rather cruelly I thought: "You should have sold out. I did."

"Easy come, easy go," my grandfather said in a nasty way. "You hadn't worked all your life in Leadenhall and then been obliged to trade off . . ."

My mother lifted her plate – we were at dinner at the time – and crashed it down on the table.

"That is enough," she said.

I had noticed before that sometimes, when he was in his right mind, my grandfather would say some apparently harmless thing which jarred upon Mother. Ordinarily she was a very calm woman and behaved with dignity, but there was something in the past and having to do, I think, with property which had left her with a sensitive spot.

When my grandfather was wandering in his mind he never offended, partly because much that he said made no sense at all, or if it did was connected with time out of memory, his own youth, how he'd gone on cloth-buying expeditions to the Low Countries, and once to France to bring back a shipful of people called Huguenots and set them up in London so that his cloth could be woven on his own premises. At such time his talk could be interesting, though never very satisfactory because he'd trail off into rubbish and call me Penelope, which was Mother's name.

Now, in his right mind for the first time in a week, he went on with his talk of war.

"The Puritans hate silk and velvet, fine leather and lace. What isn't looted will be forbidden by law."

Father said, "Well, fashion has gone to extremes. Lace-trimmed boots! And men sleeping in curling rags."

"You were partial to a bit of finery yourself once, Adam."

"Still am, if you call it finery. I like a silk shirt and good cloth for coat and breeches."

"I think I shall go to London tomorrow and sell out," Grandfather said.

It seemed to us that his brief spell of sanity had ended. The idea of his going to London and transacting any kind of business was so absurd that had it not been pathetic it would have been laughable. He could lose himself in the short distance between Minsham and Muchanger. As for Layer Wood! Mother was obliged to send a small boy to follow him, not ostentatiously, wherever he went and to appear whenever he seemed to be lost and bring him home.

Now, sticking to one subject with unusual tenacity, Grandfather said, "If it comes to war they'll commandeer all ships."

Father, using the soothing voice which we all used towards the half-demented old man, said, "That shouldn't worry you. You own no ships."

Grandfather gave his cackling laugh. "So you may think! I own two well-founded ships, *Seagull* and *Mermaid*."

"You *did*," Father said patiently.

"It just happens," Grandfather went on, "that when a certain bargain was made, property in London was a stipulation. The ships were at sea." He cackled again. "In the

40

City it was well-known that anybody had to get up pretty early in the morning to get the better of John Mercer."

Mother said a trifle sharply, "Father, Timmy is waiting to take you for your walk."

"Let him wait! I know I have lapses. I know I forget . . . But if you," he was addressing Father, "will come into the office, I will show you that where business is concerned I'm no fool. In other ways . . ."

Mother said, "Humour him, dearest."

Father gave an almost imperceptible shrug, rose and followed Grandfather towards that mysterious place at the rear of the house known as the office. In the doorway Father turned and said, "One of you ride over to Brook and tell Smith I'll be along later. I'll see for myself before deciding."

I knew what he meant. The month was May, a time when every farmer with sheep to sell had to decide which of the two fairs to send them to. In-the-wool or shorn. The In-the-wool was the earlier and meant just what it said: a sale of sheep with poor fleeces, not worth the shearing price and doomed for the shambles or, on the completely reverse side, young, potential breeding stock whose wonderful fleeces must be shown off.

I could have done it myself – I mean I could have made the decision, for I was over fourteen in that year, 1642, and ever since I could ride a pony I'd been going round with Father, keeping my eyes and ears open and my mouth shut. I'd understood quite early that neither inside the house nor out of it did I count for much. John was the precious one, the son, the first-born, the heir to what Father now owned: Pargeters, Nine Elms, and Brook. The trouble with John was that he was not interested. He had not been interested in school, either. He'd been sent to Baildon Grammar School, Father's old school, and had come home for good the previous Christmas knowing far less – I am not boasting – than I did except where Latin was concerned. Grandfather, in his better days, had taught me to read and Father had quite a collection of books, some of them banned. King James had hated Sir Walter Raleigh, had in fact had him beheaded, and forbade any circulation of his books. But

Father was a completely unorthodox character. Indeed almost perverse. Say to him not to do something and he'd find a good reason for doing it, tell him to do something and he'd dig in his heels.

Father had told one of us to go to Brook, but of course we both went. Until John went to school, and now when he had left, we did most things together. I was a year younger, but perhaps girls age faster than boys, and although we were different in character we had the bond of both being young. And lonely.

There had been a time when the isolation of our lives had puzzled me. That was before I understood about class distinctions. But all along I'd been one of those children of whom it is said that little jugs have big ears. I'd heard things, including some words spoken in anger. And now I understood.

Mother had a sister, my Aunt Lydia, who had made what was called 'a good marriage'. Her husband was brother to Sir Walter Fennel of Ockley. Grandfather had thought that by buying some land and building a rather fine house he would qualify as a country gentleman and that my mother, by far his favourite daughter, would make an even better marriage. Instead she had chosen Father, a mere plasterer. And what was more a man with no social ambition at all, and yet as proud as Lucifer. I never saw it happen, but I can imagine how hotly he would have resented the slightest hint of patronage or toleration. Yet he also had his yardstick and would do business with, be civil to but never friendly with men who would have felt honoured to call him friend.

On that beautiful afternoon I mounted my dear brown mare, Bess, and John said "Watch me!" and this time managed to vault into the saddle of his more showy mount, Sultan. I said, "Very good!" and leaning from my own saddle, released the door of my wolfhound's pen. I loved him and he seemed attached to me. I'd have had him in the house but Mother said he was quite unsuitable and that if I'd wanted a lap dog I should have chosen a spaniel of the small kind.

We went through Layer Wood because, as everybody

said, Layer was the shortest cut to anywhere, and Pargeters, Nine Elms and Brook all lay abutting it, interrupted only by a small farm called Crowswood.

Some of the rides through the wood were so narrow that two horses could not go abreast, then in places the path would widen. At one such John said: "Do you think the old man was rambling or does he actually own ships?"

"Who can tell? I think Father half-believed."

"And if there are, and they're sold, Father will somehow get hold of the money and buy some more land." John sounded disgusted. "I could understand it if he got any pleasure out of it."

"He does. In his way. Simply owning it is a pleasure to him."

"Just a lot of hard work. Overlooking this, seeing after that. I can tell you one thing, Sarah, when it comes to me I'll do differently."

"In what way?"

"Let it out – smallholdings pay best – and take the rent and enjoy myself. Or put in overseers and let them do the work. Look at us now . . ." It was plain to me that my brother, not given to much thought, had meditated over this. "Smith's a capable man. He's paid extra and has the house but when it comes to deciding about which scabby old sheep . . ."

"*None* of our sheep are scabby," I interrupted him.

"You're as bad as Father is. A real chip off the old block!" That was more like John, laughing and teasing.

I thought: There is some truth in that, but alas not in looks! Father was an exceptionally handsome man with fair hair – now silvering a little – and truly blue eyes. John was his spitting image. I resembled nobody. My hair was brown, with a tinge of red, and my eyes were gooseberry green. Mother's were emerald, exactly matching the jewel she always wore. I thought Mother was beautiful with her truly green eyes, her white skin and cloud of night-black hair.

The ride narrowed and John went ahead. I followed, thinking; from looks to marriage.

43

Although we were socially isolated, the isolation was not complete and once or twice John and I had visited Aunt Lydia; and rather more often a house at Nettleton – a most beautiful house called Merravay, owned by Sir Rawley Rowhedge and his wife, Lady Alice. They were as much unlike the ordinary run of people as we were and they had a son named Charles who at some gathering – probably a Harvest Feast – had favoured me enough to provoke some dizzying thoughts. But shortly after that he had gone up to Cambridge and doubtless forgotten all about me.

When next we could ride side by side, I said, "When you come into possession, John, I'll be your overseer."

"A fair offer," he said, and laughed. "Nothing would suit me better. But by that time you'll be married, with seven children. And fat!"

With that we turned out of Layer Wood and onto Brook Farm. And as John had remarked, Smith was a competent man. He had already divided the sheep, so far as I could see faultlessly. John barely glanced at them, he just gave Father's message. And that was unnecessary, for almost immediately Father himself arrived, studied Smith's arrangement with no marked satisfaction and made a trivial change, just about enough, I thought rather uncharitably, to show that his errand was not wasted. Then he surprised us all.

"When are the shearers due, Smith?"

"In ten days' time, sir, more or less."

"I might be away," Father said. John and I looked at each other. Father? Away? Never once to our knowledge had he spent a night under any roof but his own. "See to their welfare but no drinking until the end of the day. My son will see to their wages. Good day, Smith." He swung his horse round and we followed.

Father was lenient. I'd heard, through John who had heard from his school-fellows, of parents who were completely savage, beating their children on the slightest provocation or none at all; making their children stand in their presence until given permission to sit. Father was not like that. Nor was he the kind of parent that Grandfather must have been to his two daughters. Father always kept a certain dignity, a distance. It could be tempered by kindliness, but never indulgence. I will not say that we dared not ask about his forthcoming absence, it was simply that we felt it better to refrain. Wait to be told.

We were informed at supper-time. Grandfather had apparently produced enough evidence that he did own two ships as well as other property in London to make Father feel it necessary to go there immediately. He must be back in time for haymaking, likely to be a little early this year since the weather had been unusually warm.

When John and I were young, Grandfather had made the journey quite frequently – and always brought back presents. He had left men in London whom he trusted absolutely; it was they, or their messengers, whom Grandfather had received and entertained in his office. I cannot recall Mother making any fuss about Grandfather's going but now she was behaving as though Father were about to go to Africa and risk being eaten by cannibals. And May, she said, was such a treacherous month, Father must take warm clothes as well as light-weight ones. And finally, he must not go alone; the highways were becoming more and more infested with robbers. "All right," Father said, "I'll take Tom Markham." Tom, a day labourer at Pargeters and having no home, lived in the house, part of what Grandfather had once called in anger, 'this beggarly establishment'.

Then after supper it was Father's turn to fuss. "I want a word with you, son – and Sarah, you may as well listen, too." But though allowed to be present I was not directly addressed. Father spoke as though he were about to be absent for three months, leaving behind him a lunatic asylum with the least demented inmate in charge, aided just a little by the next least lunatic one.

"I shall despatch what business there is with all possible speed, but should I be delayed . . ." Out poured the orders, John saying "Yes, sir. I will see to it, sir," and all the time, I knew, relying upon me. But it was to John that Father handed the money for the shearers and – just in case – the extra hands needed for the haymaking should the worst happen and he be delayed.

Finally Father said, "Look after your mother. She frets overmuch."

We both promised, but it showed me how two people can live together for years without understanding each other. Mother was the least fretting person one could imagine. She left the running of the house, even the planning of meals, to Marian our cook. She liked to walk around and sit in the garden but so far as I knew never made a suggestion or planted a thing. Most mothers, I understood, saw to it that their daughters could sew, embroider, play the virginals, acquire some knowledge of cooking, preserving, making herbal brews. About such things Mother had never concerned herself, and she was equally remote from John, which was quite unusual. Her attitude to her father was similarly indifferent. When he began to behave strangely she said, "It happens. He must have an attendant." Yet she was capable of some emotion, like banging her plate down when some reference to the past annoyed her.

I must add a word about her age. John was almost sixteen, so even had Mother married at fifteen and quickened instantly, she must now be over the thirty line; but nothing showed on her face of sag, of worry or fret. I never saw her with a hair out of place, or other than beautifully dressed. Too self-contained to be lovable, and the same could be said of Father. Grandfather, for all his vagaries was more . . . more human. Still, John and I promised. Yes, we would look after Mother and see that she did not fret.

Father rode off through the light mist that promised a fine day and by dinner-time Mother had indeed started to fret. "I hope your father has found a good inn." We knew that she had insisted that he should carry some food with him, in case, as she said.

At supper-time she hoped he had found a good lodging with a well-aired bed. It went on and on, every meal the same thing, and she eating hardly at all. Grandfather still ate with us then, heartily, he was fond of his food, but usually in near silence. But one evening he slammed down his knife and said, "Ha! Trying that again are you? He wouldn't care if you starved or drowned. He's a horse-leech. And you're a fool."

Four, five days and why no message? No letter?

In our corner of Suffolk we had as yet no regular postal service yet communication was easy enough; any pedlar, tinker or mere traveller would take a letter on one stage of its journey. People who could afford to do so did it for nothing; others charged a penny or twopence. The missive then became a property, gaining value as it changed hands, so that the recipient might eventually pay a shilling or eighteen pence. People were only too glad to pay for their letter. There was a story of a girl who could not write sending a sealed letter to her mother who could not read. The mother said she could not pay the sixpence asked, so the tinker was annoyed, though he had not been obliged to take a step off his beaten track. The process was repeated and finally the mother admitted that the mere sight of the sealed paper, entirely blank save for the address, told her all she wanted to know – her daughter was alive and well.

No letter came from Father, and Mother, usually so calm, became more and more frenzied. She suggested that John should go to see what had happened to Father and John would most willingly have done so. But a search of Grandfather's office showed that every paper referring to the London premises and the ships, if they actually existed, had been removed. Grandfather could not or would not answer any questions and Mother had a fit of self-accusation. "I should have paid more attention. I do remember talk of a change of premises, but I gave no heed. I was so happy." Now she looked so extremely unhappy that I had to search for something comforting to say. I said, "I think I know what has happened. Father was so anxious to be back for the haysel that he despatched the business with the utmost speed and reckoned he'd be back before a letter could reach us."

"That is the only possible explanation," Mother said. And that day she ate a little, gave Marian, our cook, some slightly conflicting orders about a meal, hot or cold, to be ready for instant serving, and did whatever she usually did to make her hair so glossy.

John called me a meddlesome, blabbermouth fool. But for me, he said, he'd have been on his way to London.

One miserable day followed another. Father did not come. No message came. I avoided the house as much as possible – easy enough for the hay was early and, since John remained sulky and uninterested, the burden fell on me.

Now and then I did think about Father, but in a rational way. I imagined him alive and active in London, but armed with out–of–date papers, trying to trace a warehouse, some weaving sheds and two ships which, if they existed, had very common names. Even so, I sometimes thought irritably, he could have sent a message. He was not stupid. He'd lived with Mother for years and years; he must have known what I had only just realised – that she was deeply in love with him.

I was at an age where females think about love rather seriously . . .

We were all at dinner one hot day with the window set wide. We heard the creak and crunch of wheels, the slow plod of hooves. Mother sprang up and cried, "A message! Nobody else would dare . . ."

She meant that no driver of a wagon would have come to the front of the house. She ran out into the hall, threw open the front door and cried, "Well? Come forward. What is it?"

It was a very rickety old wagon drawn by a wretched horse, but a horse tall enough to momentarily obtrude between us and the man on its far side. Then it lowered its head as exhausted horses do, and there stood Tom Markham looking very wretched too.

"It's the Master. Dead. I done my best."

Mother made a peculiar sound, not a scream, and running to the wagon's tail, managed somehow to let it down; and there was the coffin. She put her arms about it and her head on its foot and so stood.

Grandfather, jerked into sanity, said, "Boy, what happened?"

"It was the plague, sir."

At that Grandfather went demented in another way.

"Stand clear," he shouted. "Penelope, come away! Even lead cannot contain it. Penelope, will you come away? I'm immune," he said. He went and took Mother by the arm. By sheer force he pulled her clear. She struggled, realised that she was outmatched, and was suddenly icily calm. "Leave go of me, you old fool." Grandfather, who adored her, looked as though she had struck him. She said, "Tom, fetch two men and bring your master into the house."

"No! No!" Grandfather's voice was almost a scream. "You don't know. It'll go through the house like fire. You'll all die. There'll be . . ." It was too much. The narrowly balanced scale of his mind tipped and he fell back into babble.

Mother said, "Tom, wait. When did he die?" Tom reckoned, as the unlearned do, on his fingers, fumbled, said, with no real certainty, "Yesterday'll be a week."

"And it *was* the plague?"

"Yes, Mistress. Bad in London it was."

"Now listen to me. You are not to mention the word. We want no panic. Go find two men. John, ride and tell the Rector and warn the Sexton. Say sudden death, a week ago. Say heat-stroke. Sarah, go into the garden and cut every white flower you can find."

For a moment there was no doubt about who was in charge.

Alone in the garden, heaping a basket with the roses and lilies which just at this moment of the year bloomed together, I had time to think and to be sad. There had never been between me and Father the close bond which can exist between father and daughter, but there had been fondness of a cool kind, and on my side admiration. He was, perhaps beyond all, such a *just* man and justice is a rare quality. Anybody who has studied the Bible – as we all did in those days – knows how rare. The Cities of the Plain, Sodom and Gomorrah, perished for lack of a few just men.

And it was strange that in thinking of Father I should refer to the Bible for, unlike anybody else I knew then, he did not regard it as Holy Writ. In fact, I do not believe that he regarded anything as holy. He never flaunted his scepticism, paid his tithes and attended church often enough to avoid trouble. It was his general attitude and a few chance remarks which showed how he felt. Somebody once spoke of a ghost having been seen in Layer Wood and Father said, "Let me hear no more of such nonsense. When people die, they are *dead*." He said that with real feeling. Of Rogation Days when parsons went around blessing the fields and asking for good crops, Father said, "Surely, if the Almighty governed such things there'd be no bad crops – and no hunger." He said these, and many similar things when Grandfather was still capable of sustaining a sensible conversation and even offering some argument.

Almost imperceptibly Father's matter-of-fact mind had influenced me, and a few quite ordinary experiences of the apparent futility of prayer had marked me too. I'd had another dog before my wolfhound Boru and when he fell sick I'd prayed very hard – even fasting, which was supposed to make prayers more effective. And when the idea of John going to school had first been raised I'd prayed again that Father might change his mind and hire a tutor instead.

The Reverend Mr Althorpe, Rector of Minsham and Muchanger, lived in Minsham, the larger of the two villages. He was not young and of indolent habit, but he mounted his old horse and came to offer words of comfort to Mother and also to learn what was known about the circumstances of Father's death. In any case of sudden death where foul play could possibly be suspected, it was the parson's right to refuse burial and his duty to inform the Coroner.

By this time Father's coffin was laid on a table in the hall and heaped with flowers whose fragrance could not quite conceal another odour, also sweet but unpleasing. And at each corner of the bier a thick wax candle burned in a silver stand. This kind of display, though not actually forbidden, was disapproved of by Puritans. And officially, at any rate,

Mr Althorpe was a Puritan though Grandfather, who hated all change, said that when he first came to Pargeters Mr Althorpe had been quite otherwise inclined.

Now he looked at the flowers and the candles in silence, just a slight frown. Then he spoke to Mother of the Life Everlasting, the certainty of resurrection and the necessity of resignation to the will of God.

Mother listened, dry-eyed, stony-faced. How she felt about these – or indeed many other things – nobody could know. I could only think of Father saying that when people were dead they were *dead*. John just looked miserable.

Then, the mystical part of his errand performed, Mr Althorpe turned with ill-concealed relief to the practical.

I'd never doubted, nor I think had Mother, that Tom Markham had told the sad truth. But . . . Father had gone to London to sell property and perhaps ships. He could have been carrying money on his return journey. It was just possible, though highly unlikely, that Tom had killed and robbed him, hidden the money somewhere and made up his tale. Slightly more likely was that Father had been set upon and robbed, and Tom bribed to tell his tale. Part of me repudiated both theories; privately I thought Tom too stupid either to invent or sustain such a tale.

Having called two men from haymaking and helped to carry the coffin in, Tom had gone to bed. Roused, he must have put his head in a bucket, but he still looked sleepy when he came into the parlour where Mr Althorpe had decided to hold the inquisition.

I had one poignant thought about Father, that just man. Father had as much natural dignity as any man I ever knew; it was dignity which had decided him to abstain from any social activity where he would be no more than tolerated. But he would not have kept an obviously exhausted man standing. He'd have said, "Take that stool."

Tom stood.

Question and answer produced a story coherent and straightforward, marred only by Tom's difficulty in re-membering times and place-names. Twothree or fourfive being a near enough measure of time; near the river or off

51

the Strand a near enough identification of place. He and Father had reached London in good time, there being no mire on the roads, and had lodged at an inn off the Strand. It was called The Woolpack and well-known. Whenever Tom thought he was lost, anybody he asked – except foreigners – could tell him how to get back to The Woolpack, just off the Strand. Every day Master had gone out on business; every day Tom had seen to and exercised the horses and then occupied himself how he would. He'd made friends with a young man who worked odd times at The Woolpack and who when he wasn't working showed him around a bit. Tom had enjoyed a river-trip and a visit to a fair twothree hundred times bigger than Baildon's Midsummer one.

"Yes, yes," Mr Althorpe said, "get along."

Well, fourfive days went by. Then Father said his business was taking longer than he had expected. "I must write to my wife," he said.

Mother said, "And did he?"

"He did, Mistress. That very night and sent it next day by a new thing, called Mail Service what stop at Colchester. But he paid for carrying it on. I seen him. Then he went about his business. This was afore we knew about . . ." Tom looked helplessly at Mother. "What you said not to say, Mistress."

Mother said, "Here you may."

Tom said, "The plague."

The effect of that one word was startling. One moment there sat Mr Althorpe, not greatly but rather suspicious of Tom, the next he was a quivering jelly of fear.

"There was plague in London?"

"Thass what I'm coming to." It was Tom's turn to sound patient. "Plague kilt Master, spite all I could do."

"Immediate interment is essential. I'll go and . . . Tonight at eight o'clock . . ."

Mother, still in full control, said, "Near the gate. By that white headstone." Then, unheard I think by anybody but me, she added, "Let his bones lie where his heart has been all these years." Then she turned to Tom and said, "Tell us the rest." And I pushed a stool towards where he still stood. He sat down on it and told us what, in a quiet way, was a story of heroism. And not without ingenuity either.

"We was well back," Tom said, "nearing that town where our barley go, brewing place . . ."

"Royston?" I asked tentatively.

"Thass it. There all of a sudden . . ."

Outside Royston Father had said, "Tom, I feel ill." It was a hot day; Tom had helped him down from his horse and laid him in the shade, taken Father's handkerchief and dipped it in a ditch, nearly dry on account of the hot weather. When such restoratives failed Tom had walked into Royston – or rather towards it. And the little town was on guard. The citizens knew that the plague was in London and wanted no contact with anybody from that direction. "I weren't the only one," Tom said. "Like an encampment it was and all on the watch for sickening. Even there, being the last comer, I weren't welcome. Specially after I'd shouted to one of the guards that my Master was sick a way back on the road and I wanted a doctor. I said I'd pay a fortune – which was a lie, neither me nor the Master heving a penny on us beyond what was needed to get us home. Still, that coulda bin took care of later. But the doctor was scared too and wouldn't venture." Tom's haggard face darkened at the memory of that rebuff. "Still, Master never suffered. There was a tinker woman sold me some stuff in a leather bottle. I give her all I had on me and towd her if it worked I'd put some money behind a milestone. Which I did, acause it did work. One dose kilt the pain and I kept him well-plied."

"Thank God for that," Mother said. The thought flashed through my head that if Father could have spoken he'd have said: Thank Tom.

Tom had rigged up a shelter of branches; cut bracken for a bed and walked miles across fields to find lonely farmhouses to buy eggs and milk and bread. "Not that he needed much at first. But he was pulling round. It was the slow sort, you see. Them lumps they call buboes *was* going down and he could swaller . . . And then . . . He just died."

There was a moment's silence. Then Mother said, "Did he know? Was he conscious?"

Tom hesitated. "Not rightly so. Sorta rambling. And, like I said, no suffering."

"You did very well. I am grateful."

I think she would have left it, but since no one else asked, I did. "Tom, what next? How did you manage?"

"Swopping. And bl— bad bargains I got. Two good horses, with harness for that old contraption – and the coffin. But I didn't hev time to haggle." He allowed himself a moment of self-approbation. "I reckon I did most of the pulling from Royston to home."

I waited again and then said, "You should go back to bed."

"No. I got Master home, I helped carry him in, I'll help carry him out."

So Father went to his grave in a way he would surely have approved. A hay wagon, hastily washed and pulled by one of his own horses, carried him to church and nobody was present save his family and such of his own workmen as could be rounded up. There was none of the panoply of grief and no tears. John almost broke down but Mother put a hand on his arm and steadied him. My chest and throat ached and tears could have been a relief, but if Mother, the most bereaved, could remain calm, so must I.

Three days later Mr Turnbull the Baildon attorney arrived, speaking words of commiseration, tinged with reproach. It was usual for a deceased man's man-of-law to be informed at once. Mother, accepting no rebuke, said, "Mr Turnbull, my husband died very suddenly of heat-stroke on the far side of Royston. His body was some days on the road and immediate burial was necessary. Things have been much disrupted."

"Naturally. Naturally. But testators often express some wish regarding interment."

"I knew my husband's wishes in that regard."

Father's Will was simple and as one might have expected, just. He left all he owned to John, but until he was eighteen

54

Mother was to be in full control. After that she could choose between living at Pargeters or going to the farmhouse at Nine Elms which was to be put into a state fit for habitation by a gentlewoman. From the estate she was to receive a hundred and twenty pounds a year. At the age of eighteen, married or single, I was to receive fifty pounds a year and at marriage a dowry of five hundred pounds. That was all.

"When was the Will drawn?" Mother asked.

"Fourteen years ago."

"And no mention of guardians or wardships," Mother said. "You see, my husband trusted me absolutely."

He had also apparently assumed that there would be no more children.

Refreshments were then offered; Mr Turnbull refused sherry wine, finding it liverish in warm weather, but accepted some of Grandfather's Rhenish. Marian had also sent in small saffron cakes which John and I were glad to see for truly, ever since Father rode away Mother's attitude towards food had made it impossible to eat heartily – except in Grandfather's case. She now for the sake of courtesy took a glass of wine, sipped it and then ignored it, accepted a saffron cake, broke it but did not eat. John and I each took a cake – very small; Mr Turnbull ate two.

That left five in the dish – with Mother's scorned pieces, six. We regarded them as legitimate prey, for we had become scavengers, sometimes even raiding the larder. It seemed despicable to think of eating at this particular moment, but as John had once said, if going hungry could bring Father back he'd starve for a fortnight; since it could not, he felt that people who didn't want to eat should not come to table.

In this instance greed was thwarted, for Mother said, "I would like now to make my own Will," and sent us away. "Don't go far. I shall need you shortly." So we went into the kitchen garden and ate some not-quite-ripe strawberries.

Presently Mother recalled us. She had in her hand Father's bunch of keys. "Come with me," she said and led the way to the bedroom which she had so long shared with Father and in which she now lay alone. There stood the chest, known as the Trunk. Such chests, nailed to the floor and heavily banded in iron and with massive locks, were a feature in any household of substance, a guard against robbers or dishonest servants. They were roomy enough to accommodate any silver articles not in daily use.

From the buckled strap which held the keys together Mother selected the largest and with a slight touch of formality handed it to John. A silent acknowledgment that though for the next two years she was in charge, he was the heir. When the lid was lifted a faintly musty odour was perceptible. The trunk contained little in relation to its size; what silver we owned was in use, and Father had never been a man for ostentation. There were several documents, paper or parchment, neatly arranged and tied with the pink tape favoured by lawyers. There was a jewel case covered in green velvet, two canvas money bags tied at the neck with twine, and below these what looked like a plain piece of wood. That was all.

Mother leaned forward and lifted out the papers.

"You count the money," she said. John and I took a bag each, emptied the coins on to the bed and counted. In variable coins each bag contained fifty pounds.

When we turned back to Mother she had evidently found the document she had been looking for. I glimpsed the words: Agreement between John Mercer and Adam . . . The rest was obscured because Mother was also holding to her chest the piece of wood from the bottom of the Trunk. It was very thick, six inches at least.

"I want these," Mother said, at once clutching and yet seeming to dismiss them. "How much money is there?" We told her and she said, "So little?" It was a justified question. Father farmed, very successfully, only a little short of a thousand acres; he lived modestly and was known to be saving to buy more land. His latest acquisition had been Brook Farm, six years ago.

"It may not be enough," Mother said. Enough for what, I wondered. "Well . . ." She paused. "I see no reason to make a secret of it. That case holds the trinkets given me by your grandfather. I have just willed them away to your wife, John." She shifted the paper and the great board she carried, and touched the emerald on its slender chain. "This I intended for you, Sarah, but if I must, I must . . ."

I was, for a moment, horribly reminded of the onset of Grandfather's failure of mind. Sentences trailing off; statements not quite linked.

"Take the money and buy Crowswood," Mother said, as though ordering a yard of ribbon.

John said, "Now?"

"Of course."

"Father tried to buy it, more than once," I said.

"Old Borley is dead. His son may feel differently."

"What am I to offer?" John asked.

"All there is. And if necessary promise further payment in future. Lock the Trunk, put the key on the strap and leave them on the table in the hall." She went away.

"Come with me," John said. "Don't you think two pounds an acre rather a lot?"

"It's ridiculous. I know Father *wanted* Crowswood but I doubt if even he would have paid that. And I'll bet you three pence that even so Will Borley won't sell."

"Taken," said John who loved a bet however small.

We clattered downstairs, put the keys on the hall table as instructed and then turned towards the kitchen and the stableyard. It was shorter than going out by the front door and around the house as Mother had obviously expected us to do.

In the kitchen she stood by the wide hearth, poker in hand. The paper roll recording some agreement between Grandfather and Adam . . . – surely Father – was flaring, half consumed already; the solid block of wood had fallen awkwardly and had not even begun to smoulder. I caught one glimpse before Mother said, "I thought you had gone."

All the way to Crowswood, which lay between our Nine Elms and Brook, John grumbled. Hadn't he got enough to see to? Did Mother realise what she was doing? I said, "Well, it would round off the estate nicely." He snorted. Estate? Did *I* know what I was talking about? Three farms or four or, come to it ten, all strung in a line along the edge of a wood didn't comprise an estate. An estate was a compact area of land . . . Look at Merravay, look at Mortiboys, look at . . . And he ended suddenly, "Look at that!"

I was already looking at a sight rarely to be seen even on an estate. Fifteen superb heavy horses in a meadow in which two or three cows could be comfortably accommodated. A real good pasture takes Heaven only knows how long to establish and once established is an asset, to be treated with care. This meadow at Crowswood was ruined. The horses had eaten the grass and their hooves – they were all shod – had churned the roots and the ground into dust.

Revealing his ignorance of such things, John said, "Has Borley taken to horse-breeding?"

My turn to snort. "Do you see a mare or a foal? And no breeder would so overcrowd."

"Let's get this done with," John said, and we rode on into the Crowswood yard where we came face to face with Will Borley who was wheeling, on a flat, two-wheeled carrier known as a sack-barrow, a load of *new* hay. I saw the significance of that and also that Will Borley looked dismayed. He quickly mastered what he felt and came forward.

"I was sorry to hear about your father. If I'd known I'd hev paid my last respects."

John said, "Thank you. It was very sudden."

"A good neighbour," Borley said. "Time I lost all my pigs of swine fever he started me off. Sow newly farrowed. Another time, too, in the drought, he gave me leave to take water from that well that never fails. Now he's gone to his reward."

The words were cordial enough. But Will Borley, usually so stolid, was ill at ease until John, anxious to have the unwelcome errand disposed of, blurted out that we had come to make another offer for the farm. Then he forgot, for a moment, the new hay and the crowd of horses and became almost eloquent. "How could I sell the place thass been in the family for years uncounted?" The Borleys had been there since it was Intake land, meaning cut out of the forest. "There ain't many places that've gone straight from father to son so many years. *And* mentioned in Doomsday Book, or so they say."

"I'm offering two pounds an acre," John said in a way which showed plainly enough that he wanted the offer to be refused. Which it was. "The money ain't minted," Will Borley said. So John, quite rightly, made no offer of further payments. He said, "I shall not trouble you again."

"Ain't no trouble," Will Borley said with as near graciousness as he could manage. "I knew how your father felt. He had some happy days here. A long time ago."

He was a great deal younger than Father yet something nostalgic in his voice seemed to hint that they had been young together. Then he said, in quite another voice: "Them horses . . . I'm keeping them for a friend."

"And that be hanged for a tale," John said as soon as we were out of earshot, back in Layer with its many paths. He sat and gnawed his thumb, a childish habit to which he reverted when perplexed. "I know what I *think* . . . Look, you go home and break it to Mother. Tell her Borley said the money wasn't minted. I'll see you at supper."

He swung his horse about and set off at a good pace in the direction of Ockley or Clevely or Nettleton. More slowly I rode towards home. I had little fancy for breaking the news to Mother; I felt John had dodged it. Also why had he not told me what he thought, then I could have told him what was in my mind.

The day had been hot and heavy, threatening thunder, and now the storm broke with the dreaded forked lightning, so much more dangerous than the sheet. We had been warned repeatedly not to shelter under trees in a thunderstorm and here was I in Layer! But I was very near the turn-off to Nine Elms and after two more flashes was in the open field making for the farmhouse where Cooper, the foreman on this place, lived with his pleasant, bustling wife. Rain was falling in torrents and out here I could feel the force of the wind. I entertained a true farmer's thought: wheat and barley, already heavily headed on account of the good weather, would be flattened irretrievably and would have to be cut by reaping-hook rather than sickle – slower, more back-breaking and more expensive.

Bess, very nervous of thunder and knowing this yard well, headed straight for a stable. The door was open and as we shot in, the dark interior was illuminated by a blinding flash. I saw what I saw without really noticing. I slithered down from the saddle and made for the house.

Cooper already had the kitchen door open and was peering out. "You, Mistress! I thought I heard . . ." Then I was inside and Mrs Cooper was exclaiming over my drenched state, stirring up the fire, running upstairs to fetch dry clothing, all too wide, and the skirt too short, but welcome, for the downpour had chilled the air suddenly.

Cooper had tactfully withdrawn while I was reclad and had had my hair towelled with just that extra touch of vigour which characterised all Mrs Cooper's actions. He now came back, said he'd given Bess a handful of oats, rubbed her down and she was calm now. But the rain was still pouring down and after a slight hesitation he invited me to share what he called, 'our humble meal'. Little did he know how permanently slightly hungry I had been since Mother started fretting, or how good his wife's giblet pie tasted.

I had, of course, been to Nine Elms before with Father and always entertained – if Father could spare the time – in the parlour, one of two. For Mother, I thought, Father had chosen well, a good solid house, spacious and not without dignity. But . . . Oh dear! Sitting there I realised that if this ever became Mother's home, it would also be mine. It was then that I knew how much I loved Pargeters.

Cooper was definitely uneasy. He kept looking out of the window. "Still pouring," he'd say. And I'd say something about the flattened corn and Mrs Cooper, who reared geese for market, said rain was good for grass.

I was their guest, I must make some contribution to the conversation. I said, "My brother and I went to Crowswood this afternoon and saw something strange. Fifteen heavy horses in his cow pasture."

It was a wrong thing to say. There was one of those awkward silences which can occur even in a parlour among equals. One does not need to see a fire in order to feel the heat and I could feel ill-ease pour from Cooper. Mrs Cooper at last said, "Fifteen is a lot."

"Yes," I said. "The pasture was bare dust. It'll be a quagmire now."

"Will Borley mostly knows what he's doing," Cooper said. It was a rebuke. Mind your own business. I said, "Yes, indeed." Then he glanced at the window again and said with the most blatant relief, "Rain's stopped. I'll fetch your horse, Mistress." I changed back into my own clothes – all light-weight linen and almost dry. Mrs Cooper made a slight protest about them not being quite fit to wear yet; why not go as I was. But I could say, truly, that all the trees in Layer would now be dripping and I should be wet again before I reached home. I thanked the Coopers very heartily and rode off, noting that the three horses which belonged to Nine Elms were in their meadow; and remembering what I had seen just inside the stable.

At Pargeters the supper table was set for two and still bore signs that Grandfather had already eaten. Nowadays, losing count of time, he often demanded food at unusual times and had developed untidy eating habits. John, wearing dressing-gown and slippers, was hacking slices from a joint of salt beef.

"Where the devil have you been? I want to talk to you."

"And I to you. I've been sheltering at Cooper's. Where's Mother?"

"In bed. She took flowers to . . . you know. And told Marian that when she came back she'd go to bed. She wanted no supper. Get out of those wet things and hurry down. I've got a lot to tell you."

I hurried away, sparing a minute to listen outside Mother's closed door. No sound. So I donned my robe and slippers and hurried down. And, Peggy the waiting maid

61

having been sent away, John and I engaged in one of those antiphonal conversations.

In our predominantly Puritan area there were the Rowhedges, the Hattons and the Helmers who were Royalist. Not in any ostentatious way, for the time had not yet come for taking sides openly. They simply paid the most resented of the King's taxes, Ship Money, with no fuss. So had Father, because he held it to be reasonable. Why should only sea-coast towns pay for the defence of the whole realm? Father was also slightly anti-Puritan because, he said, they interfered too much, and Grandfather agreed with him, having visited the Dutch Netherlands, a very Puritan country and very dreary. Still, we were not, as a family, very politically minded.

Now John said, "I went straight to Merravay and told the Rowhedges about those horses. They confirmed my worst suspicions."

"Intended for war if it comes?"

"Yes. Sir Rawley said he had already bought dozens, at very competitive prices, and sent them to the King."

"But not those now at Crowswood?"

"No. Of them he knew nothing, except that there was a concentration somewhere in the area. He rather suspected Sir Walter Fennel."

"Whose enthusiasm stops short at his pocket."

"You're right there."

"Now I'll tell you something. Cooper is in league with Borley. Helping to feed those horses with *our new hay*."

"How do you know?"

"I saw the barrow, piled high. And when I mentioned the horses . . ."

"You bloody fool!"

That was too much. I was prepared to yield a little to his seniority, and his sex. But ever since Father had left him in charge he'd been dependent upon me and I had supported him – with tact. Besides both our parents had insisted upon our being courteous to each other.

"Don't you dare speak to me like that, John Adam

Woodley-Mercer. And just bear this in mind. Next time you have an errand you don't much fancy, here's one bloody fool who won't hold your hand."

We glared at each other and then simultaneously broke into laughter.

"It's just that you've spoiled such a neat trick."

"What?"

"Well, obviously Borley is expecting somebody to collect them. Lady Alice said she'd send three men first thing in the morning, with money for their keep and some nice canting talk. Now, of course, Cooper knows you know and I'll bet they're being moved this minute."

I said, "If only you'd told me what you suspected, I'd have told you what I thought. Now, wait a minute. I said nothing to Cooper about the hay and I mentioned the horses in the most casual way. Suppose I . . ."

"Suppose what?"

"Suppose I go and pretend . . . I promise not to involve you." That was important, for in our world only men were regarded as responsible – apart from a few independent widows. What one silly girl did, of her own initiative, hardly counted.

Bess strongly – and rightly – resented being dragged out again. I'd never struck her in all the time I'd owned her and this evening I carried no crop as I often did, mainly used for defending Boru from other dogs who chose to regard him as a wolf. So I had to urge Bess on with slaps on the flank and nudges of the heel. This and agitation made me arrive at Nine Elms convincingly flustered and breathless. The long summer evening was gently fading into twilight. Mrs Cooper was shutting her precious geese in their fox-proof pen and Cooper was upending the now-empty sack-barrow in the open-fronted cartshed.

I said, "Cooper, could you get a message to Will Borley?"

"I could."

"I just heard," I said. "A plot afoot. Those horses should be moved. Tonight."

"Where to?" It was a rational question. There were not

63

many places like Crowswood within easy reach. Self-owned, secluded.

"Why not here? On Flatiron?" On most sizable farms fields and pastures had distinguishing names, all homely and often related to shape. "Could you and Borley manage?"

"Lead one and the rest'll follow." That was true. Of all horses the heavy, amber-coloured ones were the most manageable. They could pull their own weight and be guided by a thread of cotton and they did follow each other like sheep.

"But what then, Mistress?" Cooper asked.

"They will be collected. I will see to it. Tell Borley that when those who intend to fool him arrive he can say they are gone. And I must go . . ."

Bess needed no urging and I was soon home. John had gone to sleep, his head on his folded arms at the supper table. I nudged him and he roused. We laughed together at the thought of Borley and Cooper shepherding horses intended for Parliament on to what at most could be called neutral ground.

I said, "You must be up at cockcrow and ride to Merravay so that the men being sent to Crowswood will come to Nine Elms instead."

Both John and I owned watches, rare and treasured, gifts from Grandfather in his London-going, present-giving days. Mine was very pretty, as much a bauble as a timepiece. And it said, next morning, that it was four o'clock when the first cock crowed. I was awake after an uneasy night. I padded along to John's room and shook him into wakefulness.

Back in my own room I went to the window which faced East, overlooking the road which at one end stopped at Pargeters and at the other branched, left to Muchanger, right to Minsham All Saints. The church stood isolated on the boundary between the two villages. It was surrounded by trees that obscured all but the top of its tower.

I looked first at the sky; a pink dawn foretold bad weather and I was thinking of the corn flattened by last evening's

64

storm. A spell of rain now would cause it to sprout where it lay. The sky was satisfactorily grey and I was turning away when I realised that there was something wrong with the landscape. No church tower!

We speak of not believing our eyes. I did not believe mine. I blinked and stared. Then I thought of the storm. Lightning!

Sheer curiosity and the fact that I had time to spare before anybody would be stirring in the house, before John could be back from Merravay, made me dress hurriedly and set out for the church.

Half the tower lay about the graveyard, some of the stone blocks in heaps, some alone. The bell, its rope still in place, lay on its side, just inside the gate; beyond it was Father's grave and there, crushing the flowers she had brought, was Mother lying on her face.

Shock held me rigid for a moment but as soon as I could move I skirted the bell and went to her, turning her over. There was no sign of any injury and her face wore such an expression of unearthly calm as I have never since seen anywhere. I thought of what she had said about letting Father lie where his heart had been. If the position of mere bones meant anything, the same could be said of her. And that thought made me glance at Anne Borley's grave. The white headstone had split off as neatly as the shell from a walnut, leaving a grey, unmarked stone. I thought: Easily mended.

Shock can take strange forms. There was I capable of thought, even sparing one for those horses and hoping that all had gone well. And wondering what John would feel, back at breakfast and only Grandfather about. And Grandfather, so devoted to Mother; I could only hope that he would not fully realise.

I knew that something must be done; that this road was not much used except on market days when people took things to Baildon, and on Sundays. Yet when I tried to rise from the kneeling position into which I had dropped in order to turn Mother's body over, I had no bones in my legs.

The light brightened, full morning and at last I heard voices, men who lived in one village and worked in another. Loud exclamations of astonishment. I tried to call, but no sound came, so I grasped Anne Borley's headstone and with a mighty effort got to my feet, reached out and put my other hand on the rim of the bell and so stood. But unable to speak.

They thought I was a ghost and recoiled, clutching at each other. I thought of Father and his resolute rejection of all superstition; when you were dead, you were dead. I mouthed at them and then, luckily, one recognised me, plucked up some courage and ventured the few steps which brought Mother into view. Then he turned and ran towards Pargeters and the other man went into Muchanger to tell Mr Althorpe and the rest of the village.

John was so kind and so practical. He came riding Sultan and leading Bess, lifted me bodily into the saddle and then rode beside me with a firm handhold of a bunch of clothing just above my waist. He did not say much, but all comforting. Not to grieve for Mother whose life without Father had been so obviously joyless. Not to bother about anything, he would see to all. And then . . . What a good idea it had been about the horses.

When we reached home he half carried me into the dining parlour and poured some brandy. "That'll make you feel better." I couldn't even thank him, but in my dumbstruck state I decided that never, never again, no matter what he did or said, would I think harshly or speak sharply to him. And alongside this thought ran another. What about poor Grandfather whose mind, or tongue, failed him, as my voice now failed me. In future I'd be more understanding – not patient; patience includes a feeling of superiority.

John said, "I must see to a few things. I shan't be long. Would you like to go to bed?"

I shook my head; but I pointed to the kitchen where servants were stirring.

"I'll tell them," he said. "And to leave you alone. Just sit and recover."

Curiously, the idea that I might be dumb for the rest of

my life never occurred to me. It was, to me, like that numbness that can overtake a limb held too long in one position, feeling returning with the sensation known as pins-and-needles. Was one's voice to be restored in a similar way? I sat still and waited and nothing happened except that my mind went on and on, finally centring itself upon the idea that what Mother had done for Father, we must do for her.

The kitchen door opened, closed, opened, closed. I knew that Marian and the others thought I sat there griefstricken. Quite false. Father's death had hurt me more. But I knew I must move, get up and do something. At least I could cut flowers. Too soon of course, for, fast as the carpenter-joiner and his apprentice in Muchanger worked, it was evening before Mother was coffined, the flowers arranged and the candles alight.

I was still speechless, but I could write and the first thing I wrote, for John to see, was: Does Grandfather know?

"I told him myself. As gently as I could. He did not understand. He said that so long as Penelope was all right nothing else mattered."

Mr Althorpe was convinced that Mother had died of the plague, the sudden kind. Other people held that the lightning had struck her and John, urging me to eat, said that he believed she had died from lack of food. The Rector's opinion carried most weight and Mother was almost as hastily interred as Father. And though for him the bell had tolled even that small ceremony was denied Mother. It had taken six strong men to heave the bell away to allow passage for her cortège.

By that time I had recovered my voice and was more or less myself again – a stupid phrase, for who, dumb or loquacious, drunk or sober, angered or delighted, can really be anything other than himself?

There followed a somewhat confused time. Grandfather enjoyed the most prolonged sensible spell he had had for years though still convinced that I was Penelope and that it was his wife, Agnes, who had just died. There must be a suitable memorial. He planned a large table tomb of white marble, a family affair upon which all our names and the names of our putative descendants could be carved in due time, such carving to be done around the sides, the top being reserved for a large cross in relief. Mr Althorpe, whose permission was needed before anything could be done in the graveyard, said that crosses were not permissible. The Cross in any form, and the surplice, were outdated, discountenanced symbols, reeking of Popery. This verdict angered Grandfather and he grumbled on and on until he found another grievance. Why, he demanded, had he received no money for all his assets in London?

This was indeed a cogent question. Tom Markham had seemed most scrupulous about Father's possessions and surely would have brought back any papers recording a business transaction. So Tom was interrogated again.

"Oh yes, Master sold whatever he'd gone to sell. And at a good price. Once we had a drink to celebrate."

"And what did he do with the money, Tom?"

"Took it to the goldsmiths. In Lumber Street."

"Lombard Street. Thanks, Tom. That's all I need to know."

Tom looked puzzled, but no more so than John and I felt and I, at least, was not much enlightened by Grandfather's dissertation upon bills of exchange, sensible as the business seemed since it saved people carrying large sums of money about with them. "And they pay interest. So Penelope, my dear, you will never want." In or out of his mind he retained the illusion that I was his daughter. Now and then he told me that if I'd make up my mind and get married and have a son, he'd buy a baronetcy. "I have toyed with the idea, but the moment never seemed right. Now I can well afford it."

However that phase, though longer than most, came to an end and he relapsed.

In August of that year, with the unusually early harvest just ending, the final breach between King and Parliament came. The King left London, went North, hoping for a welcome at Hull which was not only a great port, but an arsenal. He was rejected there and eventually raised his Standard at Nottingham. So the Civil War began.

At about the same time a period of our life about which I do not care to think began. Father, that mere plasterer, and the besotted woman who had chosen to marry him were both dead. There remained John with his looks and his charm and his nigh on a thousand acres. Most eligible. And Wills, once they had been proved, were not private. With my certain allowance and modest dowry I also was eligible – to suitors who could not look for better; widowers with young families, younger men with squints or stammers or bad teeth.

It was Aunt Lydia who decided that we were now socially desirable and invited us to attend the wedding of our cousin Annis who had made a most satisfactory match with a gentleman from Kent. Sir Walter Fennel must have been impressed, for he offered his mansion for the jollifications which at that time still marked a wedding. I wore a green velvet dress, trimmed with cream lace and a very modest necklet of seed-pearls strung in whorls. "Not good enough," John said, and hurried upstairs. When he came down he was carrying Mother's emerald pendant. I shrank back a little. "Once she told me that it was the first thing Father ever gave her and at a time when he could ill afford it."

"All the more reason for not wasting it."

It was a very fine wedding indeed; the bride, Queen for the day, properly attended, with flowers, with music. Perhaps one of the last to be so celebrated for many a long day and I wish now that I had enjoyed it more. But Charles Rowhedge whom I knew and felt at ease with was not there.

Perhaps I was already too old to take readily to a new form of life. Perhaps I shared Father's ability to do without people except those of his family. And, no perhaps about it, I resented how Father, and Mother because of him, had been treated.

John took happily to the new régime and was relieved rather than concerned when I said, "You go, proffer my excuses. You'll enjoy yourself more if you don't have to keep looking to see if I am left in a corner."

My withdrawal was made easier by the fact that the country was now at war, taxes had risen to heights never reached before and that the first battle, fought at Edgehill in October, had been indecisive, both Royalists and Parliamentarians claiming victory. In such circumstances too much festivity would have seemed out of taste.

John and I gave one party at Christmas that year and were very merry, but it was a feverish merriment; if Parliament triumphed there would be no more merry-making at Christmas. We were, with few exceptions, a Puritan community but even here there was a feeling that extremists might take over, and the eleventh Commandment, "Thou shalt not enjoy thyself," come into force. Already all theatres were closed and the strolling players whose visits had been so welcome in country districts were to be treated as common vagrants.

Yet somehow we lived through another year of rumour and uncertainties, of placid intervals and some false alarms. Soon the King and the court were firmly established in Oxford, and on the whole events seemed to be going well for the Royalists. But to the unchanging seasons of the countryside – the sowing and reaping of crops, the begetting and rearing of livestock – war meant nothing. John attempted, not too successfully, to take more interest in his duties as a landowner, when he was not engaged in socialising with some of our grander neighbours, and I pursued my own even course. But we did not give a party for the Christmas of 1643, and we were not alone in having no heart for festivities.

As usual, the weather worsened after Christmas with occasional days when roads were impassable. Understandably John grew restive. He had never derived any pleasure from reading and at all indoor games he beat me so easily that playing against me bored him. Once, gathering the cards together, he said, "I must admit that you're unlucky. And you know what they say – you should be lucky in love. By the same token, it bodes ill for me! Not that I shall lose any sleep over that. The whole thing is overrated. Look at Father."

"Father? I always thought – at least not always, but lately – that Mother was the one who did the loving."

"Oh, that." John dismissed the long years of placid marriage, the birth of two children, Mother's extremity of grief. "I was thinking of something else."

"Anne Borley?"

"So you noticed, too . . ."

But this conversation, maybe the most promising of interest that John and I had ever embarked upon, was interrupted by Grandfather coming in and demanding supper.

Next day the weather cleared. John rode off to visit the Hattons at Mortiboys where there was a tennis court and I went my rounds. It was now February and lambs began dropping in March, so pens must be built, straw fortresses against the next harsh month.

At Brook, Eli Smith told me that he was leaving at the end of the following week. He was within his rights for Father strongly objected to the system of bonded labour whereby men and women were engaged by the year. I was still so unpolitically minded that I imagined that Smith had come to better terms with some other employer. He was a good man, fairly young, very active and completely reliable which was why Father had made him foreman at the most distant of the three farms. He occupied the farmhouse at Brook, admittedly an inferior building to the one at Nine Elms, but comfortable enough. He was unmarried and his mother kept house for him.

It was a situation which found me utterly inexperienced. Never once so far as I knew had anybody working for Father ever left voluntarily.

I wondered – no, I *knew* how Father would have dealt with this. Cool, civil.

I said, cool and civil, "We shall miss you, Smith. I hope your move will be fortunate."

"I'm going to the war," he said. "On the side of Parliament."

That, too, was his right. I said, "I hope you will come through alive and unmaimed."

"Thank you, Mistress."

"What will happen to your mother?"

"That I wanted a word about. That depends on you. And who you get in my place. I mean a single fellow might be glad of her – she's clean, and a good cook. Or I'd rent the house for her if you're agreeable. Failing which she could go to her sister, out Shelfanger way."

"I must consult my brother," I said. Smith was not a man to smile easily but a glint of amusement lightened his rather dour face. Then he went on to talk about lambing. "I been training Dick Summers and he's handy . . . And there's Cooper . . ."

Not *my* business. There was a conspiracy among men – even Father, an enlightened man, shared it. Procreation except where their own kind was concerned, was not women's business. Matings were a mystery, bulging bellies things to be ignored; then lo! Count the pretty little lambs, admire the new calf or the foal.

When I knew more I realised that the intention to conceal was well-meant.

Riding away from Brook that morning I decided to suggest to John that Smith should not be replaced. I'm as self-seeking as the next person and had my own future to look after. John, judging by what I had seen at parties, would have no difficulty in finding a bride. Not really pretty, not all that well endowed and, above all hard to please, I was unlikely to marry. I must make myself so indispensable that I need not be unoccupied.

John was very late for supper that evening and was oddly silent, not eating much, indeed pushing his food about rather as Mother had done. He was not precisely sober but far from drunk. There was a kind of suppressed excitement about him and I wondered whether he'd become betrothed to one of the girls he favoured. They were all cut from the same cloth, shortish, plumpish, very fair with kittenish faces and that manner known as vivacious.

My suspicion deepened when I told him about Eli Smith

and tentatively suggested that he should not be replaced. "We'd save his wages and we could probably let the house. It'd help towards the taxes."

"We'll talk about that . . . after," he said.

Peggy removed the last plates, withdrew the cloth and bobbed her goodnight. John refilled both our glasses with Grandfather's favourite white Rhenish. He took a long draught and I waited, wondering which of the smiling, pouting, fan-tapping, ringlet-tossing little creatures I must soon call sister.

He said, "Sarah. I want to go to the war."

I blurted out the first words that came to mind: "Oh John! You're so young." He looked offended and then laughed. "Isn't that an advantage? What use would an army of dotards be? The only thing that bothers me is *you*."

"Why?"

"Could you manage here? Or should I sell out and buy a nice little house for you and Grandfather, in Baildon?"

I considered this truly horrible prospect for a moment. "I should die of boredom. But don't let that sway you. Personally I think it would be folly to sell an acre just now when the whole situation is so undecided. People are reluctant to invest. And there's another thing: are we – I mean are you – entitled to sell before you are eighteen?"

"Have you been in communication with Mr Turnbull?"

"Mr Turnbull? I haven't seen him since the day he brought Mother's will. Why?"

"You talk like a lawyer. Well, I have seen him, this afternoon. I'm afraid I told him a lie. I said I planned a long absence combining business with pleasure – stock-buying in the West country and a possible betrothal. To a lady of vast possessions. I told him that if you accepted the responsibility, I wanted to leave you in full charge, even with power to sell land should I decide to remain in Gloucestershire. And he raised the very point you did – in the eyes of the law we are both minors. But Grandfather is adult. Isn't that the ultimate absurdity? Here am I, three months short of the age Father thought responsible yet that poor old dodderer . . ."

73

I said, "Wouldn't it be simpler to wait until after your birthday?"

I remembered wishing Eli Smith survival and no wounds, but that was mere speech. Now, John, going to the same war, was terribly vulnerable, a frail thing of flesh, bone, spilled blood.

"It could be simpler. But too late. Sarah, I want to *be* there. I want to serve under Prince Rupert."

News of the war reached us belatedly and almost invariably slanted. The occasional Newsletter was printed in London, a Puritan stronghold, and even rumour reached us after having been sieved through Puritan minds. However, even we had heard of Prince Rupert of the Rhine, nephew to the King. Still only twenty-two, he had years of experience in continental wars behind him and was the most reckless and dashing leader of Cavalry. There were those who said he was arrogant, foolhardy, over ambitious, trying to usurp the young Prince of Wales in the King's affection. He was a hero; he was a devil, he was a foreigner – no better than a hired mercenary. But he had glamour; what he said or did, even what he wore, was news. I understood how John felt.

I said, "I can perfectly well look after the farms."

It sound so prosaic, so inadequate, but it satisfied John. "I know you can. Now all we need is Grandfather's signature, just to cover the interim period. After my birthday you'll be in full control. You can even sell land if needs be." That reminded him of something else. "I wish we'd found Father's hoard."

This was one of those jokes which are not all jest. That Father should have left so little actual money in the Trunk was inexplicable. He never lent money, the only investment he believed in was land. So John and I had concocted – and half believed in – the story that he had hidden money in some secret place. It became a kind of game, we searched all likely and unlikely places. With more urgency when the taxes became so ferocious and the man who had erected that grandiose tomb had begun pressing for payment. We had never found a penny. Nor, despite Grandfather's complete faith in the honesty of the men in Lombard Street and the

74

efficiency of the bills-of-credit service system, had any money fallen like manna from Heaven.

"I must take Mother's jewels," John said. "The King doesn't need hungry men to support."

"Mother intended them for your bride."

"I shall take good care that my bride has plenty of her own. Come on, let's look."

Most of what Mother had called trinkets were just what a doting, well-to-do man might give his daughter for Christmas or birthdays; nothing showy or extravagant. The exception was a ring, an oval emerald framed in small diamonds, and set high so that the stones caught the light. "I wonder why she never wore this. It matches the pendant," I said, trying it on and turning my hand to catch the green sparkle.

"Keep that, if you like it," John said generously. I thanked him, but refused, and then, not to be outdone said, "You can take the pendant, too."

"Too grand. They say that so many families have sold jewels to buy horses and guns that the market is flooded. And only Puritans have money now. Well, except for that ring there's nothing here that the most ardent Puritan couldn't bestow on one of his wives."

That was another joke. Puritans were so devoted to the Old Testament which countenanced polygamy that anti-Puritans said it was merely a matter of time before it would be legal here. This was on a par with the Puritans saying that all Royalists were dead drunk most of the time and scented not only their hair but the manes and tails of their horses.

It was ironic, but completely in keeping, that Eli Smith could let it be known that he was off to the war and depart with good wishes and handshakes and kindly rough jokes about not arguing with bullets or sleeping in any damp beds, while John had to steal away on a pretended errand.

There was reason for such caution. Charles Rowhedge was known to be with the King; Cambridge town was for Parliament, the Colleges were not. They'd melted down their plate and sent it with dozens of young men to the King in the very first days of the war. Then there was Chris Hatton of Mortiboys; his mother was French and Chris had been staying with her family in the vine country of Burgundy when the war began. Had he stayed there? Or had he come back, smuggling some of the arms which the Queen, Henrietta Maria, herself a Frenchwoman, had gone to buy in France – with money raised by pawning the Crown Jewels? Mortiboys was actually searched, quite legally, by a deputy sheriff and a party of men, with a warrant. Their quest was saltpetre, small in bulk but absolutely essential for the activating of muskets. Mr Hatton, well known to be stupid, was said to have joined in the search, and actually revealed a priest hole that nobody knew existed, saying: "And if you're hunting my boy, too, measure the space. They must have bred priests small in those days. My boy, thank God, is man size."

The third young man from our district, mad-cap Nick Helmar, had simply said to his parents, just as John had said to me, that he was off to the war. But he said it in the presence of a servant and next day was appealed to by seven or eight men, all young, strong labourers who said they'd go with him – if he could mount them. They'd arm themselves, they said, their weapons ranging from a silver-handled scimitar of Eastern design to a bow and some arrows.

It was not an indictable offence to go and fight for the King, but in a community like ours it attracted punitive action in subtle ways. All taxes had risen steeply, but those levied on the properties of the wrong persuasion were proportionately far heavier. The market overseer at Baildon and the various auctioneers developed defective sight, and nothing from a "rebel" estate made a fair price, while anything sold to a "rebel" acquired a sudden value. The term "rebel" had become almost geographical; in the North and West the Parliamentarians were the rebels, in the East the reverse held.

John was anxious not to leave me exposed to persecution however petty, and thanks to Father's uncommitted attitude and our own caution we had so far attracted no suspicion. The true part we had played in re-directing those fifteen horses had never been exposed. So, when John told other people the story he had told Mr Turnbull, it was accepted without question.

And we were both still young enough to take a kind of pleasure in making preparations secretly. Most of Mother's trinkets we hid in the padding of the saddle John would ride – and that saddle would not be strapped on to Sultan. Rather touchingly, John said, "I should hate Sultan to be hurt." And that made me think of horses being shot under their riders. So I suggested hiding Mother's pearl necklace inside John's hat and her rings behind the buttons of his coat. A simple operation. I cut off the buttons, stitched the rings into place, held by firm stitches, and then sewed back the buttons which were of the unostentatious kind.

John fretted about the lack of ready money and one evening I thought of a possible explanation which cheered him immensely. I said, "Do you know, I think it quite likely that what money Grandfather's property made Father sent to the King through those Lumber Street people." (Another small joke. We knew the word was Lombard.)

"Whatever made you think of that?" he asked; but I could see that the idea pleased him.

"Lombard. Italy. Roman Catholic. They'd be on the King's side. And half this whole bother is about religion. Not that Father would have minded much about that but Grandfather may have given him instructions."

It was useless to question Grandfather. He was going through a phase when any mention of money evoked one of three responses. "No need to worry, my dear Penelope. You will never want." "I'll see about that when I come back from Amsterdam." "I only conduct business in the office." Yet he had signed the paper making himself responsible for everything until John's eighteenth birthday, and then me responsible during his absence, without protest or question. "Positively dangerous," John remarked, "he'd sign his own death warrant."

And then John was gone and I entered the most completely solitary period of my life. No more little jokes, or arguments. The evenings were the worst time and as the year advanced – John left in March – they grew longer.

On a few occasions I rode over to Merravay. Lady Alice, who as my Aunt Lydia had once acidly remarked was not entitled to be called more than Lady Rowhedge, was the only woman whose company I really craved. She was so different, so real; she was also knowledgeable and witty. But presently the joy of her company was denied me. One evening I thought her manner strange, not unwelcoming exactly, but uneasy, pre-occupied. When I came to take leave, she, not a woman given to meaningless gestures or endearments, embraced me and said, "My dear. It would be as well if for a short time we are not seen to be too closely acquainted. Rawley and I are under strict observation, the reason for which it is better that you should not know. If I get news of John I will contrive to inform you immediately. If you ever need help, let me know . . . This is a mere interlude: not Goodbye, Au revoir."

Then suddenly she stiffened, seemed to draw away and said, in a different voice, "Be brave. Much awaits you."

That evening I was keeping my promise to John that I would exercise Sultan regularly but there was not the accord between us that there was between Bess and me, so it was not until I was back at Pargeters that I could give my whole mind to what Lady Alice had meant. Be brave, there are better times ahead; or, Be brave, you will need all your courage.

To this day I am uncertain of the answer.

John had promised to let me know how he fared, but knowing how much he disliked writing and imagining war to mean constant battle and movement, I did not really expect to hear very soon or very often, yet that summer I found myself unusually alert for calls from pedlars and tinkers, even beggars.

But my first letter from John was brought by an old woman who sold salt fish from Bywater. She asked two shillings because Pargeters was a bit off her regular beat.

Since John had set out for Oxford, where the King was known to be at that time, and Bywater was a port under the strictest possible surveillance by Parliamentarian forces, I was surprised to receive it at all, and not surprised to see that it had been opened and read and clumsily re-sealed.

Luckily John had written cryptically.

"My dearest sister, I hope you are well and not too busy. I am busy indeed but the business goes well. It may take a little longer than I planned; I may indeed go as far as Gloucester. But travelling suits me. I never felt better in my life or did business with more pleasant people . . ."

I took this to mean that he had achieved his desire to get under Prince Rupert's command. I was glad for him, but worried. It was now being said that the Prince bore a charmed life and thus could afford to take any risk; but my brother was ordinary flesh and blood.

So time went on and the war went on with no really decisive battle. A Parliamentarian leader, Oliver Cromwell, complained bitterly about the quality of the troops he led – calling them old decayed serving men and tapsters and asking how such fellows could be expected to stand against gentlemen of quality. What Parliament needed was a new army and he was prepared to raise it. Pargeters – now more often called the Home Farm – Nine Elms and Brook lost two or three young men, ill-spared, for we were busier than ever before. Armies must be fed and neither soldiers nor their horses are really productive. I did a good deal in the way of re-organising the farms and although taxes still soared, so did prices.

I had two more letters from John; one most mysterious: it simply appeared on the table in the hall and must have been placed there by somebody whom John trusted. It was worded cautiously but the pretence of being on business had been dropped – he might have been a schoolboy enjoying a wonderful holiday. He was having a wonderful time, enjoying every minute of it. He added, like a schoolboy, that his funds were running out. I had actually about twenty pounds locked away in the Trunk but how could I get it to him? He gave no address.

His third letter came by way of Merravay, brought by an old man ostensibly bringing a cow to mate with our bull. There was a covering letter from Lady Alice. Cryptic again. "This cowherd is trustworthy. If you wish for a share in the calf he will take charge of the money."

It was a common arrangement between very small farmers who handled money as little as possible. It was unusual between places like Merravay and Nine Elms where I had concentrated my herd.

Then I read John's letter. If I heard that he had had an accident I need not worry – he'd suffered only minor injuries; his horse had fallen. He needed a new one and good horses were expensive.

The seals on that letter had not been tampered with. I wasted a minute wondering how Lady Alice had known that it contained an appeal for money. Then I thought: Probably because Charles writes similar demands to her. So the trustworthy cowherd went off with – I hope – a successfully impregnated cow and twenty pounds in what looked like a roll of sacking.

And soon after that there happened the thing which changed all.

It was St John's Eve, June 24th, and I was riding home at the end of a long, tiring day. It was the time when fleecing gangs moved about, and no doubt about it Oliver Cromwell had drained off the best of such itinerant, independent workers. And this year at Brook we had a gang not so much incompetent as careless. I had concentrated the flock there and Dick Summers, whom Eli Smith had trained and recommended to me, was in fact a good shepherd but an ineffectual person. He had no control. All that day I had been the one urging more care, noticing the little nicks which if left un-dabbed with tar could breed maggots.

I remember thinking how glad I was to be riding Bess, and that I missed Smith – and that soon I should be home, washed and changed into clothes which did not reek of sweat and sheep and tar.

We were almost at the turn-off to Pargeters when Boru

who had run ahead and was out of sight began to bark. I was not apprehensive. For one thing robbers did not frequent unprofitable places like Layer Wood; for another, had danger threatened me in any form Boru would have been back at my side, silently menacing. I rounded the bend and saw Boru investigating something in the high young bracken. He barked again, demanding my attention, and out of the green depths a voice said, "Good dog. Go away! Damn you to hell! Be off!"

I said, "Boru! Come here."

The man had been prone and I should certainly have passed unseeing except for the dog. Now he was in a sitting position, getting to his feet, reeling a little, reaching out for support from the nearest tree, yet making some attempt at a bow.

I said, "Good evening."

"Good evening. I hope I did not startle you. Weariness overcame me . . . Am I trespassing?"

Before I could explain that to trespass in Layer Wood was an impossibility since it had not had in recorded time any owner, something more than weariness overcame him. His hold on the birch tree slackened, his knees buckled and he fell.

I had by that time taken good stock of him; the ordinary seaman's rough clothes, such a sharp contrast with manner and voice, the pallor under the tan which gave his skin the colour of dish-clout.

I was out of the saddle, knee deep in the bracken. I said, "You are ill – or hurt. I'll get help. I live nearby."

"Please," he said. "I'm all right. Just ignore me. For your own sake . . . believe me, as well as mine. Just pretend you never saw me. Please."

He spoke with some vehemence, but in a weakening voice and although I had no experience of illness – we were an exceptionally healthy family – I knew that he must be very sick. Even in this cool green place his body exuded heat, his eyes were both sunken and glittering, his lips cracked.

I said, "I can't just leave you."

"You must. One thing you could do . . . Tell me the way to Merra . . . Nettleton. I seem to have lost my bearings."

"It is too far for you in your present state. Look, I live nearby, and quite alone. No one need see you."

"Servants?"

"I'll look after you myself. And if your destination is Merravay — Lady Alice is a friend of mine."

That decided him, and gripping the tree again he began to struggle to his feet. He kept his left arm immobile, the hand pushed inside the buttons of the blue canvas shirt.

"Why a nick in the arm should affect the legs . . ." he said, managing a wry grin and almost collapsing again. I moved round and said, "Put your arm round my neck." He did so and I took a firm grip of his hand to keep the arm in place. Our progress was as wavering as that of two drunken persons. But we reached Bess and somehow I got him into the saddle, and then, remembering how John had held me that morning, laid hold of the waistband of his trousers.

Most of the houses near Layer Wood have fields between them and the trees; Pargeters was different. We had only a portion of the garden. Halfway along was a track leading to the stableyard. There I hauled him down, gave Bess a dismissive pat and resuming my supporting posture somehow reached the now never-used door of what had once been Grandfather's office.

John and I had never been allowed there. It had been Grandfather's special sanctum and had remained so long after he had become incapable of transacting any business. Father had never used it. Two shelves below his collection of books in the parlour served him as office. But I knew that the key to the half-hidden door was on Father's strap which I always carried in a pouch at my waist. The door opened a shade unwillingly. The smell of a place long deserted met us. I said, "Here we are," and saw, with what delight! that the furniture in the room included a large couch. I lowered him onto it, lifted his feet in their rope-soled shoes and laid him prone. He said "Thank you," and lay still.

Then began my battle against time.

It was not unusual for me to send Bess off to the stableyard, walk through the side garden and enter the house by the front door. I was a creature of regular habits and I was well served. As I went up the main staircase, Annie would carry a jug of hot water to my bedroom; Marian would put the last touches to the supper dish, Peggy would look over the table and in ten minutes be ready to serve me. The outward appearance of ordinariness must be preserved.

So it was on this momentous evening.

I was glad to see by the state of the cloth that Grandfather had taken his supper. Peggy brought me a dish of asparagus, by many regarded as a luxury vegetable but at Pargeters it grew like weeds. It was not a dish part of which could be smuggled to someone in hiding. Cold roast fowl was. I said to Peggy, "I'm hungry. I only had a bag-dinner." A bag-dinner, or noonpiece, was portable food, mainly bread and cheese, which sustained workmen or travellers who were out of reach of the main meal of the day.

Peggy, understanding, helped me lavishly, and to bread too. Half of it I slipped down into my lap where a linen table napkin waited. Finally she put before me a dish of strawberries, a jug of cream and some well-pounded sugar. And how I wished I could transport them too.

I said, "I shall go to bed early. You need not wait."

Promising secrecy and safety I had been stupid. Thinking only of reaching the hiding place, and mustering enough strength to get him there, I had not thought of what the undertaking involved.

Food – yes, I had that. What about drink?

Grandfather had been drinking his favourite white Rhenish; Peggy had poured me a glassful and I had drunk about half. The remainder I now poured back and leaning out from the open window, set the bottle firmly. What about brandy which almost ranked as medicine? There was a bottle, half-full, on the sideboard. I put that outside too, together with the chicken and bread in my used and now greasy napkin. I took a clean one from the pile on the sideboard, crumpled it and left it in my place.

Then I went softly upstairs, found a light but warm blanket and a spare pillow and dropped them from a window that overlooked the overgrown bit of garden near the office.

By this time dusk was falling. And I thought of light. I slipped my bedside tinder-box and a spare candle inside my bodice and stole downstairs and outdoors again. Passing the window of the dining-parlour I collected the food and drink and went back to the office, quite dark now because its window was more than half obscured by the overgrown laurels.

I made a light and then saw that my one poor candle was not needed. Grandfather had four, thicker and of better quality in holders too black to be pewter. Silver, unpolished for years?

The man lay as I had left him, but the light roused him. From his flat position he reared slightly, using only his right arm as lever. He said, halting and hoarse, "If it isn't . . . too much trouble . . . could I have a drink of water?"

The one simple thing which I had not thought of.

There was water in the ewer in my bedroom, but it was rainwater which Mother had firmly believed to be better for the complexion than that drawn from the well. It was brownish and unclear, quite unpalatable.

There was always a bucket of water in the kitchen, but the three men and the three women who slept in would be there, rounding off the day with their interminable game of Noggin. And to go and ask for a mug of water to drink would be unusual; only the really poor drank water just as it was.

There was a well full of water in the yard, but the yard was near the kitchen; the bucket and chain would rattle, Bess would whinny, Boru greet me from his pen.

I said, "Could you drink wine? From the bottle?" I had not thought of bringing a cup. A fine conspirator I should make! Then I wondered whether perhaps Grandfather might have provided himself . . . And, bless him, he had. His sloping-topped desk stood high; one pedestal held four drawers, the other a cupboard and inside the cupboard were four matching glasses, several bottles, white and red wine and brandy and a tobacco jar, with alongside it four new clay pipes. So I could offer my guest a drink in civilised fashion. He really was thirsty. Thirsty enough to have drunk the dark rainwater had nothing else been available. He emptied his glass twice, pausing only to say "Thank you," and "You're marvellously kind."

I then, rather shame-facedly, offered the food. "The best I could manage at such short notice."

"Bless you. I'm starving. I think hunger is my trouble. At a critical moment I found myself without money. And I daren't beg. There had been, you see, a . . . scuffle. People may be on the look-out for me."

He wolfed the tepid chicken and greasy bread.

I grappled with another problem, any overnight guest's needs. What was one supposed to say? In the end I decided to be blunt. I said, "I dropped a blanket and a pillow into the bushes. I will now fetch them and show you the place of easement."

Grandfather's firm resolve to keep business apart had extended to the provision of a separate such place, set amongst the laurels. I went with him almost to the door. He seemed rather firmer on his legs and I remembered how Grandfather had always claimed that good wine put heart into a man.

I retrieved the blanket and the pillow and returned to the office which felt different now; welcoming, glad to be part of life once more.

He'd spoken of a nick in the arm and inside the blanket I had wrapped the only available medicament that I knew – a pot of something known as Old Mother Nelly's Ointment. It was regarded as a cure-all for anything short of a broken bone, the pox or the plague. The old woman died before I was born; some people said she had been a witch and the ointment had magic power. She was supposed to have whispered the secret of its making to somebody from her deathbed. Father once said that he knew that was rubbish.

Various people made it and sold it, so it varied in quality. It was unusual for a house like Pargeters to have only this one curative within its walls, most ladies prided themselves upon their skill as herbalists. But Mother had spent her youth in London, with a doctor at one corner of the street and an apothecary at the other, and had never bothered. Or indeed needed to.

Back in the office and suddenly intimate and easy, I said, as I might have said to John, "Now, let us look at this nick in your arm. I have an ointment, said to be magic. And a clean bandage could only be advantageous."

He had kept his arm concealed, but inside the slashed sleeve of his shirt I glimpsed a soiled, bloody bandage.

"I thank you again. But I think I'd better not. Last time I saw it it was not something I would wish to show to a lady."

I should have been the last to deny that I was a lady, but I knew, even then, that I was more.

I said, "I am more. More even than a farm-wife. For a long time . . . ever since my brother . . . No, before that. Since my father died before the war began, I've been dealing with sights usually regarded as unsuitable. Come, let us not be silly . . ."

It was a gash about five inches long in the fleshy part of his upper arm and it was a horrible sight, the lips of it puffy and inflamed and gaping apart. It oozed a little blood and a great deal of thick, yellowish-greenish slime which stank, faintly sweet, wholly corrupt. All around it his arm was swollen and red. I had heard of simple injuries, even scratches that were said to have "gone bad", but I had never seen one before, and despite my bold words about experience in unsuitable sights I was appalled, not least by my own impotence. I had a vague idea that wounds should be bathed, but I was still without water.

"Just cover it again," the man said.

A phrase from the Bible slid into my mind. The Good Samaritan had used oil and wine when he helped the man who had been robbed and wounded. I had no oil, but thanks to Grandfather there was no shortage of wine. I soaked my handkerchief and dabbed gently.

"I hope I am not hurting you too much."

"Hardly at all," he said. But he said it between clenched teeth. And I doubt that even water could have made a clean wound of this; so soon I desisted, applied a lavish dressing of the ointment and the clean bandage, trying to make it firm enough to bring those gaping lips together without being too tight. Then I remembered one of Grandfather's stories of a man whose foot had been trapped under a beam in a burning house. "It was cut him free or leave him to frizzle," said Grandfather, who had a way with words which at the time neither John nor I were mature enough to appreciate. The gist of the story was that before the barber-surgeon came to sever the foot the man had been so plied with brandy that he felt nothing. So I said, "Would you like some brandy?"

"If . . . you . . . have it."

I poured for him and then for myself. Why not? Ladies did not, except when recovering from a swoon, drink brandy, but I needed as much bracing as though I had swooned at the sight of a mouse.

The stuff ran through me, banishing worry and bewilderment and weariness.

I remember saying, "Do you feel easier now?"

"Thanks to you, yes. I feel I could sleep for a week."

He was at least arranged comfortably now; the pillow under his head. I spread the blanket. I said, "Good night. Sleep well."

"I can never thank you," he said, and reaching for my hand kissed it, not the mere stylised brush of the mouth that in the case of unmarried women was permissible only to old acquaintances, but with some fervour. My heart gave a jolt but I thought, He is grateful; and so he should be. Little as I had done, I had done my best.

I remembered to retrieve my own candle and tinder-box and stole out, closing but not locking the door. There was little likelihood of anybody entering this out-of-the way, almost-forgotten door amidst the overgrown laurels.

But I had again been stupid and forgotten one vital thing. When I had stolen softly around to the front of the house, the main door was bolted on the inner side.

In our quiet corner this bolting of doors and latching of ground-floor windows was as much symbolic as realistic, but Grandfather, a Londoner, had started it, Father and John had continued and since John's going Tom Markham had assumed the male duty of locking up. "I'll see to bolting and barring," he had said.

So here I was, locked out. Unless I could be successful as a burglar I had the choice of spending the night in the garden or returning to the office.

I began to prowl around the house, temporarily at least my own, like a housebreaker, and when I found an entry I knew that I owed it to Grandfather and his overseas connections. Several plants in our garden were rare, brought in by ships which had traded with Holland. One of these was a pretty thing, half-tree, half-creeper which grew by walls and produced pale purple flowers, not unlike bunches of grapes; it was called Wistaria and when it grew it certainly grew, throwing out tendrils very quickly. One such tendril had invaded the rear window of the parlour just at the top corner, not far above the hinge; this had prevented the casement from closing completely so that the latch, though in place, hardly met its socket by more than a fraction of an inch. It yielded under the slightest touch. I climbed in.

Out of doors the moon had served me, indoors I lighted my candle and made my way into the kitchen which had three doors, one to the yard, one to the dining-room and one to a kind of lobby out of which rose the back stairs and out of which a number of doors opened, larder, dairy, wine store, and the office. This door also had its bolt, on the lobby side. Many years must have elapsed since anyone had touched it and it was literally rusted into place.

I was anxious not to make the slightest noise which might wake or alarm the man on the other side of the door, so I fetched some lard and worked it into and around the bolt, and while it did its lubricating work I busied myself by collecting a breakfast which would make up for the paucity of the supper, nourish and please him, and all without drawing Marian's attention to any depredation. Apart from some ham and bread my basketful consisted mainly of delicacies, one at least very rare and specially intended for the ailing.

Then I worked at the bolt and after what seemed an infinity of time edged it free. I now had – as Grandfather had had in his time – access to the office from inside the house.

Farm work in the summer months begins very early, but I intended to forestall everybody. I was anxious to know how his wound did; it was imperative that my day's routine should seem just as usual. I imagined myself carrying my basket, collecting a jug of water – after all, he had asked for water – going through this door, tending to his needs and being back in my room by the time Annie brought me my warm, morning wash water.

Absurdity! In fact if one's life can have a keynote word, mine is absurdity. Sleeping so slightly as almost to have derived no benefit, I was up and dressed at first light, by my watch just after four. Going towards the kitchen I could smell frying which must surely be fancy. But was not. There at the kitchen table sat Grandfather and over a newly kindled fire in the wide hearth, Timmy was frying eggs and bacon in a pan.

I'd sworn to myself to be more patient and understanding towards Grandfather and just then, because of his office, had especial reason to be grateful to him, and Timmy was a workhouse orphan whom I had always thought fortunate to have such an easy job, at the same time pitying him for the boredom, the near slavery of being subject day and night to an old man's whims.

But just then I hated them both. Really *hated*.

Grandfather was back in the past, making an early start to catch the tide. "I'll bring you something pretty, Penelope, my dear."

Timmy went on frying. Only my presence in the kitchen needed an explanation. Timmy led a separate life from that of the other servants but when he had a chance he talked, in a mildly complaining way. I could just imagine his saying that he'd been up at first light – "and the mistress came down . . ." Then somebody would wonder why. Ordinarily it would not have mattered a pin but until the man was safely out of the house I dared not take the slightest risk.

"I'm going to Brook," I said. "The shearers are inclined to be laggard in the morning."

"You shouldn't go out on an empty stomach, Mistress," Timmy said. "Hev one of these." He held out the pan, bacon cooked just enough, eggs basted so that the yolks looked pinkish. "Time you eat I'll harness Bess. If you'd just keep an eye . . ." He nodded towards Grandfather who, having set about his early breakfast with zest, paused and said, "Don't say I didn't warn you. And don't talk about love. I *know*." He resumed eating. My food lodged behind my breast-bone and turned into red-hot cinders.

Then Timmy brought Bess to the door and I took up my basket. "Tell Marian that I shall not be back to breakfast. And dinner I don't know about."

I rode Bess out of sight amongst the trees, tethered her and ran back through the dew-fresh garden.

The air in the room was more tainted with that sweetish, corrupt stench and after the morning brightness seemed almost dark.

He lay on the couch but the blanket was on the floor and the bandage, though not entirely off had been disturbed, loosened and pulled down so that part of the wound was exposed, looking uglier than ever. He could have been asleep, or unconscious. Not dead; he was too hot and flushed to be dead; and he was breathing, in rapid, shallow gasps.

I could think of only one person who could help, and could be safely asked to do so. I picked up my skirts and ran to where I had left Bess and, wishing heartily that I'd been riding Sultan, set out for Merravay.

One fear that rode with me was that the man might regain enough strength to make a noise.

Plainly he was fevered and in fever people raved. Two doors and the lobby separated him from the kitchen and while breakfast was in progress and while pots and pans clattered no sound he made would be noticed. But if one person went into the lobby to reach dairy or larder . . . Oh dear! Oh Bess, please produce a turn of speed.

Past the turn-offs to Nine Elms, to Crowswood and

Brook. Past the pool said to be haunted by the ghost of a girl deserted by her lover; past the place where three paths met – one leading inland to Baildon. Of what we called Our Villages, Nettleton was farthest from Pargeters and even then the house stood apart with a long drive of elms between it and the village. If only I knew a short cut. But Layer Wood was in itself a short cut and I was so ignorant of the geography even of this limited region that I dared not risk experiment now. Suppose the man died? Suppose he had been discovered, waking up and shouting as people just recovering consciousness were said to do? Where am I then?

The morning promised a fine hot day but it was still early enough to be cool, yet I sweated from anxiety, and urging Bess. Then we came to another place where three paths met and Bess, a gregarious animal, pricked her ears. I heard thundering hooves and had just sense and power enough to pull Bess to the side of the little clearing when Lady Alice on her great black horse burst out of the path which led to Merravay.

No greetings. She said, "Is he dead?"

"No, but very ill. A wound gone wrong and much fever."

"I'll go ahead. Barbary cannot tolerate a horse ahead of him. Don't worry, child. It will be all right."

Where the paths or, as some people called them, rides were only wide enough for one horse and rider, conversation was impossible; in wider places we could exchange a few words. For the ridiculous thing was that Bess, getting old – she was eight when Father bought her for me – staid, accustomed to a jogging pace, suddenly produced that speed which slaps and gentle kicks and urgent words had not produced. Perhaps she, like Lady Alice's great horse, had a keen sense of precedence.

When we did draw level very few words sufficed. I told her what had happened, what I had done, what I feared. And I said, "How did you know?"

"I sometimes see things," she said with a kind of reluctance. "Never very clearly – and never in time!"

Then as we neared Pargeters, she said, "This had better

be done openly. We met and you invited me to breakfast."

In our stableyard the big black horse caused quite a stir. He was already something of a legend for speed and power and for being quite unmanageable except by his owner, towards whom his behaviour was lamb-like. The men, now mustering for work, stood and stared, but kept their distance, and Job the boy whose duties included looking after the stables, with priority given to visiting horses, busied himself ostentatiously with Bess.

Lady Alice dismounted, patted the black neck and said, "Wait here for me." She detached from the saddle a bag, beautifully embroidered, of the kind in which ladies carried their needlework or knitting, their smelling-bottles, scent-bottles, even a change of head-dress.

She said, "It is so kind to ask me to breakfast. And to see the peonies." Her voice, not loud, was exceptionally clear and I felt that she spoke with purpose, explaining to anyone who might be interested the reason for her presence here. We then walked round to the front of the house and into the dining-parlour where Peggy was hastily setting the table. Servants are very conscious of rank and afterwards Marian was to reproach me for bringing Lady Alice to breakfast and on a morning when I said I should myself be absent for the meal. Had she only had warning she could have produced a far better meal.

I could barely eat what was provided I was so impatient to get her into the office. She took her time, chatting mainly about gardens, and when the last crumb had been eaten saying, as one lady-of-leisure to another, "And now, if you will show me the garden . . ."

Outside, she said, "We show ourselves in parts that are overlooked. Working towards those laurels you spoke of. Perhaps it would look well if you gave me a few peonies." I plucked some so impatiently and roughly that several roots came up too. But at last, at last we were amongst the laurels and into the room where the man lay.

Instantly her whole manner changed. "Mortification already! Ah well . . ." and then in a different voice, "Eddy Lacey! Oh dear!" But she wasted no time on lamentations.

She set her pretty bag on a stool and opened it, displaying contents as different from the usual as she herself was; flasks and flagons and jars all slotted into little pockets, and on the stiffened bottom bandages and tools.

"We must see how unconscious he is," she said. She pulled up an eyelid, smacked his cheek sharply, said, "Eddy! Eddy! Wake up! It's Alice!" There was no response and she said, "I think he'll do. Are you squeamish?"

I said, "No," but possibly my face gave me the lie. She said, "Stand on the other side of the couch and hold his shoulders down. If he groans take no notice. If he shouts and struggles, hold this under his nose." She handed me a little phial and with a final command, "Look away!" set to work.

I did take two furtive glances; the first informed me that the discoloured wound now had some black about it; and the second that blood was flowing under the blade of a shining silver knife. Squeamishness, a thing I felt that Lady Alice would despise, almost overcame me then; my stomach heaved, my head dizzied, but I fixed my eyes once more on the laurels outside the window, drew some deep breaths and did not disgrace myself.

Lady Alice said, "It is done! Now we *must* rouse him. He needs a febrifuge and unconscious men can't swallow. They choke."

She took another flask from the pretty bag, unstoppered it and held it under his nose; she shook him and slapped him and when he groaningly came almost to himself, called as though to a dog gone astray. "Eddy. It's Alice. What have you to tell me? Eddy, this is important."

At last he said in a faraway voice, "That anchorage . . . No longer safe . . . Betrayed."

"I understand," she said. "Now drink this." She had the draught ready; it came from one of the bigger flasks and was a pleasing pale green. He gulped at it. "I was thirsty. Very good wine . . . but not the same."

I cried in self-abasement, "I forgot the water last night. This morning I was thwarted. But I will get some." I could have wept with chagrin.

"Please," he said, "don't distress yourself. You did so much. And I lived." He managed a smile.

Lady Alice, instantly understanding, said, "Is there an empty bottle? Bring it and see me off. I would like just one word." It was more than one, but hardly a dozen, for she was with me almost at once, clutching her flowers. We appeared to stroll into the stableyard, one lady being courteous to another, but as we went she poured forth instructions. Another dose around noon; another if necessary, at sunset. Invalid diet today, some good broth perhaps. If he complained of pain one of the pellets from the brown jar. "I shall not come again unless I am needed. If I am . . ." she paused and bit her lip, "send a man, any man who can ride, to tell me the calf is ready. Now we water this so-dangerous horse."

She simply called him by name and he came. "Move over," she said, and he moved so that his bulk was between the well and the kitchen window. Not that there was much to see. I lowered the bucket and there was all the noise that I had not dared to make in the night. It came up brimming. But no animal ever drank from the well-bucket which also brought up the household water; so she fetched another, said, "Give me the bottle," filled it, with a dexterity I did not possess. Even so, some spilled so Barbary had but a small drink. "Never mind, darling. You can drink when we get home," she said, speaking as though he were human. She mounted and I handed back the flowers which I had held while she manipulated the buckets and the bottle. From her height on the tall horse, she reached down and touched my cheek. "I didn't want you involved. But you have done marvels. If he's found, he'll hang, so be careful. God keep you. I'll go by the road."

Then she was gone and I was left, holding a bottle of water in the meagre folds of my workaday skirt. And so fast had time sped that it was now eight o'clock. In summer the beginning of a working-woman's day. And all must seem ordinary; so I spared only a moment to dart into the hiding place and set down the bottle of water within reach. Eddy – at least I now knew his name – was again somnolent, but differently; easy. I said, "I'll be back as soon as I can. If I am not here by midday take another dose of this. And if pain strikes, one of these. And if you should be hungry, eat anything in the basket – except the ham. All the rest – especially the orange concoction – is good for the ailing. Eat freely of that."

Job, if he had been in hiding, had emerged, Bess was saddled and ready, Boru out of his pen, cavorting around. An ordinary morning. Everything must seem ordinary.

I rode straight to Brook and was the unwilling spectator of about the worst shearing session anybody ever witnessed. That morning I realised that life must be lived on various levels, the personal and what I can only call the professional. I said to Dick Summers, "Did you speak to him?" I meant the leader of the gang, an enormous man, rightly called Samson.

"Mistress, I did. He just laughed."

"Oh. Then I must speak to him myself," I said. And I was rational. I thought, I admit, less of sex than of size and the fact that a person mounted always has a certain advantage, so I mounted before calling him over. He came, but insolently, taking his time. It was still well short of noon and he was already half drunk.

This in itself was a breach of rules. One tankard at breakfast, one at dinner, one in the late afternoon if work was prolonged. During and after supper the gangs were allowed to drink as much as they liked – or as much as was provided. On many farms the amount was limited and the liquor of poor quality, a weak brew called small beer. But, adhering to Father's custom, I had provided beer of market strength. At Brook they were well fed too and comfortably accommodated in the house which was still occupied by Eli Smith's old mother. So getting tipsy early and doing bad work smacked of ingratitude too.

"I am dissatisfied with your work," I said.

"I bin leading this gang sixseven years now and never had no complaints."

"I am complaining now. Your men make too many nicks

95

and your tar-boy misses too many. We shall be breeding maggots wholesale."

I waited for him to apologise and promise to take more care, but he merely stood there, looking amused if anything.

"Very well," I said. "From now on for every nick above three on each sheep, and for every wound left untreated, I shall deduct one farthing from the wage packet." Being so transient, shearers were paid by the day, the gang-leader taking the whole and dividing it in pre-arranged proportions.

"You'd best not," he said. I realised that he was not now looking at me, and slightly amused, but at the pouch I carried at my belt. And there was menace in his voice. I suddenly felt vulnerable. As was seemly, I had called him away from the shearing pen – nobody should ever be rebuked before his subordinates. Dick Summers was busy, concentrating on moving the sheep along, concentrating too on ignoring me. I hadn't even Boru, for whenever I came to Brook, where I had concentrated the flock, I left him in the kitchen of the farmhouse so that there was no bother with the sheep-dogs. I was alone. I was rather frightened. Possibly people who claim that they have never felt fear are telling the truth. I rather doubt it. They wish to forget the weak moment, or perhaps they lack imagination . . .

Samson said, almost genially, "One swipe of my fist and you'd be down off that nag. Nasty accident, that'd be; and five men and a boy to swear the horse shied at a rabbit. So less not hev talk about knocking off farthings. Tell you suthin else. Women should stick to women's business – and that ain't round shearing pens, interfering. Pay me now. We look to finish tonight. Or leave it with that weak thing you call your foreman. And you stay away."

I suppose this was one of those moments when anyone not brought up by Father would have said, silently, God help me, and exercising faith would have expected divine intervention. To me such happy expedient was denied. How mean to apply for aid from a power to whom one had never owned any allegiance. All I had to fall back upon was anger, which can run hand-in-hand with fear. I think it was being told to stay away from what was virtually my own land . . .

"I meant what I said," I said with a mixture of stubbornness and bravado, and prepared myself for the blow.

But then as in a well-managed masque the whole scene changed. Samson touched his hat and said, "Yes, ma'am, I'll see to it at once," turned and began to move briskly away. Astounded by his metamorphosis I turned and saw, just on the other side of the gate, Sir Walter Fennel on his stout grey cob.

I had no reason to like him and in fact did not. But I was mightily relieved to see him, representing as he did Authority.

"Good morning, my dear," he said briskly, "was that man bothering you?"

"We were having . . . a slight argument." I was remembering with some discomfort our last meeting, when he had said that the pretence of John's being absent on business was known to be nonsense; he was known to be at the war. And of course no woman could run three farms, but he would find me a good overseer. I'd rejected the offer.

Sir Walter did not now waste time saying, I told you so. That could wait. Far more urgent was the exercise of authority.

"Come here, you. Yes, you. Uncover when you speak to me. Why were you arguing with this lady?"

"About the work, sir." Samson shot me a look of pure venom. "She don't know about shearing. How could she? I was just pointing out . . ."

"Is that correct, my dear?"

"More or less," I said. I did not wish to prolong this scene. My flush of relief was ebbing and I felt that Sir Walter was being rather free with the 'my dears'. Despite our slight connection by marriage he had never been anything but formal with me. And I had remembered the secret hidden at Pargeters and Sir Walter's reputation for spying. But, give the man his due, he was thorough.

"I take it that the quality of your work was being questioned?"

"That ain't so easy, these days, to get a good team together."

"You are admitting to bad workmanship? Therefore this lady, as your employer, would be justified in dismissing you out of hand. You would then, however briefly, be vagrants and I, as a magistrate, could order you all a sound whipping."

Samson seemed actually to shrink in size and muttered about doing better.

"That would be wise," Sir Walter said. "I shall look in myself, later in the day." When Samson had gone Sir Walter said, "I have a matter of some importance to discuss with you."

I thought, He can't *know*! But how could I be sure? I knew that Lady Alice distrusted Sir Walter; I had heard Eddy say: Betrayed. A few minutes ago I had felt physical fear, now I felt the other kind. Lady Alice's words rang in my mind: If he's found, he'll hang . . .

I said: "I am willing to discuss anything, Sir Walter. But first may I thank you for your most timely intervention. That man thought I was ignorant, which I am not. All in all I suppose I have been at more sheep-shearings than he has had hot dinners. But it is hot here in the sun. Shall we go into the house? The parlour is comfortable and the beer good."

I meant, of course, the farmhouse, so nearby.

He said with a kind of dreadful playfulness,

"Are you denying me the hospitality you extended to Lady Alice this morning? I rather hoped you would invite me to dinner."

I said the only thing left to me to say: "But of course. Please come to dinner. I must warn you, it may be a scanty meal." I knew that though he was a Parliamentarian, a Puritan, he was addicted to the pleasures of the table and liked his wine. Extreme Puritans had strict views about wine-bibbing as they called it and some, it was said, even deplored beer-drinking. Well, at least at Pargeters we were well-stocked with wine, for Grandfather had been fore-sighted.

As we rode Sir Walter chatted in a light way. Evidently he had encountered Lady Alice with her drooping peonies. June, he said, was no time for transplanting anything; even he, no gardener, knew that. And from that to the weather, the harvest prospects. And so we came to Pargeters, and the outjutting piece of the house in the laurel thicket seemed to my disturbed mind to leap up, huge, red, fiery, as much demanding of attention as a Guy Fawkes bonfire. Yet he seemed not to notice. I led the way along the path to the stableyard and then, on foot, to the front door. The cool of the house was welcome, but to me it felt dangerous. The office and its secret seemed to scream. I could almost smell the man. Pouring the pre-dinner wine my hands were so unsteady that Sir Walter noticed. Fortunately he attributed my condition to the wrong cause. "Allow me," he said, taking the bottle from me. "That oaf has thoroughly upset you. I shall be very stern with him this afternoon." He sipped some wine and went on, "You may remember that I told you that you were assuming too heavy a burden."

"Part of my state is due to surprise," I said. "My father died two years ago. Since then I have dealt with many men, but never before have I encountered insolence. I shall certainly not engage that gang next year."

"Ah, next year," he said and sipped again. "We shall see many changes before then." I knew what he meant. The end of the war. Both sides at that point were confident not only of victory but of a swift conclusion. "This morning's incident," said Sir Walter, "makes it the more difficult for me to state the nature of my business which, to be blunt, would reduce your regular work-force – but at the end could work to your advantage. You have heard of Cromwell's Ironsides?"

"Of course."

"Recruits are still needed. Cromwell, himself almost an East Anglian, favours men from this district."

I stared at him in bewilderment. Had I suddenly gone stupid? Was my mind too much occupied by the thought of

99

Eddy Lacey hidden away there in the back of the house?

"You control three farms. And so far only one man, Eli Smith, has enlisted."

"Can I be blamed for that? All our men are free. We have no tenant farmers to be coerced."

"Men can be influenced. And with your brother's known allegiance, certain inferences must be drawn."

"Quite falsely. Eli Smith was my best foreman, but I did nothing to dissuade *him*. What is more, his mother chose to remain in the house at Brook and although rent was offered, I have never taken a penny."

"Certainly to your credit," he conceded and then, changing his manner again, "How many men sleep in the house?"

"One – by Oliver Cromwell's standards. Tom Markham. There is a boy – the one who took your horse. His name is Job, a workhouse orphan, slightly dim-witted and undersized. The third, an aged man, a good gardener but much crippled by rheumatism. And Grandfather's Timmy."

"A modest household."

"As you probably know, Sir Walter, my father was averse to ostentation."

As though to prove what I said, Peggy began to serve the very modest meal – eminently suited to a hot midday for people who worked in the afternoon, but again reflecting upon Marian's prowess as cook. Two unexpected guests in one day, and both titled, and not so much as a custard pie! Not that it mattered since both Sir Walter and I were preoccupied. I with Eddy Lacey – had he remembered his midday dose? And Sir Walter with his next move.

"Have I your permission to speak to your men?"

"As I said before, they are free men."

He gave a nod of satisfaction. "That is wise. The end cannot be far off and a Roundhead victory is certain. A war, however justified, engenders ill-feeling. Someone might say that you had been – shall we say? – obstructive. Asking men if they wanted to kill their young master. Such sentimental talk has been known. On both sides."

"The thought never occurred to me, Sir Walter. Ask any of my men. Recruit whoever is willing to go."

My uneasiness in having him under my roof was increased rather than alleviated by something in his manner. Out of character. Why should he, of all people, bother about what people said or thought about me in the future? And of course I resented his complete assurance that the war would end with Parliament triumphant. I thought: Oh, go away, go talk to the men; get on with whatever you want to do and leave me free to tend my business.

But he went on eating the strawberries with a slow, gluttonous appreciation. And then he asked a question that startled me. "When your brother went to the war, how much power did he leave you?"

"Complete," I said, rather proudly, for John had indeed left me in a position which most men denied their wives or their widows.

"Then may I suggest that you sell Brook Farm?"

All that I had suffered that day, and it seemed to have lasted a lifetime, rose and broke the surface of my hard-held self-control. I said, "Sir Walter, I should not dream of parting with one acre of the land which my father loved." Something perverse in me kept me mentioning Father. If Sir Walter had been a little more yielding, less proud and aware of his rank, life would have been different for us all.

Yet now, in his way, he seemed concerned for me.

"I think," he said, "that I put the fear of the law into that man this morning. I shall threaten him again this afternoon; but perhaps you should take a man with you if you go to Brook again before the shearers have gone."

"I will," I promised. Anything to get him away.

At last he was gone and I was free to steal away through the laurels.

Eddy lay on the couch, but at sight of me jumped up and bowed. "My good angel," he said. "I am incredibly restored."

"I am glad. Did you take another dose?"

"At midday, so far as I could judge in this gloom. And I ate well, too: much regretting your order about the ham!"

He gave me a cheerful grin which changed abruptly to a grimace of pain. He sat down suddenly.

"Your arm hurts still?"

"Much less. Much less."

"There are pills for the pain."

"I know. But they bring drowsiness. If I lie and doze I shall weaken. And I must think of being on my way."

"Not yet," I said quickly. "We'll talk about that later. I must go now. I'll come as soon as I can this evening."

Everything must seem ordinary, and on an ordinary afternoon I should have been supervising the haymaking at Pargeters and Nine Elms and then the shearing at Brook. But I had given Sir Walter permission to go anywhere, to speak to anybody and it would be better to stay out of sight. And I had the perfect excuse; this was the kind of afternoon when one washed one's hair and dried it in the sunshine.

Ordinarily either Peggy or Annie helped with this process, beating the egg and the soft soap together and applying it, then rinsing it off with vinegar water. This afternoon Marian took it upon herself and seized the opportunity to scold me as far as a servant can scold an employer. She chose pathos as her text.

"I know I'm old and once you're old every little thing'll count against you. Just get a twinge of toothache and people think you should be in an almshouse. I can still cook, given the wherewithal. But twice today, twice in one day, I bin made to look silly."

Head bent over bowl, a position that leads to breathlessness, I muttered, "I didn't know myself . . . I was surprised, too . . . Marian, don't rub so hard! You're not kneading dough."

"I bin here a long time. Afore you was born, Mistress. And never a complaint that I know of."

"Nobody is complaining now. Except you."

"I know how people talk. People of quality. A bit of brawn for breakfast – and the bread stale. A bit of cold ham for dinner. Next thing you know they'll say how ill-served you are and their cook got some relation would do better. And they know a nice almshouse in Blind Row."

"That is nonsense, Marian. Rinse me now. I'm getting a crick in my neck."

Dowsing me thoroughly, she went on: "Almshouses is all very well for some – the useless sort. But I ain't like that. I gotta lot of work in me yet. What is more, how could I live on a shilling a week, with prices gone up so cruel?"

She finished the rinsing, gave my hair a rough towelling, spread another towel over my shoulders, spread my hair over it and stood back. Turning on the stool, I saw that more than vinegar and water had gone into the rinsing. Marian's eyes were full of tears and her cheeks were wet. I said, "Marian, you are silly! Conjuring up bogeys to scare yourself. I give you my solemn word that so long as I have an egg to boil, you shall boil it for me. And when you are truly old – say a hundred – I'll boil you an egg."

I went along to Father's shelves and chose a book at random and then, in the garden, took a seat in the full sun. I gave the book scarce attention, my mind too busy with other things. Grandfather's voice, coming from behind me, gave me a jolt. "Penelope! Oh, how could you? You naughty, naughty girl."

I twisted round and saw that he was regarding me with great disfavour, almost with disgust. I had the absurd but nonetheless genuine feeling that somehow he knew. What else could account? In his right mind he had been fond of me, and then when he confused me with Mother, fonder still. I thought: He has wandered into the lobby and noticed that bolt! And was Timmy with him?

That seemed to me to be the crucial question. Grandfather easily forgot; and if he didn't, if he babbled, who would believe? I looked hastily at Timmy and learned nothing, for his face wore that deliberately absent, nothing-to-do-with-me expression which he assumed whenever there was somebody else to give his charge any attention.

"Your hair! Your beautiful hair," Grandfather said. "Oh, I know it was fashionable once. Queen Elizabeth had red hair, so every woman must copy it. Henna," he said, as though naming poison. "I imported it myself. A profitable side-line . . ." He seemed to lose the thread of his discourse, groped for it and for once succeeded. "Bad women, prostitutes. It is their trademark. And you . . . you had such beautiful black hair."

When he had first confused me with Mother and called me by her name I had tried to explain, but that had only led to further confusion. Was it worth trying again now? Before I could decide his mind had slipped again. "I want my supper and I want some proper food. I get quite enough cold provender aboard ship."

I went indoors and, as I coiled and pinned my hair, thought of many disconnected things. How strange that Grandfather should only today have noticed that my hair was not black; Sir Walter's advice to take a man with me if I went to Brook, and his suggestion that I should sell it; my own immediate plans for the place. Obviously Dick Summers, good shepherd though he might be, was a pusillanimous fellow, quite unfit for his present position. I thought: possibly Tom Markham and then, immediately: that is if Sir Walter's recruitment campaign hasn't netted him, a promising fellow and able to ride. I also thought, of course, of Eddy Lacey and, taking a last look in the glass, with one of my rare flashes of self-approval, that my newly washed hair though not black was pleasing.

The boy Job, who at busy seasons often helped in the fields, was back on duty in the yard and I said, "I'll take Sultan this time. Have they finished in the Paddock?"

"Just about."

I sensed a difference. In his near-simpleton face, in his brisker gait. It was as though something pleasant had jerked him out of his usual apathy. I remembered that girls worked in the hayfields; perhaps one had smiled at him.

I had decided against taking a man with me to Brook; I'd take Boru and instead of leaving him in the yard at Brook would take him into the field with me, but with a rope attached to his collar. Even that precaution was unnecessary. Samson and his gang, completely unsupervised, were subdued, working away steadily and well. Anyone with half an eye could see the difference between the sheep shorn that afternoon and those dealt with earlier in the day. I imagined that Dick Summers, knowing that I should come back to do the paying, had been ashamed to face me.

Two sheepdogs came, stiff-legged with challenge, towards Boru and I threatened them with my crop – I carried one when I rode Sultan who resented me and indeed any other rider than John.

I said, "I have come to pay you." Samson, hat in hand, standing to attention, said, "Thank you, Mistress," and took the money without counting it and without looking at me. It was difficult to believe that the scene this morning had ever taken place.

"When do you expect to finish?"

"Tonight. We shall work while the light lasts."

Two impulses immediately went to war within me. Reason said that had the earlier work not been so hastily and badly done the gang would not have been able to move on tomorrow; memory of Father answered back. He'd always had a weak spot for seasonal workers, mainly homeless men, always uncertain of their future and so frequently exploited. Father won. I said, "In that case I shall owe you a little more," and put my hand to my pouch.

"No. We got our orders," Samson said. I thought: Sir Walter must have kept his word about putting the fear of the law into him.

"In that case . . ." I said and turned away, but not soon enough. I saw Samson's eyes fixed on me with a look of such virulent hatred that a sword thrust through the breast could not have made more impact.

I know that some people were said to have the Evil Eye, but this, like every other form of superstition, Father had derided. As his true daughter I should have thrown off the thought that a rogue's angry look could do me injury. But the idea rode with me and as I tussled with the wilful horse and Boru, free again, loped a few yards ahead and then ran back to see that all was well with me, I reckoned my vulnerable points. My brother away at the war, and Eddy Lacey hidden in the house.

Then I realised that this weakness of spirit owed something to physical exhaustion and strain of mind. Look what

I'd been through since yesterday at about this time. And the day was not yet over. I needed something to revive me, and having handed horse and hound over to Job, who still wore that strange look of exhilaration, I went indoors and poured myself a measure of brandy.

Slightly fortified, I went upstairs, shed my working garb and washed, then went to the closet where my dresses hung on pegs. On impulse I lifted down the green velvet which I had worn for my cousin Annis's wedding and so seldom worn since.

Is this acting as usual? I asked myself. Caution said: No, but vanity was stronger. Strong enough to make me go to the Trunk and take out Mother's emerald. In so doing I noted that the Trunk held just fourteen pounds in cash, a sum which must last for everything, wages and household expenses, until the fleeces were sold.

Supper, always the most substantial meal during a busy season, had for its main dish that evening stewed mutton, Marian's famous dumplings, new peas and young carrots. Earlier in the day I had worried about broth, but Eddy had seemed so almost miraculously better, hankering for ham, that I had ceased to fret about that.

When Peggy first came in to serve me she had given me a long, assessing look and I said: "They say everything goes in threes and twice today I have been caught unawares. So this evening I've made myself grand."

"Marian was right upset."

"I know. Has my grandfather had his supper yet?"

"One of them. Then he went to bed." Grandfather's eating habits were not approved of by the servants.

"He may want another soon. Fetch a deep platter and give him a good helping with plenty of the gravy. Then stand it aside. He won't mind it being cool." I was thinking that if the fever had returned and Eddy could not eat solid food, the gravy would serve as broth.

Next time Peggy came in she said, "Mistress, Tom Markham'd like a word with you after supper."

I could not go to Eddy yet; I had ample time.

"Tell him to come in when you come to clear the table."

As though to show what she could do, Marian had made one of what Father always called kick-shaws. This was a concoction of crushed strawberries, sugar, whipped cream and gelatine. We called it Strawberry Mould. I told her to leave that on the side for Grandfather, too. I was quite safe in tampering with Grandfather's supper. Even if he remembered and complained, nobody would believe him.

Tom Markham came in. Like me he had washed, and was wearing his best clothes – a white shirt and grey breeches. It shot through my mind that he was about to ask leave to marry and bring his wife to Pargeters. And to that I had an answer. Father had never allowed it. Any married woman, he said, would try to lord it over the servants.

Tom said, "I wouldn't want you to think, Mistress, that I *wanted* to be the one to tell you this. We took a straw vote on it and the lot fell on me."

"I understand, Tom. Bad news?"

"Sir Walter said you knew about it and had give him leave . . ." There was some reproach in his voice.

"I was more or less obliged. To have refused would have given an unfavourable – and quite wrong impression."

"I reckon so. But to my mind we was jogging along all right as we was. Now we're losing seven good men – I ain't counting Job."

"Are you one?"

"No. I ain't. I ain't easily bribed. Thass all it is. Sheer bribery!"

I noticed that he was shifting from foot to foot. Tired? Embarrassed? Both?

I said, "Sit down, Tom. Now tell me everything."

He began by listing the men who had volunteered. Jerry Cooper, my manager at Nine Elms. I should miss him; he was a good all-round man, absolutely reliable so far as work was concerned. Dick Summers. I doubted if he'd make much of a soldier and I was thinking of demoting him anyway; but a good shepherd. Two Minsham men, one with a houseful of young children and a scold of a wife; Cromwell's army would be a refuge for him; the other rather over-fond of his beer; how would he fit in? Three Muchanger men, one a good carpenter. "And Job," Tom ended. "Sir Walter promised *him* a drum." There was a note of mockery in his voice though his face remained sombre.

"What did he promise the others?"

"A new Garden of Eden, more or less."

I never knew what mandate Sir Walter had had, or how far his desire for recruits had run away with him. There was the pay, three or four times what a man could earn as a labourer; allowances for dependants; pensions for wounded men; and a vast re-distribution of land, five acres for every man with a clean record – that is, one who came through without drinking, smoking, swearing or whoring. And for those who already owned five acres or more, a cash gratuity.

As I listened, Tom ticking off items on his fingers, my wonder was, not that Sir Walter had lured in so many but that I had an able-bodied man left. I also thought, idly: All material things. No mention of an ideal, a Cause. But the war was now almost two years old. The Parliamentarians who had taken up arms for a Cause had been expendable. With the Cavaliers, as the King's men were now called, it was different. While the King lived . . .

I said, "Thank you, Tom. Sir Walter certainly made a good haul. I shall have some rearranging to do. I wish you would reconsider your refusal to take charge of Brook."

I had offered him Eli Smith's job before. This time he said: "I bin thinking, though I don't know no more about sheep than I did then. But we can get a good sheep-hand and I'll take charge. But I don't want the house. I *like* living here."

"Old Mrs Smith is held to be a good cook. And one day you'll want to get married."

"Time enough to deal with that when the day comes. I'll look after Brook and come back here at nightfall." Something in the way he spoke enlightened me suddenly; he did not wish to leave me with no man about the house.

"I understand. And I do appreciate your consideration, Tom. We'll call it a bargain and pledge it properly." I rose and went to the sideboard and poured two glasses of wine. He stood, and I did not resume my seat.

"Good luck and good health, Tom," I said.

"Mistress, I wish you every good in this world."

He spoke with such sincerity that I felt Samson's curse on me had somehow been cancelled out.

Tonight I was not flustered so I loaded my tray carefully: the food, knife, fork, spoon, a jug of water from the bucket in the kitchen, a freshly lighted candle. Quite a load, which I balanced on one hip as I opened the door to the office. Eddy did not have to get up, he was already on his feet and, reaching out both hands, took the tray from me.

"Your arm is that much better!" I exclaimed.

"Unbelievably better. I've been exercising it all afternoon. My legs, too. I think I must have worn a groove in the floor. And I've eaten the ham!"

"I hope you still have appetite. Cold mutton stew is not very enticing – but it was the best I could manage."

"You've managed marvellously. I can find no words with which to thank you."

He was obviously a tidy-minded man; the blanket, neatly folded, lay on the end of the couch. All the containers which had held delicacies were back in the basket. He said, "You sit on the couch," and placed the tray on the stool, seated himself on another and began to eat, still voracious but in mannerly fashion.

A person not eating when another is should talk, as entertainingly as possible. I said, "I have had an exciting day. Sir Walter Fennel, generally regarded as a spy, invited himself to dinner."

"God! What a strain on you. What a nuisance I have been. But I'll be off as soon as I have finished this."

"You can't," I said sharply.

"Why not? Is somebody on the prowl?"

"No, but I should be so dreadfully worried. The cure was too sudden. Unnatural. I should imagine it wearing off and you collapsing again – with no one to help. I should not be able to sleep or eat . . . or attend to anything. Some people hold that Lady Alice is a witch and magic cures can wear off as quickly as they come. Please, please wait just one more day."

He stopped eating and was regarding me sadly. Yes, sadly. Yet when he spoke his words were formal.

"I should indeed be very sorry to inflict an additional worry. But I must get another ship as soon as I can. I must get back to Bristol."

I thought for a moment. "You would get there sooner if you had a horse. And I have one to spare. But it is a very *good* horse. In your present garb and your face neither shaven nor bearded, you would draw attention. Everybody would think you were a horse-thief and a witless one at that. Rest until tomorrow and I will bring you a razor and some decent clothes."

"But not tonight?"

"No. Not tonight."

"Blackmail!" he said, and laughed. Yet I could see by the relaxation of his muscles, his very expression, that the respite was not unwelcome.

So we talked and drank wine together. He told me almost nothing. I was garrulous; telling him about John; about Sir Walter's errand and his culling of seven good men and a half-wit, and his remark about the war ending soon with the defeat of the Cavaliers. And he astonished me by saying, "We may lose . . . But we must do so in such a way as to show the world that a belief in a Cause carries more weight than superiority in numbers. There are precedents – Christendom itself, founded on the faithful few. Or look at Hastings. Harold was defeated, and his faithful few dead with him – but we are speaking English today, not Norman French."

He was putting into words something I had thought in my muddled way about ideals and bribes.

"*If* defeat should come, what will you do?"

He laughed: "Turn pirate if I have a ship under me. I'm a younger son. The ship was my portion. What will *you* do?"

"If my brother survives, run the farms for him. If not, run the farms."

"What about marriage?"

110

I lied in my teeth. "I have never yet seen the man with whom I wished to spend the rest of my days. Are you married? Betrothed?"

"I have never . . ." He paused and went on, "had anything to offer."

"Yourself?"

"Fathers – fond or otherwise – look no higher than a man's pocket. The worth of a man himself has been plainly shown since they – no, I must be fair – since both sides started selling prisoners. In Virginia or the Bahamas, as I sit here now my worth is exactly forty pounds."

"I did not know that prisoners were sold."

"They were not, at the beginning. Something of chivalry remained then. Prisoners were often exchanged and the dead decently buried. Men on both sides remembered that they were fighting Englishmen. But war is a debasing business."

Suddenly he ceased talking, stood up, flung his arms about.

"Look, I am cured. No excuse for lolling about. Be as kind as you were yesterday. Give me now what you would have given me tomorrow – and let me go."

What could I do but creep about like a thief, find Father's razor, and some of John's plainest clothes? I took from the Trunk the most I could spare without embarrassing my affairs – ten pounds; a small contribution towards the ship he needed.

Old houses are supposed to creak, giving rise to what Father had always scorned as stories about ghosts walking; and Pargeters was really a new house, less than fifty years old, but that night every board I trod on seemed to scream. However, I collected what I needed, went downstairs again, handed in the razor and the clothes and said, "I will pack you what we call a bag-dinner." I took up the tray and paused, imagining again, as I had imagined last night, Bess whickering, Boru banging against the slatted door of his pen. I had more resources now, and on the narrow part of the desk, just a ledge above the slope, I laid out the mutton bones and one small crust of bread. Then I went into the kitchen, washed the platters, set the tray back in its place and, proceeding to the larder, selected not only the delicacies, but some more solid fare. People often make mock of Suffolk cheese, calling it hard-tack, saying that never having been edible, it could never become otherwise. Certainly it never went mouldy.

If I chose to be romantic or poetic, I could say that I packed this food alongside my breaking heart. But with me, as always, reality would take charge. I thought: Mrs Cooper made this cheese, and immediately the surface of my mind began to be busy with what Tom Markham had told me, planning, rearranging . . . but back in the office another kind of reality took control. He was about to leave; I might never see him again; and I loved him.

Not for his looks, though they were good enough despite the harshness of the lines between the eyebrows and beside the mouth. And how could I be in love with his quality of character? Literally all I knew about him was that he was brave. Nor could my malady be that thing so beloved by poets, Love at First Sight. On the previous evening, which now seemed a lifetime ago, my feelings had been limited to pity and concern. But I loved him, and he was leaving and I must make the best of it.

His thoughts were practical too. "I'm wondering. How will you explain the absence of the horse?"

"I shall think of something."

"For the love of God, not theft. Horses are worth their weight in gold and there'd be a hue and cry out from here to Land's End."

"I shall not report a theft. Mention of worth makes me think of money. This is all I can spare – to help you secure a new ship." It seemed such a pitiable offering and he seemed both astounded and grateful. On impulse I unhooked the link of the pendant's chain and held it out.

"I can't," he said. "I can't rob you of your pretty things."

"It is for the Cause. And I never liked it. Rid yourself of it as soon as you can. I don't think it is a very lucky thing."

Father's bride-gift to Mother; more than he could afford. And what happiness had it brought her who knew where his heart lay? And what good had it done me? Eddy had not even noticed my changed appearance. I never wanted to see that pretty thing again; or this dress; or this room. Oh never, never again this room. But suppose a search party arrived?

Lady Alice had taken away that bloodied, stinking bandage, saying, "I will dispose of this." I now took up the discarded clothes. Tomorrow I'd weight them with stones and drop them into the nearest Layer pool. The blanket and the pillow I could leave; they betrayed nothing except that Grandfather had liked his little nap.

I said, "We'll go out through the house. Can you carry the tray?"

In the little lobby I carefully edged the bolt into its old position. Eddy set the tray on the table. I put the bundle of clothes by the dresser, ready to snatch up when I returned – alone. Then I blew out the candle, for it was a night of bright moonlight.

I opened the kitchen door and stepped out into the yard.

Grandfather when he built Pargeters had had a free hand; no house, no buildings except a farm had occupied the site before. It had been desirable to have the stables near the well, but the doors faced away from the house. I said in a near whisper, "Sultan is a difficult horse."

"The best kind – properly handled. I know horses."

Boru threw himself against the bars of his pen and I pacified him with the bones. Bess whickered and I gave her the crust. And Sultan behaved like a lamb. I thought: Of course, he can smell John's clothes. All ready now; the last moment had come. Eddy turned to me, took both my hands and would have kissed them. But I went crazy. It was like having a convulsive fit. I threw my arms around him; I clung. Our mouths met and our hearts. I was shameless, saying, "I love you. I love you." And there was a moment, a second, a century during which I know he felt the same.

In the long aftermath I was obliged to hold to that thought, otherwise I should have been diminished in my own esteem, for a female to love unloved and to say it was the ultimate disgrace.

He detached himself, gently, but very firmly.

He said, "I shall remember you always. And if I live, I will come back."

I had already told him to keep to the road, the way through Layer being confusing to strangers. I'd said: "At the church turn right, that road leads west." So he went.

Crying may be a habit. One I had never acquired. John was older and he was a boy and the rule ran that boys didn't cry. To stay even, I must not cry. Father had died; and Mother, and I had not wept. Now, when I needed to, I could not. The pain in my chest and my throat, the desolation in my mind must remain uneased by the shedding of tears.

I stood there and grew old. Then a sound roused me. Somebody in the yard, hidden from me by the jut of the stable. My instant thought was: A spy! Somebody who had missed his quarry by a matter of minutes. Yet how could anybody know or guess? Even had Eddy's presence been suspected who could possibly know that he was leaving tonight, or that I had given him a horse?

Moonlight can play strange tricks; the man who rounded the corner looked enormous and faceless. And menacing. But it was only Tom Markham wearing just his breeches and a pair of the slippers which stood just inside the kitchen door. Booted feet – except those of the family – were not allowed to tread on Marian's floor.

"Mistress!"

"Tom!"

"I thought I heard something." He had armed himself with a stout cudgel. Had Eddy not warned me, I might then have said: You did. So did I. But they've got away with Sultan. As it was, another lie formed in my mind and slid, smooth as cream from a pitcher, out of my mouth.

"A man came to collect Sultan. I sold him. I meant to tell you Tom, and ask you to hand over. But you had so much to tell me, my mind was diverted."

"You should've called me."

"I know. But the man was so late and since I had not told you . . ."

"What make of man was he?"

"A most respectable man. I should not have sold Sultan to just anybody, difficult as he was."

"Any trouble tonight?"

"No. Surprisingly docile."

"Ah," Tom said. "Somebody give him the word." I knew then that in his mind Lady Alice's visit and Sultan's docility had meshed together.

We were then in the kitchen. Tom said, "Nonetheless . . . Another time call me. Thass what I'm here for. Bear that in mind and don't go venturing out, nigh on midnight."

"The situation is unlikely to occur again. But thank you, Tom. The man was late; but he had underrated the distance. He came from Thetford."

"Want a candle?"

I said, "No, thank you. The moon will serve."

Ever since we had stepped into the kitchen I had been aware of that tray on the table. Given time, I intended to make all good. My trouble was that since the moment I had found Eddy in the bracken, I'd had no time at all. Now a bleak empty space stretched before me.

I was unwilling for Tom, already so disapproving, to see the tray, and be told another lie – that I had offered the Thetford man some refreshment. Let Annie find the things in the morning and think in her dull bovine way: A bit more for me to do!

Next day was Wednesday, market day in Baildon, and the first of the fleece sales; most of the wool on offer coming in from small farms whose owners, living from hand to mouth, needed money immediately. Dealers took advantage of their necessity and prices were always low. But they were an indication of the trend of the market. So I rode that morning into the space behind The Hawk in Hand where the auctioning was under way. And I had been there a bare ten minutes before Lady Alice arrived. She reined in alongside, greeted me with a mere nod and fixed her gaze on the man who was saying, "Four shillings, I'm bid. Any advance on four shillings?"

She said, not looking at me, hardly moving her lips: "All right?"

"Cured. On his way."

"Look in at The Old Vine," she said, and edged the big black horse away.

I knew the place; in fact it stood on the way I took coming and going to Baildon. It was an old, handsome house and as a hostelry had a good reputation but Father had never patronised it, preferring The Hawk in Hand which was more central and where more general business was done – like this morning's fleece sale.

Now, approaching it, I was aware of embarrassment. It was all very well for Lady Alice to say: Look in. Respectable women did not look in at inns unaccompanied. The Hawk in Hand was different, it served so many purposes. I thought, rather peevishly, that Lady Alice should have told me more; her very anxiety not to involve me, afraid even to be seen addressing me in public, left me in an awkward position.

However, it proved not to be awkward at all; it was, in fact, like arriving at a private house where one was expected. The yard was vast, but very quiet. An old man, almost as crippled as our Old Harry, hobbled forward and took my horse and a boy appeared from nowhere and said, "If you would come this way, Madam." He led me around the side of the sprawling building, opened a door and there I was in the presence.

My good memory had served me well, and riding along I had remembered that the landlady's name was Kentwoode and I had prepared a few fatuous words: I would like, please to speak to Mrs Kentwoode. I had no need for them. She said, "I am glad you could come," and led me into a parlour, pretty though furnished in an old-fashioned way.

I said, "You know me, Mrs Kentwoode?"

"Oh yes. This is my private sanctum. I do not invite strangers into it. Please sit down." She went to a corner cupboard, produced a letter and gave it to me. As I recognised John's writing, she said, "Excuse me. I am needed in the kitchen."

The outer cover of this letter was very clean; it had not been much handled. I broke the seals and read the words on the inner page. One could hardly call it a letter. Two terse sentences. "The need for money is desperate. Sell Brook."

I felt no dismay. I was not disconcerted. What I felt was bewilderment. Whom did John trust so absolutely to get the money to him? And then I thought: How curious, only yesterday Sir Walter suggested the same thing. Remembering how I had answered him I did feel a pang of sadness; Father had so valued every acre. Still, he was dead and his aspirations with him. The land was John's now. He and only he had the right to say what should happen to it. One hundred and fifty acres of land, "in good heart", as the saying went. Worth what?

Mrs Kentwoode came rustling back. She said, "Not bad news, I hope."

"No. Merely puzzling."

I looked at her half angrily. She was august, dignity and authority were stamped on her. They must be defied. I said, "Nobody tells me anything and yet I am expected to act as though I were well informed. It makes life very difficult. How much do *you* know about this, for instance?" I tapped the paper on my lap.

"I can only *infer*. It was sent by somebody who preferred not to approach you openly. If it resembles others that pass through my hands it contains a request." A small cold smile touched her lips. "And the sender knew that anything entrusted to me would – short of disaster – arrive safely at its destination."

"You control an underground network?"

"I am one link in a chain."

"You could forward money?"

"Far more easily than most things. Does your garden produce any special delicacy?"

The question took me by surprise.

"We grow good peaches."

"Send me six. Get a small basket, wrap the money well;

117

place some leaves over it and arrange the fruit. Have you a trustworthy messenger?"

"Yes." I thought of Tom Markham.

"Tell him to hand them in saying that they are especially for me. There is one more small matter. If I ever have another communication for you I will place this –" she indicated a bowl, very pretty and of unusual design and filled with pot-pourri "– on the window seat of the room to the left of the main entry. Look for it as you pass."

I said, "Sir Walter, yesterday when you suggested that I should sell Brook, I rejected the suggestion. But you recruited so successfully that I now have little choice. I wondered if you knew of anybody who would buy it without much delay . . . The thought of selling is still painful to me, I don't wish to prolong the agony."

"I know the very man. I had him in mind when I spoke. A very decent man indeed and certain to be a good neighbour. His name is James Clover. He is a lawyer, connected in some way with the administration of University property."

"And he wishes to be a farmer?"

"He is a far-sighted man – and a staunch Presbyterian."

It sounded like a non sequitur, but even to my ignorant ear it made sense. At the beginning there had been those for the King, those for Parliament. Now the latter party, having no core, were beginning to splinter. Presbyterians were comparatively moderate, a minority but a powerful one. If the Roundheads won and some more extreme group gained control, Mr Clover would lose whatever office he held.

I said, "He sounds acceptable. Would he buy without a lot of chaffering?"

Sir Walter slipped in one of his cunning questions.

"You are in need of ready money?"

"I soon may be. I need new men, and what you said yesterday about pay in the Army is bound to reflect on wages. Also, earlier today I was at the first fleece sale. Bidding was slow and prices deplorable."

"So I heard. But I can assure you, Mr Clover would not haggle and he can well afford . . . What is the extent of Brook?"

"A hundred and fifty acres."

"With a dwelling house?"

"Yes. Modest, but sound. Father was very averse to dilapidations."

"Well, my dear, if you care to leave the whole matter to me, I will arrange it as profitably and expeditiously as I can."

It sounded kindly and to an extent I was grateful, for I knew nothing about selling property; but I could not bring myself to trust Sir Walter whole-heartedly. Why should he do me a favour? My hesitation must have shown for he said, with undiminished amiability, "Perhaps you would prefer Mr Turnbull. My own experience is that lawyers move slowly. Of course, we shall need him to make the whole thing legal in the final stage, but I doubt very much if he could find you a buyer so quickly."

In other words, if I chose Mr Turnbull we should not have a buyer ready and waiting. Mr Clover, something to do with the University at Cambridge, was not a very exact identification. Mr Turnbull and I should find him hard to trace.

I also saw something else; Sir Walter was not doing me a favour; he wished to ingratiate himself with Mr Clover.

I said: "Oh no. I should be most grateful if you would arrange it all."

"Very well, I'll bring him over tomorrow afternoon." I stared. Cambridge was twenty-six miles away. "He is staying in the district," Sir Walter said.

Surely no property was ever so casually inspected, so hastily approved, so quickly decided upon. Mr Clover, a conspicuously neat man, all in grey and rather delicate looking, said, "Exactly what I was looking for," which is hardly the way to set about striking a bargain. Of the house he said, "It could be made very comfortable." In the land he showed no interest whatsoever, though Brook was in some ways unique because it stood on a gentle slope, the higher portion eminently suitable for sheep, which had only to stroll down to the stream to drink, then uphill again to the dryer space which suited their feet better. The remaining acres grew good wheat and barley.

Within twenty minutes of his arrival, Mr Clover said, "And when could I take possession?"

I remembered the word *desperate* in John's note.

"Immediately."

"That suits me well. And the price?"

"A hundred and fifty pounds," I said. I thought of Mother's attempt to buy Crowswood.

Sir Walter gave a slight gasp but Mr Clover said, imperturbably, "Very well." Taking advantage of him I said, "That does not include the sheep, or the standing corn. The sheep I can move tomorrow, but the corn must wait till harvest."

He then showed that he was more observant than he appeared to be. "I have no objection to the sheep. The fold is well away from the house. A shepherd would not impinge upon the privacy I desire. Take the harvest at your leisure. I should, however, like to start upon the house as soon as possible."

"Tomorrow, if you wish."

"I assume that you have the deeds and that they are in order."

"I brought them with me," I said.

Sir Walter who had said very little, now spoke in a most self-congratulatory way. "I told you that if you liked the look of the place, everything would go smoothly."

"You did indeed, and I am most grateful. Now all that remains is to find a lawyer in general practice."

Mrs Kentwoode had mentioned peaches. Either she had not expected me to find the money so soon or she did not know much about gardens. Our peaches, espaliered against the south-facing wall, looked pretty enough but were as hard as stone. However, I chose six of the most forward, arranged them as told to and entrusted the basket to Tom Markham.

After that nothing much happened except that the

recruited men went off and I found a new workhouse orphan to take Job's place. He was far more intelligent and was, incidentally, a living example of what good food can do. In his first month at Pargeters he grew eight inches and fattened out as well. He'd been given the name of Thomas and was always called by it because Tom Markham was Tom, and the other diminutive, Tommy, was not sufficiently unlike the Timmy who was Grandfather's attendant.

What else do I remember of that lull?

Mr Clover's work on Brook, which I heard of but did not see, remembering what he had said about privacy. He had kept old Mrs Smith to cook and housekeep for him.

Oh, and Mrs Cooper came to see me, offering to pay rent now that her husband had gone.

"If I could keep the yard and just a strip of pasture at the bottom of Pond Field, I could build up a business, Mistress. I've always sent a few fowls and geese to market in Baildon. Now there's turkeys, too." Her eyes shone with enthusiasm. "That Phyl Whymark drives stuff up to London fairly regularly. She'd take mine."

"You can have that bit of pasture and welcome. But tell me. I understood that dependants of men in the Army were to be given allowances."

A cynical expression, strangely at odds with her open countenance, crossed Mrs Cooper's face. "I'll believe that," she said, "when I see it. I mean, Mistress, how could they? There must be thousands of women and children far more dependent than I ever was. Besides, Parliament and the Army are two different things, or so we hear. And Parliament holds the purse strings." I reflected that she was better informed than I was. In a predominantly Puritan area like ours, anti-Royalists could meet and talk freely; I was cut off, Lady Alice was afraid to be seen talking to me and Mrs Kentwoode wished only to communicate by signs. I was wondering how soon I might expect some sign that the Brook money had reached John. Or whether – I dared hardly frame the thought to myself – I might ever expect a message from Eddy. He had not said: I love you. He had not said: I'll write. But surely he might feel inclined to let me know whether he had reached Bristol, whether or not he had obtained another ship.

Mrs Cooper brought me sharply back to the present; "What rent would you be asking, Mistress?"

"Nothing. That strip of grass, two yards wide, between ditches is quite useless – except for fowls." She thanked me heartily and then, perhaps as a token of gratitude, gave me a surprising piece of information.

"Did you know Will Borley went, too?"

"You astonish me. I'd have said he was too old. And who will look after Crowswood?"

"His Missus. And her eldest, girl though she may be, and the boy about twelve. . . ." Mrs Cooper gave me a look, half mischievous then sliding into gravity. "The fact is, Mistress, whether you know it or not, you've set us all a sort of example. Mary Borley told me herself that when they was arguing she said if you could run three farms she could run one. And that was really what put into my mind to set up in business and not wait to see the promises kept."

I suppose I should have been flattered, but I had felt so many things in so short a time that I was incapable of feeling anything much, especially anything new.

The weeks went by and I seized every possible excuse to go into Baildon, often taking Tom Markham with me as I had in the past taken Jerry Cooper. I controlled the farms, made the decisions, accepted responsibility, but I had never hardened myself sufficiently to go alone to any gathering where I should be the only female. So he was with me on the October day when I saw the pot-pourri bowl on the windowsill. I reined in immediately and said in a falsely weak way: "Tom, you were right when you said this was no day for me to be out. This is a killing wind. I shall ask Mrs Kentwoode to let me sit by the fire."

"You all right? Want me to see you in?"

"Oh no. You go to the sale."

"What about your own errands?"

"Nothing urgent. They can wait."

The Old Vine yard was busier than it had been on my

former visit, but it seemed almost as though Mrs Kent-woode had been on the look-out for me . . . I was hardly out of the saddle when she appeared at the side door, shrouded in a shawl like a work-woman. It did nothing to detract from her dignity. She said, "Go to the fire. I'll be with you in a minute." She was rather longer than that and I stood by the fire wondering whether I was about to receive a message from John or – remote possibility – Eddy.

When she came in she dropped the shawl on a chair, went to the cupboard and brought out first a squat bottle and two glasses. She poured the brandy, turned back to the cup-board and produced a letter. Handing it to me she said, "Drink first."

Fear struck. What did she know? I said, "Is it bad?"

"I don't know. If it isn't it is an exception."

I looked at the cover. John's writing. As usual just my name. I felt the disloyalty of disappointment, instantly regretted.

It was John's usual, cautious letter, longer this time, at least addressing me as "Dearest Sister," and hoping that I was in good health. "My own is excellent, but I am again in sore straits for money. Your last kind loan, for which I thank you, simply melted away. Can you help me again?"

"Bad?" Mrs Kentwoode asked.

"No. Though of course one can never tell. There is no date. Anything could have happened while this letter was on its way."

"My son – my only son – is with the King."

"I did not know that. I'm sorry."

"You have a request for more aid?"

"Yes." It was such a relief to talk about it. I told her about selling Brook and my rooted objection to selling more land. "Wool prices were low this year," I said. "I have not yet sold the corn; prices always rise after Christmas. I have beasts for slaughter in the market at this moment . . . But then there are the taxes."

"There are indeed. What about jewels?"

"All gone to the war."

"Silver plate?"

"Some."

About this, as about so many things, Grandfather and Father had taken opposite views and I think that what silver there was at Pargeters had been in Grandfather's possession before my parents married. Father thought it ostentatious.

"Send what you have – or what you can spare. Send it here – I have means of forwarding even things of bulk."

I thought of servants. Of course, by this time everybody knew that John was fighting for the King and accepted the fact. But servants did not tend to talk. Marian never left the house, Peggy, another workhouse orphan, formed only fleeting attachments to young marriageable men, but Annie was one of a huge Minsham family with sisters in service in many places. She had only to say that heaven be thanked she'd have no silver to clean in future . . .

Sir Walter Fennel knew I had sold Brook, but he had himself suggested it and it served some unfathomable purpose of his own to have Mr Clover there. Selling the silver from one's very table was a different matter and might invite retaliation.

"I know a man," Mrs Kentwoode said, "who makes perfect replicas. Base metal, lightly brushed with silver. Every piece I have is fraudulent." She broke off and frowned thoughtfully over her brandy. "This tiresome matter of communication," she said. "And spies. I have one under my very roof at this moment! I plan to outwit him, of course; but another will be sent. So have you no man about you whom you can trust *fully*? In an inn-yard a man is so much less conspicuous."

"Tom Markham is faithful," I said. "But not very . . . clever."

"A messenger need not be clever – look at carrier pigeons!"

We managed a little laugh together. Then I said: "Mrs Kentwoode; you implied that on the whole the news was bad."

"How could it be otherwise? War is no longer one man facing another, or even facing great odds with but courage and endurance. It is a matter of resources. Parliament can levy taxes, the King depends upon gifts. And the loyal parts of the country, the West and North are the poorest. His allies have failed him. And I am not alone in thinking that Prince Rupert is as much a liability as an asset."

"In what way? My brother is with him."

"Out of date," she said. "Brilliant and brave but quite undisciplined. More than one engagement which could have been a victory proved indecisive because he would not turn back and co-operate with the infantry."

She sounded so well-informed. But of course she spent her life in the company of men and was obviously at the hub of an intrigue.

"You think we may lose?"

"Not if we can hold out long enough. Already there are rifts on the other side. They will widen. The Presbyterians, for example, have no quarrel with the King, only with the Bishops. They'd make peace tomorrow . . . So you see," she said more brightly, "why every silver spoon must be melted down."

On the way home I took Tom fully into my confidence and he showed great understanding. "Visiting The Old Vine ain't gonna be no hardship," he said. "I'd do more'n that, if you arst me to."

Next morning I discovered, with surprised satisfaction, that Pargeters was better furnished with silver than I had thought. Grandfather had not been averse to ostentation; but Father's prejudices had been paramount, especially as the old man's mind began to fail. And Mother had had no will but Father's. (I was a step nearer now to understanding her attitude, poor woman!) I found in the back of a cupboard a number of pieces, long unused, completely black; a set of six porringers; two very elaborate candlesticks and a centre-piece for a table, a sailing ship, beautiful in its workmanship. I held it for a moment, thinking what a pity to melt such a thing down. Then I remembered Mrs Kentwoode's words about holding out long enough.

Marian not unnaturally took an interest in my activity. "Are you looking for something, Mistress?"

"Nothing you could help me to find," I replied with

marked lack of graciousness. "Really, this cupboard is disgracefully untidy."

"Girls get worse every year. And I'm making damson cheese." Considering this a sufficient answer, she waddled away.

I thought my finds were enough for one smuggled consignment. Once I had told Mrs Kentwoode that I thought I knew a trustworthy man, she had given me exact instructions. Tom was to deliver sacks of completely ordinary things: hay, turnips, cabbages, beans, but only into the hands of the old half-crippled man, or those of Mrs Kentwoode herself.

I put that day's loot into a small sack, wrote a note to say no duplicates were needed and then hesitated over ready money. The animals for slaughter had sold well; I had the fleece money, disappointing as it was. Taxes in December – but then I could sell the hoarded grain. I suffered a twinge, not conscience exactly, but I *had* sent Eddy off with ten pounds and Mother's emerald. And what I was dealing with now, was it not John's own? I sent ten pounds as well. (It shows how fundamentally impractical I am that I completely forgot that I would soon be eighteen and by Father's will entitled to fifty pounds a year of my own.)

The business of getting duplicates made was not unduly bothersome. Most of our silver in daily use was slightly rickety, one candlestick I dropped. The duplicator worked with incredible speed and incredible skill. I sometimes suspected that he kept a stock of silvered frauds. By the last week in November when the winter set in early and the first snow began to fall I had literally nothing of convertible value left; and no idea that another responsibility was moving towards me.

In really bad weather Grandfather did present a problem. Even with his erratic meal-times, he couldn't eat all day and although he slept in snatches, he had wakeful, restless hours with nothing to do, nowhere to go, nothing to think about nowadays, for increasing lengths of time, nothing to say.

Even his disconnected reminiscences seemed to have failed him. When he did speak it was usually to complain.

"I'll try the beads." These were the cheap clay beads of the kind sold as fairings. They were vividly painted and were kept in a wide shallow box. Sometimes Grandfather would sort them out according to colour, putting them into a tray with compartments. At other times he merely counted them – his arithmetic was still amazingly accurate. At other times he would string them; using a large needle and coarse thread. Timmy often wore three necklets.

I was sorry for Timmy; but at least he was indoors on a foul day, he was sitting down by a good fire and had biscuits to nibble.

I was crossing the hall on my way to the parlour when the door-bell rang. I opened the door, a cold blast swept in and some snowflakes, so that for a second the small figure on the step seemed to have materialised from the storm.

From the depths of the sodden hood a small – I thought childish – voice asked, "Is this Pargeters?"

"Yes." My heart jumped a little; I thought: A message!

"Are you Mistress Woodley-Mercer?"

"Yes."

"Oh, thank God," she said and began to cry.

I drew her in. By this time Peggy had arrived to answer the bell and I said, "Mull some wine, quickly." I guided the sobbing, shuddering child into the parlour, lifted away the hooded cloak and sat her down in front of the blaze. As soon as the hood was removed I could see that she was not a child; eighteen at least and when not exhausted, half-frozen and in tears would be very pretty.

I said, "Don't cry. You're all right now."

She said, "Johnny . . ." and cried even harder.

"My brother. What about him?"

"Dead," she said. "And me as I am."

For a moment the significance of the last statement eluded me and I could only take in the fact that John was dead. My brother, the only companion of my youth. And even if we had had some differences of opinion, in the end he had trusted me as few women have ever been trusted.

I would have wept if the gift of tears had not been denied me. I beat down once again the sheer physical discomfort of tearlessness. My heart cried out, Too young to die! My head replied that men, however young, who went to war were likely to be killed. He had done what he wanted and in the doing had died.

Just then Peggy came in with the hot wine. I said, "Make a room ready – the one opposite mine." By that time I had rallied and saw what I had missed when I removed her cloak and she slumped into a chair and wept into her hands. She was heavily pregnant.

"Drink this. It will warm and hearten you," I said. She sipped, then as the liquid cooled, gulped it. She stopped crying and was calm. I waited, trying to study her without staring. I had noticed, without noticing, that her cloak was of the best quality cloth and silk-lined. Her dress was of fine linsey cloth with narrow, plain linen collar and cuffs, considerably soiled. Her shoes were fragile, intended for indoor wear; dampness and some walking on rough roads had ruined them, and the heat of the fire towards which she had extended them, was making them steam.

Everybody believed, or pretended to believe that to sit in damp footwear was a sure way of getting a head-cold; so I knelt, removed the shoes and stockings, rubbed the cold small feet briskly and wrapped them in the little shoulder cape which I wore indoors in chilly weather.

She said, "Thank you," and gave me a slightly unsteady smile.

"Now, tell me everything."

"It is so difficult to know where to begin."

"Well. Is it John's baby?"

"Oh yes. It is John's baby. And he said if anything happened – bad, I mean – to come to you."

"Did he know about the baby?"

"Oh no. I didn't know myself then. And when it started – I mean the baby – I thought it could be shock. You see, my father was killed in the same battle. Marston Moor that was. In July."

"How dreadful for you. I am most truly sorry."

I had noticed that she wore no ring. But she hadn't told me where she came from and it could have been a place where the parson wouldn't allow wedding rings, since they were a symbol and all symbols were Popish.

"It was horrible," she said. "You see, Mother was always a bit of a Puritan and after Father was killed we went to live with her brother, my uncle who is very Puritan indeed."

"Were you and John married?"

After the briefest possible hesitation she said, "No. But we were betrothed. I mean *really* betrothed. You see, there was no time."

Betrothals no longer held the importance they had once done. I could remember Grandfather, in his good days when he liked talking, especially about the Tudors whom he greatly admired, saying that Henry VIII had ended a marriage that displeased him by claiming that his so-called wife was party to a betrothal, never cancelled. And Father had said it was a good thing betrothals were losing force; in the old days children had been pledged in their cradles!

But even when betrothals were legally binding it had been assumed that a marriage must preface its consummation. By old standards or new John's baby would be a bastard. What was more, the new laws, aiming at making people virtuous by legislation, were brutally strict about any sexual irregularity. Harbouring a woman about to bear an illegitimate child was a punishable offence.

"That must be a secret between us forever. Nobody else must ever know. What is your name?" I could hear myself sounding like something out of the Inquisition.

"Cynthia Hastings."

"From this moment on you are Cynthia Woodley-Mercer. My brother's widow. I will get you a ring."

"Oh, but I have one," she said. "I mean a ring." She dived behind her collar, hauled on a piece of string and fished out a ring which, if it were not Mother's was an exact duplicate; the most modest and least valuable of them all: a plain gold circlet set around at intervals with tiny pearls. "I thought it better not to have anything of value about me while I was on the road."

"Very wise," I said.

"Johnny had it hidden so cunningly. Behind a button. I cut it off and sewed the button back again. Then we were betrothed with my Father and the other man . . . Captain – Captain Fraser as witnesses. But my uncle didn't believe; I mean he chose not to. And as soon as it began to show he was *furious*. He called me the ugliest of names. The poor baby, too. And made me stay out of sight. And I know he and my mother were planning to send me away. So I came."

"You did absolutely rightly. You'll be safe here. We'll all look after you – and the baby, too, in due time."

I accepted her story then without a quiver of doubt. There was only one tiny discrepancy; she referred to John as Johnny, a name he had always for some reason detested. But if she had used the diminutive no doubt it had sounded beautiful to him. Some people reduce Sarah to Sal and little as I liked Sarah, I liked Sal less, but if Eddy had called me Sal it would have been like music in my ears. Indeed my experience with Eddy, brief as it was, affected my relationship with Cynthia. How could I hold against her that loss of virginity before marriage when, but for Eddy's control, I'd have lost mine, down on the straw in the stable?

Grandfather would have nothing to do with her and his dislike was based on the colour of her hair. "Yellow," he said. "Never any good. Keep away from me, young woman."

I could only conclude that at some time in the remote past a yellow-haired girl had rejected his advances or played him false. It was a pity because had he taken to Cynthia they might have enjoyed each other's company. He was in his second childhood and she – I came to realise – had not yet outgrown her first. Unkind? I admit it, but the truth was that once established, safe and comfortable, Cynthia lapsed into the role of little girl – and a spoilt one at that.

She was a babbler, and that was something new at Pargeters where talk had usually been serious and purposeful. Much of her talk in the early stages was concerned with the work she was doing to convert Mother's clothes to her

130

own use. Mother had been tall, so everything must be shortened and what Cynthia intended to wear immediately had to be enlarged about the waist. This she did most competently, inserting gussets, or even whole panels. Some dresses – the prettiest – she refused to convert. "After all, I shall be my proper shape one day. What a pity that your mother did not like blue."

"It did not suit her. Her hair was black and her eyes were green."

Something jarred on me slightly but I thought with satisfaction that at least I had made her understand that there would be no money for new clothes for some time to come. She had naïvely thought that if you lived in a big house and owned land you were rich. The ever-looming threat of taxes, the more intermittent but no less serious threat of a crop failure she did not understand. She had led a sheltered life, though not as I had at first guessed, in a town.

She had, in fact, never volunteered the name of the place from which she had come; but I asked and she said, "When my father was alive we lived in York. At least near York. My uncle's house was nearer Tadcaster."

It was vague, but in many areas she was vague. I asked when the baby could be expected.

"I don't really know. It takes nine months doesn't it? About April."

There was now no real reason for Tom Markham to visit The Old Vine; I'd sent what I could and John was no longer alive to ask or to receive, but I clung to the faint hope that one day there would be a message from Eddy. So though it was the dead season of the year I encouraged him to go into Baildon regularly, visit The Old Vine and bring back snippets of gossip. He was never late back, he was never in the least bit tipsy and he was now my chief, indeed my only foreman, so that it was an understood thing that on Wednesday evenings he should come into the dining-parlour and report to me, drinking a mug of ale as he did so. He'd admitted to me once that he didn't care for wine much. I sipped brandy, of which, thanks to Grandfather (and for once Father had not argued), we were still well supplied. The import of luxury goods was now forbidden and the irony was that whereas in the past smuggled brandy had been cheaper than that upon which import duty had been paid, smuggled brandy was now very costly. However, the cool room facing North which served Pargeters as a cellar, was still well stocked.

Tom told me this and that, nothing of interest. Then he said, very ill at ease; "I did hear suthing made me think a bit. I don't aim to offend you. Or upset. The young master's death was blow enough. We all saw you grieving and getting thin as a rake . . . Mind if I arst you a question, point-blank?"

I said, "Tom, you have done confidential errands for me. You know I trust you. How could you offend me?"

"All right then," he said with the air of a man preparing to plunge into deep water. "Did that young lady bring you any proof she was Master John's widder?"

The question hit me in the midriff. With what little breath I had left I said, "Ample proof." Then I drew another breath and said, "What in the world, Tom, made you ask such a question?"

"Suthing I heard tonight. There's a trade in it now. They go about the battlefield – women I mean – and look for young men that look worth a bit. Then they take suthing, a ring or a button – lock of hair even. There's families being proper took in."

"But how can such women know which family?"

"They're still buried. All in the same grave nowadays, they say. But names still read out."

I thought of John being tumbled into a communal grave and winced inwardly. But what did it matter? As Father had said, once you were dead you were dead. Another aspect struck me. I said, "Tom what happens if one of these harpies turns up claiming to be the wife of a man already married?"

"Well, she ain't got nothing to lose, hev she? And men maybe gonna die next day . . . You can't be too strict."

"I can assure you, Tom, my sister-in-law satisfied me absolutely."

"Got her lines and everything?"

"Oh yes. I must say, Tom, I should like to know what put such a notion into your head." I asked not in rebuke but from interest. I knew the flaw in Cynthia's façade, but how had anyone else even guessed?

Tom took his time over that question.

"Well, behaviour mostly. Not that I see the young lady much, but the girls talk. *She don't act like a widder.* I mean . . . laughing and talking and preening about in new dresses."

"She happens to be a very brave lady," I said with some warmth. "As for the clothes. She arrived with nothing and is making over a few of my mother's old dresses. Isn't that better than sitting about and crying and making everybody else miserable?"

"If you say so. It was just that I wondered, and then I heard that tale. I wouldn't want you to hold it against me."

I assured him that I did not but I went to bed thoughtful. It was almost impossible to imagine Cynthia in the role of battlefield ghoul but somebody could have gone for her. The man responsible for her condition? What was the name she had stumbled over in her first account to me? Captain Fraser! He could even have been one of John's comrades-in-arms. How easy, how dangerously easy it was to fabricate a whole story.

I thought of her vagueness: '*near* York', '*near* Tadcaster'; any hamlet of five cottages had a name! She was equally vague – or was it evasive? – about the time when the baby could be expected. And she called John 'Johnny', imagining it proof of intimacy.

On the other hand she was the very epitome of all the girls whom John, during his brief social life had admired: small, fair-haired, blue-eyed, pretty chatterboxes. And I had really nothing concrete upon which to base my suspicion. Just Tom's retailing of a story. And Cynthia's behaviour. I had noticed it myself and likened her in my mind to a stray cat, cold, wet, wretched; taken in, cherished, installed and happily making itself at home. Anyway, as Father had sometimes said, when in doubt it is better to err on the lenient side.

That was in every sense a long, hard winter. Two or three times, after a heavy snowfall, we were cut off completely. Tom Markham literally forced his way through waist-high drifts to Brook where, taking advantage of Mr Clover's offer, I had, maybe foolishly, left the sheep. He came back full of praise for Mr Clover and Eli Smith's mother who had helped him to carry the hay, stored for such emergencies.

The tax-gatherers came with demands which exceeded my worst expectations.

And for the first time I found the evenings tedious beyond belief. I had formed the habit of reading; the end-of-the-day, cosy-by-the-fire escape from sad thoughts or present worries. But now there was Cynthia, exercising upon me that most desirable social asset – the ability to talk about nothing. She had now started on making Mother's fine underclothes into a layette for the baby. I'd read half a page of, say, Hakluyt's *Voyages* and she'd ask me whether single or double feather-stitching was to be preferred. There was also a process known as drawn-thread work, I must admit very pretty, giving plain linen the look of lace; but it took four hands, two to hold the linen taut and two to loosen and pull the threads. And she talked. Once or twice, after Tom had alerted me, I asked questions, as tactfully as I could. York Minster is a building so famous for its beauty that even I had heard of it. "Oh yes," Cynthia said, "it is pretty." One of her favourite words.

"Did you attend service there?"

"Oh no. We didn't live *in* York . . . Sarah, that candle! I can hardly see what I am doing."

She was an only child. To an extent she talked freely about her hateful uncle – but never giving his name. When I asked whether her mother would worry about her disappearance, she said, "Oh no . . . They'd be so *glad*! They were trying to put me away. Oh dear, now I've dropped a stitch!" She knitted as well as she sewed. I often felt sad for

John who should be sitting here in my place, listening to her cheerful prattle and looking forward to the birth of his son; they would have been a happy couple. But if Cynthia could be so unwidowlike that even servants commented on it, I must resist morbid thoughts.

She *was* brave. She would talk and talk about the baby's clothes and how lovely it would be when he was here. (She never doubted his sex.) But she never mentioned what must happen before there was a baby to wear those dainty garments. Of childbed I was equally ignorant in practice, but I'd heard of women dying or made invalids for life, and although all the men, from Father to Tom Markham, had kept me away from the sight of a parturition I knew that even animals sometimes died in the act of giving birth. In Cynthia's place I knew I should be terrified. She never showed a flicker of fear, and as the year turned upwards again, with the days lengthening and the ploughs out, Cynthia's thoughts were all on the cradle. "But surely, Sarah, there must be a cradle somewhere. Every family has a cradle. *You* must have had one."

No doubt I had; but by this time I knew enough about my parents to guess that John had been welcome, every man wanting a son. Then I had been born and I could well imagine that Mother had decided that enough was enough.

Marian, who must have seen me in it, disclaimed all knowledge. "There was one, that I do know. Rather pretty if I remember right. But what happened to it I don't know no more than the Man in the Moon."

"A baby must have a cradle," Cynthia said, and I agreed, secretly grieving about the expense. The taxes had frightened me and I had set myself a course of rigid economy. The man who had done general carpentering jobs had gone to the war. So, doubtless, had many others, and those who remained would charge what they liked.

Little Thomas saved me that outlay. "In the workhouse, Mistress, there was an old man I used to help a bit, cutting pegs, he never would use nails. By cradle you mean a box on rockers. I reckon I could make one."

It began as a box on rockers, very sturdy, but plain.

Cynthia transformed it. She could quilt as well as she could do most things with a needle, and using an old satin skirt of Mother's – possibly a bit of bridal garb – she lined the cradle beautifully, made a matching cover, and changed an ordinary-sized pillow into a small pillow and mattress. My contribution was to bespeak Annie's mother who, when not actually in childbed herself, assisted at others and had a very good reputation.

"Of course me mother'd come here first," Annie said agreeably, "but there's several due this time of year. If you could give just some *idea* . . ."

"It should be some time in April."

"Is that the nearest she can reckon?"

I was instantly on the defensive. "This is Mrs Woodley-Mercer's first baby," I said stiffly. "She has no experience. And there was the shock of bereavement. Ask your mother to hold herself in readiness for the whole of April. I will pay her."

But it was March, the eighth to be exact, at the end of a pleasant day. The banks of the little stream that ran through that part of Brook which Mr Clover had lent me – refusing any rent – had been all starred with primroses. Tom Markham had gathered me a hatful and they were there in the false-silver bowl on the table. I remember their faint, sweet, outdoor scent.

Cynthia said, "Sarah, dear. Next time you go into Baildon, will you buy some blue ribbon?"

"If I can," I said. What strict Puritans called fripperies were beginning to be in short supply. She began to make the hoary old joke about blue for a boy, and stopped, staring at me with utter astonishment and clapping both hands to her distended body. "I think . . . it's begun."

It had begun and it went on for an incredible thirty-six hours.

I sent Tom helter-skelter to fetch Annie's mother and bring her back, riding pillion. She took complete charge, the one experienced person in the house, enjoying her little brief authority. I remember her saying. "No need for such haste. It'll take till tomorrow." Next day she said,

"Well, she is a bit narrer and by my reckoning thass a big baby."

We all admire qualities we do not possess, and Cynthia was *brave*. I stood or sat there, an impotent witness to such pain as I had not imagined could exist and which eventually even the midwife admitted was exceptional. She had exerted all her skill, made sure that there was no obstruction and that the baby was in the right position; she'd persuaded Cynthia to take a little wine, a little broth – strength must be kept up; sometimes a few steps helped. A 'groaning chair' had been known to work. I asked what a groaning chair was. Just an ordinary chair with a hole in the seat through which the baby could fall. It took Thomas less than an hour to convert an ordinary chair. Quite ineffectual; as were such tricks as a pinch of pepper to provoke a hearty sneeze and a jug of well-cold water dashed into the sufferer's face to administer a shock.

Annie's mother was not yet defeated. When the longest twenty-four hours in the history of time had elapsed she took from her shabby little bag a small bottle. "I ain't often driven to use this," she said, her authority slightly tinged with apology. I noticed how carefully she measured the dose, drop by drop. She added a little water and said, "Here ma'am, drink this and it'll soon be over."

It was not. I began, belatedly, to think about doctors. I knew there was not one in Baildon; what about Bywater? Thetford? I said, "Could a doctor help, Mrs Meecham?" She scowled. I thought: Professional rivalry! But the thought which could have caused me some amusement, failed to do so just then. "There's an operation called a Seezer but thass too late now. And they can use a sort of grappling iron, which *we* ain't allowed. That mean a dead baby nine times outa ten. I agree this is stubborn, but so long as she don't weaken . . ."

Cynthia may have been weakening in body, in spirit, no. She writhed, she moaned, at times screamed, but always trying to muffle the noise, biting her hands, the pillow, the edge of the sheet.

I realised that I didn't care whether this baby were John's

or not. It could have been a blackamoor's baby if only it would get itself born and end this torture.

I also realised that I loved my near-sister-in-law. She had bored me by her chatter, often incensed me slightly by her trivial, childish attitude; irked me by her vanity; baffled me by her evasiveness; excited my suspicion . . . Now I knew that if she lost the fight which she was waging so heroically, I should be again bereft.

Mrs Meecham believed, quite rightly, that a midwife merited plenty of nourishment and some little what she called cat-naps. These she took in a chair with her feet on a stool. "You go to bed," she told me. "My Annie can keep watch and wake me if there's any change." I knew that to go to bed would be as useless as attempting to eat had been. So I resorted to brandy, to Mrs Meecham's disapproval. "I bin on a lot of cases," she said, "but I never seen nobody, no, not even a husband carry on like you're doing."

She had the enviable ability to sleep as soon as she closed her eyes and wake just as promptly. And she was imperturbable until at last, in the grey dawn of the second day, Cynthia began to fail, the moans and cries dwindling to low mewling sounds, rather like those of a kitten. Once she said, quite clearly and with a touch of defiance, "All right then! Kill me!"

"No help for it," Mrs Meecham said, not flustered exactly, but with her calm beginning to crack. She took up the bottle and this time poured a massive dose, not counting the drops, adding no water.

Perhaps another five minutes passed; then Cynthia gave a scream and a heave – and the population of the world had increased by one.

"A boy," Mrs Meecham said as though she were personally responsible for this satisfactory outcome.

When all was tidy and Cynthia was asleep, Mrs Meecham sensed that her reign had ended; but she still had advice to give. After what Cynthia had been through there wasn't much likelihood of her being able to feed the baby. Mrs Meecham knew a very decent woman with enough milk for two. "Just let me know." And when the baby was weaned, goats' milk was a lot better than cows', that had been proved by experience. I accepted that and thought happily that goats' milk would be available. If you kept a herd for breeding as well as for slaughter, you always ran a few goats as well because they ate some weed which made cows abort.

I paid, without grudging, what I had promised the midwife, full pay for April.

Cynthia, when she woke, took a good look at the baby and made a very characteristic remark. "You see, he is a boy – and we never got that blue ribbon." It was the kind of remark which would once have annoyed me, but I knew I should never be annoyed by her again. And she said that of course she could and would feed the baby. "You never know. I heard of a wet-nurse who had fits. Nobody knew at the time, but the baby she fed turned out to have fits too."

Before Puritanism became so powerful a christening had been a great occasion, second only to a wedding. I could remember several, it being considered civil to invite one's employer and his family. Father had always found some excuse not to attend but he invariably sent a gold piece worth ten shillings, to be placed in the baby's hand. I could remember his saying, "It's supposed to ensure that the child will never lack money, which is, I suppose, as sensible as the idea that a three-week-old baby needs cleansing of original sin." And once, sending the sixth such tribute in just under six years to the same family, he'd said, "Really, I wish I employed eunuchs. But they are expensive, I believe."

Grandfather, in the old days, had been the great one for any kind of jollity, and with him John and I had attended many christenings. There'd been flowers – if any were available; music from the organ; Mr Althorpe in his shining white surplice; and of course, every member of the baby's family who lived within walking distance. All in their best clothes. Afterwards a feast, with food very plentiful, because many christening gifts took the form of food. Grandfather always warned us to eat sparingly but to praise lavishly. "You have a good meal awaiting you. This they've saved up for." Once he added, "If the peasants in some of the countries I've seen could see how ours live even on festive occasions, they wouldn't believe their eyes."

Now all was altered. Bit by bit all ceremonial had been eroded. New babies were named and registered as baptised, almost as casually as I put down in the stud book the fact that one of the Frisian cows had calved.

Mr Althorpe wore no surplice, just a plain black garment, known as a Geneva Gown – no surprise to me, of course, for the Sunday Observance rules were back in full force and stricter than ever. Not suffering from age or infirmity, I had attended morning service and avoided fines. I knew that the altar under the East window had long been disregarded – rather too solid to be removed, so shrouded with a black cloth. Its function had been usurped by a plain wooden table just inside the main West doorway.

The font, rather a beautiful one, said to be a good deal older than the church itself and possibly brought from Baildon when the Abbey there was demolished, stood slightly to the left; and not having attended a christening lately I was surprised to see that it was not to be used. Instead, on the table which at least had a white cloth, was a bowl. Just a shallow crockery bowl like those used in dairies for milk, so that the cream can rise to the top and be skimmed off. It was about half full of water.

I wondered then and have wondered since why Puritans clung to some observances while discarding others. Why, for instance, bother with any water ceremony at all?

At least we had chosen the right names, and with the minimum of fuss. There was as yet no actual rule that Christian names should be of Biblical origin, but they were in favour. The baby, named for his father, was to be John Adam.

All would have been well but for Grandfather. I had not wanted him present and saw no reason why he should be. Apart from his first derogatory remarks he had seemed oblivious to Cynthia's existence and he had made only one comment about the baby, who happened at that moment to be crying: "Good lungs at any rate."

I knew that everybody employed either permanently

or temporarily would be in the church that Sunday afternoon, for nowadays christenings were performed then, after the compulsory catechism session for children and servants. Also there was the matter of a kind of loyalty, and there was habit, and curiosity. I'd planned a modest, very modest feast, to be held in the barn and I'd tried to use my imagination to compensate for the lack of expenditure. Very few labourers' cottages had ovens so I thought pastry would be a treat. Marian, far too lame to attend church, had worked for days making her famous pork pies. Of all farm animals the pig, being the most prolific, was the most expendable. It would not be a feast as the word had been understood before Christmas fell into disfavour, but with two casks of good beer it would not be altogether dreary.

Mr Althorpe just dipped the tips of his fingers in the dairy bowl and shook two or three drops on to the baby's forehead; "I name thee John Adam . . ." Then, somebody roared, literally *roared*, and there was Grandfather, forcing his way through and brandishing his stick. Now and then, when he needed to think, Father would do a bit of carving, mainly sticks and pipes. He was slightly fanciful about wood, saying, "This lends itself . . ." and I remembered that particular stick because Father had said it lent itself to a handle like a mermaid – a creature in which Grandfather believed and Father did not. It had delighted Grandfather and the stick had remained his favourite. He had come to rely on it and lately on Timmy's arm as well. Now, strong on his feet, leaning on nothing and red in the face he forced his way to the table upon which he smote so heavily that the dairy bowl jumped.

"Now do it properly," he said. "Go on, do it. Sign the child with the Cross."

The Puritans for some reason which I never fully understood had a marked aversion to what was after all the very symbol of Christianity. Even market crosses had been truncated. Graves marked with a cross as many were, lost their identity, a church window showing the cross in any form must be smashed. None of it concerned me, but I thought it silly to regard a cross, even made in the air across one's chest, as a symbol of Popery. So far as anyone could *know*, the cross, a horrible form of execution, was much older than the Papacy.

Mr Althorpe who was holding John Adam quickly handed him to me. The business of godfathers and godmothers had been abolished. Thus disencumbered he faced Grandfather and said, "I should be deprived of my living."

And it was true; I'd heard, but noted only on the periphery of my mind, of clerics being expelled because they were backward looking.

Grandfather said, "I'll see you deprived all right, you mummer! Just wait."

Of course he was still confused, for swinging round to me he said, "Bring your baby, Penelope. You," he addressed Cynthia, "bring that bowl."

Cynthia could no more have lifted the bowl than she could have flown through the air. She was making such a slow recovery that it could hardly be called a recovery at all. She'd regained her shape and a touch of her petal pink colour, and she ate heartily of the food which Marian took pains to make tempting, but she was not regaining strength properly and any exertion made her turn pale. She never complained, but when asked said that she sometimes had a pain, "not much, just a stitch," in her side.

Mrs Meecham lifted the bowl and Grandfather made his way to the font and indicated that the water should be transferred. The surface levelled out, scummed with dust and bits of cobweb, two or three spiders scuttled to safety.

Grandfather made the sign of the Cross over the water and then on his own chest. Then I knew a moment of fear lest he should attempt to take the child from me. He was going through what looked like a flash of sanity – of a kind – but that could not alter the fact that he was old and shaky. I could imagine the child's head in contact with the stone. I tightened my hold, prepared to resist. However Grandfather made no such move. He said in a firm loud voice, "In default of an ordained priest . . ." and stopped. I thought: Poor old man, now he has forgotten. But the pause was deliberate and he repeated the challenge. "In default of an ordained priest, but with the consent of those here present, I baptise thee, John Adam, in the name of the Father, the Son and the Holy Ghost." The dirty water made the sign visible on the baby's forehead, and he cried out. The correct response: Satan fleeing and howling as he went. I noticed a good many women, and some men, crossing themselves.

I looked at Mr Althorpe. He stood by the bare table, wearing the most deliberately neutral expression I have ever seen on any face. He had acted according to orders, and by the prevalent view outrage had been committed in his church and he had done nothing to prevent it. He had as far as a man could do without moving, absented himself.

Mrs Meecham, important again, took John Adam from me and I turned my attention to Cynthia who had gone very pale and was pressing her hand to her side. As we passed Mr Althorpe, I said, "You are coming to the house?"

"It was my intention. Now it would not be . . . seemly."

Outside Tom Markham was waiting to lift Cynthia into Bess's saddle.

I could hear Grandfather declaiming. He was back in his sea-faring days. "Sailors don't like carrying a priest, a donkey or a corpse, so maritime law allows captain or owner to officiate. I've committed several good men, and married some too . . ."

In the barn a lovely, touching surprise awaited us. I never knew whom to thank since everybody I accused – the word wrongly used – denied it. The place was ablaze with daffodils. Many were the wild ones which grew in Layer, but not a few were bigger, deeper coloured ones that grew in cottage gardens.

And perhaps it was as well that Mr Althorpe had absented himself, for Marian's pork pies were what was often called raised pies, sides and lid meeting in crimps, rather like the crenellations of castles. And in the centre of each lid was a hole to allow cooking steam to escape, and every hole was in the exact centre of a cross.

So far as we knew nothing was done or said about

143

Grandfather's behaviour. After all, everybody knew that he was out of his mind most of the time. And there were stories of even more dramatic happenings at christenings; in one village blows were actually exchanged.

One day Tom Markham who had come to enjoy calling in at The Old Vine came home with the startling news that the inn was closed. We all knew that Parliament disliked inns and had made life difficult for those who kept them, mainly by restricting drinking hours. Some small places simply went out of business; others were closed for infringing the rules, or for keeping disorderly houses.

"Why? And what has happened to Mrs Kentwoode?" I was genuinely anxious about her.

Tom grinned. "Mistress, you'd never guess. She's gone and got married again and her husband don't like inn-keeping. They say he's gonna turn the place into a school."

"I hope she will be happy," I said, and I meant it. The closure of The Old Vine, the breaking of a link in a mysterious secret chain of communication meant nothing to me. John was dead and the hope that there would one day be a message from Eddy had faded, slowly but completely. Either he was dead, too, or he had forgotten me.

The next news from Baildon was terrible.

I don't suppose the whole truth will ever be known. We heard bits and pieces, rumours, garbled accounts. The Rowhedges had obviously been smuggling in supplies from the Continent and providing transport for the first and most dangerous stage of the journey towards the West. There may have been another betrayal. An ambush. Sir Rawley was dead, together with several other men – all strangers. There was a burnt out wagon nearby and some evidence that it had contained explosives. Was there, however, evidence to connect Lady Alice with the smuggling? When whatever happened on that road from Bywater occurred, she was entertaining Sir Walter Fennel and a Roundhead captain to a supper while a sergeant and eight troopers were enjoying hospitality to the rear of the house. After supper, said to have been a gay meal, she'd gone into the yard and was making her big black horse show his tricks. And he'd bolted with her on his back.

Then – and here came the rub – nobody could go in pursuit of her. Not a horse in that yard, however beaten or prodded, would move. Black magic? And how much easier to accuse a woman of witchcraft than of smuggling, which, if she had ever been guilty of, she might plead had been done under coercion from her husband.

Some old stories were dragged up. A dog had once run into a harvest field and told her that her father was dead. She'd gone into a burning stable, called to the trapped horses and led them out unscathed. And she had made draughts and salves which had worked wonderful cures.

I must be fair; most of the people who spoke of the cures did so in the belief that they were defending her. But as Father had sometimes said, the prejudiced eye takes a distorted view. And Puritans were as fanatical about witchcraft as they were about crosses and surplices.

She was tried and condemned to be burned next Wednesday – the trial ending on a Friday. When Tom told me I imagined the four days and nights intervening. And I imagined what death by burning meant. I began then to suffer the vicarious pain which is about the most useless thing in the world.

I know all the derogatory terms for those who drink too much: toss-pots; wine-bibbers; swill-tubs. I'll grant that some men drink for pleasure as others over-indulge in food – and with much the same results. But how many drink to escape?

That evening I had no other resource. Talking about it would have altered nothing, but it would have been a relief to me. Cynthia? However, I knew well enough by then that her mind was limited. She'd say, "How horrible!" and that correct contribution made, resume whatever she was doing. And why not; she did not know Lady Alice. Also, she probably believed in witches and thought they should be punished. I'd caught enough scraps of conversation amongst the servants while the trial was on to know how *they* felt. A half-pleasurable excitement, almost a wish to believe. Magic was magic, a touch of excitement in hum-drum lives.

And even had Father been alive still and I could have talked to him, it would not have helped Lady Alice. What I needed was *power*. A posse of armed men to storm the old Bridewell in which she lay.

Cynthia still went to bed early. I said, "I still have work to do. Kiss John Adam good night for me." I heard Tom make his round. Then I sat in silence and drank brandy with the deliberate intention of dulling my mind to the point where I could go to bed with some hope of falling into a sodden slumber.

That longed-for moment never arrived. My mind grew livelier and livelier, its imaginings more and more grue-some, widening out from Lady Alice's blood boiling in her veins and her flesh charring, to the appalling vista of all pain through the ages. Like everybody else who could read and was allowed access to it, I had read Foxe's *Book of Martyrs*. Bad enough, but limited. What about the early Christians, thrown to the lions in the Roman arenas, or soaked in pitch, burned as living torches to illuminate gladiatorial shows? What about St Peter, the rock on which the whole Papacy was founded, being crucified upside down because he re-quested it, feeling unworthy to suffer in quite the same way as his Master. What about the Crucifixion itself? A blame-less man who, believing himself to be the son of God, could have commanded a squadron of angels with flaming swords . . .

Perhaps Father shouldn't have said it in my presence, but he had. "That would have impressed even the Romans. And saved a great deal of trouble."

Suddenly I realised that I had been a fool to try to drink myself silly down here. My head was spinning, the two candles I had kept burning swung and danced, each in its nimbus. I thought: I must get to bed while I can, and in an attempt to rise, to press my hands against the arms of the chair, my feet on the floor, realised that I had no hands, no feet, no power at all, and after that last panic thought, I am dread drunk! no mind either. Nothing.

146

Next day was Saturday, which in Baildon was a kind of secondary market day. No livestock, just a few stalls selling produce, crockery or oddments. At one of these I made a purchase – my ostensible reason for being in town that morning, at last some lengths of blue ribbon, the lack of which Cynthia mentioned almost every day. At any other time I should have been pleased at obtaining such a rarity. This morning my mind was elsewhere. And I thought that the whole market had a strange atmosphere, not a hush exactly, there was noise enough, but subdued yet vibrating. I glanced at what remained of the market cross. If I failed, next Wednesday, somewhere near there . . . I must not fail.

Yet what had seemed so simple and easy in my drunken stupor now seemed impossible. And I felt suddenly conspicuous, as though what I planned to do was written in letters of fire above my head. But the stall-keeper, drawing a not altogether false inference from my purchase said, "Lady, how about a nice rattle? Real ivory and the bell's silver." Like a juggler, he produced it. A pretty thing indeed, a globe of ivory – or bone – carved as finely as to look like lace, the little shining bell imprisoned inside it and the handle just right for a teething child to bite upon.

"How much?" I asked.

He assessed me in a flash; good horse, good clothes. Father had been averse to showiness but had insisted upon quality; and except for the green velvet, never to be worn again, I had made no addition to my wardrobe, not needing to, being full grown when he died.

"Two pounds. To *you*, Lady."

"Too much," I said, with a crazy kind of laugh welling up inside me. Here I was on a life-or-death errand, bickering about the price of a toy which, if I failed, John Adam might never see. And doing so, said the cool voice in my mind, because you are afraid, putting off the moment you fear.

"Say thirty-five shillings, then," the man said, slightly but not too severely disappointed.

My hands shook as though I had contracted palsy. And small wonder, after last night's debauch!

The pretty toy just fitted into my pouch which widened at the bottom and was now empty except for the ribbon and the screw of paper which I took out and held in my left hand. Ready, so that if all went as it had last night, when I planned it, it would be only the work of a second. I nudged Bess into a gentle trot and set off for the lane, just off Friargate where the Old Bridewell stood. I had never seen it in actual life.

Baildon and the cluster of villages around it was not populous enough, perhaps not wicked enough, to warrant a place of detention for long-term prisoners. It was merely a place for people awaiting trial for offences within the jurisdiction of the local magistrates. Witchcraft was such an offence. (Had Sir Rawley been taken in the act of smuggling, thus giving aid and comfort to those whom the Parliament called rebels, he would not have been dealt with so summarily but sent on to Ipswich to be dealt with by a judge on circuit.)

The Bridewell offered to the street a heavy, iron studded door, a stretch of flint wall and a window, slightly higher than most, out of easy reach for anyone on foot in the lane. The window was unglazed, but well barred, the bars no more than four inches apart. I had no means of knowing whether she would be in the space behind this barred aperture. In my trance, my drunken stupor, my somnambulistic state, she had been there, almost seeming to expect me. But this was real life! I wondered what to do if she were in the rear of the building. Was the gaoler bribable? And me with nothing, my last coins spent on a stupid toy!

I said, "Lady Alice!"

The floor inside must have been above street level. Her face, ghastly white, appeared at the window. She said, "Go away! At once!"

I shot out my left hand. I said, "Your own." I could hear hubbub, vague but increasing, somewhere behind me, at the end of the lane.

She said, "Bless you. Now go!"

And I had no choice. Bess shed ten years and sprang into action like a four-year-old. The lane ended as so many do, in a communal dungheap, and she went over it like a bird and there we were back in Friargate.

Bess resumed her sedate pace and I rode home deep in thought. Was there a rational explanation of what had happened? There I'd sat the previous evening, too drunk to get myself out of my chair. Yet I had, and taking a candle, gone across the kitchen, into the little lobby and on into the room I had sworn to myself never to enter again. And there was Lady Alice's pretty bag containing exactly what I knew I should find – a very small stoppered bottle labelled with one word, 'Lethal'. The stopper resisted me but finally gave way and I tipped the contents into my palm. Four pills, round, slightly flattened, a palish green in colour. I would have taken them all, but whatever had me under control said, Two will be ample and easily passed.

It could very well have been a dream except for the fact that when I woke there on the table by my bed, near the candlestick, were the two pills and in my hand was the precise knowledge of what I must do and how to do it. I also realised that I had been in that office room and never spared a thought for Eddy.

The legend of Lady Alice went on. First the manner of her death. They said that a dog, apparently mad and running in circles, was her familiar, sent by Satan to spare her an agonising death in public. There may well have been a dog, many dogs go mad in warm weather. I'd have said myself that even had she put her hand between the bars of that window it would have been out of reach of a dog. And who ever heard of a bite from a rabid dog bringing instantaneous death? The old gaoler rather muddled his stories; at first he said she took a convulsion and dropped dead. Then he reported a few last words; I thought as an embellishment.

The other story told about her was the haunting of that stretch of road along which she had taken her last wild ride. From time to time various apparently sensible people, reported uncanny experiences there. Nothing ever seen – at least by a human – but the sound of galloping hooves and very odd behaviour by other animals.

However, the whole thing was overshadowed by news of the Battle of Naseby which, strictly speaking, was the end of the war as ordinary people understood it. There were to be other battles, but the Royalist cause was lost there; Cromwell's New Model Army proved its worth. Royalists and those with Royalist leanings bore in mind that many of the Roundheads – men and horses – were freshly come to the fray, whereas the Cavalier ranks were debilitated by three years of war.

At Pargeters life went on; time marked by the seasons, by the farming procedures and the steady growth of John Adam who cut his teeth, took his first steps, spoke his first words.

Sometimes, half ashamed of myself, I looked at him as he developed, for some sign of a resemblance to John, to Father, Grandfather, Mother, or even myself. Nor did he resemble his mother who was so exquisitely fair. Cynthia herself once commented upon the fact that he was like nobody on her side of the family. "None of us were swarthy," she said. I said, "My mother's hair was jet black, but not curly and she certainly wasn't swarthy, very pale, with green eyes."

"Like yours, Sarah?"

"Not at all. Really green – and beautiful."

"But I think your eyes are pretty," Cynthia said and proceeded to talk about something else.

Perhaps it was left to Grandfather to say the ultimate word about the boy he had himself christened. It was one of those occasions when Grandfather's eccentric eating times coincided with the family dinner, always rather tricky times. Suddenly he said: "He's a changeling." Another ancient belief. That the Little People, the Fairies, sometimes stole a human child from its cradle and left one of their own, with, so far as happiness in family life was concerned, most unfortunate results.

Even to a believer in such fantasies the idea of John Adam being a fairy child would be difficult to accept because he was so large and solid. A big baby, growing into a big boy with a truly enormous appetite.

Of food, at that time, we were never short. On some things I was bound to economise, because the taxes grew worse, harvests were variable, and Parliament, now in full control was trying to keep down farm prices. I could no longer afford such luxuries as sugar and dried fruit or spices, though these were on sale again, after a lapse. I could no longer afford to have a calf killed for veal, or a tender young lamb sacrificed for household consumption. Marian and Grandfather were the only ones to complain openly. "How am I gonna make my long-keeping cake?" Marian demanded. Grandfather would say, "Salt pork *again!* Don't I get enough of that aboard ship?"

One morning – harvest time in the year after Naseby, that is 1646, Tom Markham said, "Will Borley's home."

"For good?"

"Yes. Discharged. Suthing wrong with his innards."

In his talk with me Tom was always prim, and innards, by his standard, was a more polite term than bowels.

"Dysentery?"

"Some such word. I ain't seen him myself but Mrs Cooper hev and she say you wouldn't reckernise him."

When Tom chose to give me this information we were on the sheepland from which one could look down upon Brook and I had the irrelevant thought: Nobody would recognise Brook, either. Mr Clover must have spent a small fortune on it, not so much enlarging, though there was one addition to the side; but on beautifying it, the old thatch replaced with rosy tiles, the windows enlarged and the walls painted white. Now I saw that a garden was being laid out.

Then I thought again of Crowswood and could see no reason why I should not just look in on Will Borley – the only man I knew who had actually been to the war and seen a battle. There had never been any ill feeling between us; he'd refused to sell Crowswood, but that was his right; as it was his right to go to the war on the side he favoured.

And once or twice during his absence I had helped his wife, mainly through hints and advice I'd given through Mrs Cooper. In fact we three, all women trying to shoulder men's jobs, had formed a kind of alliance.

I have known several disillusioned men but never one more embittered than Will Borley; now, as Tom had said, unrecognisable as the sound, upstanding man he had been. All skin and bone, like a tinker's donkey, and his skin, greyish-yellow, looked scaly.

"And I can't buy arrowroot now," Mrs Borley said as soon as the greetings were over.

I said, "We may have some. I'll look and if we have I'll send it over."

"I shall be all right now I'm home, with proper food," Will Borley said. "The worst of this is the way we been treated. Lied to. Made use of. Get ill, with the rotten food and . . . other things. Get wounded even and you're chucked on the midden. I'm luckier than . . ." He made the precipitate departure his disorder demanded.

"He mean he got something to come back to," Mrs Borley said with a touch of justified complacency. "But no gratuity as promised. I tell him, forget it. Thass whass turning your bowels sour."

I said I would look for arrowroot and rode home using, as usual, the way through Layer. And as I entered the yard from the garden side a woman on a horse and a boy on a donkey came in from the entry from the road.

Talk about family resemblances! The boy was so like Eddy – he could only be his son; and the woman? Eddy had left me with the impression that he was unmarried. Mistress, then! But how old. How plain. But with dignity, even a kind of stateliness – something which made me feel that I should stay mounted, meet her more on a level.

I said, "Good morning. I am Sarah Woodley-Mercer."

"My name is Katharine Bowen. I am Eddy Lacey's sister. This is my son – Edman."

I gave myself away at once; I said, "You have news of Eddy?"

"Alas, no. Had I had I should have informed you somehow . . . And before I say another word I must tell you that we are paupers, asking charity."

I said, "Welcome to Pargeters." I slipped to the ground and would have gone, as courtesy to a welcome guest, and to an older woman, to help her alight, but the boy forestalled me. And then I lost all mannerliness in surprise, in an almost horrified staring. She was so deformed. In the saddle she had looked normal, even imposing; standing she was all twisted as though her trunk had been severed from her legs and then replaced but all askew. I had the idiot thought that so twisted a body could never have given birth to a baby. Yet she had said, 'my son'.

She said, "My appearance is misleading. I am strong and healthy and do not propose to be a burden. And young as he is, Edman can earn his keep."

She walked with a limp and a lurch but with a kind of determination.

I led the way through the kitchen, that being quicker, and into the parlour where Cynthia was sewing some new garment for John Adam and at the same time amusing him by throwing a tethered ball for him to retrieve.

I made formal introductions, describing Cynthia as my sister-in-law and Katharine as a very old friend, who, with her son, had come to stay. It was still some time to dinner, so I slipped into the kitchen and was slightly amazed to see that Marian had already unstoppered the crock in which the very last of her long-keeping cake was stored. It kept so well because it was so stuffed with currants and raisins and contained so many eggs and so much rum. In bringing out the last, knowing that it would probably never be replaced, Marian was paying Katharine a very great compliment indeed, recognising quality, even clad in homespun.

I could not very well tell Marian that Katharine was an old friend, but I could and did say that she was a distant relative of Grandfather's.

"They'll be staying, I take it," Marian said, making it easy for me. I said I hoped so. Peggy came through with a jug of the small beer which was now the staple drink for everyone but Grandfather – my sense of justice demanded that what wine remained, should be reserved for his enjoyment.

I was aching to be alone with Katharine; I had a thousand questions to ask her, but not in front of Cynthia who had never heard of Eddy's existence.

I began to slice the cake. Katharine said, "A very small piece for me . . . Sarah, please," But Edman's prematurely solemn face brightened at the sight of such food. I cut him a good wedge. John Adam made a demanding noise and I cut him a reasonable portion which he wolfed with his usual avidity. Cynthia refused, with one of her rather plaintive references to her poor appetite. I had often lately thought that it was strange that she who had been so brave under positive torture, should have become something of a whiner as soon as John Adam was weaned. I knew that she did not feel well, often had pains and I wished there were a doctor whom I could consult. I wondered about that last massive dose which Mrs Meecham had administered – and with such success. And one morning, after church, I had a word or two with her. Naturally she was not going to admit that she had been at fault. "Thass early days yet," she said rather heartlessly. "She'll pull round; don't you fret." But the pulling round seemed to be taking a long time.

Now, John Adam, having devoured his cake, made a grab for the uncut remnant on the platter which stood not quite in the centre of the table. In doing so he knocked over Katharine's tankard of small beer. Much of the liquid ran about the table, but most of it went into Katharine's lap. She gave vent to an exclamation of annoyance and gave John Adam a look which showed me that not all the lines on her face had been engraved there by the years. Cynthia, in return glowered. An apology would have been more apt; but it was left for me to make. I said, "I'm so sorry. He's very . . . young." I could hardly say small; for John Adam, aged nearly two, looked three at least.

Katharine said, not very heartily, "It is of no matter," and shook off as much of the small beer as she could. Cynthia took her son by the hand – allowing him to retain the cake, and led him away. Katharine said, "Edman, go see to the animals – and bring in the bag. Presently."

I asked my urgent question. "When did you see Eddy last?"

"In July last year, the fifteenth or sixteenth. It was then that he told me about you – how marvellously kind you had been. Thanks to you he had a ship of a kind and some crew. All starving. I had nothing of my own, but I had access . . . You might say I occupied a position of trust. So I stole. I sent him away with provisions for a fortnight. I am not ashamed. I do not regret it. Except that it lost me my post and what roof remained. But Eddy knew then that my position was very precarious and that in a case of real need, you or Lady Alice Rowhedge would help."

"Lady Alice is dead," I said. And alongside the thought of how and why there ran a tiny thread of gratification that both the men I loved, John and Eddy, had trusted me to do my best for those whom they loved. "But please believe that you are *entirely* welcome here."

She said, "Thank you . . . I rather hoped that *you* might have seen my brother. Or had some message."

"Nothing."

"Then I am afraid we must face the worst. And I often ask myself which he himself would prefer – to be dead or a slave."

There was a silence. Then she said, "What is certain is that those of us who are left must struggle on and stay alive if we can. The other thing that is certain is that this cannot last. There is so much dissension. I know! I've lived in very close quarters with Roundheads. You might almost call me a camp-follower," she said with a grimace which was not quite a smile, "except that the camp never moved and I never slept with a soldier. They don't enlist blind men."

I must admit that I liked that light-hearted reference to her stern lined face and crooked body.

Bit by bit she told me what had happened to her since the war began. She was completely unlike Cynthia, nothing evasive at all. She'd lived at Brigstowe; seven miles from Bristol. "It was called Brigstowe Castle but except for a

155

gateway and a tower and some crumbling walls there was nothing left of the fortified place it had once been. We had a comfortable house." She had a husband, Arthur, and two sons, a boy named for his father, but known as Son, and Edman, named for her favourite brother. Her husband and Son, not yet seventeen, had both fallen at Edgehill.

She recounted this double loss without visible emotion, then went on: "Of course, at that time we all believed that the war would soon be over and that the West would see no fighting at all; but the Roundheads came on, like an evil tide. They took Brigstowe. Every inch of the land I had tried to make so productive. They made the house their headquarters. One must speak as one finds, I suppose," a certain regret tinged her voice. "Colonel Godwin said he did not make war on women and children, but he requested me to leave, which I was desirous to do. My own family lived at Hayes Barton, midway between Exmouth and Honiton. Then I had my accident." She explained that the grounds at Brigstowe were scattered with ruins and that Colonel Godwin's men, planning an assault on Bristol's walls, were practising mining operations, later to be used against what remained of the city's walls. "Colonel Godwin had most generously told me that I could take one horse; too old and decrepit even to be a baggage animal any longer. I'd stabled it apart, in the old dove-cote – part of the ruins and throughout the three days allowed me, I had been cosseting it, the poor thing had no teeth. I was on my way to collect it that morning . . . Have you ever witnessed an explosion? Then it is difficult to imagine. The earth rocked, I seemed to fly into the air, lost my senses and came to pinned under a great stone." She paused again and I saw the lines in her face deepen. "Nobody could have been kinder. Or more clever. It was an army surgeon who put me together again as well as he could which, we must admit, was very well indeed. He even gave me opium pills to spare me pain. All things considered," she said with that smile which was not quite a smile, "any good Roundhead might be correct in regarding me as an ingrate traitor. It was from their stores that I provisioned Eddy's ship. On the other hand I've washed and mended, made possets for men with head-colds, treated minor wounds, held dying hands. Perhaps I am a two-way traitor." She brooded for a moment. "They're only men, very few actually *bad*. Merely deluded."

I thought of the men who had gone from my employ – and of Will Borley.

"And some are to be bitterly disillusioned," I said.

"That is what I meant by saying that whatever régime they establish cannot last. They're squabbling already about whether one should take Holy Communion standing, kneeling, or sitting, whether men should wear or not wear hats in church; should an ordained man be called parson or minister. And there is also the little matter of property. There is one group, small, but vociferous, Levellers they call themselves, who believe no property should be privately owned. And meanwhile the ordinary fellow has his pay months in arrears."

This was the kind of talk I had so missed since Father died. A snippet here and there with Lady Alice, then forbidden; a few words with Mrs Kentwoode, also curtailed. I realised just how limited conversation had been; Cynthia with her preoccupation with clothes, with John Adam and her little ailments; Tom Markham, so sensible, but with so small a vocabulary. With Katharine I was like a glutton, long starved, suddenly confronted with a laden table. And I was insensitive. I failed to notice that Cynthia now felt herself excluded and was suffering from jealousy.

"Are they going to *stay* here?" she asked in a voice which informed me that a negative would be pleasing.

"Oh yes. They have no home. And we have plenty of room."

"Have they no relatives?"

"Not now. Even her elder brother went to war as soon as Exeter was threatened. He is now dead. And her younger brother – nobody knows quite what happened to him."

"Her elder brother must have been very old."

"Not necessarily. Katharine is much younger than she looks. The last four years have been hard on her."

"She is not the only one."

I think that Cynthia resented the fact that Katharine had come so well-armed with credentials. Her own marriage lines, several birth certificates, the deeds of Brigstowe Castle – a bulky roll. In fact the single bag which was all her luggage consisted mainly of papers. They would all be needed when order was restored, she said. Cynthia who had arrived with nothing concrete even to identify her was bound to feel the contrast. Understanding this, I tried to be patient.

Edman helped in the garden or in the yard and was always ready to amuse John Adam who, not unnaturally, adored him. There was some ill feeling about that, too. And once some open bickering at table. Edman said: "I'd like to take John Adam for a ride on my donkey."

"Impossible," Cynthia said. "He's far too young. It would be dangerous."

"I'd hold him very carefully," Edman said mildly. "And Balaam is very docile."

"I don't want John Adam to grow up bow-legged from riding too young."

Katharine laughed. "Stand up, Edman. There, is he bow-legged? I assure you, he was on a pony when he was John Adam's age – and about half his size."

John Adam, sensing the purport of the argument, began to shout, "Want ride . . . donkey . . . want . . ."

Katharine said, a trifle too sharply, "It is not what *you* want, young man. It is for your mother to decide."

Cynthia did not welcome this support; she hated any criticism of John Adam, however indirect it might be. She took refuge in the now familiar way; placing a hand to her side she asked to be excused. "This pain again . . ." There was often nowadays a hint that any little argument exacerbated the pain. And she could not say to Katharine, as she had once said to me, "You cannot imagine what real pain is like." Anybody who had been so broken and then put together by an army surgeon must know only too well.

Katharine was, I admit, rather hard where Cynthia was concerned, inclined to think like Mrs Meecham that I over cosseted her. "She'd be better with more fresh air and exercise."

"She'd take both if she felt able," I said. "She really is incredibly brave." I told her about the difficult birth. "Most surprising," Katharine said.

But Katharine and I did not often discuss Cynthia. We had so much more to talk about. She had taken, as soon as she had rested up a bit, to riding with me on my rounds. She was very knowledgeable about land and stock, having been in my position, a woman in charge – for some time; but far more short of labour. Her husband had gone to Nottingham at the head of thirty men; all tenants, Brigstowe being run on the old-fashioned lines, the open field system.

She had quite a pleasing little anecdote about the horse she rode. I had noticed that first day that it was a mare of quality, though too thin and not well groomed.

"As I told you, I gave Eddy provisions from some stores of which Colonel Godwin had put me in charge. It was easy to do, for Eddy knew about the little creeks, quite near the house. Nobody actually suspected me at first. How would I have disposed of so much stuff? I was camp mother as it were – but also a prisoner. Colonel Godwin had been moved by that time and Colonel Piggott was far stricter. He was suspicious of some of the men and there was talk of flogging. Have you ever seen a man flogged? Well, I have, it is not . . . pretty. So I confessed. Colonel Piggott was a stickler for rules but even his book gave no precedent for the case of a woman who had done what I had. He'd gladly have flogged me, but I think there'd have been a mutiny. So he ordered me and Edman to leave at once, carrying nothing; nothing whatsoever. Under the prevailing conditions that was a death sentence. So Edman and I set out – it was about ten in the morning. There is a long avenue at Brigstowe; ordinary troopers were not supposed to use it – except to cross it at certain points." She gave a brief laugh. "At one such point a man walked briskly across, dropping something as he went. My bag with all my papers, some bread and cheese and eleven shillings in small coinage. That he had

had such instant access to the papers proved that he was on the office staff. He may even have been the man suspected of the pilfering. I shall never know . . . Then, at another permitted crossing space there was a trooper, with a horse, this horse. He ducked away through the trees, leaving the horse behind. He may have been one of the several for whom I had written letters."

"What a story," I said. "You have accounted for everything except the donkey!"

"He cost me two shillings. Grossly extravagant! But . . . well, troopers' saddles were not designed for disabled females and with Edman riding pillion behind me the discomfort was considerable. Besides before we were near Reading I knew how to earn a bare subsistence." She gave me a curious look. "Did it never occur to you to wonder why it took us so long to reach you? The answer is that we all worked. I noticed as we came eastward how little the war had affected ordinary life. Elsewhere it is different. Such a shortage of work animals, and in places, of men. We helped with harvests, then with early ploughing and several funerals. I lived in a state of perpetual terror – less of pursuit as time went on, than that somebody might steal Sabrina. More often than not Edman and I slept in stables."

Our conversations were not all about the past or even the present. Katharine's view of the far future was sanguine, but there were grim years ahead. And she worried about Edman's education. At Brigstowe there had been a tutor who, having almost finished with Son, had just started on Edman. "But old as he was, he must go to the war. I did my poor best, but I'm no scholar and after Brigstowe was taken, I've had so little time."

I said that of course Edman must go to school. I said I was sure I could help. I remembered what Tom Markham had said about The Old Vine becoming a school and I thought of the Baildon Grammar School at which both Father and John had been educated. Actually I had no choice, for The Old Vine was not yet established. Secretly, I was rather glad, a temporary loyalty need not war with family tradition.

I went to the Grammar School full of confidence. Father had been a pupil there and though poverty had prevented his going on to some profession which would reflect glory upon his old school, he had never disgraced it in any way and had ended as a man of considerable property. He had been generous, too, always responding to any appeal. John, less of a scholar, had never infringed any rules, and he too had been generous. When the school moved from its old, cramped premises to the spacious building it now occupied, he had sent men, horses and wagons to assist in the move.

I gave my name to the hall-porter and was invited to wait; then informed that the Headmaster was not available, but that Mr Ashford would see me. He was a civil man, though stern-looking.

I wonder now at my naïveté. I answered every question as fully and honestly as I could. I had even thought to bring Edman's birth and baptismal certificates. I admitted that there was no kinship; that the boy and his mother were domiciled with me. I said I would be responsible for his fees. I said that Edman enjoyed excellent health, and had received some education already.

Mr Ashford appeared to take note of my answers, at the same time making a pattern of little squiggles on the margin of his page. With the last question asked he glanced at his handiwork, then at the open window and appeared to go into a trance. Waking from it he looked at me and said, "I am sorry. I can assign no place to Edman Bowen. The school is already overcrowded and there is a long waiting list."

"Circumstances existing when I entered this room," I said bitterly. "Why waste your time – and mine?"

"It is customary," he said mildly. "I do not make the rules." In his voice there was just the faintest hint that had he had more authority the verdict might have been otherwise but I was too angry and disappointed to care about potential goodwill, even if it existed. I snatched up Edman's documents and went out to where Bess waited, tethered in the shade of a great chestnut tree. I put the precious documents into the saddle-flap and then stood for a moment, leaning against Bess, too dispirited to mount.

How was I to tell Katharine? After sounding so confident. My common sense protested that she could not, would not blame me for the failure. Look what I had done for her and Edman already? And, casting back, into another sphere, for Eddy . . . And that horrible, self-derogatory voice in my mind said: Ah! What you feel now is hurt pride. For too long you have exercised absolute power within your small sphere. I admitted the truth of that, but was not healed.

"Miss Woodley-Mercer . . ." A man's voice, faintly familiar. I raised my face from Bess's mane, turned and saw Mr Clover, clad in his sober grey and mounted on his staid grey horse.

"Are you all right?"

"In all but temper," I said, still furious and shamed and defeated.

"I rather feared you might have been overcome by the heat."

"No. A slap in the face."

"Speaking figuratively – I hope."

"Indeed yes. Nonetheless painful." However, to show that I was all right, I got into the saddle and we rode together out of the Grammar School grounds. His appearance there did not surprise me because the main building stood back from the street and all the space which had once been dense shrubbery had been cleared and made into a forecourt. He could well have used it as a place to leave his horse or ambling along Northgate, he could have seen me leaning against Bess and turned in.

Our relationship was rather unusual, good neighbours to a degree but not friends. He was a Presbyterian which to me meant the other side, and he was an associate of Sir Walter Fennel. Also he owned Brook which I grudged being obliged to sell. On the other hand he allowed my sheep to remain on a piece of Brook for which he had no use. I had always tried to repay by sending gifts of such things that Pargeters produced and Brook did not – asparagus, peaches, plums and every time we killed a pig he had fresh pork. All duly acknowledged with thanks in little notes, most beautifully penned. That was the extent of our contact. So why, on that sunny afternoon, confide in him? Probably he would think, as the school authorities did, that Edman, son of a Royalist and sponsored by the sister of another, had no right to an education.

Instead he said, in words that have stayed with me ever since, "Principles and prejudices should not be confused." Then, after a pause he said, "I should be most reluctant to raise any false hopes, but I will see if anything can be done." He began hastily to talk about other things and I thought with deep gratitude that he had at least deferred the dreadful moment when I must tell Katharine that I had failed. I could truly say that I had not been able to see the Headmaster, only an underling who had no power to make decisions. So we must wait.

In fact the waiting was not long. Within ten days I received a communication informing me that an unexpected vacancy had arisen and that Edman Bowen had been given the place. Enclosed was a list of rules to be observed and a reminder that the slightest infringement would result in instant expulsion. There was also a list of what a boy must take with him, clothes, bed-linen, blankets and table napkins. Another piece of paper mentioned fees – in Edman's case high, since he was not Suffolk born or living in Baildon.

"So, after all," Katharine said, torn between joy and anxiety, "we are being a burden. I'll sell Sabrina."

"Oh no! My Bess is ageing. Besides, look what a versatile horse yours is." It was indeed rare if not unique to find a saddle horse, ex-Cavalry at that, willing to pull a wagon or a plough.

"Then I must find some gainful employment."

"You have been so helpful to me. Ever since your arrival."

"Sarah, I said *gainful.* I hope I have earned my keep, but I have not contributed a penny piece. Now, with this . . ." she tapped the paper concerning the fees, "and taxes likely to rise again."

"They may not. The war is virtually over."

"My dear, I am old enough to know that war or peace, glut or famine, taxes never go down."

Anyone less stupid than I would have been warned – though foresight is as futile as hindsight. There simply was in our area and at that time no gainful employment to be had, though Katharine was as versatile as Sabrina. There were surplus women in every household and in every occupation. Widows who had taken refuge with their families; women whose men had gone to the war and who disliked living alone, not to mention a whole crop of girls who during the war had reached marriageable age and must wait until putative husbands came home. (I was myself in that category.) Nobody needed a nursemaid, a cook, a milkmaid or washerwoman. Between Edman's going to school in mid-September and coming home for the winter vacation – the word Christmas now dropped from the calendar – Katharine had earned in coinage less than ten shillings; five for a fortnight's work in a cook-shop in Cooks' Row while the proprietor's wife had a baby, and four and sixpence by doing a man's work at the mill during the busiest three weeks of the year.

Men were coming back though Parliament was still conducting a kind of war against the Scots and meditating war with Ireland. Ironically enough the men first to be demobilised – apart from those invalided out – were the ones who had made the New Model Army the success it had been. Katharine who knew far more than I did about such things said that Parliament was afraid of that army and wanted something more malleable, composed of younger men, less opinionated.

Of those I still thought of as my men Jerry Cooper was next to come home, sound in health but just as embittered as Will Borley. He came to see me almost as soon as he was back, ostensibly to thank me for helping and encouraging his wife.

"The boot is on the other foot, Cooper," I said. "When I was . . . obliged," Heavens, I had almost said reduced, "to sell eggs and poultry your wife was most helpful to *me*."

"She done well," he admitted. "But you let her stay. She've saved a bit. And me, what hev I got? Five acres they promised. They can argue theirselves black in the face, but that was what Sir Walter said that day. I reached sergeant's rank and never a black mark to my name. And they owe me thirty pounds in back pay!" He spoke with great venom.

I had some difficulty in finding quite the correct response to that complaint. The natural retort was: Well, what did you expect? But I liked Cooper and also I wished to preserve my middle-of-the-road balance. So, before I could reply, Cooper spoke again.

"Do you want me back?"

I tried to remember whether one of the promises had concerned the keeping of jobs open. Or was there some new law about the matter?

"Oh dear," I said, "that is hard to answer. You were so good a manager, but Tom Markham has been so good, too. And my friend, Mrs Bowen, is most helpful. And I was obliged to sell Brook."

"So I heard. Well then. Me and my missus talked this over and wondered if we could come to a sort of arrangement. Would you let us stay in the Nine Elms house and hire us half Little Paddock? What she've saved we need for stock – turkeys mainly – but we could pay a bit of rent and I'd turn to and work for you busy times. Or whenever you arst."

"I can see nothing against that." No hurt feelings on Tom Markham's part, or Katharine afraid she was not earning her keep, and less need for outside labour at haytime and harvest.

"God bless you," Cooper said and almost in the same breath, "How much?"

I thought of so many jumbled things: Father's dislike of tenants; Mr Clover's generosity over the sheep-run; Cooper's disillusion with the Army he'd served; and the fact that he would have to fence off his half of the three-acre meadow. I said, "Your help in a busy season will be sufficient."

Then came the time when two ugly words, 'Malignant' and 'Sequestration' came into common usage. A Malignant was anyone who had fought for the King and Sequestration was the forcible seizure of property belonging to the King's supporters. In our area Merravay – beautiful Merravay – was the first to go, a fact which saddened but neither surprised nor alarmed me. Lady Alice and Sir Rawley were dead and were known to have been active in the smuggling. Charles, their heir, had vanished, much as Eddy had done. Such an estate could not remain ownerless; so it was divided off and sold, the house and some thirty acres going to a woman of known bad character who had friends in the Army. England was now under military rule, for in the struggle for power between Parliament and the Army which it had called into being, the Army had won.

The degree of severity with which the new rules were applied varied from place to place, known Royalist areas being most oppressed.

Katharine and I and sometimes Cynthia talked about the future, usually in a rather detached way. Once Katharine said, "Well, I hope they cut Brigstowe into a hundred holdings and each hedged. I am in favour of enclosures. So when Edman comes into his own the estate will be worth more than it was when we were kicked out."

"John Adam . . ." Cynthia began and then went on in the sourish voice she often used towards Katharine. "You are fortunate to have papers to back your claim."

"Have you none?"

"Nothing. Nothing at all. Nor would you have had but for that man who worked in the office."

"True. Having the papers eased things. But there are other sources of identification, Parish registers, tax records, family graves – even people's memories."

Cynthia turned pale and excused herself abruptly. When she had gone Katharine said, "As a matter of interest what did happen to her papers?"

I invented rapidly. "I think there was a fire . . . We never talk about it. They were not of much importance. Everything relevant to John Adam's inheritance is safely here upstairs, in the Trunk. With yours."

"She mystifies me a little. The other day I just suggested that it might be time to start teaching John Adam his letters. I don't think she knows them herself."

"Few people think girls need education," I said.

"I'm not talking about education, Sarah. What I am saying is that it is . . . unusual to find a lady of any standing who could not write 'This be quince jelly' on a pot of the stuff."

I had learned by that time not to take sides though I preferred Katharine's company and conversation; so I slithered away with some remark about the poor prospect of anybody making quince jelly this year, the spring being so tardy.

And it was on a day far more like February than late April that two Roundhead soldiers arrived.

The elder, solid, red-faced and not unamiable in expression, introduced himself. "Major Harrison," he said. "And this is Sergeant Silver." The sergeant was thin and lanky and wore no expression at all. He carried a large folder of stiff canvas tied with tape. I imagined that it had something to do with billeting, though we had never been imposed upon before, we were so remote. But now men were being demobilised in greater numbers and many, of course, East Anglians.

I led the way into the parlour, offered seats, sat down myself. The major said, "We are here to discuss the taxes."

"They are paid. On the first of December."

"The ordinary taxes, yes. This is the tax levied upon the property of Malignants. You have the papers, Sergeant?"

The sergeant read in a rapid monotone which seemed to come from a great distance. "Property of the late John Adam Woodley-Mercer, Captain of Horse, serving with Charles Stuart: Pargeters, three hundred acres; Nine Elms, two hundred and thirty; Brook, one hundred and fifty . . . Total assessment, one thousand five hundred pounds."

I thought: I am going to be sick! Not here. Not in front . . . I pressed my hand across my mouth and waited. When the upheaval had subsided slightly, I said, "There is some mistake. Brook Farm was sold some time ago."

"But since the outbreak of hostilities? Exactly. If all the land sold since August 1642 were exempt the pickings would be poor indeed. The levy is made retrospectively."

"But I cannot possibly pay."

With the weariness of having heard – and said – the same things before, the major said, "Everybody says that. But in most cases some means is found. Even now there are undisclosed resources. Jewels, silver, standing timber." Standing timber meant trees of at least twenty years old. Pargeters had none. Grandfather had evidently considered that he was near enough to Layer Wood not to need trees in his garden. Of the nine elms which had given the other farm its name only three now remained.

"I have nothing," I said. "Except the land and if I sold every inch, I could never hope . . ."

"Excuse me, sir," said the sergeant. He selected a paper and handed it over.

"Ah! Restricted . . ." He did not say he was sorry, such polite expressions were probably forbidden, but there was almost an apologetic note in his voice as he explained that I must not sell the land. I must raise that iniquitous sum of money or the land would be confiscated.

I asked a ludicrous question, "How long am I allowed?"

Sergeant Silver consulted his papers and said, "June thirtieth, sir."

Not that it made any difference. I couldn't have raised the money in a thousand years.

I asked a sensible question: "And the house?"

Again the sergeant, after checking, gave the answer.

"No specific mention, sir. Left to the discretion of the new owner."

Utter despair has a climate in which the human spirit cannot for long exist. Unless some hope of a hope seeps in from somewhere men take to the rope, women to the nearest water. I sat there seriously contemplating suicide.

And whom would that profit?

Only myself.

And why not, just for once, something for me? Peace forever. Walk up through the garden, into Layer and into the pool where some other unfortunate woman had found release. As Father had said: When you were dead you were dead.

But I didn't move. I sat there and the frail hope came creeping; *if* I could somehow keep the house – or part of it; the garden, or part of it . . . Who else was in a position to bargain with the new owner, whoever he might be? Katharine had no rights at all and Cynthia's were dubious. In fact any new owner would have been completely justified in refusing to have any truck with them at all.

So sanity came back and when I joined the others for dinner I explained that the soldiers had called because the ordinary tax commissioners had made a blunder and failed to note that Brook had been sold.

"Then you may have been over-paying for years," Katharine said.

"It is possible. I shall go to see Mr Turnbull about it tomorrow."

Mr Turnbull to whom I could tell the whole story, said: "Legal? Legality was once easily defined. A measure became law if it had the approval of a majority of Members of Parliament; or, in another sense, if a ruling monarch, governing without Parliament, had the power to enforce his will upon the country. Now Parliament makes the laws and what was illegal on Monday is legal on Tuesday. Since Parliament agreed that known supporters of the King should be fined – the men who called upon you were incorrect in referring to taxes – then, yes, the demand is legal. With what degree of severity or leniency such a law is applied depends upon the interpretation put upon it by individuals in power – that is, the major-generals. Fifteen hundred pounds is certainly excessive. And the inclusion of Brook Farm smacks of skulduggery, which is of course, rife. Even so, it occurs to me that somebody must want all, or part of your property very badly. Unless. . ." He paused and held the pause so long that I said, "Unless what, Mr Turnbull?"

"I have no wish to offend you. I am merely seeking for an explanation for such extreme vindictiveness. Did you, yourself, ever engage in any activity inimical to the Parliamentarian cause?"

"No."

"Nothing which, however seemingly innocent at the time, could now be construed otherwise?"

"Nothing," I said, denying John, denying Eddy. And frightened. Suppose somebody – I visualised a small, rat-faced fellow – really went to work on me. It might seem strange that the wife and daughter of a man of property should not have owned even the smallest trinket and that his silver was base metal, thinly disguised; that the money obtained from the sale of Brook had simply vanished, the sale not even mentioned on the page labelled 'Income' in my otherwise meticulously-kept account book.

The use of torture in order to extract confessions had largely fallen into desuetude – except in the case of witch-craft, but so far as I knew it had never been withdrawn. I sat there in Mr Turnbull's quiet office and asked myself how well I should stand up to physical pain, deliberately inflicted. The answer was badly. I should tell all. I might mention Lady Alice, whom nothing could hurt now, but my reputation would be further blackened. I should mention Mrs Kentwoode – now Mrs Flowerdew. I might even involve Tom Markham!

My really intolerable distress must have shown on my face, for when he next spoke Mr Turnbull, that grey, impartial man, sounded almost kindly.

"You came, Miss Woodley-Mercer to ask my advice about the legality of the demand made upon you and I can only tell you that as matters stand today it is legal. I am not so sure about the inclusion of Brook Farm in the assessment. There I see a possibility of some easement. Upon what terms are you with Mr Clover?"

"Good. I might say excellent. He once did me a singular favour."

"And he is a Presbyterian," Mr Turnbull said with seeming irrelevance. He proceeded to explain. "Apart from those who call themselves Independents, the Presbyterians form the largest, most coherent and articulate party in Parliament today. Their goodwill is much desired. And Mr Clover, though now largely retired, is a man of influence. If you could persuade him to *complain* that the inclusion of Brook, even retrospectively, seemed to cast some doubt upon his ownership or affronted him in any way, the fine might be reduced."

"Even then I could not pay."

"I suppose not," he said. The silence that followed was uncomfortable. In the circumstances it seemed absurd for *me* to feel sorry for Mr Turnbull, but I was. I thought: Poor man, he's suggested the only thing he can think of and wishes I'd go away. But I was struck by that familiar feeling of helplessness.

"What will you do?" he asked.

"I don't know."

"You have no relatives to whom you could go?"

"None." My Aunt Lydia's so-well-connected husband had died and she had gone to her so-well-married daughter in Kent. They'd had little desire for my company when I was independent; they certainly wouldn't want me now. With Cynthia and John Adam, and Katharine.

Then Mr Turnbull said an astounding thing. "You are young and of pleasing appearance. Much the best thing for you to do would be to marry – preferably somebody in good odour with the government. I assure you there is no alternative. There are thousands of women in your position. The proud ones starve; the others take to . . . a way of life which, frankly, I cannot recommend."

This stilted, earnest euphemism for prostitution somehow revived me, made me capable of rising, thanking him and taking my leave. My inner voice rebuked me sharply; fancy being *amused* by a turn of phrase when things were in such a desperate plight. There were precedents for it, of course. Anne Boleyn, told she was to be beheaded, laughed and said that she had but such a little neck; Sir Walter

171

Raleigh, facing the same fate, had called the axe a sharp cure for all diseases and Sir Thomas More had made his quip as he mounted the scaffold. Tonight I should have to tell Katharine the truth, but we should laugh together over Mr Turnbull's description of harlotry.

He had, however, said other things, too, calling Mr Clover a man of influence. I knew that he was a lawyer, not in the ordinary way but employed in the Bursary Department of King's College at Cambridge. When I had gone to thank him for getting Edman a place at school he had explained, off-handedly, that Baildon Grammar School owed a lot to King's both financially and otherwise; so one word to the Governors had been sufficient.

On that occasion – high summer of the year before last – he had been in the garden when I called and we had talked there.

Today, taking the turn-off to Brook, I was not very hopeful of much help from Mr Clover, except that if he could make a protest, raise a question, it might delay things a little. Just possible, but unlikely, that if what Mr Turnbull called skulduggery was going on, the excessive nature of the fine might be exposed.

Old Mrs Smith opened the door to me. I'd never liked her much; even in Father's day she'd never been welcoming or friendly. She was a small woman, bolt upright; age had simply shrivelled her, hardened her. I knew that she had the reputation of being a good cook, though her appearance belied it – but then I was accustomed to Marian.

Mr Clover was in his study, a spacious room in the new outbuilt wing but incorporating, if I remembered rightly, part of what had been the old farmhouse kitchen. The walls were almost lined with books, with some new 'scratch' panelling between the shelves. There was a huge hearth with a good fire going on it, a new square-bowed window, with brown velvet curtains, looped back. In front of the hearth was a large, gaily coloured rug on which stood a settle, comfortably padded, a chair with cushions and a small table bearing some objects unfamiliar to me.

I took in all this detail while Mr Clover rose, greeted me,

friendly but a trifle guarded, I thought, and said, "Another cup, please, Mrs Smith." He indicated that I should sit in the chair, pulling it a trifle nearer the fire with a comment upon the unseasonable chill of the weather. "It is warm in here," he said. "And a cup of tay will warm you still further. May I take your cloak?" He took it and hung it over the back of the settle while I wondered what tay might be.

Mrs Smith came in and set down the extra cup with such ill-grace that Mr Clover said, "Gently. Gently! They are very fragile."

They were really small, shallow basins with matching saucers, and made of porcelain so fragile as to be almost transparent. They were beautifully painted, with small sprays of flowers which also decorated as much as I could see of the container, which was shaped rather like a pear, its lower half encased in a kind of basket work, very fine, and white in colour. The basket had a handle; the container a lid and a spout.

"It is an infusion," Mr Clover said, lifting the container and pouring a pale amber liquid into the cups. There was a touch of ceremonial about the action, something that reminded me of Grandfather, in the old days, opening a bottle of wine which he thought rather special.

"I have never heard of it," I said.

"I don't suppose half a dozen people in England have. A colleague of mine at Cambridge has some connection with the East India Company, and obtained a small sample to try. He says it is the beverage of the future, having great medical virtues. It comes from China."

I sipped. To me it was almost tasteless, and to drink it was difficult since the frail cup offered little protection from the scalding liquid. Mr Clover chatted on about tay, and China, and the East India Company; then the weather, his garden, some new bulbs he had ordered from Holland, almost as though he knew that I had come to him bringing trouble and he wanted to defer the mention of it for as long as possible. This gave me an opportunity to observe him and to wonder whether if it came to the pinch I could take Mr Turnbull's advice and marry him. I thought how amazed he

173

would be to know that behind my wide-eyed attention I was assessing his possibilities as a husband.

Old. Getting on for fifty, I guessed, but not in the least decrepit. Besides, I was myself no longer so young.

Clean. Extremely clean both in person and in clothing.

Kind. I had good proof of that.

Well-to-do. Well-educated. In every way most eligible. That thought made me consider myself.

Of pleasing appearance. That was the most Mr Turnbull could say of me. I should have no dowry and I had dependants. More serious, perhaps, was the fact that I had no skill in the art of pleasing men. Mother had been too much preoccupied to bother to train me in the only career open to women. And during that brief emergence into social life my Aunt Lydia had offered nothing but criticism, even saying that I was too tall – as though I were to blame for that as well as for my lack of vivacity. I was not even domesticated. I was a freak, a good female farm foreman, an asset not likely to carry much weight with a man who had no farm.

Mrs Smith came and removed the tay tray and as soon as she had gone, I said, "Mr Clover, I'm afraid I have come to bother you again." I then told him everything, noticing that his expression grew more grave as I proceeded, and when I had done, he said, "This is iniquitous. I suspect that some extremist covets your property very much . . . I cannot help. Believe me, if I had fifteen hundred pounds I would lend it. But what capital I had I have spent. Here. I have made a farmhouse into a comfortable dwelling and a paying farm into a pleasure garden. My sole income is my pension."

"I did not come to borrow, Mr Clover," I said, mustering a smile. I told him what I had hoped for and he said, "I'm sorry. I fear it would have no effect. Law is no longer law as we once understood it. Military rule opens the way to many abuses. The latest proposal, I understand, is to bring the King to trial for treason . . ."

I listened as he explained that it was upon this issue that Presbyterians disagreed with other brands of Puritan, but my mind had reverted to my own problem and I soon took my leave. He came with me to the stable where I had left Bess; and I saw Mrs Smith watching from a window. Her expression reminded me of Samson the shearer when we had our dispute. I thought: She has an easy job, she would of course resent any woman who threatened it however indirectly.

I rode home feeling very miserable, a mood which just suited the time of day and the time of year. There is always something sad about the lighter evenings and the burgeoning trees when the weather remains cold and grey.

I told Katharine and Cynthia the whole story after supper that evening. Cynthia began to cry and Katharine turned chalky white and was silent for a long time. Then she said, "I suppose it was inevitable." It was left for me to say, not with hope exactly but with at least something that was not quite despair, "Everything depends upon the new owner. It might just be possible to come to some . . . arrangement." My idea of what such an arrangement might be was very hazy. I improvised as I spoke.

Compared with many houses Pargeters was of moderate size but the new owner unless he had an exceptionally large family could easily spare one bedchamber, into which three women and a three-year-old boy could squeeze. We could live in the kitchen.

He might be a man with no experience of farming, in which case he might be glad to employ me.

Mrs Cooper had kept herself – and saved ten pounds – by rearing poultry for market.

Grandfather and Timmy could live in the office.

And what of the garden? It was very large and over-productive, for it had been laid out when Grandfather had grandiose ideas. The new owner might be willing to rent me part of it.

Everything depended, as I had said at first, upon the disposition of the new owner.

Cynthia listened, sobbing and sniffing. Katharine said, "It might work. He might even employ me. Believe me, I can plough a furrow as straight as I myself am crooked."

"What we must not do," I said, timing the joke badly, "is

to take to a way of life which frankly Mr Turnbull would not recommend."

Katharine saw the point and laughed. Cynthia said, "How you can laugh . . . with the workhouse staring us all in the face!" Sobbing, she clapped her hand to the pain in her side and drifted away.

"She'll cry herself to sleep. She's very childish," Katharine said rather callously. "Sarah, one thing strikes me. To have rigged this whole business so brutally, somebody must want Pargeters and possibly Nine Elms very badly."

"Mr Turnbull and Mr Clover said precisely the same thing."

"He must also wield a great deal of power. Can you think of anybody?"

"Not a soul. Everybody I know – apart from Jerry Cooper – has as much land as he can handle."

"Have you an enemy?"

"Kat, when Mr Turnbull asked me that, I said No. And I meant it in good faith. But at Brook, not long ago, I *was* reminded that I once had a dispute with the leader of a shearing gang. But he was a lout and incompetent at that. How could he ever achieve any power?"

"Scum tends to come to the top," Katharine said.

Father had dismissed ghosts in the ordinary sense of the word as superstitious nonsense. But there are ghosts of another kind, those who tread the corridors of the mind. And I must admit that during the following days I was haunted by the memory of Samson; the hatred, the actual physical threat, the impotent ill-will that had made me be cursed.

I defied that ghost and went about my preparations with order and energy, though without much confidence.

For possibly the last time in my life I had labour at my command and I made the most of it. May is a relatively easy month in a farmer's year; hay not ready to cut, sheep not ready to sheer. In a surprisingly short time the garden was transformed.

I left the space between the front of the house and the road untouched. It was largely devoted to roses. Alongside the house was the less formal space, part lawn and part flowers and flowering shrubs; that also I left. It was in the space behind that, nearer the rear of the house and in the kitchen garden that changes were made. I had all the laurels rooted out – no small task since they were twenty years old. Here I intended to keep my fowls, with the former house of easement, considerably enlarged, serving as a roosting place, safe against foxes. I took from the side garden a stretch of lawn as pasture for geese. This was all railed in just as Jerry Cooper had railed in that piece of the Little Paddock which he now occupied – rent-free. He came to help with the making and planting of the rails. He owed me a few days' labour he said. He showed concern for my future but regarded his own with assurance. The new owner or owners of Pargeters and Nine Elms would certainly be Puritans, of one kind or another and unlikely to be hard on him. "Though nobody'll be as good as you bin," he said.

The path which I had made did not bisect the kitchen garden and railed in on both sides did not make an equitable division, nor did it run quite straight. It gave me rather more than half the asparagus bed. But unless the new owner had been a prolific and successful breeder of children, I should be responsible for a larger family than his. And I should be growing the stuff for sale. The 'crowns' as asparagus roots were called, were now as wide as a man's shoulders, alive and full of promise, but they had to come out to make way for the dividing path. I had them set again in a freshly dug and well manured space, an extension of my share of the original bed. It was late for such transplanting, but I could only hope. It was late, too, for the planting of potatoes, a new and, it was said, delicious vegetable now being introduced to our area by a Clevely man. I'd never tasted one, but Father had said the potato was a mere fad – a tasteless thing and connected with a silly superstition; it was said only to flourish if planted on Good Friday.* So Pargeters had never grown a potato, but I was willing to try.

* Even now, in the 1980s, this belief persists in rural areas.

177

The new path, curving slightly, divided the strawberry bed, this time to the new owner's advantage, but that I could bear since strawberries are such temporary things.

Of more durable produce division was impossible; the new owner would have all the carrots, I the onions.

I planned in a kind of daze, in my mind always conducting a senseless argument with a faceless, nameless man – the New Owner and with myself. I kept hearing the lanky sergeant say, "No specific mention, sir. Left to the discretion of the new owner." Now and again, in nightmares, Samson the shear-master came. Far worse than the faceless man.

Cynthia rallied and invoked my admiration again. "The one thing I can do better than most people," she said, "is to sew. And sew I will. Puritans disapprove of lace, but they wear cuffs and collars. I'll produce some that would not offend Cromwell's self."

Using linen from the finest sheets of which we had plenty she produced, with unbelievable speed, sets of matching collars and cuffs that were beautiful for their workmanship. Edged with drawn threadwork, or that form of embroidery which consists of tiny holes with their edges sewn round with tiny stitches, or with feather-stitching, double or single. She even made them adjustable by an arrangement of buttons. Katharine and I, unskilled at such work, admired hers whole-heartedly.

But where did one find an outlet for such things? The man who kept the shop from which in the past we had bought ribbon and lace and material by the yard had become discouraged and retired and his premises were now occupied by a butcher. All I could think of was the stall which dealt with what Father had called knick-knackery. And the owner had two faces, one for would-be buyers – amongst whom until that moment he had reckoned me – and one for would-be sellers. Oh yes, he said, they were pretty enough but it would take time to get people to look for such things on his stall; and to display such things properly took space of which he had little to spare; and to be made to look their best they should be pinned out on a

178

board, preferably covered with black velvet. On and on until my temper, very short these days, gave out and I said "If you don't want to handle them, stop mauling them about with your filthy hands!"

He then shot a barb which hurt. "I always thought you was a lady. I was mistook!"

Now I had to go back and tell Cynthia that what she had made wasn't wanted. Quite impossible! She'd cry. So I made up a lying tale; the work, I said, and the idea had been much admired and would be offered for sale, but no money yet; not until the man who had taken them to try to sell them had tested the market.

"That is reasonable," Cynthia said. "Meanwhile I will make some baby clothes. There must be a market for those."

It was a lovely summer but I could take no pleasure in it. I had to decide about the hay. If on the thirtieth of June both Pargeters and Nine Elms must change hands, why bother? But, as Katharine had said of people, scum rises to the top and a hayfield neither scythed nor grazed quickly reverts to the wild, the tougher grasses and the weeds overcoming the ordinary grass. It hurt me to think of that happening. On the other hand why should I suffer the commotion of haymaking for the benefit of the new owner? Yet again, I wanted to please this unknown man and make him agreeable to our staying. In the end the haymaking took place as usual with the weakest of small beer and no saffron buns and not quite the usual gaiety. Everybody knew what was likely to happen to me, and though I may have had an unknown enemy in high places I had none in the immediate vicinity.

The dread day came and went but on the third of July Major Harrison came again, this time accompanied by four troopers which made me think – with no amusement – that he could have expected to ride away with fifteen hundred pounds and needed a guard.

It was a brief visit. He asked if I had the money and I said I had not.

"Nor any hope of raising it?"

"Absolutely none."

"Then the law must take its course."

"I know. Major, there is one thing I need to know and perhaps you could tell me. Who is the new owner?"

"I cannot. How should I know? I fought from Edgehill to Uttoxeter and am now a glorified rent-collector!"

He spoke very sourly and I thought: Yet another discontented Puritan!

After that nothing happened for about three weeks and then Jerry Cooper came to see me, looking excited and displeased and bursting into speech as soon as we were alone.

"Hev *you* bin taken over yet? Well, we was. Today. Me and the missus in the backhouse, plucking fowls for tomorrow's market and in he come. He say, 'I'm the new owner,' he say. 'Captain Bennett,' he say and he prod at a nice pullet and say, 'Just right for supper. Get it on the spit, woman, right away.' My Martha never been spoke to like that in her life. Then he turn on me and say, 'You come and show me the boundaries, I take it you know them.'"

All local men knew the boundaries because the old custom of blessing the fields at which Father had mocked, had changed into a kind of sport, hilarious for all but the victims. It was called Beating the Bounds. Where the demarcation was a waterway, boys were pushed in; where there was a hedge they were thrust into it – and most hedges were of quickthorn or briar – and if the boundary was vaguer, the line between two stones or two trees, the boys were bent over and beaten on the buttocks. Boundaries were remembered!

"Captain Bennett," Jerry went on, "he gotta kinda map. He kept saying 'Correct' or 'In order'. Just like being in the Army again . . . So then we come to the bit you so kindly let me hev. And he say we can keep it and still live in the house but I must work for him full-time and Martha gotta cook and keep house, putting him first."

I said, "Well, I suppose it could have been worse. Captain Bennett has no wife?"

"He did, but she died and small wonder, poor soul. He's a

Calvinist and they don't rate women much higher than dogs. All the time he was guzzling that pullet he was grumping about it not being stuffed. My missus simply hadn't had time . . ."

"Well, at least you have a home and employment," I said. "I shall miss you at harvest. But by then it may not be my harvest."

"Thass all a bloody – pardon me – shame. I'd never hev gone if I'd seen the outcome of it."

I reported this conversation to Katharine and asked what exactly a Calvinist was.

"The worst of the lot," she replied without hesitation. "They aren't even Christians. They believe that you're judged at birth; either saved or condemned and nothing you can do will alter it. And Cooper was right about their attitude to women. If *we* get a Calvinist we have no hope at all."

Another week passed and the weather turned blisteringly hot. Tom and I had spent the afternoon inspecting the corn fields and decided that the barley was ready to cut. "And no help from Jerry Cooper this year," Tom said gloomily, and began to reckon in his mind which of the casual labourers we'd employed while Cooper was away at the war was best – and likely to be free.

I followed my usual routine, wash and change before supper. After the open fields the house, with every door and window open, seemed deliciously cool.

I was halfway down the stairs when I saw that there was a man on the step beyond the open front door. The sun, still bright, was behind him, so that all I saw for a second or two was a dark bulk. A thickset man of medium height, looking taller because of the high-crowned hat which had become the headwear for Puritan men. I was across the hall, almost face to face with him before I recognised Eli Smith who had been foreman at Brook and had gone to the war early and of his own accord.

It sounds absurd, but one's reactions are unpredictable and attitudes acquired in youth are not easily shaken off. My first thought was that he should have gone to the *back* door.

I was civil, however. I said, "Hullo, Smith. So you're home now. I hope I see you well."

"Thank you; yes. I have a good deal to talk over with you." Part of my mind noted that his voice had become far less rustic. Part of my mind remembered that during the last few years merely courtesy titles had been dropped; nobody said Mistress or Madam any more, even hereditary titles had been abolished; Mr and Mrs and occasionally Miss were retained. Sir was reserved for the army. Part of my mind thought: If he has come to complain about what has happened at Brook, he'll get a tart answer.

And while I thought, Smith said, "No need to ask me in. Pargeters is mine now."

PART THREE

When I told Katharine and Cynthia what had been said and arranged, Cynthia, as might be expected, began to cry. Katharine became angry and rebellious.

"You must be mad, Sarah. Stark raving mad. I never heard of anything so monstrous. Well, I won't be a party to it. At Brigstowe we always paid our poor rate. I'll go into Bristol workhouse. I couldn't bear to stand by and watch – leave alone seem to condone . . ."

I managed a rather shaky laugh. I said, "If you do that then Eli Smith and I must haggle again. You see, you were part of the bargain."

"Bargain!" She spat out the word. "That in itself is an obscenity."

"Why? Most marriages are bargains. With the bride having little say. Fathers name dowries, would-be husbands make marriage settlements. The only difference that I can see is that I had some say; and on the whole, I think I did rather well."

Considering the weakness of my position, I *had* done rather well. In the cut-throat game played out between me and Eli Smith, I'd held only two cards, one of dubious value. He had admitted that he had always had a fancy for me, back in Father's day. But he said it in an unfeeling way, much as a man might say that he preferred carrots to cabbage. It was not a compliment and bred no confidence in me.

My other card, much stronger, was my obstinacy. If he wished to marry me he must accept those for whom I regarded myself as responsible: Cynthia, John Adam, Katharine, Marian and Old Harry, and, of course, Grandfather.

He'd jibbed. He said he did not intend to feed a lot of useless mouths. I argued back; the only useless mouth was Grandfather's – even John Adam would soon be able to collect eggs or firewood. Grandfather I could not argue about, but I could, and did say, "If Grandfather goes, I go with him." And I meant it. So, very grudgingly, Eli Smith conceded that point, saying that old men didn't eat much. He had then gone on, stating his intentions quite plainly.

Now, reporting to Cynthia and Katharine, I could tell them how I had argued and what I had promised in order to keep a roof over our heads. To Cynthia I said, "I explained that though you were unfit for outdoor work, you could earn with your needle – and keep an eye on Grandfather, and mend."

To Katharine I said, "You and I, Kat, are to become labourers. I think that Eli Smith intends to run Pargeters with only Tom Markham to help, even in the busiest season. And Marian will be alone in the kitchen."

"I don't shirk work. It is the idea of your marrying the man I can't stomach."

"You've never seen him," I reminded her.

"I don't have to. I know enough about him to know that he is thoroughly unsuitable. He's a Puritan. He's taking advantage of your misfortune. And look at his way of taking over. Simply arriving and dictating terms. No decent man of whatever creed or class would have behaved in such a way." Suddenly Katharine rounded upon Cynthia and said, "If you must snivel, go and do it elsewhere. You rasp my nerves."

This was grossly unfair, for Cynthia had the ability to weep without making a sound, or distorting her face. The tears welled up and spilled over; they never even reddened her eyelids.

When we were alone, Katharine said, "I was never one to make a display of my feelings, but Sarah, I've become so fond of you. I simply can't let you act so precipitately. Marriage is for life. And it involves such . . . intimacies. Men can be so demanding. And there's another thing, too. I once said I felt that somebody wanted your property very much. Now I see it was *you* this man wanted."

I strove for a lighter note. "Oh, of that he made no secret. He declared himself. He'd always had a fancy for me. Very gallant!"

186

"So he schemed and used either influence or money to get your fine hoisted to a height where payment was impossible. Darling, I'm sorry. I don't think I could stay here and watch you being . . . degraded. And all the time feel that I had helped to bring it about. No, let facts be faced. You have supported Edman and me, and you have spent coined money on him. But for us you could perhaps have offered an instalment and staved off the vultures."

I said hastily, 'Kat, I never mentioned Edman's existence. I soon saw the trend of Eli Smith's thoughts and he'd see in Edman another source of cheap labour – and probably demand back those pre-paid fees. As for your staying or going, only you can decide. I must stay. There's Grandfather, Marian and Old Harry, as well as Cynthia and John Adam."

Katharine drew a deep breath.

"Then I must stay too and help as much as I can. I shall not be a useless mouth, I assure you. And I will be civil."

The next three weeks – the time needed for the calling of the banns – were very curious ones, a kind of Limbo. Rather like one of those fogs which occasionally swept inland from Bywater, blotting out details, leaving big, solid things vaguely visible.

I remember two very painful interviews in the first days of Eli Smith's ownership. The first was with Marian who had an almost uncanny way of knowing things. (While I had Eddy hidden in the office I had gone in dread of her intuition.)

She came straight to the point. "Mistress if you're doing this to keep your promise to me, you forget it. I'd sooner go to the almshouse twenty times over than see you marry Eli Smith, just to keep a roof over my head."

I said, rather unkindly, "Marian, your need of a roof had no part in my decision. There are others. And I have myself no fancy for being homeless."

The know-all expression crossed her wrinkled face and

she used one of her favourite expressions. "I happen to know," she said, "that *you* was offered a home – and a comfortable one. But for yourself only."

"Gossip," I said. Annie had so many sisters, all in service around nearby villages. But in this case gossip was correct. As soon as my coming ruin was known about, Sir Walter had offered me a home at Ockley, as companion, a kind of lady-in-waiting, to Lady Fennel, a woman I disliked. I had explained then about my dependants and he had tried to argue them out of existence. What were almshouses and workhouses for?

Now, talking to Marian, I thought, not entirely with displeasure, of Sir Walter's shock when he heard of the mésalliance that I planned. He'd say: Like mother, like daughter! Mother had married "a mere plasterer" and here was I doing even worse.

"My chief concern, Marian, is Grandfather."

"Ah, yes. But I do sometimes wonder whether, apart from food, he notice much now."

"Even so, workhouse food is said to be bad. So, Marian, we must all hold together and prepare to work very hard. And try to please Mr Smith."

It was the first time I had spoken of him in that way. And it brought home to me the fact that I should be sharing a name with that unlikable, hard-visaged woman at Brook.

During the interval Eli's behaviour could not be faulted. His control of everything had begun with his arrival, but he confined his activities to out-of-doors. He lodged with the Borleys at Crowswood – as Father had once done. This was rather surprising, since his mother was housekeeper at Brook and there were three bedrooms there. But perhaps Mr Clover, a Presbyterian, disapproved of other brands. There were spare rooms also at Nine Elms, but Captain Bennett was a Calvinist and the question of rank was involved.

Everybody knew that Eli Smith was now master, that he planned great changes. The news that he was to marry me took a little longer to spread and it was not until the third day that Tom Markham asked to see me, in private, after supper. I said I would see him in the other parlour, since the dining-parlour table was in use. Cynthia, at one end, was cutting out cuff-and-collar sets, at the other Katharine was attempting to teach John Adam to write his name.

I innocently imagined that Tom had come to tell me that he wished to leave, finding Eli Smith impossible to work with. I dimly remembered that in Father's day when the labour force between the three farms was mobile, Tom avoided, so far as his not particularly inventive mind served, going to Brook. I now thought that if Tom said he wished to leave I could say in all honesty that I was sorry, and refer him to Eli Smith. Instead I went to face a scene that I was to remember for a long time.

First, why was he clad in his Sunday best, and at this latish hour, freshly shaven? Servants about to give notice did not bother with such niceties. Secondly, why was he so nervous? He was a typical East Anglian, straw-coloured hair, flax-blue eyes and solid features, the nose dominant. His disposition was East Anglian too – Oliver Cromwell had recognised the virtues of men who told to stand, stood, told to advance did so, often in the face of seemingly impossible odds; when a man fell, they simply closed ranks.

Tom said, "Mistress, is it true what I hear?"

Striving for the light note again, I said, "That rather depends upon what you have heard, Tom."

"They say you're gonna marry Eli Smith."

"That is true."

"Christ!" The single expletive was eloquent. Father, unbeliever that he was, had the strongest objection to using the name of God or of Christ in that way; and Father had known how to make his wishes felt.

"You can't do it," Tom went on. "I 'on't let you. I'll . . . I'll kill him first."

"That wouldn't help. We might get somebody worse."

"They don't come no worse. A wolf in sheep's clothing if ever there was one. He's mean. He's cruel. He deceived even your Dad what reckoned hisself a good judge of men and was – as a rule. You've only to see him with animals

. . . or day labourers that can't answer back. The idea of him and you . . ."

Tom seemed about to choke. I said, "Tom, getting excited is no use. I have given my word. Look on it this way. I'm not marrying the man, I'm marrying Pargeters and the shelter it gives me and six other people."

"But that ain't right. Times like these, living sacrifices ain't expected. Them that can fend for theirselves should do it; them that can't there's allust somebody to aid them. You gotta think of yourself. Or me if you like. I been in love with you since you was a tiddler, and fit to marry a lord. There's a bit in the Bible. Rose of Sharon. You been that to me all these years. My lovely Rose of Sharon. I never looked at another woman, at least not serious. I could've gone to the war but I stopped here to help and keep you safe. Now, if you can think about marrying Eli Smith, why not me what worship the ground you walk on?" He shot out a big brown hand and took my wrist in a hold that left a mark that lasted a fortnight. "Marry me. I'd do right by you. While I have breath in my body, you'd never want. We'll go to Yarmouth. I'll join the herring fleet. They earn good money. And I'd treat you like a queen. Queen of my heart."

It was touching. In decrying Eli Smith Tom may have exaggerated, in describing himself he had been truthful. I thought of all those secret errands he had made to The Old Vine.

People speak of the heart as the seat of the emotions; they say, My heart rose; or fell; or broke. Mine never even fluttered. It had turned to stone when Eddy rode away and I could think quite coolly. Think: if all things were equal I would much prefer Tom Markham to Eli Smith. But I had no choice.

I said, "Tom, any man offering marriage to a woman does her honour. I do feel honoured and most grateful for all that you have done over the years – clear back to what you did for Father. But you must see that I am already committed. I have responsibilities – and I have given my word."

He was still holding my wrist. Now he turned my hand over and kissed my palm. Deep inside me something stirred, but that womanly part of me which should have responded to such a caress had gone, with Eddy. I withdrew my hand: "Tom, you and a few people close to me know why I must marry Eli Smith. He knows himself but I suppose that, like everybody else, he has his pride. I'd prefer that my reason was not generally talked about."

Tom said, speaking with dignity: "This conversation never took place. I never bared my heart afore and I shan't start now. Nor I shan't stay here. Mebbe I could get a job with Captain Bennett at Nine Elms. If not, remember this. I'll always be within call and if Eli Smith don't deal rightly with you, God help him."

Eli and I were made man and wife in a ceremony shorn of all beauty and ritual and dignity. It suited Eli's Puritan principles; it suited my mood.

And afterwards . . . Well, there are matters of which it is better not to speak, and the performance said to make two people one flesh is such a matter. I had disarmed myself by making the bargain and I think that Eli was afraid that by showing any fondness or tenderness, any ghost of the fancy he had once had for me, he might weaken his position. It was a cold and joyless business. He claimed his right to possess; I surrendered. That was all.

I do not know whether Eli tried to replace Tom Markham or not. Harvest was nearly upon us and labour was temporarily in short supply; but it was also possible that other men felt as Tom did about Eli and did not wish to work for him. All I know was that in that year the good harvest at Pargeters was gathered, carted, stacked by one able-bodied man – Eli – and two women new to the scythe. Katharine, despite her deformity, did better than I. She had done manual work before and developed some muscle in shoulders and arms; I had none. My chief memory of harvest 1648 was of utter weariness and such pain from stiffness that it was difficult to find a comfortable position even in bed. But I would not be outdone and Eli encouraged me roughly, saying that stiffness wore off with more exercise and strength came with practice. He did the work of three men and seemed never to tire.

This year there was no harvest ale, no saffron buns and no gleaners. From time immemorial, back even to Biblical days, as soon as a crop was carted the gleaners came. A woman with some lively children could pick up enough fallen ears to make a sack of flour; older, solitary persons retrieved enough to feed a few hens.

This year the only approach to a gleaner was John Adam. "I was earning when I was his age – and not so well-grown. Stone-picking, rook-scaring. Anything for a halfpenny." It was one of Eli's rare references to what must have been a hard childhood. And of his war-time experiences he never spoke at all.

Old Harry was not conscripted for field work. Perhaps when I was pleading with Eli to let us all stay and try to make a living out of part of the garden, I had planted a seed in his mind. Garden produce could be sold and make profit. Therefore Harry, gnarled and bent and sometimes groaning with pain, must tend the garden.

Indoors, economy must be the watchword. No more egg and bacon breakfasts; no more white bread – the dark kind, known as "black" though actually a brownish grey, was fully as nourishing and far cheaper.

The spit apparently was to go out of use. No more fowls or large joints of meat were to turn there, sizzling and appetising.

I sat there and remembered how my brother had complained about school food and Father had listened saying that in his day things had been rather worse, and then sent John off with money to buy extras. Edman, inured to hardship, had never once complained.

Bit by bit Eli's plans for the future were revealed to us. Perhaps the near-impossibility of cultivating Pargeters with only two women to help had dawned on him. He proposed to convert a good deal of the acreage into a dairy farm and to take a stall on Baildon market place as an outlet for his produce. "Light indoor work," he said, explaining what was expected of us. And it was true that most dairy work was done by women, but not on the scale visualised by Eli. A few farmwives with a pint or two of butter to spare – butter though a solid was measured by the pint – would go and stand on the steps of the Market Cross which was still called the Butter Cross by some people, though the Cross had been hacked down years before.

Pursuing his plan of campaign, Eli built out of the wreck of an old wagon a light cart.

He was handy with tools and ingenious. This contraption would not be required to carry much weight, so although he retained two of the wagon wheels, he used a plane on their heavy spokes. He used the same method of lightening the half-body. The result was a vehicle fully capable of taking anything our garden or dairy, however much enlarged, could produce. At the front of it Eli rigged a seat, also light-weight, being contrived from a cane-seated bench.

At intervals while working on this, he rode about the countryside buying cows. The time was apt for him for the season was approaching when every animal not needed for breeding went to the butcher, and everybody enjoyed an orgy of fresh beef, before out came the brine tubs and beef was salted down. Winter feed was unknown except for hay, and that was needed for horses. Offering a price very slightly above that paid by butchers, Eli acquired some remarkable bargains.

Unlike sheep, cows have no set breeding season and Eli's herd included cows in calf, cows whose calves had been weaned, a few with calves at heel. Such calves were quickly weaned and taken to the butcher; never a scrap of veal found its way to our table. Almost the same might be said of any pig Eli sold. The smoke-house with its huge chimney and slow, oak-burning fire was no longer used for the curing of hams or whole sides of bacon. Eli sold the pig to the butcher and then bought back the head, the feet – called trotters – and a quantity of belly pork, known as fat-and-lean which in most cases consisted of fat with thin veins of lean running through it. Plain boiled it was unappetising, salted down rather worse, though Marian did her best. She went to endless pains making a pig's head and trotters into brawn, boiling them until every last shred of flesh could be picked off, adding it to the liquor in which the meat had been boiled and then turning the whole brew into moulds. "I could make a decent pork pie, too," she said, "but for that I need proper lean meat and white flour."

During this interim Eli suffered three blows which he bore with stony fortitude. Mr Clover at Brook wrote in his beautiful script that he could no longer afford to lend the sheep-run; he must let it at a rent of five pounds a year.

Eli actually deigned to consult me about this. "What do *you* think?"

I said, "My father never held with having all one's eggs in one basket. He was a great believer in mixed farming. And wool is a cash crop."

"He's a Presbyterian and I'm an Independent," Eli said. "So naturally he hates me." He brooded, scowling for a moment and then said, "All right. I'll pay."

Eli's next rebuff came from the Market Overseer and was perhaps inexplicable to anybody outside Baildon. The butter women with their wide wicker baskets were mere transients, as were hawkers, or mere entertainers with their poor cowed dogs. But the right to set up a stall, a board supported by trestles, was different. It could even go with a house, or be mentioned in a will. It was in fact a property. But there were other spaces which could be hired. Eli's first application was refused. Perhaps the Overseer had a different brand of Puritanism, perhaps he, like other people, resented Eli's sudden emergence as a man of property; most likely of all he was holding out for a bribe.

So at Pargeters we suffered from a surplus of milk. Butter, particularly if salted and well-casked, will keep for a time; we therefore churned butter and also made quantities of a more long-lasting comestible, cheese. Marian was the only one of us with any experience of dairy work. In the old days we had always kept two house cows and she had overlooked, rather than worked at, the making of butter in what was called a paddle churn a tall, narrow lidded jar with a four-bladed plunger with which one of the maids used to agitate the cream into butter. Eli had gone to a sale and bought, very cheaply, one of the new-fangled end-over-end churns, a barrel slung between struts and activated by a handle. One knew by the sound when the butter had 'come' because the sloshing sound changed to a gentle thud.

We had never made what was called hard cheese at Pargeters. On this point Grandfather and Father had been in agreement. Both had eaten it in the past – Grandfather in his sea-faring days, Father at school, in lodgings, on journeys. The most that could be said of it was that it satisfied hunger and kept one alive. Give them soft cheese, made from whole milk, with more cream added. It was delicious but it would not keep. We made none of it while Eli was waiting for a site on the market. Instead we made hard cheese, a process ruinous to the hands. Milk, soured naturally or by the addition of rennet – a substance taken from a calf's stomach – curdled and formed clots which had to be broken by hand. Very bad for the nails and fingertips. The effects were contradictory, nails softened and broke off, fingertips hardened and grew rough.

Meanwhile Katharine and I had been taught to milk cows, an art in itself and I can only hope that the cows were grateful for our gentle handling. As Tom Markham had hinted, Eli was hard on animals, treating them as insentient things. He had appropriated Katharine's Sabrina and was, she said, ruining her mouth and her temper.

Apart from that remark Katharine was scrupulously careful not to make any derogatory reference to Eli, who was, after all, my husband. She once said to me that his table manners were unexpectedly good. "Possibly at some time during the war he consorted with gentlemen." In his presence she was usually silent, and if addressed, invariably polite. Once the subject of clotted cream came up. I'd never seen or even heard of it. "As a West country woman, Mrs Bowen, you know all about it."

"I've eaten it certainly," Katharine said. "It is delicious. And it sours less readily than ordinary cream, I believe."

"That is what interests me. It'd be a marketable thing. But how is it *done*?"

"I'm sorry, I can't tell you, Mr Smith, because I don't know."

"Yet you've eaten it." He made it sound like an accusation.

"Yes. But you see, until I came to Pargeters I had never set foot in a dairy."

"Parasites," Eli said, becoming unusually voluble. "Living off the fat of the land and never doing an honest day's work. I don't altogether go along with Lilburne and his Levellers but some of his ideas aren't far out. The idle rich are as useless as the idle poor that we call paupers."

"I cannot help the station to which I was born, or my upbringing, any more than you can help yours, Mr Smith. And I resent being called idle."

Perhaps Eli realised that his hold on Katharine was tenuous and that as a source of unpaid labour, she was, for all her crookedness, my superior in every way. Somebody once said that only a well-bred person can apologise gracefully. Eli did his best but it was not gracious.

"I wasn't speaking personally," he said. "Forced to it, you're a good worker. There're exceptions to every rule." Then, as though making that much of a concession had irked him or the mention of Leveller ideals had inspired him, he said, "In future we all eat and live in the kitchen."

I had nothing against the kitchen; I'd spent happy hours there. Marian had been a kind of substitute mother to me and made me gingerbread men and allowed me to clear out, with a spoon, basins and saucepans in which she had made delicious things.

And Eli's decision was sensible, for we had come to the time of year when the evenings were chilly and there was now nobody to lay and light a fire or clear the ashes in the morning. The kitchen was at all times warm. I was very fond of Marian and I liked Old Harry and yet . . . Yes, I did feel degraded. And irritated with myself for so feeling.

Eli was at Baildon next day, making another attempt to get a market site, so I said to Katharine, "At least we can make the kitchen more comfortable." We dragged in another settle and some chairs, gathered some cushions and spread a rug in front of the wide hearth. Then I looked at the wide mantelshelf which for years had been the repository for things which had no other place, a jumble of useless objects all thick with dust.

Marian, who had watched disapprovingly said, "Anything you put up there ma'am'll be filthy in no time. And the same can be said of that rug. S'pose I spill something."

I said I would be responsible for dusting the shelf and that nothing she spilt would show much on the rug which was mainly dark-hued and intricately patterned. "Or," I said, "we could roll the rug aside while you are actually cooking."

I moved on to the mantelshelf two of the worthless candlesticks and three very gaily painted bowls which had always stood in the dining-parlour. Grandfather had bought them in Amsterdam long ago and said they came from China.

Then Cynthia complained. How could she possibly do her delicate work at a dirty kitchen table? Marian asked leave to say that her kitchen table had never been called dirty before. Didn't she scrub it every day? Then Cynthia said something which was to have fateful consequences. "What I really need is a good big bag to hold all my stuff."

I thought instantly of Lady Alice's pretty bag still lying in the office, a place now doubly haunted for me. I did not believe in ghosts in the ordinary way; Father had liberated me from such credulous fantasies; but there are other hauntings. When Eddy left I knew that I never wanted to see that room again and it had taken another strong emotion – the wish to spare Lady Alice an awful death – to get me there just long enough to snatch a couple of pills.

Now I said, "Kat, do an errand for me," and asked her to fetch the pretty bag.

I carried it up to what had been my own rather starkly virginal bedroom which had a walk-in closet with pegs for clothes and a high shelf. In the far corner I noticed, with a little jolt, a bottle of brandy. I must have put it there some time ago. I now placed on the shelf the little flasks and jar which the bag had held, pushing the jar marked 'Lethal' into the far dark corner beside the brandy. I hadn't time just then to examine the contents of all the other containers.

Eli came home in which, for him, was a jubiliant mood. He had obtained his site and another study of the market had showed him that a stall such as he planned would have no serious competition. At this turn of the year people were selling apples and pears and damsons and onions, but mostly in small quantities. There was a stall which sold cheese, but cheese only. There was nothing of such variety or on the scale which Eli planned. In this good temper he did not criticise – or perhaps failed to notice, my attempts to make the kitchen more comfortable. Towards the end of supper – a better meal than usual – I saw him eyeing us all more intently than usual, as though assessing us. He discarded me quickly but between Katharine and Cynthia he hesitated; then announced his decision. "You," he said to Cynthia, "will be in charge of my stall."

It was an apt choice. She was very pretty and had when she chose to exercise it, a pleasing manner. And she had often expressed a wish for more company. "Nice easy job," Eli said. "And you can take your work. If trade slackens off you can put in some stitches."

Cynthia looked pleased. Eli transferred his attention to Marian. She and Old Harry had been the ones most discomfited by the shift of family life into the kitchen. It was an invasion of their privacy, and throughout the meal neither had spoken.

"Riding home," Eli said, addressing Marian, "I had some further thoughts. Those famous pork pies; they'd sell. So would your brawn. And that cake that'll last a year."

"I couldn't make such things without proper materials which I ain't got now."

"You would be provided."

"But I only got one pair of hands, one pair of feet; and I ain't a witch. I can only be in one place at once. All this extra in the dairy . . ."

"We shall all have more help. My mother is coming here to live. Tomorrow."

Life which had been difficult, was much worse after Mrs Smith came. She seemed to disapprove of everybody in the world except Eli, and I think she took pleasure in being tyrannical and in scolding and in practising parsimony for the sake of it. Like her son she seemed to be tireless and had no sympathy with lesser mortals whose energy flagged towards the end of a long day. Unlike Eli, whose work took him out of doors, she was always there. She was completely illiterate and thought all books – except the Bible – were rubbish. Now and again, my stint of work done, I would take a book and try to escape for ten or fifteen minutes. "Is it there ain't any mending?" Mrs Smith asked in her rasping voice. She dominated me as easily as she dominated the others. And I think the only time I opposed her was on behalf of Marian whom she bullied worst of all, largely I think because she was jealous of her. One day when Mrs Smith had been particularly nasty to Marian, I said, "Perhaps you should be a trifle more careful, Mrs Smith. What Marian makes has a ready sale, and she is not chained to Pargeters as the rest of us are."

I was chained. I'd forged the links myself. Which did not make the slavery more acceptable.

After that Mrs Smith – and I also was Mrs Smith, our roles much confused – was still nasty to Marian but less aggressively so.

The point of dispute was they could both cook, but in differing ways. Mrs Smith had been reputed a good cook, and she could, it is true, hammer a bit of tough meat into subjection; her dumplings were edible though made with the cheap dark flour. Marian was now again cooking for more delicate palates.

It was in the dairy that Mrs Smith reigned supreme. She knew how to make clotted cream, and soft cream cheese and a delicacy known as sage cheese, seemingly much in demand. In the dairy I was literally her handmaiden. And I heard a great deal about a substance known as elbow grease. Anything I did with less than her own violence brought the admonition to put a little elbow grease into it.

The stall was a success. Cynthia for a few weeks was

happy to get away from Pargeters. Eli went with her on the first Wednesday but no more; he held that a man should go to market only when he needed to buy something; other visits were simply time wasting. Katharine looked forward to Wednesdays too, for market day was a half-holiday for the Grammar School boys, and Edman sent messages and sometimes a letter.

Then, inevitably, the weather became cold and Cynthia grumbled to Katharine and me. "If I get chilblains, how can I sew?" she asked tearfully. I sympathised with her, knowing how shrewd the wind could be in open spaces. Not that the dairy was warm, built as it was to face north and with a window barred, but not glazed. And my own hands were so ruined by cheese-making, scrubbing and scouring that chilblains would hardly be noticeable.

I thought of the old days when goose-grease was a guard against chilblains or a cure if they had been contracted. We had a few geese at Pargeters, but they were for the market. It was over this simple substance that I had, without recognising it, proof of Marian's power to work, if not magic, something very near to it. I merely said to her in a casual way, "I wish we had some goose-grease," and the next day but one, choosing a moment when we were alone, she handed me a jarful.

I said, "Marian, who on earth . . ."

"Least said soonest mended."

"Mrs Cooper?" I hazarded a guess. Mrs Cooper still reared geese, and doubtless Captain Bennett commandeered one when he felt so inclined.

Marian then took refuge in one of those obscure local sayings which I, born in Suffolk, fathered by a Suffolk man, could not understand at all.

"Lay-overs catch meddlers," she said, and moved purposefully to the oven.

My hands were past redemption and Katharine said hers must surely be immune by now, so the precious goose-grease was reserved for Cynthia's use, and she did not develop chilblains. And on the next Wednesday we saw to it that she went off warmly clad. Katharine and I each contributed a flannel petticoat – the hems taken up – and in addition to the good cloak and hood in which she had arrived, she had a thick, fleecy shawl once Marian's in her going out days. Cynthia had complained that the cloak impeded her movements. "I have to reach this way and that." A shawl worn over the head, crossed in front and with its tapering ends tied behind the back was far more practical; it must have been a working woman who invented that garment.

"But it makes me look so ugly," Cynthia wailed.

Katharine said, "Does that matter? *You* are not for sale."

That was a horrible winter and not only for us . . . The King was a prisoner and all but the Presbyterian element in Parliament wanted him tried for treason.

In a way, we at Pargeters were better informed than we had been in the past, for every Wednesday the one thing Cynthia was allowed to buy was a Newsletter. From this, for his mother's benefit, Eli read aloud. It was, of course, violently partisan – only Puritan publications were allowed to circulate, and considering that Katharine, Cynthia and I had lost dear ones fighting on the other side it showed as much as anything else the complete lack of sensitivity of both the Smiths who gloated openly and made comments that would have been offensive even to moderate Puritans. The pathetic, last-hope gesture of the Prince of Wales who from his exile sent a blank page, signed and sealed, so that Parliament could write its own terms in return for sparing the King's life, brought nothing but derision from Eli and his mother.

These reading sessions always took place on Wednesdays in the interval between the early dark and supper. January of that year, 1649, was bitterly cold and the kitchen was the only place where one could be moderately warm. I could sometimes escape, making Grandfather my excuse. More and more he fell into my care, though for six days a week Cynthia, by Eli's decree, was supposed to look after him. He grew more and more difficult, and sometimes Cynthia said he frightened her. But he was quite harmless, though since Timmy had been sent away he had led a life calculated to drive even a sane man idiotic. Twice he'd wandered, and

Eli had said we had no time to spare searching for idiots. So he was locked in and when the cold weather came kept to his bed for warmth. Yet he tried to hold on to human dignity and to avoid the chamber pot or the chaise percée. With a little help he'd struggle to the nearest privy.

Once, when I had coaxed him down to supper, he made a commotion, his mind flitting back to the past when he was master of himself and of his small world.

"What is this?" he demanded after two mouthfuls of one of Mrs Smith's better offerings, meat and onion dumpling with the emphasis on onion. "Is this an emergency? Send Captain Waters to me *at once*." He glared around. "And who are these people? Stowaways? I have no objection to honest refugees. Stowaways I will not tolerate." Then his wild eye rested on me, with the half recognition which was familiar. "Penelope! My dear, my dear, what are you doing here, eating this muck?"

Mrs Smith was irretrievably offended – I suppose we all have our little vanities. She decreed that in future Grandfather should eat in his room. Such scenes, she said, upset Eli and that she could not tolerate. Eli was the one surviving son of several and his father had died of worry and over-work. That mustn't happen again.

Truly, for a moment the woman seemed almost human.

After that Grandfather ate in his room and so meagrely that he should have starved. But he did not.

On 30th January 1649 the King was beheaded outside the Banqueting House of his own palace at Whitehall.

I remember the date for a purely personal reason; my second miss. That, and the fact that I had felt sickish in the morning, convinced me that I was pregnant. And hardly any woman, even a prostitute whose livelihood was threatened or the mother of twelve, ever welcomed pregnancy less.

I remembered Cynthia's hours of torture. To go through *that* in order to produce another Smith was abhorrent to me. And I was grossly ignorant on the subject of human reproduction. I knew about animals. Pregnant mares should not drag heavy loads or be ridden at a fast pace; cows in calf should not be hustled; as for sheep, it needed only a fright to make a ewe abort.

I could talk to nobody about my state. Katharine, though she was tactful, was, I knew, very religious – almost, if not quite, a Catholic. She believed in God and would, I knew, regard my condition as God-sent. Cynthia would point out what a comfort and joy she derived from John Adam.

So all alone I moved beds about, jumped down the last few stairs, sneaked off once in Layer Wood and ran as though fleeing from some terror. I thought of suicide; Top Pool was near at hand; but the moment I was dead six people would be homeless; Mrs Smith's spite would see to that.

So I waited, while a beautiful spring moved over the England which was now a Republic, and in high places the Parliament and the Army struggled for supremacy.

I began to show about mid-April, and Katharine was the first to notice.

She and I did the milking, starting at six every morning and beginning the second milking at four o'clock in the afternoon. Due to her shape and her gait she was unable to carry the milkmaid's yoke with a bucket on each side, so that task fell to me.

Milking was not an unpleasant job, cows are amiable, well-disposed creatures and they exude warmth. The milking times could have been a time for conversation but Eli was often about, measuring out the food which the cows knew awaited them in the next shed; or gathering muck as he called it, to add to the manure heap. So our conversation was guarded.

But on that morning, after we had said how nice it was to have daylight at six o'clock, and definitely, definitely warmer, we sat on the traditional three-legged stools and, across an intervening cow, Katharine said, "Sarah, I don't wish to pry but . . . are you going to have a baby?"

I said bitterly, "Is it so obvious? Yes, I am. I absolutely dread it and the idea of bringing another Smith into the world revolts me. Another Eli. Another Mrs Smith. What could be more horrible?"

Katharine said; "Need that be so? Characteristics, even physical features can skip a generation. The Smith blood can be only one small strain in the blood of any child you bear. Darling," she said, and she did not use endearments freely, "this should be such a happy time for you. Don't make what seems to be bad spoil your gratitude towards what may be a great blessing."

"I'm not the only one concerned. Think what a life the wretched child will have. Look at the way they treat John Adam."

"They may absolutely dote on a child of yours. Besides, everything may be changed soon. We have another King, in the Lowlands, and some day he will come into his own – that I truly believe." Then her voice changed. "What must at all costs be avoided is a miscarriage or the chance of a malformed child. You must not strain yourself in any way."

"Tell Mrs Smith that. I'm sure her recipe for easy child-bed and a healthy baby is the more liberal expenditure of elbow-grease."

There I was wrong. Neither Eli nor his mother was capable of showing joyousness or enthusiasm; but Mrs Smith said I must do light work only and try to eat rather more; and Eli's gratification showed in the after-supper ceremony which he called Evening Prayer. This consisted of a straight man-to-man talk with his God which to me resembled nothing so much as a chat between neighbours over a boundary fence – one neighbour doing all the talk-ing. Eli was often perilously near scolding Jehovah, as he might have scolded a disobliging neighbour who refused to lend a scythe. Eli was always conscious of his own virtues; he was law-abiding and hard-working, he abstained from what he called strong liquors, and from tobacco and from swearing or frequenting 'strange women'. And in return he expected God to treat him properly; if not, the rebuking tone crept in, often with some reference to Job, another worthy character who had been unjustly afflicted. This extempore prayer – the only kind allowed by extreme Puritans – combined arrogance with sycophancy. The neighbour over the fence was of uncertain temper, so even complaints must be carefully worded: Thou knowest, oh Lord . . . Or, Thy will be done, and then the nudge.

On the evening of the day when my pregnancy became known, Eli said, "We thank thee, oh Lord, for the promise of a new life to be devoted to Thy service."

Nothing much of note happened during my gestating time. Mrs Smith proved an adept at finding light work for me and I spent more time with Grandfather since even a pregnant woman could pick peas and at the same time keep an eye on an old man who had outlived his wits. He only once showed any awareness of my condition and that was sudden and disconcerting. "Pray for a boy, Penelope. Girls are a sore burden."

I did not pray but I hoped for a boy. I thought that on the whole, in a drear and ill-organised world, the male stood a better chance and had an easier life physically. None of this being tied to the moon's cycle, with aching head and aching back, to be ignored because the whole matter was unmentionable. And no man ever needed the attention of a midwife, or the use of a groaning chair. Yes, given any choice in the matter, I'd have chosen to bear a boy; but towards the end of my time the placidity of a breeding animal overcame me. It was almost like having a holiday. From myself. From my surroundings and circumstances and all responsibilities.

Even my memory of Cynthia's long agony seemed to fade. I did not, in the last month or so, live in dread. And in the event there was nothing to dread. On a very sultry afternoon, Katharine and I milked as usual – milking, since it is done sitting down, was counted as light work and I had strict instructions not to lift a bucket. Katharine could carry one at a time and trudged to and fro, occasionally helped by Eli, even more occasionally by Mrs Smith.

We were on our way back to the house when thunder growled, far away behind Layer. I said, "A storm would cool the air a bit." Ordinarily I rejoiced in hot weather, but I was now so bulky that I found the heat burdensome. As I spoke I felt a sharp pain; it was like being impaled by a sword. I stopped and bent over.

"Is it here?" Katharine asked.

"I think so."

She set down the bucket and took my arm. The pain eased and I straightened. "I'm in my old room," I said. "Kat, you could deal with it, couldn't you? *She's* the last person I want around me at such a time."

I had once raised the question of bespeaking Mrs Meecham, but Mrs Smith said when they lived at Stonham she had acted as midwife and layer-out.

"I know how you feel," Katharine said, "but I daren't take the responsibility. I haven't the experience. And if . . . I mean . . . Mrs Smith would feel slighted."

I had been sleeping alone for some time. Eli had ceased to exercise what he called his conjugal rights as soon as he knew that I was pregnant, and there was nothing else to hold us together – no companionable bedtime talk, none of the gestures of affection which I imagined more happily married people enjoy. He had made no protest when I said I was now too bulky and restless to make a good bed-fellow. I had resumed my habit of reading in bed and it was typical of Mrs Smith's spite that she begrudged me a little candle-light. First she chided, then she acted in an unbelievably petty way. My candlestick never held more than half an inch now, even if I left far more overnight. But Marian was aware of what was going on – very little escaped her – and every now and then I'd find a whole new candle tucked just inside my bed.

Now I was taking to my bed, not to read and fall asleep, but to suffer, to be humiliated all under Mrs Smith's unsympathetic eyes.

In fact my suffering was very brief; all over in two hours. My baby was exceptionally small and seemed to slide willingly into the world.

Her welcome from her grandmother was; "A girl! And a poor, pingling thing at that. You could put her into a pint pot."

Katharine said, "What a lovely little girl." But that, of course was the correct thing to say.

And from me, at first, the poor child had nothing but rejection. I hadn't wanted Eli Smith's baby in the first place. And I hadn't wanted to have a girl. A big lusty boy such as John Adam had been, would, I somehow felt, have given me status. I turned away, and slept and woke in the same mood.

Katharine was there when I woke and at first she was patient, though firm. "Of course you must see her, Sarah. You must feed her. You can't imagine Mr Smith hiring a wet-nurse, can you? If you don't feed her, she'll die."

"That would be far the best thing."

Katharine said slowly, giving weight to every word; "I've known you a long time, Sarah. I know you have no religion. Would it surprise you to hear that more than once you have shaken my faith by being kinder and more honest and braver than anyone I ever knew? Now when it comes to a really moral issue, I see the weakness of your case. You are prepared to commit murder, in cold blood. Murder I said and murder I meant. Unless that child is fed, it will die. I know a few – exceptionally hardy – will survive sucking a flannel rag soaked in cow's milk. But your baby is frail. Unless you feed her – and soon – she will die. And I shall never respect you again."

I lay there and knew that a whole way of living, of thought was being challenged. I said, "All right, Kat, you win. Give her to me."

So I looked on my child and was lost.

Possibly every woman thinks her first-born something exceptional and beautiful. Mine truly was, even from the first never red-faced and wrinkled and bald. She was like a beautiful little doll. So far as she resembled anybody, it was my mother, but prettier. She was born with hair, just enough, very black and inclined to curl; and when her eyes lost the universal slatey blue of the new born, they were, like Mother's, truly emerald, and she had the same skin. If she could escape smallpox, with its disfiguring scars, she would be a beauty. But as often as I thought that I had the disquieting thought: To what end? In a Puritanically minded society beauty was not valued – was indeed rather distrusted. Clothes and hairstyles were all designed to make even pretty women look plain. Often during those early days I would be overwhelmed by the sense of my own helplessness. I wanted so much for my child and had so little to give.

I was worse off than most working farmwives who were allowed to keep at least some of what they earned; egg-and-butter money was the usual name for it. At Pargeters nobody but Eli ever handled a penny. Even Cynthia who, by her needlework and her stall-keeping, was an active money earner was never paid anything. Eli knew to a penny what the stuff on the stall should fetch, and what the things Cynthia was commissioned to buy should cost. Once she confessed to Katharine and me that she was often tempted to cheat, but was terrified of the possible outcome.

I had been right in my premonition about how Eli and his mother would treat a girl-child. In fact, if I remember rightly, the only interest they showed was over the choosing of her name. It must, of course, be Biblical and I had rather hoped for Elizabeth; Elizabeth was the mother of John the Baptist, and Grandfather's memories of Elizabeth Tudor had all been to her credit. But Eli and his mother settled upon Dorcas, a New Testament character famous for her good works. And since so many girls were now being named for virtues, Faith, Hope, Charity, Prudence and Diligence, I accepted their choice.

In an offhand way Mrs Smith did once make a reference to her granddaughter. She said, "At least we know now that you are capable of child-bearing." A plain indication that she expected a grandson within a year of Dorcas's weaning. I would myself have welcomed a boy. But I did not quicken again. And no doubt, God, the neighbour over the fence would have been rebuked about this failure to oblige, had the whole matter of sex not been unmentionable even between man and his Maker.

I devised a way of carrying Dorcas about with me slung in a shawl which I could put down wherever I happened to be working, or carry on my back when I moved from place to place. Mrs Smith disapproved; why not leave her, well wrapped, in some room where she would be in nobody's way?

"She might cry."

"And what would that matter? Nobody would be disturbed."

"Nor would she be comforted," I said. And Mrs Smith did not labour the point. Perhaps she sensed that there was a point beyond which I could not be pressed. I was committed, a meek, obedient wife, and where I myself was concerned I never demurred; but I had put in a word for Marian and probably I looked as though I might put in more than a word for my baby. Cows with calves can be as dangerous as bulls.

So time jogged along. I noticed, if nobody else did, that Eli's resentment over having no son took the curious form of disliking John Adam. Here was the son such a virtuous man should have had, had indeed every right to expect. Eli had never been more than tolerant of him but now the wretched boy could do nothing right. He changed from the spoiled darling he had been, and worked hard at any task he was set, but never to Eli's satisfaction. Not surprisingly the constant and often unjustified nagging soured the boy's temper and his handsome face often wore a surly expression.

Now that I had Dorcas, I could sympathise fully with Cynthia's worry about her son's future. She did not share Katharine's faith in the return of our King-in-exile and the changes it would bring about. "I don't mind admitting," she once said to me, "that I hoped to re-marry. I still have some looks."

"You're very pretty. But so many men died in the war."

"I wouldn't mind somebody older. Anybody who'd give John Adam a chance." She then added something, the significance of which escaped me at the time. "I should have realised that decent men don't look for wives on the market place."

We had as near neighbours two bachelors, Mr Clover and Captain Bennett, but in their different ways they were both too comfortably ensconced in their celibate state to be considered eligible. Mr Clover had replaced Mrs Smith with a married couple and, although he was officially retired, still spent a good deal of time in Cambridge. Captain Bennett was snugly tucked in at Nine Elms, marooned in his Calvinism and letting the farm go to ruin.

Cynthia's chances of remarriage were poor and I could offer nothing but hollow-sounding phrases such as: We must hold on and hope for the best, and: We never know what is around the next corner.

What was around the corner for me was bad. Eli made an attempt to break the bargain we had made.

There were several contributory and converging reasons: the time of year for one – haymaking and sheep-shearing often coincided and on a place so undermanned as Pargeters had become this presented problems.

I was back in harness again. Dorcas had been weaned in November. I then returned to the big connubial bed and Eli had exercised his conjugal rights with vigour. But it was now late May and there was no sign of the longed-for son.

Marian's legs had failed her in a manner which even Mrs Smith could not ignore. Pain she would have decried; "Work it off!" but feet and ankles grossly swollen could not be so lightly dismissed. Marian, rather tearfully, said that once up and downstairs was as much as she could manage, and that meant that she could not take her turn at dealing with Grandfather.

Marian was now of considerable importance, for in the season when the garden had little to offer and even milk production tailed off slightly, there was a steady demand for the things she made. Therefore her well-being, if not her actual feelings, must be considered and Mrs Smith actually suggested that she should move into the office and thus avoid stairs altogether. Marian refused. Sleeping alone, so far from everybody else would make her nervous, she said.

So who, when we were all facing the busy season, could take Grandfather for his necessary little walks, and carry his tray?

Eli found an answer and broke it to me one evening when we were undressing for bed. "There's only one thing to do. He must go to the workhouse."

"So! You would break your promise to me."

"I was not on oath. I made no bond. In a moment of what I now see was weakness, I made an arrangement. It now suits me to make an alteration."

"That's the argument of a dishonourable scoundrel. A decent man's word *is* his bond."

In over a year of marriage we had never quarrelled. I'd bitterly resented his bringing Mrs Smith into our household; I'd objected to many things – even the choice of my daughter's name; but I had accepted, having no power. I'd bitten back sharp retorts, remained civil if cool. I'd looked on myself as a model wife. I was mistaken. Eli now proceeded to enlighten me. It was almost laughable, yet there was just that little nub of truth in almost all that he said.

"We struck a bargain. And you was the first to break it. I gave you my name, a place in the world, and I agreed to feed all the useless mouths you'd been harbouring. And what did I get in exchange? A wife? A woman in a bed – and about as much use to a man as a sack of flour. I reckoned you might come round, you never did . . ."

Oh dear; it went on and on. I'd known, he said, how anxious he was for a child, but had I told him? No; I'd told Katharine Bowen, who'd told his mother, so that he, who should have been the first to know, heard at third hand. And then I'd gone about looking like somebody sentenced to death. And what had I given him? A girl and a poor specimen at that. Then his target of grievance shifted. Where he had made his mistake was in coming to any arrangement that included Katharine and Cynthia. We thought ourselves superior; he wasn't deaf, he'd heard us whispering and laughing together. We'd managed to make him feel an outsider in his own house; at his own table. I was not to think he hadn't seen us exchanging looks.

And finally, to get back to the matter in hand, how could anybody have known that the old idiot would live so long?

I ignored that and fastened on the words 'useless mouths'.

"Our bargain, which included my grandfather, has been much to your advantage. It would interest me to know how you could have run the dairy, and the farm, and the stall without the help of those you insult by calling them useless mouths. We all earn far more than we eat."

"Barring the fancy stitching, one good strong girl, reared to work, could do more than the lot of you put together. And life'd be easier."

That was probably true. A good workhorse of a girl, a younger version of Mrs Smith – probably even chosen by her – would have suited him better. And there'd have been none of the friction.

My all-too-ready self-blame became active. Perhaps I should have pretended more. To what? Affection, when Eli had from the first acted so unlovably? To passion? How could I?

Perhaps the Poor Law Authorities were in fact over-burdened or perhaps one of the Board of Guardians looked on Eli with little favour. Grandfather was refused a place in the workhouse. He was Eli's father-in-law and Eli was responsible for him.

"One of the Guardians," Cynthia said with her pussy-cat smile, "said that he was surprised that Eli, a man of property, should even think of putting a relative into the work-house."

"Who on earth told *you* that?"

"It was common talk on the Market," she said, reverting to her characteristic vagueness. Indeed as time went on she became more and more reticent about the Market. There were even times when Katharine was obliged to ask had she seen Edman.

Eli never again mentioned Grandfather and the work-house to me.

He did mildly reproach God for not seeing fit to lighten his load, "But Thy will be done."

By the following summer his references to the much-afflicted Job became slightly more justified.

It was the last Wednesday before full harvest but at Pargeters we were always a week ahead and Eli, Katharine and I had been cutting barley all day. I had stuck to my rule about taking Dorcas with me wherever I went. She was still short of a year old, but she could walk quite well. I had devised a kind of harness for her – a little knitted belt with straps that went over her tiny shoulders and crossed at the back going under the belt and then joining into one strap with two tails which could be tied around any firm object. There was no risk of her strangling herself.

She was a singularly untroublesome child. I believe that animals know things outside their experience and perhaps children do, too. It sometimes seemed to me that she knew she was unwanted and must make the least of herself. My only other experience with young children had been with John Adam, imperious and aggressive from the start. Dorcas fretted quietly if I were out of sight, but I seldom was.

Cynthia had made her a little sun-bonnet, apologising for its plainness. "I'd have embroidered the frills a bit, Sarah, but They wouldn't like it and Mr Smith does hound me so. I sometimes think I shall go blind."

Her eyes certainly did look rather inflamed and I said, "Well, the market harvest lull will soon be here. That may give you a chance to catch up and ease off a little."

When I did field work I carried a stake with me, drove it into the ground and tethered my child. I made certain that no dangerous weed or hedgerow berry was within reach and left her with the only toys she had – a wooden spoon, I think whittled by Father, and the rattle I had bought for John Adam on that morning I chose not to remember. She also had a double baked crust, provided by Marian.

It was an uneventful day and at four o'clock Katharine and I went in to do the milking. Eli continued to work, with John Adam, making sheaves ready for stooking.

Katharine carried both our scythes and I carried Dorcas. In the milking shed I tethered her again.

Then, making our last trip, I with the yoke and two buckets, Katharine with one and a hand free for Dorcas, we were in the yard and Cynthia drove in.

She was crying. And the cart still contained practically all that the Pargeters dairy had sent to market that morning.

"What happened?" I asked.

"There was another stall, selling cheaper . . ."

I supposed it was inevitable. Whatever one man did and made a success of, others would copy.

Mrs Smith bustled out and took charge, admirably, I must admit. With a sweeping glance she divided the immediately perishable from what could be salvaged. Nothing, no amount of cooling would keep clotted cream or full cream cheese until next market day. "We must eat them ourselves," she said in a voice more suitable to someone self-condemned to live on nettles for a week. But the butter, even the unsalted kind, would be more durable if lowered into the well. As for the hard cheese, it was indestructible, and next week, with harvest starting and hirelings to be fed, people would be clamouring for it.

Poor Cynthia. She had good reason to cry. She tried to avoid a confrontation with Eli; "I've had a terrible day. I have a headache. I'm going to bed," she said. But escape was not so easy. "Fetch her down," Eli said. His fury was like a cold blast.

"Now. Who did this other stall belong to?"

"I don't know."

"And didn't think to ask. Was a man or woman behind it?"

"I don't know."

"Couldn't you look?"

Cynthia showed a spark of spirit.

"You know the Market, Mr Smith. Thieves just waiting for you to turn your head."

"Then how did you know about the under-selling?"

"From the first of my regular customers. Collecting an order and saying he was sorry he gave it, because just across the way he'd have saved sixpence. So . . . so the word spread, and except for Marian's stuff I hardly made a sale all day."

"And I suppose it never occurred to you to cut our prices down? No. I always knew you were a fool."

Mrs Smith remarked that blubbering never helped anybody or anything; and then the rest of the miserable meal was devoted to a conversation between mother and son as to the identity of the rival. Eli had already convinced himself that a secret enemy must be at work. Mrs Smith, in whose eyes he was perfect, could not believe this. "You never harmed anybody. You always bin honest. Who'd want to hurt you?"

"There's always envy. And whoever it is he's ready to lose money to ruin me. And he's local. Five miles is as far as dairy stuff'll travel in this weather. If only she," he gave Cynthia a contemptuous nod, "had showed a mite of sense we might hev a clue. Somebody on the Market would hev recognised. And if she'd bothered to look we'd know what the charges were. And what sort of stuff was going so cheap."

The Evening Prayer after supper was even more self-pitying and admonitory than usual while at the same time enlisting the good neighbour's help against the hidden enemy; and another reference to Job.

Next morning, as we milked, Katharine said, "Well, the boils are yet to come." Her brand of religion set little store by the Old Testament. I gave the little laugh that was expected and then said gloomily, "We should suffer most."

All through the next week Eli displayed the energy and the singlemindedness that must have made him a model soldier. He scythed like a fiend, not even stopping to eat his noonpiece; then, when it was supper-time, he took a piece of bread and cheese and, eating it, mounted Sabrina – searching the whole area within a five mile radius of Baildon for some clue to that secret foe. Of whom he asked his questions, and how truthful the answers were I could only guess; for the one open squabble between us – that concerning Grandfather – so far from clearing the air had worsened our relationship, and I only knew from what he said to his mother, and to his God, that his search had been unavailing. Nobody in the district had suddenly taken to dairy-farming; no pasture, so far as he could see contained any unusual number of cows; nobody could, or would, give him any information.

On Wednesday morning Katharine and I milked as usual and then Eli said to me, "Go and make yourself tidy. You're keeping the stall today."

Making myself tidy meant donning one of the summer dresses left over from my girlhood, a time now infinitely remote, changing into my Sunday shoes and putting on the only form of head-dress approved of by Puritans. This was a strip of linen which could be opened out flat to be washed and ironed. One of its longer sides had a fold over piece, the other a wide hem through which a tape could be threaded. In wear the folded-back piece framed the face; at the back the tape was drawn tight and tied, its ends neatly tucked in. Not a hair showed, and I doubt whether Cleopatra herself would have looked very enticing in such a strict framework. Cynthia had once confessed that, on days when she knew Eli was not at market, she discarded the thing and shook her hair free. In me vanity was dead. I took a little longer over dressing Dorcas in a pretty dress, made for her by Cynthia from one of my old ones.

When I went down, the cart, with my dear old Bess between the shafts, was already loaded and Eli was climbing into the driver's seat.

"You're not bringing her," he said.

"I'm not going without her."

Our eyes did battle. I quailed inwardly. All power, all authority was his. He was physically a very strong man. He had only to jump down, separate us forcibly, throw me into the cart and push Dorcas into Mrs Smith's untender care. And I knew where Dorcas would spend the day; Mrs Smith had once suggested it when Dorcas first began to toddle and finger things – the cold bare room which had served Grandfather as a cellar. "There's nothing there she could meddle with and no harm could come to her. Carting her

216

around as you do is sapping your strength and making you round shouldered."

So, though fearful, I stood my ground and Eli said; "All right then, get in."

A paltry triumph and soon cancelled out because Eli took out his temper on Bess. Father had always said: The best whip is in the manger. Meaning that a horse given enough oats and corn and hay, needed no urging.

I said nothing, however, it would have angered Eli more.

Baildon Market so early in the morning was pandemonium, but organised pandemonium if that is not a contradictory term. I had never seen it in this state; I had only visited it as a customer, often mounted; sought after, respected. Now I was one of a crowd, ruled over by the Market Overseer, who was probably applying laws going back to the times of the monks but using his own methods. He knew that thieves – mainly boys – haunted the Market so he had organised a group of supposedly reliable boys who, when they were employed, were very highly paid indeed. Five minutes of their time cost a penny at a time when a day labourer earned fivepence a day. Doubtless a good share of this money found its way into the Overseer's pocket.

No animal was allowed to stay on the market after nine in the morning; nor were people selling from baskets or barrows allowed to remain in one place very long. The Overseer favoured people who had a site and hired the trestle tables which were stored in his shed.

One of the honest boys was obviously waiting for Cynthia, who when she came alone must have needed his services. Eli was quite capable of fetching the trestles and the board himself. I spread the white cloth. At Pargeters cloths were no longer used at meal-times. Then we unloaded; all the dairy stuff at one end; Marian's pies, brawn and cake at the other; in between, displayed on a square of black velvet, the two collar-and-cuff sets which were as much as Cynthia had managed that week. And the Price Slate. This was obligatory for all regular traders for Parliament itself was alarmed at the way prices were rising. Food prices. People selling what were called fripperies could charge what any fool was prepared to pay.

With Cynthia in charge, the slate had always been filled in. This morning, it was blank.

Presently Eli, who had been looking round as he helped to unload and arrange, said, "They're here. A man and a woman, and believe it or not, their stall ready set for them! Bribery and corruption! Now listen . . . You just walk across. Take a basket. Look like an early customer. And notice their prices. Above all, find out where they come from; and who's behind them. Your living as well as so many others depends upon this. Sell at a loss if you must."

From the church tower that dominated the Market, nine strokes boomed. Eli said, "I must get back. The horse and cart will be at the Hawk in Hand; and for twopence one of the accredited boys will help you clear up. Hi, you boy," he raised his arm and snapped his fingers. "Take care of this while my wife does a bit of shopping." He gave the boy a penny, and then, after a slight hesitation, two more. "She may need a bit of help later. You see to it, or you'll never get your badge again."

The badges were bits of wire, twisted into a numeral, slung on a bit of dirty string. The Overseer issued them to boys he believed to be reasonably honest. They were much coveted. My boy was number 6. He slid behind the stall; Eli drove away and I, taking Dorcas's leading rein in one hand, slung a basket on my arm and went towards the rival stall.

It was being kept by a young couple who struck me as being rather shy. Cynthia had said that it took a little time to get used to addressing customers. The young man went on arranging their goods on a cloth of very fine linen, but the young woman smiled at Dorcas. I ran my avid eyes over what they had for sale. It consisted only of dairy stuff, some eggs and a few fowls ready-dressed for spit or oven. It was all of superb quality and the prices chalked on the slate made my heart sink. I knew enough about costs to realise that this stall even were it completely cleared, could show no margin of profit and that if I undersold them, as I had been ordered to do, I should show a loss on everything except what Marian had made.

I said, "It's going to be another hot day." I knew that a remark about the weather was always acceptable even between strangers.

"Good harvest weather," the young woman said and somehow I knew that she would have been happier in a field, binding sheaves, making stooks. I also realised that despite my basket, I was not behaving as a putative customer. The young man gave me a suspicious glance. He was not entranced, as the young woman was, by Dorcas. She said, "What a very pretty little girl." Feeling like Judas, I said, "She's had quite a long drive . . . Have you come from any distance?"

"Only from . . ." She stopped. I think that the man had kicked her. "Not far," she said, deliberately vague. "And now ma'am what would you like?"

I thought: How astonished you would be, dear girl, if I told you the truth – I would like to banish you and him, whoever he is, and this stall and all that is on it, to the furthest ends of the earth.

I said, "I was just looking," beating a hasty retreat, and carrying Dorcas, for genuine customers were now beginning to arrive.

Back at my stall I wrote the figures – burned in fire on my brain – with cold chalk on cold slate and with my heart even colder. I remembered Eli's words about my living and that of many others being involved. It was true. And I began to suspect that his suspicion about an enemy was justified. I thought of all those cows, of Mrs Smith and me in the dairy. I thought of Father with his firm belief in mixed farming. Eli had upset the balance, and some of the best arable land in Suffolk was now reverting to the wild. He had set up something immediately profitable but very vulnerable. Yet, I thought angrily, fair competition we could have faced. This was unfair. This was ruinous.

I even spared a thought – half-pitying – for Eli. He'd set himself to walk home; five miles was nothing, he said.

I was not entranced by the customers who did halt by my

stall. I detected in their attitude something of contempt for me. They seemed curiously all of a pattern, smug, self-satisfied housewives, many of them accompanied by a serving wench or a young apprentice to carry the baskets. One or two of them commented on the revised prices, "And about time too." Dorcas's harness attracted some attention, especially later in the day when women with less leisure came shopping. I actually took ten orders. I sold the collar-and-cuff sets and everything of Marian's making. Otherwise my sales were negligible, though twice I sent Boy Number 6 across to read the prices on my rivals' slate and reduced mine until we were all in the ludicrous position of giving stuff away. I sat there on the three-legged stool which was provided with the trestles and the board and I thought of how angry Eli would be, though I had obeyed his orders to the letter; and thought that he had been right about his conviction that he had an enemy. A very powerful one, too . . . I was of divided mind. I hated Eli, especially when he was exacting his conjugal rights, but he was Pargeters.

A shadow fell across the stall, and looking up, I saw Mr Clover, whose grey clothes matched his grey horse. I suppose that white caps constituted a uniform; for he looked surprised. "Ah, Mrs Smith . . . I trust that Mrs Woodley-Mercer is not unwell."

"No, it was just that it was my turn, to keep the stall."

"I see," he said. He looked disappointed and ill-at-ease. "I frequently buy some of her work. They make acceptable gifts. You have none today?"

"Two sets, but I sold them early."

"I am on my way to Cambridge," he explained unnecessarily. "I may even have to proceed to Lincolnshire."

He did not ask me to pass on this information to Cynthia, but I felt the request was implicit. "I wish you good-day."

He raised the high-crowned, bandless hat which Oliver Cromwell had made fashionable, and rode away. Had my mood been less glum, I thought, I would tease Cynthia about her elderly admirer. As it was I could only think that once, in an attempt to save Pargeters, I had been willing to marry him myself.

Now all about us the food stalls were ready for the dinner trade. Over charcoal braziers, sausages and slices of bacon were being fried, very tantalising to the palate so long denied them. There was a stall selling cold viands too, great pink hams and joints of beef. Almost next door to me was a stall which sold sweetmeats, squares of gingerbread, saffron buns, marzipan slices.

Dorcas and I ate what we had brought with us, dark bread and cheese, but she had a bottle of whole milk – whole meaning not yet skimmed of its cream. The one advantage I could see of working in the dairy and thus under Mrs Smith's hard heel was that I could, and often did, sneak some whole milk, even sometimes a spoonful of cream, for Dorcas.

Soon after the dinner hour the schoolboys came. They wore uniform, black, bat-like gowns and caps that fitted the head and then went square and flat, with a tassel in the centre. They erupted, making for the food stalls, but one stopped by me.

It was Edman. And it was two years since Katharine and I had decided not to mention his existence. He was now so like Eddy that my heart jolted.

He said, "Aunt Sarah! I wasn't expecting to see *you*."

While I was saying how glad I was to see him, how much he had grown, how well he looked – all the trite things, I thought: How thin, all growth upwards; and how shabby! In that moment of emotion I could not recall exactly the terms of the agreement I had made, plumping down my money in advance. Something about that uniform; but that probably meant the gowns and the mortar-board hats. His shirt sleeves were too short by three inches, and frayed and his wrists were mere bone.

"Look," he said, using Eddy's word, Eddy's voice. "I did so want to consult you. Mother's letters told me nothing and Aunt Cynthia was evasive. Is something terribly wrong at Pargeters?"

Nothing that he could deal with; so I said, "No. Your mother is well. Our reasons for keeping you away still hold. We are sorry about the holidays, though."

"I don't mind. Several boys don't go home."

Dorcas, who had been taking a little nap in the shade under the stall, woke and hauled herself up.

Edman said, "I knew you had a little girl. Isn't she pretty?" He smiled at her and she smiled back. Young as she was, she never smiled first but waited for the other person to make the first overture. Eli and Mrs Smith had never smiled at her; she was used to unfriendly faces.

Edman handed me a letter. "It's for Mother, but it concerns you too, Aunt Sarah. I'd have liked to talk it over with you, but the boys want to swim. And I'm in charge. I'm a prefect now."

Recklessness overtook me. All the boys had been eating and I thought: Edman has never had any pocket money. I also thought that Eli would be so angry about the stall's failure, for which he would blame me, that a shilling would make no difference. I dived into the pouch, which by now should have been bulging but was not, and took out a shilling.

Edman said, "Can you spare it? I mean, I'm all right. I don't need . . ."

"If you don't hurry all the sausages will be gone."

"Thank you more than I can say. Give my love to Mother." He swung away and I saw that the tassel on his hat was made of silver threads. It marked his rank as prefect, I supposed.

And what did he do with the first and probably the last pocket money he ever had? He spent at least a third of it on the most expensive foodstuff on offer, a marzipan slice. He pushed it into Dorcas's small hand.

I could have wept.

My next visitor was different. No lesser personage than Sir Walter Fennel himself. He was mounted, of course, and able to look down on me. "This," he said, "is the final ignominy! I did not believe my ears. I came to see for myself. Even now . . . I know that man is a rogue and more mercenary than most. But you are his *wife*! That he should so degrade you . . ."

I said, straightening myself, "I see nothing degrading in trying to make an honest living." I saw him glance at my unsold goods. "I do find it mortifying not to be able to do so because of unfair competition. A rival stall has been under-selling me all day."

"Where is it?" He had helped me once; maybe he could again; I turned, prepared to point. There was no stall. Two of the Overseer's trusty boys were each carrying a trestle and one end of the board.

"They've sold out and gone home," I said, bitterly wishing that the same could be said of me.

"I never imagined," Sir Walter said. "I did offer you a home."

"On terms I could not accept," I reminded him.

"You prefer this?"

"It suits my purpose better."

"Then on your head be it," he said, and turned his horse and rode away.

I looked about me and saw that market day was to all intents and purposes over. Even the poorer people who shopped late in the hope of bargains had gone. I began to pack up and to look about for Boy Number 6 who was at least honest. He came running towards me. "I'll give you a hand across to The Hawk and put the rest away after-wards." I felt so reduced, so desolate that I was grateful for that crumb of goodwill and was meditating giving him an extra penny when another horseman drew rein by my stall. Looking up I saw Tom Markham.

I had not seen him since he had left Pargeters though I knew, through Marian, that he had worked for Captain Bennett only briefly. Where, after that, he had gone I had not been told, or bothered to enquire. Now I remembered his remark about herring fishermen making good money – but not the kind of money represented by the clothes he wore, or the horse he rode.

He said, almost word for word, what Sir Walter had done, "I hardly believed my own ears. I shouldn't have thought even Eli Smith . . ." He dismounted nimbly. I stopped putting our rejected offerings into the smallest possible space and stacking the dishes and plates on which they had been so uselessly displayed and said, "Hullo, Tom. You look well."

"I wish . . ." he began, and checked, aware of the boy, hovering.

"Decent boy?"

"Most helpful. All through a rather horrible day."

"Good," Tom said, and produced a shining two shilling piece, probably more than Number 6 had ever seen in one coin before. "You take all this and have it put into Mrs Smith's cart. We'll be along."

Then Dorcas made a diversion. That almost uncanny talent she had for knowing friend from foe informed her that here was a friend. She could not yet talk, but she could gabble, and did so now, with an entrancing smile and lifted her arms indicating a willingness to be picked up. Tom hesitated for a moment, looking acutely uncomfortable. I could guess what was in his mind. Eli Smith's child begotten of my body! Then he relented and heaved her up, keeping the rein looped over his left arm. She reached out and touched the horse. "Gentle as a lamb," Tom said quickly. Dorcas crowed with delight. One stranger had given her something delicious to eat, another offered her something new to explore.

The Hawk in Hand prided itself on catering for all comers and towards the rear, overlooking part of the yard, was a room where females were welcome. At this time of day it was occupied by women awaiting their husbands. Tom tethered his horse and we went in, giving the deceptive appearance of being a family. Tom ordered wine.

Now the memory of our last meeting hung between us. Aunt Lydia had once told me that a lady should always be ready to open a conversation; and that men always enjoyed talking about themselves. She would have approved of what I said.

"You didn't stay long at Nine Elms. Where are you now, Tom?"

He answered with a seeming reluctance. "Flaxham Park. Mrs Watson was wanting a foreman."

"It's a huge place. I went there once with Father." But other things surfaced on my memory. Mr Watson, hoping for an heir, had married a young wife. No heir had been forthcoming and he'd left one of those spiteful wills – if his widow re-married, she'd lose all. So she stayed a widow and employed foremen!

Tom said, "It is huge as you say, and Mrs Watson is a lonely woman. There'd been several before me, and they'd all robbed her blind. The place was going to rack and ruin, till I took over. She's . . . grateful."

"She's fortunate," I said. The wine was having an effect on me, unaccustomed as I now was. I leaned my weary back against the well-padded settle, and even the thought of Eli's cold rage eased away.

"You said you'd had a horrible day," Tom said. "Apart from being stuck there behind that stall, anything special?"

I told him about the rival stall. "You must have seen how much stuff I have to take back."

"I wasn't paying much heed." He looked thoughtful. "I could buy it . . . But that wouldn't stop the same thing happening again. Looks to me like somebody trying to put Eli out of business. Somebody with a deep pocket, too."

"Eli speaks of a secret enemy. I believe it now. It was unfair competition."

"I've no doubt Eli Smith hev trod on a good many people's corns," Tom said. "I'm main sorry though if you're gonna be hurt, too. Thass nobody round Flaxham way. I'd hev heard. I dessay lots of people grudge Eli getting Pargeters so easy – but they're all smallish. Not men with money to fritter away. Will you be on the stall next week?"

"There's the harvest lull for three weeks."

"Ah, I was forgetting. To tell you the truth I don't use the Market much. If you're big enough, buyers come to you. Not wishing to boast . . . But I've kept an eye . . ."

Two women came in. One said, "Good afternoon, Mr Markham," and gave a summing-up glance. It was unlikely that she would recognise me, for I had not been in Baildon since my marriage, but suppose somebody remembered that Tom had once worked for me, and left abruptly as soon as I agreed to marry Eli? A choice bit to gossip about for those who enjoy such things. Mrs Smith, lolling about, after market hours, drinking wine with Tom Markham at The Hawk in Hand.

I straightened my back and then stood up, saying I must go. I said, "Thank you, Tom. It's been a great relief to talk things over. I hope you have a good harvest."

Boy Number 6 had either misunderstood or determined to earn his unexpected bonus. He had loaded and harnessed the cart and stood waiting. The contrast between the two horses hurt me. Tom's mount so sleek and glossy, my dear old Bess bony and dull-coated. She had enough Thorough breeding not to look quite a peasant's drudge horse, but she was perilously near it. Both she and Sabrina were doing heavy-horse work on scanty rations. Katharine and I grieved and grumbled between ourselves, but dared not expostulate.

Because of what had happened to Boru.

Eli – like Mother – disapproved of dogs in the house, but during that first harvest he had not openly objected to Boru's presence in the field while I worked. Then one morning my beloved hound lay stiff and dead in his pen. It was just at the corn-storing season, when all good farmers waged war on rats. There was poison available. But I had no shred of evidence, and was indeed at that time trying desperately to make our marriage, not happy, but peaceful. It was Eli who betrayed himself, saying complacently, "Well, he wasn't any use."

So I never asked that Bess should be spared or better fed. I did not want her to end in the special slave-horse market where the lame, the outworn, pitiable crocks changed one merciless master for another, at the cost of a few shillings.

Now and again Katharine and I tried to smuggle a handful of oats or a wisp of hay. However, Eli shared with his God that all-seeing eye a representation of which, worked in crudest cross-stitch, now hung above the kitchen

hearth at Pargeters, with its legend: THOU GOD SEEST ME.
We were usually caught. Once Katharine, at heart a devout
woman, said, "The spy service between Pargeters and
Mount Sinai is very efficient."

That evening Eli's rage was intense. He could not blame
me, as he had blamed Cynthia, for not reducing prices. I had
done exactly what he had told me to; yet I felt that the
shilling I had given Edman, the time I had spent drinking
wine with Tom, must somehow show on my face. But his
inner eye was fixed upon that secret enemy. This proved it!
"I am afraid that it does," I said.

I managed to give Katharine Edman's letter, reserving
talk about him until we were milking next morning. I
passed on Mr Clover's message to Cynthia who said, rather
off-handedly, "Oh yes. He has an aged relative in Scunthorpe. Quite wealthy, I believe."

All through the gloomy supper and the long God-chiding
prayer, with Eli likening himself to David confronting
Goliath, "But Lord, thou knowest, David could *see* his
enemy." My mind kept reverting to Sir Walter's visit to the
stall, the way he had looked and spoken, the seeming horror
at finding me in charge. And then Tom Markham echoing
the words about not believing his ears. Was there something shameful, something I didn't know about, in standing
behind a stall? I remembered, too, Tom's words about the
enemy having a deep pocket.

My thoughts were quite incoherent and I longed to
clarify them by hearing them put into words and examined
in the light of Katharine's cool judgement. But that too
must wait until milking time tomorrow; and even then be
deferred, for Katharine had a problem of her own – nothing vague or speculative.

"It's Edman," she said as we settled down. "You must
read his letter. I'll give you the gist. He wants to leave
school."

"But I thought he was doing so well; sure to get a
bursary . . ."

"He has. I mean he has qualified; but he doesn't wish to
take it up. He says he hears such strange things about

Pargeters and he is now ready to take a clerk's job and . . . and support me. Or better still he could come here and help shoulder the load. He says that when we get Brigstowe back it would be useful for him to have some firsthand practical knowledge of farming."

"That," I said, "is absolutely impossible. Eli would work him to death and be vile to him. And how could we ever explain why his very existence has never been mentioned?"

"I think even Eli is beginning to realise that he can't run Pargeters aided only by a monstrous regiment of women."

That phrase had been coined by John Knox, one of the founders of Calvinism. Other Puritans made free use of it. Knox had been referring to Elizabeth of England and Mary of Scotland – very different from us, so down-trodden and overworked.

We took our filled buckets and placed them near the door, inside, out of the sun. Settled again, I said, "Kat, we'll talk more about Edman this evening – he won't expect an immediate reply. Now just listen for a moment and tell me if this idea is too absurd. Could Eli's enemy be Sir Walter Fennel? He much resented Eli marrying me, and he is rich . . ."

There was silence; then Katharine said, "I think it quite likely. With people of his kind, family ramifications run deep. If you had made what he considered a good marriage he'd have basked in reflected glory. As it is he feels shamed. He did offer you a home, remember. He'd gladly ruin Eli."

"But why *now*? Why wait two years?"

"I can think of a number of reasons. Maybe he hoped that Eli would ruin himself – a good many Jumped-up-Johnnies have done. Or it may be that he is mean. Mind, I don't know the man, I can only judge from what I hear. He could have been waiting until he could see a way of hurting Eli without much risk of loss to himself. Or he may be at heart a timid man and was waiting for a lead from somebody else."

"I thought of such things. But Kat, one thing remains a puzzle. If my marriage to Eli Smith, who ostensibly owns Pargeters, caused such shame, would rendering him a pauper – and me with him – do anything to improve the situation?"

There was another pause; then Katharine said, very firmly, "Yes. I know how the minds of petty country gentry work. Eli Smith has now so far committed himself that without the stall, which had a monopoly, Pargeters might not be a viable proposition. Then he'd move – Sir Walter would hope to some place where the relationship, vague as it is, would not be known about."

I said, "Thank you, Kat. Now I know what to try."

Ockley Lodge was far grander than its name implied, it had been a hunting lodge for some sporting Abbot of Baildon in medieval times and was a palace in miniature. I rode boldly to the main door, dismounted, shook out my skirt and rang the bell. A surly-faced footman opened the door to me and I said, untruthfully, "I have an appointment with Sir Walter," and stepped inside. From some distance inside the house came the sound of music and voices singing – Lady Fennel's ladies, of whom I could have been one. Cutting through this sound, the jangling of a bell being furiously shaken by hand. I said, "My horse will stand." As indeed she would, not because I had magic power as Lady Alice was supposed to have had but because for Bess, these days, just to stand was luxury and, going on an errand approved of by Eli, and in his interest, I had ventured to snatch a good handful of hay and a few almost ripe summer apples.

I disliked the way the servant looked at me though I understood it. I said, "If Sir Walter is in his library, I know the way. You may answer the other bell."

"But I have instructions . . ." the man said. I headed for the library, down one of those long corridors which Grandfather in building Pargeters had avoided.

"You took your time, damn you. I was beginning to think you were all stone deaf," Sir Walter snarled. He sat in a high-backed, padded chair, so set as to give him no view of the door but an excellent one of the garden, which at this time of year was lovely to look at and lovely to smell, the window being half open. His left foot was propped upon a stool and covered by the lightest possible knitted shawl. Within reach of his right hand was a table bearing everything that a pipe-smoker could require, a carafe of clear water and a small silver dish bearing three tiny cubes of the solid opium to which only the very rich now had access. Nearer the centre of the room was another table upon which stood, on a silver tray, two decanters and several elegant glasses. In his hand Sir Walter held a silver bell.

I had now moved into his range of vision and the expression of anger with which he had been prepared to greet a tardy servant did not relax. It hardened.

"Come to gloat, eh? This is *your* doing." He indicated his afflicted foot. "I don't care what anybody says. My gout always follows an upset and yesterday you upset me thoroughly."

"Not intentionally, Sir Walter." I spoke meekly, thinking this an unpromising opening to what at best would be a tricky interview.

"Oh, I don't for a moment expect that you got up yesterday morning with the intention of shaming me anew, but you put yourself into a position where it could happen. By the time I reached home, I was in agony."

"I hope it has eased now. I wanted your advice. Perhaps even your help."

"Make yourself useful then. Put that tray on *this* table. Those damn women! One says the good wine of Oporto causes the gout. One says that to mix wine and opium will induce a stroke." He set the bell back on his handy table and cleared a space.

This evening there was something slightly different in his manner, something that made me suspect that he could have been making free with the little opium cubes. His speech was less stilted and though I was, I sensed, still in disfavour some barrier inside him was weakening.

"Pour for us both," he said, "the red wine for me. Then sit down and tell me what tomfool situation you've got yourself into now. But don't expect help or even sympathy, after yesterday's disgraceful exhibition."

My guilty conscience imagined that he had heard about my drinking with Tom Markham; but I took a heartening sip of the brandy I had chosen and said: "What did I do yesterday that was so disgraceful?"

"You exposed yourself in the open market as a woman of dubious reputation. Don't play the wide-eyed innocent to me. You managed for years on your own. Even if that lout you chose to marry may not have known or cared, you should have. It is common knowledge that any woman under fifty alone at a stall is as much for sale as the goods she displays."

I almost choked on a mouthful of brandy and Sir Walter, as though provoked to fresh pain, reached for and swallowed one of the opium cubes, washing it down with a gulp of port wine. I thought: It may be true! I tried to remember what stall-keepers I had noticed; the women alone were all oldish and drab; the sausage stall – target for men – could show a pretty, be-ribboned girl but with a stern chaperone. Even our rival stall had been manned by a pair.

"It was bad enough when that flibbertigibbet sister-in-law of yours was selling butter-pats and flaunting her curls. But for you . . . you . . ." Perhaps whoever said that opium and port wine should not be mixed were in the right. His reddish complexion darkened to near purple.

I said: "I was there yesterday because my husband thought me more capable of dealing with a problem that arose last week: a rival stall, Sir Walter, deliberately bent upon our ruin. Last week their prices were so unrealistic that my sister-in-law brought back most of our dairy stuff. Yesterday every time I reduced a price to meet theirs, they undercut again. So I am here now to ask . . ."

He said, slightly too quickly, "I have nothing to do with any market stall."

"But you know who has?"

Unfair in a way. He was, after all, a man with a Puritan conscience. The lie direct did not come easily to him; evasions and some pretence but no downright lie. And he was under the influence of opium, and of wine . . .

"What makes you say that? Doesn't every successful

231

enterprise invite competition? And why should I concern myself with how Eli Smith makes a living?"

"Because of the relationship, distant and hardly acknowledged but sufficient for you to feel affronted even – as you yourself now admitted – it was only my sister-in-law behind the stall. I am asking help now, Sir Walter. Eli has made our farming so dependent on the dairy that without the stall we shall be ruined. I know that a monopoly cannot be expected to last forever, but if I knew who was responsible for the other stall we could at least arrange to live and let live – agree prices beforehand perhaps."

"That sounds sensible. And you are correct in thinking that your stall irked me. But I never took any action."

His eyelids drooped. I thought angrily that he was evading me by pretending to fall asleep, a way of escape open only to the elderly with rank enough to protect them from a shaking and a command to wake up. So all my errand had brought me was a confirmation of my suspicions – and a glass of brandy.

Then his eyes opened wide and he said in a rather far-away voice: "In truth all I did was to oblige an old friend. Richard Hartley. Colonel Hartley. A man with far more reason for hating Eli Smith. I suppose you understand the word blackmail? I see that you do. A nasty word is it not? Yet every day, at every level a form of blackmail is being extorted; the half promise, the half threat. But in this case open and crude. I think I am about to become indiscreet." He reached a rather unsteady hand towards the decanter in which the ruby-red wine glowed. I stretched a steadier hand and poured for him, and brandy for me. He took a gulp and proceeded to be very indiscreet indeed.

"Richard Hartley is an old friend and slightly related by marriage. A very decent man but a sad womaniser. Always was, and even General Cromwell knows by now that you can't legislate people into virtue. The low fellow you chose to marry, my dear, had some administrative job with plenty of time for spying and sneaking. And he found out something about Captain Hartley as he then was which if divulged would have led to disgrace, not promotion. So he levied blackmail. Part in money, part in the allotment of sequestrated land when the time came. As we know it did. And we know *where*, don't we? And you fool enough to play straight into his hands! My friend Hartley has land out Ingham way and left the Army last year. He bore a grudge, not only about the blackmail but I think because the affair thus rudely interrupted concerned a lady who . . . Hrumph. Even womanisers have favourites. So, when my friend Hartley realised how well Eli Smith was doing and how much I was against the stall itself, he asked me to do him a favour. House a small herd, lend my dairy. He sent his own staff. He reckoned he could put Eli Smith out of business within a month. And when I saw *you*, poor Lydia's niece when all is said and done, thus exposed, I knew that for me it could not be too soon." He was beginning to slur his words a bit.

I said, "And now I hope you realise that your plot has failed."

"You just said yourself how successful . . ."

I said, "Sir Walter, make an effort and stay awake while I say something. I hold no brief for blackmailers. But in defence of my livelihood, I should be quite ruthless. And Eli Smith is not a mere thickheaded peasant. He left the Army with an unblemished record; now he is being slandered. He'll fight. Your Roundheads keep records of everything. Somewhere it is all written down in black and white, how Pargeters was allocated. I remember a Major Harrison. He could be traced . . . Also, Eli has an excellent memory. If your story is true, he will remember the name of the . . . lady concerned. A tasty tit-bit for the Newsletters."

Poor old man! He said, "But surely you understood that I was speaking confidentially. Merely trying to explain . . ."

"I am quite unscrupulous," I said. "Even had I taken an oath not to reveal anything you said, I should not stand by it. If that stall appears on the Market Place when it re-opens after harvest, I shall urge Eli to take legal action, and I shall distribute papers explaining why we are being ruined. I wield a good pen and nowadays one in ten can read."

"You are venomous."

"Yes. As an old friend of Colonel Hartley you should warn him."

I rode home with a sense of triumph. I did not expect further competition from that quarter. I could even imagine Sir Walter and his friend falling out over what the latter could rightly regard as a breach of trust.

There was however a slight melancholy in my mood. It was a sad reflection on my marriage that I never once doubted the statement that Eli was a blackmailer and now I intended to give him only a very limited account of my talk with Sir Walter. To know something about Eli which he didn't know I knew might one day bring me some advantage.

I arrived home to find the place in an uproar and all on account of Mr Clover, who had gone neither to Cambridge nor Lincolnshire but had returned to Brook, taken counsel with himself and decided to ask Cynthia to marry him.

This Cynthia was one I had never seen, gay, excited, her confidence in her power to attract fully restored. She herself told me the news, babbling almost incoherently. Katharine looked pleased but with a glint of irony.

And food for irony here there was. The Smiths, with their dislike of useless mouths, had made no secret of the fact that only by stitching herself almost blind could she avoid being damned by that epithet; now the thought of her going angered them and they spoke of ingratitude, lack of thought for others, of rats deserting a ship not yet wrecked, but threatened. "Just when that boy was beginning to be useful!" Eli said. Mrs Smith remarked gloomily that she could knit if she must but was too old to learn fancy needlework. Proof of Cynthia's diligence lay on the dresser; I had taken the orders for child-harness only yesterday, and she had completed six sets.

"And what about *you*?" Eli asked, swinging round on me. "More bad news?" He had been reluctant to allow me to go to Ockley at all.

"No. I think rather good. I shall be surprised if that stall makes a reappearance. I was right in assuming that Sir

Walter knew something and he will bring influence to bear."

"We shall see how much or how little that means," Eli said. "Now, let us pray." That evening the minatory tone of his conversation with his Jehovah was very prominent.

At next morning's milking Katharine and I talked. A little about Cynthia, "Quite the best thing that has ever happened to her," Katharine said. I agreed and then said, "I wonder about the future. The stall. Apparently Sir Walter has felt shame at even so remote a relative as a nephew-by-marriage's widow standing behind a stall." I told her of the market women's sorry reputation. She said, "If only I could go. Surely I'm old enough and crooked enough to escape calumny. And I should so welcome an opportunity to see Edman once a week. I'd sit on hot coals."

I said, "Have you written to Edman, telling him that he must stay at school?"

"I wrote and finished the letter while Mr Clover was proposing to Cynthia. He said he'd see that it was delivered."

So that was that. A happy outcome for Cynthia and John Adam – I was particularly pleased about him. His nature was being rapidly soured. Mr Clover also should find Cynthia's company agreeable, she would be grateful and eager to please: she was very pretty to look at and she would handle his precious things gently. And with regard to Edman, I was sure that a sensible decision had been reached.

There followed the harvest, hard work for us all and then some rather frenzied blackberry gathering so that Marian could make gallons of cordial. The rival stall had rather shaken Eli's confidence in purely dairy products and he was looking about for other things to sell. Any fruit cordial, properly matured, had almost the restorative quality of wine and in a society where alcohol was almost forbidden this new offering was likely to sell well.

Except that we were all now two years shabbier, Cynthia's wedding was a replica of mine, but when we left the church there was a surprise. A light carriage, of a kind as yet unknown in our district, stood waiting. It was not unlike the cart which Eli had made, except that the body work was mainly of cane, and it had proper seats, velvet padded. Before Cynthia was helped into it, she embraced me tearfully. "I shall never forget your kindness," she said. "I shall visit you often." That I rather doubted without in the least resenting it. Why should she not forget, as speedily as possible, a place which had been at best a shelter, and at worst a place of misery?

More often than not in this life things happen untimely, but within two days of Cynthia's leaving something happened at Pargeters which was most apt.

Evenings were beginning to draw in, but with harvest over we supped rather earlier and it was still fairly light as we sat down to eat rabbit pie, tasty enough so far as the meat was concerned but covered with Mrs Smith's dark heavy crust. The table-talk – if such it could be called – centred about who was to keep the stall now that the harvest lull was over. I had told Eli something that was almost half true – that we could not count upon Sir Walter's co-operation if his family feelings were again outraged by my appearance on the market, and for some reason of her own Mrs Smith, usually in such full agreement with her son, was reluctant to accept his suggestion that she should take charge. She argued that she could not be spared. So that left Katharine. She had not volunteered, nor had I suggested her, we both knew by now how perverse Eli could be. Just why Eli was so unwilling to put her behind the stall he never explained and we never understood until much later when his cold anger got the better of him.

At the table on that particular evening while I hoped, and I have no doubt Katharine prayed, that he would say that she must go, there was a sound of movement in the yard, and the door opened. There stood Edman, looking rather bigger than he had done on the Market and with his leather valise tucked under his arm. His face was disfigured; one eye black and half-closed and his jaw swollen.

Katharine said, "Edman?" and lurched towards him. He

said, "Mother!" dropped the valise and embraced her. They stood, hugging each other, and then at arms' length took stock. Katharine said, a choke in her voice, "How you have grown!" He gave a shaky laugh and said, "Well, it's been a long time. Oh Mother . . ." I knew what he meant; the long time and the hard work had aged her.

Eli said, clumsily sardonic, "And now perhaps we could be told who this is, walking in as if he owned the place." Katharine became exceedingly formal. "This is my son, Edman Bowen. Edman, Mrs Smith, Mr Smith." Edman bowed to Mrs Smith and said to Eli, "I apologise, sir, for entering so abruptly. I should have knocked."

Hostility was taken for granted and I had no doubt at all that had Edman arrived four weeks earlier, Eli would have ordered him out.

"Where've you come from?"

"School, sir. I have been expelled."

"Expelled! What for?"

"Brawling, sir." Edman indicated his disfigurements and gave a lop-sided grin.

"Brawling!" Again Eli sounded outraged. "You should be ashamed of yourself."

"I am afraid I am not, sir. There is a limit to the insults one can accept. And the other fellow looks worse than I do."

It was a touch-and-go situation. Such jauntiness! I think that even then Eli would have cut off his nose to spite his face and said, "Get out", but Mrs Smith for once took the initiative, extending, not too graciously, a form of hospitality. "I reckon you'll be hungry," she said. "Hand me a plate." She cut him a generous wedge of pie. She at least saw Edman's potential value, particularly as a stall-keeper.

Hungry he may have been but mannerly he remained, first greeting me with a kiss on the hand and a murmured, "I'm sorry, Aunt Sarah to have gone against your wishes," and then greeting Marian and Harry by name. They responded, pleased but slightly uneasy, and in fact they were often in an uncomfortable position. The Leveller theories, all men equal in the sight of God, all work, all eat together sounded better than they were in practice. I had often been aware that Marian and Harry would rather have been elsewhere. But Eli's rule, nobody to retire until Evening Prayer was finished, and the prayer following immediately after supper, had Marian and Harry trapped, forced to witness and hear things which belonged to the family.

Katharine was, for the moment, aware of nothing except the sheer pleasure of seeing her son again. She could not take her eyes off him and I could imagine how she longed to touch him, to examine his hurts.

Edman appeared sublimely unaware of any undercurrents. He ate hungrily, seeming oblivious to Eli's angry glower. He did not know the rule that at this table all conversation must originate from the master of the house and he did remember that only animals ate in silence. So, hungry as he was he made a few remarks. "Where is Aunt Cynthia?"

"Married on Saturday," Eli snapped. Edman stared for a second and then laughed, quite heartily and yet, I realised, with something of self-mockery, a thing only possible to the truly civilised person. I guessed then that the brawl had had some connection with the reputation of market women.

"I hope she'll be happy, and I hope, sir, that you had a good harvest."

"If you'd eat up and chatter less you wouldn't keep us all waiting," Eli said.

"I am sorry, sir." The cunning boy turned his disfigured glance upon Mrs Smith. "This pie is too delicious to hurry over." He ate in silence after that. When he had finished, Katharine and I cleared the table; Mrs Smith lit a single candle and then Eli said, "Let us pray."

He was slightly confused in his neighbourly chat that evening; he sought strength to subdue the unruly spirit of the stranger within his gates; he asked for patience in training the young tree as it should grow and curing its wilfulness, but most earnestly of all he besought sympathy for himself, surrounded as he was by deceitful women, forced through no fault of his own to live in a house divided against itself.

I noticed that he did not thank his good neighbour for providing him with a substitute for Cynthia.

When we were all on our feet again, Katharine, Edman and I carefully avoiding one another's eyes, Marian and Harry scuttled off as quickly as their aged legs would carry them. Mrs Smith lit about a half inch of candle and said, "I'll find you a bed." Edman hugged his mother, kissed me, this time on the cheek as he had done when he was a child, and bade Eli a courtly 'Good night, sir'.

Then the storm broke. Anyone walking in just then might have found difficulty in deciding just what heinous offence Katharine and I had committed. We had conspired, gone behind his back; I had behaved as no decent wife should, Katharine had poorly repaid the hospitality she had received at his hands. And why? Why? Katharine said that she had not wished to intrude further upon Eli's hospitality. I said, "Edman was not included in the bargain we struck. He was already at school – and I knew how you felt about useless mouths."

To that Eli retaliated, "And who paid his fees?"

"I did," Katharine said. "Years ago, well in advance."

That lie, which spared me, would not trouble her conscience, religious though she was – almost, if not quite a Catholic. The deity she worshipped was altogether more lenient.

Eli said, "All right, he can stay and earn his keep though he'll be useless till he's trained. And I will not hev all that la-di-da behaviour. Mark that. Kissing and cuddling and whispering, I ain't gonna allow."

Nonetheless something had walked into Pargeters that evening which had brought about a subtle change. Eli hated Edman and treated him abominably and Edman, warned by Katharine, conformed outwardly for the sake of peace, but he was never cowed. He had youth, and the confidence of it, and also the confidence derived from the certainty of being able to make a living anywhere; he was a very good scholar and in a short time had acquired a sound knowledge of practical farming. So when Eli shouted at him and called him stupid and idle – both most unjust accusations – he could afford to allow his emotion to show on his handsome face. His eyes would flash and his lips press together in a way which betrayed that had he spoken the words would be scathing. Or he would look amused, as though Eli's display of ill humour were a show being put on for his benefit. Anything more exasperating to a man of Eli's kind it would be difficult to imagine. Edman could also say the polite word 'sir' in a way that made it an insult.

At first I was afraid that he would overtax his strength, for Eli was very demanding and Edman, in show-off fashion, took malicious delight in doing that little bit extra. He had attained man's height but was, to my eye, over-slender. But Katharine reassured me. "Edman is now as old as Son was when he went to the war – in full armour. And if he had stayed at school that extra year he'd have spent his free time playing football or some such."

I said, "I only wish the food were better," and she said, "It is probably as good as school food, or food aboard a ship and you may have noticed that of anything Mrs Smith dishes out Edman gets slightly more than his share." Then she added, "Anyway, Sarah, this cannot last long now." Most of our conversations ended upon that hopeful note.

PART FOUR

In imagining that Cynthia would forget us I had wronged her. She came often and always with gifts. Every bit of warm clothing that Katharine and I wore during the next few winters was given us by Cynthia, who said that James liked to read in the evenings – sometimes aloud. "Most of it is well over my head, so I like to have a piece of work on hand." And when Edman's wardrobe was actually in tatters, she brought along a whole boxful of Mr Clover's clothes. "He's beginning to put on weight," she said.

She also brought food, usually meat and always with an excuse which took the sting of charity out of the offering. James had suddenly made up his mind to go to Cambridge, or Lincolnshire, and the couple now employed at Brook, the husband tending the horse and the garden, his wife the house, couldn't possibly eat this joint while it was still good. I sometimes thought that Mr Clover's financial circumstances must have improved considerably since the evening when he told me that he was totally dependent upon his pension.

At first such presents were made openly, then suddenly Eli objected. "The next thing we know'll be people saying I don't feed or clothe you properly and we're dependent on a Presbyterian. A man to whom I pay rent!"

After that Cynthia's visits became furtive. She knew our timetable and she'd leave her light carriage in the road and trudge, bringing gifts, to the milking pen, the one place where Katharine and I enjoyed the priceless gift of privacy. This led to some ludicrous situations; Katharine and I would eat our fill and then secrete about our persons slices for Edman and Dorcas. What remained we'd put into a flour bag and hang from a nail in the wall. And if Cynthia brought an article of clothing, we would smuggle it in under whatever we happened to be wearing.

As Dorcas grew older and gained more mastery of speech, I lived in apprehension lest she should mention these surreptitious tit-bits. Eli had never forgiven me and Katharine for our secrecy over Edman and made constant references to conspiracy and going behind his back. In a female this inability to let a subject drop would have been called nagging and led to a ducking in a scold chair. I knew that the child had only to say that she liked ham and Katharine and I would stand condemned as the worst conspirators since the Gunpowder Plot. Yet it was difficult to impress upon a child the need for secrecy. We left that to Edman who had somehow acquired a hold over her, not completely explained by the fact that they were the only young things at Pargeters; there was in it something of the relationship which exists between a person and a favourite animal. Somehow he managed to impress upon her the fact that nothing she ate except at table must ever be mentioned. And it never was.

Eli's particular brand of Puritanism was adept at seeing evil where no evil was. One thing Dorcas enjoyed was to be hoisted up on to Edman's shoulders, and taking a firm grip of his hair be given a ride, with a bit of chanted doggerel: "This is the way the ladies ride, trip, trip, trip. This is the way the gentlemen ride, gallop and trot, gallop and trot. This is the way the farmers ride, bumpitty, bump." When Dorcas was about four Eli decreed that it was not decent for male and female to be in such contact and the game was forbidden. "Ah well," Katharine said, "the most famous order of chivalry in the world has its motto: Evil be to him who evil thinks."

Cynthia was often away as the years went on; the old wealthy relative in Lincolnshire liked to be visited and Cynthia liked Scunthorpe. Then the old man died and left everything to his grand-nephew, James Clover, and for about a year Cynthia and Mr Clover oscillated between Scunthorpe and Brook, trying to decide where to live. Brook had the advantage of being nearer Cambridge where Mr Clover's heart was, despite his being retired. Also from what Cynthia said I gathered that he felt himself too old to take over a house which Cynthia called vast and all the responsibilities of a resident landlord, however good an agent he employed. But Cynthia much preferred Scunthorpe.

In the end they compromised; going to live at Scunthorpe but not selling Brook which would be let to someone who did not wish to farm seriously.

Cynthia came openly to say goodbye though she was laden with parcels; meat – a ham and a sirloin of beef, both cut into – another parcel of clothes for Edman and the prettiest possible sprigged muslin dress for Dorcas. She came at a time when she knew Eli was there – the midday dinner-time – and presently the reason for her boldness was revealed. "And today, Mr Smith, I have something for you." She handed him a paper which he accepted with a scowl, and read, the scowl smoothing out. As well it might, for in legal phrases and beautifully penned it gave Eli the tenure of the sheep-run at Brook free of charge for as long as the property remained in Mr Clover's possession.

"Very generous," Eli said. "Please tell him I'm grateful and wish him well in his new place." That was as near as Eli's dour nature could come to graciousness; but when Cynthia said she must go and Katharine rose to go with her, saying, "I want a word with Cynthia," Eli made no objection, though it was haymaking time and Katharine should have gone straight from the table to the field. As I did, wondering what in the world Katharine could have to say to Cynthia. They had never been friends as I understood the word, though there had been since my marriage a kind of alliance against Eli, the common enemy. However when I crossed the yard on my way back to the hay and only waved, my farewells having been said in the kitchen, Katharine and Cynthia were standing together by Cynthia's lovely little carriage.

Hours later, when Katharine and I were milking, she explained.

"Sarah, I think I scared Cynthia."

"Scared her? How? Why?"

"I've thought long and hard about this; ever since Mr Clover inherited his fortune, and formally adopted John Adam and sent him to Eton. It seemed so unfair that John

Adam should have Pargeters as well. And you and Dorcas nothing. So this morning I pressed on her weakest point. I told her that when the King returns from exile he will wish to disturb as few people as possible, and that claims for sequestrated lands would be most thoroughly investigated – birth certificates, marriage registers and so on most thoroughly searched. She was shaken to the core."

I said, into the cow's flank, "I imagine she would be."

"Anyway she gave me her word not to make, or allow John Adam to make, any claim to Pargeters and she'd get Mr Clover to put it down in writing."

It then occurred to me, since self-blame is my weak point, that perhaps I had done Cynthia an ill-service, in the long run, by pretending that she was John's widow. In Mr Althorpe's register, as in the banns, she was Cynthia Woodley-Mercer, widow of this parish, enough to make her marriage illegal if anyone ever tried to discredit it. Not that anyone was likely to; Mr Clover's old relative had no other kin, and he had managed to weather out the war without obviously taking sides – rather like Sir Walter. Scunthorpe had never been sequestrated. On the whole, I thought, comforting myself, Cynthia was safe enough.

Some days later a letter arrived, addressed to me. In proper legal terms it renounced any claim which John Adam Clover, formerly John Adam Woodley-Mercer, had to Pargeters, in the parish of Minsham St Mary's in the County of Suffolk.

Of course Eli seized upon the letter and made it the subject of a tirade. What a waste of good paper! What claim could a schoolboy or anybody else have on Pargeters which Eli had bought with coined money? Pargeters was his and his . . . Oh dear, his scornful glance flicked over Dorcas. I had a momentary flash of sympathy for him. I knew that the poorest peasant with nothing but an acre and a decrepit donkey to bequeath wanted a son to inherit. As a wife I had failed.

Time went on. The Restoration in which Katharine so fully believed was like the rainbow's end; there it was, many-

coloured, seemingly fixed, tangible at a certain point, but
never there when you reached it. John and I had chased
many rainbows in our time. For Katharine and thousands
like her almost everything that happened at Westminster
was a rainbow; this or that must surely provoke foreign
interference or encourage rebellion from within. Yet the
rainbow steadily receded and the Commonwealth, as England was now called, prospered mainly I think because Lord
Protector Cromwell was a man of good sense and understood the value of money, for before the war he had not
been a rich man, just a very modest country squire.

Yet despite the general contentment there were plots
against him; he was said to wear armour under his clothing
and sleep in a different bed every night and there were
constant rumours of his failing health – very bright rainbows indeed.

Pargeters – or Eli – shared the prosperity and in Edman
he had a most valuable slave and stall-keeper. Never once a
penny out. One Wednesday he was even a shilling over and
Eli, instantly suspicious, said, "How did you come by
this?"

"I sold a blue dish, sir. The one on which Marian's
brawns are displayed."

As Edman and all of us realised, nothing Edman did
could ever be right.

"What a witless thing to do," Eli said. "So now we are
short of a dish. And dishes that size are not easily come by."

Mischief gleamed in Edman's eyes, but he spoke gravely.

"I fully realised that. But the customer was very persis-
tent. She had just bought a turkey and really needed a big
dish."

"That is no excuse for selling one that we need
ourselves."

"Ah, but you see I bought another, brand new, not even
chipped as ours was. I charged the insistent lady two
shillings. So that, sir," he indicated the disputed shilling, "is
sheer profit."

Just for once Eli was speechless. I thought Edman was a
fool not to have spent the shilling on a good square meal for

himself, but when I said so to Katharine she said rather haughtily, "My son does not need THOU GOD SEEST ME, badly embroidered, to remind him that he is a man of honour."

The next what I call market-day row was less light-hearted. Eli went to market very seldom, he held that most men made market day an excuse for gossip and drinking; but he was obliged to go in for such things as the fleece sales. They were always held on a Wednesday, but our two conveyances went separately, Eli driving the wagon, pulled by Sabrina and Edman the cart, laden with the usual produce. Even then, as soon as the Pargeters wool was sold Eli came straight home, and on one such day he came back looking so thunderous that I feared wool prices must have fallen disastrously. But he said nothing, went upstairs and put the money in the Trunk, ate a belated dinner and returned to work. In due time Edman arrived, stabled Bess, pushed the cart into the open-fronted cartshed and, carrying all the dishes, bowls and basins used for the transport and display of goods, came whistling in, said he'd had a good day, put the money pouch on the dresser and went upstairs to wash and change.

Supper was begun in gloomy silence, broken only when Dorcas said, "Did you see anything amusing today, Edman?"

"Lots of things. I'll tell you about them later. While we work."

He had often reported something he had seen or heard, not particularly hilarious, but made to seem so by his own lively sense of humour and gift of mimicry, but Eli had not approved. He said Edman went to market to tend the stall, not to gawp about. That was the kind of unjust rebuke he enjoyed administering, for though Edman might observe what went on around him, he always sold all there was to sell.

"And now, perhaps," Eli said, halting his knife, "you can explain what I heard this morning, about you hanging about the yard of The Hawk in Hand when you should be on your way home."

"I don't hang about, sir, I work. And pretty hard too."

"And are paid?"

"Not in money. I have an arrangement with old Job Handy. In return for a bit of help during the busiest time of the week he allows me to stable Bess in the With Bait place."

The Hawk in Hand made as sharp distinction between animals as it did between its human customers. A rider spending money inside the inn was permitted to leave his horse on the hitching rail, as Tom had left his on my one stall-tending day. Then there were stables, with bait, stables without bait and mere accommodation in an enclosure where no blade of grass grew. That cost twopence; without bait was fourpence, with bait a lordly sevenpence, but the oats in the mangers there were of high quality. The irony was that the animals most in need of oats went into the bare enclosure while pampered, well-fed ones had the run of their teeth. But, as Father had once remarked, between them the Bible and Shakespeare hit every nail squarely on the head. And the Bible said, "To him that hath shall be given and from he who hath not shall be taken away."

Eli said, "You have blackened my name. Think how it *looks*. You live here, you keep my stall, but you're so poorly paid that you have to hire yourself out to that ungodly place."

"A statement very easily confuted, sir. I am not poorly paid. I am not paid at all. Mother, please excuse me, but the time has come for plain speaking. Since you never hire labour you may not be aware of the increase in wages. An able, willing worker now earns sixpence a day and often a cottage, free milk and an occasional joint. My mother works equally hard, though I spare her so far as I can. But I'm not tied here. I could get a job tomorrow as a labourer or, with luck, as clerk or usher at a school. Mother has a great attachment to Aunt Sarah and some for this place. That alone constrains me."

Eli was adept at ignoring what he wished not to hear, and for twisting an argument to suit himself.

"I know many a man who if his *own son* was expelled

from school for brawling would not have taken him in. I took you in when you were ignorant and unhandy, what you know about farming I taught you. And what thanks do I get? None. Black ingratitude. You even manage to make it look as though I don't feed my horses enough."

"In my opinion, you don't."

Katharine said, "Edman, *please!*"

Afterwards she confided to me that she dreaded Eli and Edman coming to blows. I shared that dread. Eli would fell the boy like an ox. Another thing concerned me, too, comparatively trivial, but lively. Dorcas had grown in beauty and was still lovely, despite her grandmother's steady discouragement of what she called vanity – the screwing back of the luxuriant curly hair into a tight plait tied with a scrap of rag, the refusal to let her wear any of the pretty dresses Cynthia had provided, at least until they had been so transmogrified as not to be becoming. Such petty afflictions, and unjust scoldings, the child bore with stoicism, the more touching because it was so premature. But on the evening when Eli and Edman quarrelled about The Hawk in Hand I saw Dorcas look at Eli with the very face, not simply the expression, which I had seen when Mrs Smith looked at me through the kitchen window at Brook. I realised then that half my daughter's blood came from the Smith side. I also realised that the atmosphere at Pargeters, despite what Katharine and Edman and I could do to mitigate it, was bad enough to distort the happiest nature.

Brook's first tenant was a colleague of Mr Clover's, now retired. I never saw him, for neighbourly calls were a thing of the past, and he was crippled enough by rheumatism that like Marian and Old Harry, he was excused from compulsory church attendance. He was attended by a man-servant who occasionally spoke to Eli when he made his daily visit to the sheep-run. The tenant greatly enjoyed Brook with its gardens and grounds during the summer and had installed several seats upon which to rest his stiff limbs, but he declared that winter in our part of the world was far colder than at Cambridge, and he proposed to end his tenancy at Michaelmas next year.

After that the house stood empty for some time. And then one morning Eli came in to dinner with something about him which might, in a less dour and stolid a man, have been a kind of suppressed excitement.

He said, addressing his mother, "Well, I've seen the new tenant at Brook and you'd never guess who it is."

"Anybody I know?"

"You did, once." His voice was almost playful.

"I'm no good at guessing."

"Liz Cauldwell," Eli said.

Mrs Smith dropped the ladle back into the saucepan from which she was dishing a vegetable and barley stew with a few well-hammered bits of shin of beef in it. Her face, always sallow, turned ashen. She recovered herself quickly and gave her whole attention to allotting the right quantity and proportion to each. Eli received, as always, most of the beef, then Edman – they were male and must have preference; Katharine and I were served alike, and Dorcas, despite the fact that she was growing, received least of all. I had tried in the past to pretend that I had received too much and would pass my uneaten portion to her, but that had drawn first black looks and then a reprimand from Mrs Smith; if she had helped me too heavily, I had only to say so.

Now, having given Marian and Harry helpings slightly larger than Dorcas's, but with no meat at all, she said, "I hope you didn't speak to the hussy."

"I did. At least, she spoke to me. We had a long talk. Old Cauldwell did right by her in the end. She's got a carriage, a man to see to the horses and garden and a maid."

"More than she deserved," Mrs Smith said. She looked as though she could have said much more but was conscious of her audience. And indeed we were all agog. Our lives were so deadly dull that the word 'hussy' was in itself intriguing, and it was most unusual for the Smiths not to see eye to eye upon any subject. Our curiosity went unsatisfied however. Mrs Cauldwell did not, as we hoped, appear in church. Marian, who seemed to have some mysterious sources of information, said that she went to Nettleton church.

Edman who sometimes went to the sheep-run with Eli, actually saw her and reported that she was rather old. Katharine and I discounted that, knowing that at his age anybody over thirty was an ancient. He thought she could have been pretty before she became fat; she had a lot of yellowish hair. And she was well-dressed, wore a silk dress even in the morning: "violet-coloured. And a gold chain." Obviously a hussy! But what had impressed Edman most was her good nature. "She invited us in for lemonade and cake. He, of course, refused with his usual elegance. We had no time, he said. And she laughed and said it was an open invitation."

Yet there must have been invitations which Eli accepted. Several times in that year 1658 – in the little lull between hay-making and harvest – he was late for, and once actually absent from, supper. He made his gruff excuses not to me, but to his mother. Mrs Cauldwell's cow or her horses were ailing, and her man was quite useless where animals were concerned. Or she needed a letter written or advice on this and that. 'A lone woman,' he once called her. It was interesting to see that with the word 'hussy' a breach had opened which widened steadily as the summer progressed. The Smiths were no longer in full accord.

Katharine and I were far more concerned with what was happening in the outer world. That year it really seemed that the Restoration, in which she at least had never lost faith, was about to happen. Cromwell, in poor health himself, had spent a fortnight by the bedside of his favourite daughter, who had died earlier in the year, taking with her, it seemed, her father's will to live. In September he followed her to the grave.

He had refused the Crown of England, but had taken to himself the privilege of naming his son as his heir.

"He'll last about a month," Katharine said. "Even his friends call him Tumbledown Dick. The King will be home by Christmas."

She set about making plans; she and Edman would go straight back to Brigstowe and if necessary live upon charity there until their rights to the estate were acknowledged. "There will naturally be some inquiries, but our papers are all in order."

One evening when we were milking, she was talking in this happy strain when a wave of bitterness swept over me and I said, "I hope it all goes as you plan, Kat. For myself no Restoration can make any difference. I shall still be married to Eli, and that makes him owner of Pargeters."

"I wonder. Believe me, I have given this some thought, too. After all, your brother died for his King, you merit some consideration. It was a marriage made under duress – Cynthia and I could testify to that. And the wedding was not properly conducted – no ceremony, no ring. Charles the Second will restore the Church of England and I think it quite possible that marriages such as yours will be treated as non-conformist marriages were before the war. Hedgerow weddings they were called, and they were not regarded as legal."*

"Then Dorcas would be a bastard. I wouldn't want that."

"Would it be worse than the future that awaits her if things stay as they are?" Katharine gave a little laugh. "I think you'll find that bastardy will become very fashionable." The Puritans, of course, had always made much of the Prince's womanising, as they called it. Attitudes towards bastardy were dependent upon class. Most kings and members of the aristocracy bred illegitimate children with impunity, and among the lowest classes a bastard was acceptable. It was the middle class who regarded the thing with horror.

That particular conversation was interrupted by the arrival of Edman, who from the first had taken on the job of carrying the yoke, a great relief to me, a milkmaid needs plump shoulders. With Edman came Dorcas, his faithful shadow. She was now nine and had her set tasks which she performed with something of John Adam's surly

* Well into the present century a marriage performed in a non-conformist place of worship was not regarded as legal unless a Registrar were present.

253

resignation, except when she was, in her own words, helping Edman. To begin with, of course, she was more hindrance than help, but his patience seemed limitless. When she was eight her father and grandmother decided that she was big enough to carry a full bucket of milk, or water, or pig-swill. This worried me, I feared the strain, and the possibility of her growing crooked. Then Edman came home from market one day with a small pail made of tin, far lighter than a wooden bucket. He explained airily that he had earned it by keeping an eye on the tinker's stall while the man went to the horse market. Armed with that, she really felt that she was helping Edman, but, since Mrs Smith, to her credit, was very particular about any utensil used for dairy work being used for that purpose alone, it did not solve the problem of water and swill-carrying. Edman, however, usually managed to forestall Dorcas, or go to her aid saying, "You help me, so I must help you."

The Restoration did not come that year. Richard Cromwell, however reluctantly and ineptly, took his father's place so far as civil affairs were concerned; to the Army he meant nothing, being openly averse to bloodshed. Soldiers regarded General Monk as the inheritor of Cromwell's mantle. Katharine never lost hope or faith.

In the spring of the next year, 1659, I was taken ill in the night. I woke with a jerk, feeling terribly sick. I dared not wait to make a light. I thought I could feel my way to the washstand under which stood the slop pail – after all, I had shared this room with Eli for more than ten years. But the floor came up and hit me and I vomited where I lay. I was still sensible enough to feel distress at the mess I was making. I thought, I must get up very early and very quietly, in order to clear up and not be humiliated in Eli's eyes.

But this was no ordinary attack; I went on retching and heaving long after my stomach was empty. I was never a bilious subject and the food that day had been particularly spartan, barley broth without meat for dinner and bread and hard cheese for supper.

The idea of being pregnant again shot through my mind, but that had not been so gut-ripping as this. Nor so weakening. I had fallen quite near the bed, I could reach the post with my hand, but had not the strength to grip. So I abandoned all hope of heaving myself up. It was cold on the floor and a shivering fit took me; but that passed and presently the only physical thing of which I was conscious was a tingling in my fingers and toes, the sensation one calls pins-and-needles.

I remained conscious, however, thinking thoughts which would have been morbid except that I felt so peaceful. What dire disease began with extreme nausea and then proceeded to lack of all strength? I could think of none. And suppose I died here. My poor Dorcas! Not that I had ever been much use to her; the slightest sign of affection between us was regarded as pampering. Katharine, I knew, would do her best for my child, as I had done my best for hers, but what power would Katharine have? If this long-deferred Restoration actually came Katharine would go back to Brigstowe, and by that time Dorcas would have some value as a drudge. Eli would certainly marry again and stepmothers were notorious.

And Grandfather, part of what I now saw as a fatal bargain. He'd simply die of neglect. Marian would be tolerated so long as she was useful. Harry would be cast out.

At last the cock crowed, the pre-dawn call which country-bred people ignored. Then grey light showed at the window and the cock crowed again. Eli stirred.

I managed to say in little better than a whisper, "I'm here. On the floor."

"What happened?"

"I felt sick and tried to get to the washstand. And fell down."

He ran his hands over me then, assured that nothing was broken, lifted me into the bed, on the side still warm from his body. Then he dressed hastily and said, "I'll send my mother." Not the person I wished to see at the moment. I said, "Katharine, please."

"She'll be milking."

So Mrs Smith came, bringing no word of sympathy but all her energy and thoroughness. Without actually saying so, she managed to imply that the accident and the resultant mess was something I had wantonly devised in order to make work for her. As a final gesture she flung the window wide. "This room smells foul." A cutting wind, straight from the East blew in. I cowered under the bedclothes and slithered away into something that was not quite sleep.

From it I was roused by Katharine, all concern and sympathy but making no display. She put her knuckled hand to my neck, held it there, waited and said, "No fever. In fact you are cold." She closed the window. "Do you feel like talking?"

"To you, yes." She found my dressing gown, put an extra pillow behind me, raised me a little and wrapped the old garment around my shoulders. "Tell me what happened." She was more experienced than I in the number of illnesses which did show themselves first in an attack of nausea. It was a longish list, including one particular form of stomachache. None seemed to fit my case. I had no fever, my bones didn't ache. "Kat, I have no bones. Just a tingling in my fingers and toes." She said she had never heard of that as a prelude to any ailment. She made me take half a beaker of water, heavily salted. "The best known emetic," she said. I gave a weak laugh and said, "The last thing I need." She said that something of what had caused the upset could be lingering and would be better brought up. But no nausea followed, so, having helped me into a clean shift, she went down and presently brought me a bowl of bread and milk. "As healing to the stomach as a bread plaster to a wound." I ate, but languidly, enjoying the warmth rather than the substance. Watching me, Katharine said, "That little room adjoining mine. If you could move into it, I could look after you in the night. And we could *talk*."

Nobody who has not been deprived of it could understand what a luxury casual talk can be. All through the years of Eli's dominion mere chatter had been frowned upon and since Edman had come home any words exchanged between Katharine and me had been regarded as plain proof of conspiracy. So only when we were milking had we been able to talk.

"They'd never allow it," I said.

"Actually, I think they would. Eli Smith is terrified of infection and I think Mrs Smith is, too. You will believe that I have said nothing to allay their fears!"

Soon after midday Katharine came to move me into a small room with a freshly-made, brick-heated bed. The room had two doors, one opening into Katharine's own room and one on to the landing towards the rear of the house. Katharine had practically to carry me there, I was so weak. There was no great distance between the rooms for Pargeters was a compact house. As Katharine, unexpectedly strong, hauled me along she told me that both Eli and his mother had welcomed my banishment from the conjugal bed. "They pounced on my suggestion," she said. "The only time I have ever said a word that has been heeded. And it is true, isn't it, to say I don't know what ails you."

Moving about, in the house which Grandfather had built and possibly planned, had reminded me of his existence. I said, "Grandfather! Who is seeing to him?"

"I am. Helped by Dorcas and Edman. Don't worry, Sarah. You have no strength to spare."

So I sank into lethargy and slept until roused by the sound of human voices. I orientated myself and realised that in this small room I was almost exactly over half of the kitchen. But the sounds reaching me were distorted; I vaguely imagined Eli chiding God his neighbour for rendering me useless. But Eli's communications with his unreliable neighbour were monologic; this was not. It was a medley; several voices.

I remembered that at some time during this very curious day, during which nothing had conformed to any known pattern, I had just managed to say, "Keep Dorcas away." And Katharine had agreed. She herself during those two years at Brigstowe had been exposed to every contagion or infection known and regarded herself as immune, but she agreed that Dorcas and Edman should hold aloof. "Because," she said, "we don't yet know, do we?"

Yet my first nocturnal visitor was my daughter. My Dorcas. My beloved. But seldom have a woman and her child lived in such propinquity with less show of affection. I had done my best, but what a poor best. I had never really provided for her, once she was weaned, nor properly protected her. She had not suffered from actual ill-treatment, which might have inspired me to retaliatory action (I like to think that even in my reduced state, I should at least have done that); but I had handed her over, a living hostage to my policy of peace at any price, let's not make bad worse.

She was carrying a candle in one hand and in the other a small pottery jar containing a few primroses. She said, "Aunt Kat and everybody said I was to keep away, but I had to see for myself." She set the candlestick and the flowers on the chest by the bed. "Mother, please don't die."

On the last words her voice broke, betraying her usual precocious, unchildlike control, due not to lack of feeling but to having been reared in a household where any display of emotion was sternly disapproved of.

"I'm not dying," I said lightly. "I had a bilious attack in the night. I shall be perfectly well in the morning."

"But they all said . . ." She burst into tears and threw herself upon me, hugging me, kissing me and speaking between sobs. "I just couldn't bear it. Mother, I couldn't. Left alone with . . . them. If you've got something dangerous – Aunt Kat said it *might* be – let me catch it and die too."

I did my best to soothe her, holding her close, administering little pats and speaking comforting words. Amongst the things I said was something I wished I could believe. "In any case, darling, you would never be left here with *them*. Aunt Kat would see to that." Dorcas stiffened.

"Aunt Kat and Edman are leaving tomorrow."

"What?"

"There was a most terrible quarrel. Edman said Mr

Smith had worked you to death and would do the same with Aunt Kat unless he got her away at once. And Aunt Kat said she wouldn't leave you, especially now when you were so ill. And Mr Smith said a lot about black ingratitude and harbouring beggars. And Aunt Kat got angry too and said that she'd always earned her keep and more. And she wanted an egg."

"An egg?" Of all the bathos!

"It was for *you*. So then Mrs Smith said that if you were as ill as Aunt Kat pretended it would be a waste of an egg and if you were idling you shouldn't be encouraged. And Aunt Kat said . . ."

"That you were to keep well away from this room," said Katharine's voice from the doorway. She spoke quite sternly. I gave Dorcas a last convulsive hug and said, "Run along, darling. Thank you for the posy. And don't worry. It'll take more than this to kill me." I saw Katharine cross herself. Dorcas took her candle and slipped away.

"If she has been worrying you about us leaving," Katharine said, setting down her own candle and testing me again for signs of fever, "dismiss it from your mind. I only said it to cause a distraction. I live in dread of Mr Smith and Edman coming to blows. I have no doubt that Edman would give a good account of himself, but Mr Smith would fell him – and take pleasure in doing it. But I hope you know that I'd never willingly leave you. How do you feel?"

"Quite well. Just weak and with pins and needles still. I shall be quite all right tomorrow."

"Let's hope so. But you have no reserve. I didn't fully realise how thin you are. And this is the best I could do." She offered me a slice of dark bread and a wedge of hard cheese. "With eggs at a farthing each," she said in a tone of disgust. "And a dairy full of milk! I wanted to bring you an egg whisked in milk."

When I had choked down the unappetising fare, Katharine undressed, the candle she had carried set in the communicating doorway and dimly lighting both rooms. Then we went through the process of, in her own words, making me comfortable for the night, a service I should have found hard to accept from anyone of whom I was less fond. After that we talked, ranging from subject to subject but always reverting to the political situation and the eventual Restoration. Finally she went to bed, leaving me with a clean slop pail within reach and telling me to call her if I felt even slightly indisposed.

I was almost asleep when the door to the landing opened, there was a streak of light and some movement, almost soundless. "Are you awake?" It was Marian's voice. I said, "Yes," and she came in, candlestick in one hand and a flattish basket in the other. In the basket lay a pork pie, a perfect miniature of those made for market, but in four sections and a slice of that solid orange preserve which was special invalid diet. Also, wrapped in a towel to keep it upright, a glass of what looked like froth.

"The swizzled egg Mrs Bowen was wanting for you, Mistress. And you must eat this too. The pie is for the Old Gentleman."

"I've often wondered," I said. "Marian, how do you manage it?"

She grinned; "If the years don't make you crafty where's the use in getting old? I been doing this for years."

She handed me the glass and the orange preserve and then from under the towel, produced a stub of candle which she lighted from her own. "I'll pick up the crocks on my way back," she said, and moved away, silent as a ghost. Grandfather's room was much nearer to that used until today by Eli and me, and to the one occupied by Mrs Smith. The thought made me sweat slightly until I remembered how very valuable Marian with her various skills now was. The same applied, surely, to Katharine and Edman and myself, yet the Smiths had in them a kind of perversity and such faith in their God that they could all too easily indulge in the luxury of cutting off their noses to spite their faces. However Marian came back, collected the glass and the plate, wished me good night and blew out my bit of candle.

Next day I had no fever, no signs of rash or of swellings anywhere, so although Katharine begged me to spend another day in bed I got up and worked much as usual, though slowly and feebly. One of Mrs Smith's over-used expressions was 'elbow grease'. What she meant was her own method of working, attacking inanimate objects as though they were personal enemies. She was constantly urging me to put more elbow grease into such and such a task. That day I had none, and it was typical of the Smiths that they should regard me on Tuesday as a dangerous source of contagion and on Wednesday as capable of work as usual.

Should I, I wondered, be expected to return to Eli's bed? But nothing was said and as soon as Eli had ended his conversation with God I slipped away to the luxury of a room of my own.

Katharine was exuberant that evening for the Newsletter which Edman had brought back from market had reported divisions in Parliament more serious than usual. So virulent that violence threatened and Richard Cromwell had said that sooner than see one drop of blood shed he would resign.

"So it can't be long now," Katharine said once again. "We have only to hold on."

So we held on. I never quite recovered my full strength, and something had happened to my hair; it grew lifeless looking, like a cheap wig, and it came out in handfuls. I could well understand Eli not wishing me as a partner in the exercise of his never very amorous conjugal rights.

Five or six weeks later I had another attack, more severe than the first, but less miserable because the slop-pail was handy and Katharine came as soon as I whimpered. And I was not lying on the floor in the cold night.

She fetched the salt emetic, but it was again ineffectual. After a time she sat on the side of my bed and said, "Sarah, I have no wish to upset you, but has it ever occurred to you that you may be being poisoned?"

When I could speak, I said: "But why? Who would benefit from my death?"

"Eli Smith." In the early days of my marriage she had most scrupulously refrained from saying anything derogatory about Eli, but his behaviour, and my attitude towards him, had changed that. She hurried on, "He must know, as we do, that the Restoration is very near now. And Pargeters belongs to you."

"And we all know that, unless special safeguards are made, a wife's property becomes her husband's."

"After a properly solemnised marriage. Which yours was *not*. I've said this before. And if you, because of Dorcas, wouldn't ask for your freedom, I damned well would. For how could I be happy at Brigstowe with you here in this miserable servitude? As for Dorcas being illegitimate, at Brigstowe who would know? I'd say she was a relative. And she's so pretty and old for her age, she could be married at fourteen." Suddenly almost bashful, quite out of character, Katharine looked down and began pleating the bedcover between her fingers. "I never made a song and dance about family connections but once back at Brigstowe I shall be . . . well, rather important."

I understood her reticence. She was fond of me and in a way I had been her benefactor, but my father was a "mere plasterer" and my grandfather a merchant.

I said, "In my more morbid moments, Kat, I have hoped you'd take Dorcas. But would they allow it? She is getting useful now."

"We'll deal with that when we come to it. I wish I knew more about poisons. They say that for every one there is an antidote."

Suddenly the blanketing dullness of the brain which sheer physical toil can impose, lifted. I said, "Kat, there might be. In Dorcas's room, in the closet on a high shelf. Stuff that belonged to Lady Alice."

She stole away, another soft-footed night prowler and was soon back bringing with her a bottle of brandy, all shrouded with cobwebs and furry with dust. "*This* is all there was on that shelf. And how glad I was to see it. Just what you need."

I refused to drink alone, so we shared the glass in which she had brought the salt water and grew rather tipsy. I was inclined to discount the possibility of Eli trying to kill me. It sounded far-fetched and I couldn't see what opportunity he had ever had. He had nothing to do with the preparation of the food and very little to do with the serving of it – except for the bread which always stood on a wooden trencher at his end of the table. But to poison one slice and leave the others uncontaminated seemed to me to call for a sleight of hand he was unlikely to possess. Also, although his religion was so repulsive to me I did not think that he, or his mother, would deliberately break a commandment. Katharine and I often made wry jokes about Eli's close connection with Sinai but there was no denying that the laws of conduct, said to have been handed down from there, were fundamentally sound, and Eli obeyed them. The blackmail he levied, the ruthless exploitation of everybody at Pargeters were things Eli's Jehovah would not condemn.

I put this point to Katharine and she said that Puritans could always justify themselves in their own eyes, which were synoptic with their God's.

I said, "Well, obviously no precautions can be taken, if it really is poison. What worries me more is the thought of two truly lethal pills lying about somewhere in this house. Who could possibly have taken them?"

"What pills? And how do you know they are lethal?"

Suddenly I heard myself telling her the whole story, the story I had never told, never meant to tell to a living soul. I ended, "I took only two pills and the gaoler said Lady Alice died instantaneously. Two were left . . . and where are they?"

"Not being used on you, that is certain. Yours is being made to look like a natural illness."

"And it may be, Kat. Maybe I am having what they call an early change."

I'd always been too busy to give much regard to the female link with the moon, mysterious, infuriating and unreliable. A girl could become nubile at eleven, and some women could still be capable of child-bearing at forty. But these were extreme examples.

Eventually we talked ourselves back to the possibility of Eli attempting to poison me, and the need for vigilance. It was true that nobody saw him cut the bread; our attention was focused on Mrs Smith, doling out the regulated portions; it was also true that Eli never passed the trencher around; he cut a slice, speared it on the point of the knife and handed it to the recipient. "He only needs two fingers well impregnated with poison, held aloof from the other slices and well rubbed on yours. I could do it myself, unhandy as I am," Katharine said.

"Then I'm doomed," I said, with a curious detachment for which perhaps the brandy was partly responsible. "And honestly, Katharine, if I could be sure that Dorcas was safe with you I'd be glad to die."

To my astonishment Katharine began to cry. "Don't say that. Don't even *think* it! Sarah, after all you have done, all you have borne, if you don't see the Restoration and somehow, *somehow* get Pargeters back, I shall lose faith in God."

"We're both maudlin," I said.

Next day I was even weaker than after the former attack. My bones were jelly; the tingling in my extremities was worse than before. But this time I was not suspected of being a dangerous carrier of pestilence and Mrs Smith herself brought me something to eat at midday, a slice of bread and a wedge of hard cheese. She said a few harsh, bracing words; lolling in bed was a weakening process; I was making a great fuss about nothing; I must pull myself together. I must realise that lazing here in bed I was casting a burden on everybody else in the place.

I ate the cheese but not the bread. I thought, for perhaps the hundredth time, about Katharine's theory and one thing stood out – almost, but not quite irrelevant. Eli no longer washed his hands before meals, nor had done for some time. In fact, over the years, by almost imperceptible stages, he had shed that thin veneer of civility which he had acquired during the war. Even his speech had coarsened.

Next day I struggled into my clothes and weakly tried to resume work, though Katharine argued against it, saying I looked ghastly. Our efforts to be vigilant where bread was concerned were futile and indeed rather comic if looked at impersonally.

"Change with me, Sarah; I like crust." Bearing in mind what she suspected, I thought it was brave of her and made the exchange with reluctance. That time she ate it – as an experiment, she said; and suffered no harm. But that proved nothing and it was not an experiment that could be repeated very often since we ate bread always twice, sometimes three times a day.

Spring, starting tardily that year, ushered in summer with a rush and there came a Tuesday when most of us, apart from our routine jobs, were cutting asparagus and lettuces and gathering strawberries.

And that day a pig died, a really valuable boar, worth as breeding stock at least four pounds, and as meat, because so heavy, almost three.

Eli was lamenting all through supper saying that he'd heard of no swine fever or other pig disease in the area. "Have you?" he demanded of Edman, who was so much more in touch with the outer world.

"Not a case, sir." Edman said, adding maliciously, "And nobody could say your pigs were ill-fed."

Eli glared, ate a couple of mouthfuls and said: "Added to which, I *know* about pigs and their ailments. That boar was all right this morning."

Suddenly the unprecedented happened. Marian spoke, at table, without being addressed, and in view of what pre-occupied Katharine and me her words had a curious ring.

"Poisoned, most like."

"Who'd want to poison a pig, woman?"

"You bin poisoning rats. Rats run about. One could've dropped a bit of poisoned bait."

Eli considered this and said, "I suppose that could happen."

And at that moment there came into my mind a suspicion amounting to certainty of who could have poisoned – not the pig, whose demise was probably coincidental – but me. Who, in this household, might not want to kill me but disliked me so much that to cause me pain and sickness would be a source of pleasure? And the answer came back: Mrs Smith. Eli's mother would not wish me dead, for then

265

he would be free to marry Liz Cauldwell, whom she probably hated worse than me. The fact that I had not had a third attack might be because the first two had weakened me to an extent that my capacity for work had suffered. So I was probably safe henceforth. I found a grim humour in the thought, but Katharine would be angry for me.

Marian was speaking again.

"Whaddyou gonna do with that pig?" I had known Marian all my life and recognised the faint challenge. Eli did not, and said in the most matter-of-fact way, "Send it to the butcher, of course."

Most pigs that went to the butcher's shambles walked there because they had been reared by cottagers or small-holders who owned no wagons. A few were slaughtered where they were bred and sent in by wagon – a dead carcass being more easily handled than a squealing, resisting animal. But there was an unwritten law, firmer and older than any Parliament could enact, that such pigs must be healthy, and dead because their throats had been slit. A pig dead from natural causes was suspect, and pig diseases were known to be most contagious, some even affecting human beings.

"A pig that could be poisoned?" Marian asked quite quietly, "and could poison anybody that ett it?"

"There is nothing to prove that the beast was poisoned. Just a fancy bred in your maggotty brain. So shut your mouth."

"*All right!*" Marian said less mildly. "If you don't bury that pig, you and me's through. And don't talk to me about the workhouse. I shall hev an almshouse. And I shall take the Poor Old Gentleman with me, so you can't take it out on him. And believe me, I'll let everybody know just what happened. I'll blacken your name for you."

She was using precisely the same weapon as I had used against Sir Walter and his friend. But she carried more weight. Her pies, her cakes, her cordials contributed largely to the success of the stall.

Then – and not for the first time, Eli showed what I can only describe as the shallowness of his mind. He ignored the main issue, the pig, and settled for a jibe. "And how will you get to Baildon? D'you expect me to lend you the cart?"

"I'm not that much of a fool, but let me tell you, I got friends. I only got to flick a finger and by midday tomorrow a carriage'd be here for me."

It sounded an absurd boast from an old woman who had for so long been cut off from the world and whose friends, when she had them, were of the humblest kind, yet she said the words with such assurance that disbelief wavered. I was not even certain that she had ever seen a carriage, yet I found myself thinking that just possibly somebody, realising what a superb cook she was, had sent her a message, by Edman. And Edman was going to market tomorrow! It made sense. I glanced at Edman, but his face was blank.

Then Old Harry began to cry and scrabble at Marian's sleeve. "Take me, Marian. Please, take me too. Tell 'em I don't look handy, but I can potter for hours." And that was true. He was bent and twisted and his hands with their swollen knuckles were useless for small jobs, but he could dig, prune, and spread dung and do a dozen other things, slowly but efficiently. At table he never spoke, had until this moment been a nonentity.

Marian said, "We'll see about that Harry, when the time comes."

Perhaps any belief, held strongly enough, can be as catching as measles. Affected by it, Eli was torn between rage and cupidity. He looked at Marian with sheer hatred but he said, "We'll bury the thing after prayers."

The neighbour-over-the-fence had a lambasting that evening. His faithful servant, already much burdened and sore beset, had now been stabbed in the back by a traitor, by one to whom nothing but kindness and charity had been shown. A Judas at Job's very table. Naturally Eli allowed that his God knew best, but His faithful servant had been sorely tried already and now for this to happen! However he was certain that he would be granted the patience and fortitude . . .

It was almost comic. So small a sum was involved – always assuming that the butcher adhered to the rules. Even

267

if Eli cut the dead boar's throat no blood would flow and the carcass would be suspect; a nervous or conscientious butcher might very well say, "Take it away." But it was a long time since I had dealt directly with butchers and conditions could have changed.

Wednesday was a beautiful morning, just right for hay-cutting and for sheep-shearing which so often coincided and demanded extra, hired labour. Not at Pargeters! On that morning with the cuckoo still loud but beginning to stammer in Layer Wood, and the whole of the house so sweetly as almost to be sickly scented by Marian's strawberry cordial, Katharine and I were moving hay. Eli was at Brook. He was an expert shearer and Dorcas was now a competent tar boy. Mrs Smith was taking advantage of the near emptiness of the dairy to do a bit of limewashing. She had a belief in whitewash as a preventive of mould.

Because the hayfield was so near the house it had not seemed worth while for me and Katharine to take a bag dinner, so we were there in the kitchen, eating the inevitable bread and cheese and – let's be honest – deliberately postponing our return to the field. I said to Marian who was straining the next batch through the muslin: "Marian, why were you so firm about that pig last night? You always said you dreaded the almshouse."

"I still do. But when I was a tiddler, in the workhouse, I seen what bad meat can do. People died like flies and not a nice way to die either. Besides, the poor Old Master . . ." She never finished that sentence, for Dorcas appeared in the kitchen door way and said, "Mr Smith is dead."

It was surprise which held us all so silent that from the dairy the regular slap, slap of the whitewash brush was audible. At last I said, remembering that she had never seen a dead person, "How do you know?"

"I went down to the house and Mrs Cauldwell came out, with both her servants. They all said so. And took him on a hurdle into the house."

My first feeling was of liberation. I had not lost a husband, but a taskmaster. I felt like a slave who had been manumitted. Eli had been hard-working and God-fearing, but these were not grief-provoking qualities. I looked at Dorcas, standing on the threshold, utterly calm and despite the heat of the day and the distance she had come, quite cool. In a child not yet ten, who had not been trained from babyhood to show no feeling, I might have attributed the rigidity to a state of shock. Not grief; I don't think she had ever used the word 'father'. In his presence she hardly ever spoke and out of it used the 'Mr Smith' which Katharine and I had adopted in a subtly derisory manner.

Now even in the half second while I wondered about the effect of so sudden a death on so unprepared a mind, she moved. Slowly, deliberately, she removed the bit of rag from the end of her plait and shook her hair free; the transformation was instant. She then divested herself of the smocklike garment, smeared with tar and a few bloodstains.

Katharine had not spoken. She shot out her workworn hand and took me by the wrist in a steadying, eloquent grasp. She shared my feelings – whatever they might be. I heard the whitewash brush again and said: "She must be told."

She had lived at Pargeters for hard on ten years and never once done or said a thing to endear herself to me; she had made a hard life worse by constant nagging and criticism; she had, quite possibly, administered rat-poison to me; yet now I thought: He is her son; how should I feel if somebody came and told me that Dorcas was dead? Ill news should be broken gently, but how can any gentleness soften such a blow?

She saw me and attacked at once. "I *thought* I heard chatter! I was coming when I reached that corner. Thass always the same as soon as I take my eye off you. Just because I came straight back to work you and her think you can loll about for an hour."

In order to reach the ceiling she stood on the third or fourth rung of a short ladder.

"Mrs Smith, you had better come down. I have something very serious to tell you."

The fact that I answered back must have impressed her,

for she did step down. In an ordinary place I'd have said sit down but although there were many jobs which could be done sitting down, no seat, not even a milking stool was allowed in our dairy.

"Eli is dead," I said and wished, actually wished, that I could say I was sorry, but the words would not come. The whitewash brush dropped, with a squelch, to the floor. Her always sallow face turned grey. She looked stunned but she managed to say: "Where?"

"At Brook."

She pushed past me and went out just as she was, wearing a head rag which protected her white cap from the whitewash and an old smock almost stiff with the stuff.

I went back into the kitchen thinking woodenly: The hay still matters, and then being ashamed of the thought and then wondering, Why be ashamed? Dorcas had moved and Katharine had her arm around her, speaking generalities, meant to be comforting though Katharine knew as well as I did that no comfort was needed. But there was a conventional streak in Katharine. I heard her say, "Happens to everybody, Dorcas, dear. But being so sudden, it must have given you a shock."

Marian said, "We've *all* had a jolt. Come here, dearie." She whispered in Dorcas's ear and Dorcas, her hair bouncing, set out for the back stairs.

Katharine said, "There is still the hay."

"Wait," Marian said. "Like I just said, we've all had a jolt and I know the remedy. Get your weight off your feet and just wait." And in a matter of minutes Dorcas was back, bringing a bottle of Marian's most-sought-after cordial, the blackberry. Even if it were of the latest brew – and who could tell how far back Marian's secret hoards extended? – it must now be almost ten months old, and no wonder the people who scorned beer and wine bought it readily! I found myself able to say, "Darling, could you tell us exactly what happened?"

"Oh yes . . . We worked and it was hot. So he said we might as well eat our noon-piece while there was a bit of shade. So we did, under those trees. You know. He ate very quickly and jumped up and said to me come on then and then he sort of stumbled and spun round and fell down. And was dead."

Marian said, with no sign of repentance, "It could've been my doing. I made him angry last night. Now an ordinary man, given to cussing and swearing'd work it off, but with him it turned innards and brung on a stroke." (Up to a point she was foretelling general opinion; Eli had brought on a stroke by overworking in the heat of midday. And he was inviting disaster by having for help just a child, being too close-fisted to hire a man.)

We drank Marian's heartening brew and the work habit being strong, returned to the mowing until it was milking time. Dorcas came with us, making haycocks, so we did not talk much until we were milking and I had sent Dorcas into the garden to tell Harry to gather any pea-pod which showed signs of having a pea in it, and herself to pick all the strawberries which had ripened during the day. It felt very strange to be giving orders again. And such orders! The peas would be at their best by next market day and the strawberries, when fully ripe, converted into cordial.

In the milking-shed I gave voice to a thought which had been with me ever since Dorcas made her announcement.

I said, "Kat, has it struck you that poison has figured rather largely in our lives lately? You thought I was being poisoned, Marian was sure the pig had been. What about Eli?"

"I might share your suspicion, except that each case is so dissimilar. You were ill, dear, with many symptoms which were indicative of arsenic. The pig wasn't ill; it just died; and where Eli is concerned I think Marian wasn't far out, I mean about the stroke. How old was he?"

"I don't know. He was about in his mid-twenties when he came to work for my father, and I started going round with Father when I was very young. He'd be well over fifty."

"An age when many men have strokes, whether or not a servant has annoyed them." She was prepared to close the subject on this note of amusement, but for some reason my mind would not be diverted. I kept thinking of that little container marked 'Lethal' and the two pills it had still held when I placed it, with the other contents of Lady Alice's pretty bag, on that high shelf. Everything else from that shelf had vanished, except the brandy. And ours was not – or at least was no longer – the kind of household in which, every spring a great cleaning and throwing out of unwanted objects took place. Nobody had time or energy for such rituals.

I said to myself: This is sheer nonsense and in any case what does it matter? And I was immediately struck by the memory of what the gaoler had said at the inquiry into Lady Alice's death; he'd said 'a sort of convulsion' and she had mentioned the dog. Dorcas had said Eli had stumbled and spun round before falling down.

Before the milking was finished I knew why the manner of Eli's death mattered. Suppose there were an inquest? The incumbent of a parish had only to refuse to bury a corpse and an inquest was inevitable. How should I, the only person to benefit from the death, stand in the eyes of the Coroner?

Not well!

A Coroner had the right – indeed the duty – to pry. Nobody in my household would betray me wittingly, that I knew with the utmost certainty, but something might be let slip. And although the near isolation of our lives had precluded ordinary gossip, there had been talk. Edman had said so that market day and I had always suspected that his brawling had been connected with Pargeters.

Eli and I had been married for eleven years and had one child, now almost ten, and no more. In fact we no longer shared a bed. Damning evidence of estrangement; of an unsatisfactory marriage, at a time and in a community where a so-called happy marriage between apparently heal-thy couples produced a child, or at worst a miscarriage, every two years.

Milking away as though in a trance I could imagine with what gleeful spite Mrs Smith would condemn me and how political feeling would seep in. I was, being John's sister, a Malignant, Pargeters had been sequestrated and I had married Eli to keep a roof over my head. And that there was no denying.

We heard the cart rattle into the yard, and in less than a minute Edman was at the door of the milking shed, ready to shoulder the yoke.

I said, "Edman, Eli died today."

He was not much practised in hiding his feelings and his face lit up, as though he had just been given an unexpected but most welcome present. Then he had control again and said, "Aunt Sarah, it would be humbug for me to say that I am sorry. If . . . if his death has caused you the slightest grief, then I am sorry. For you."

"You need not be," I said.

"Is there anything I can do? Where . . . Where is he?"

"In the house at Brook. He died there, he just fell dead in the sheep–run and Mrs Cauldwell's servants carried him in."

"I could take the wagon and fetch . . ."

"Mrs Smith went there straight away," Katharine said. "We shall know more when she comes back. Meanwhile, there is the milk."

All laden we set out towards the kitchen and out from the door Dorcas flew. Flew. It must have been the loose streaming hair, the way her feet in their clumsy shoes seemed not to touch the ground that gave that illusion, for her ugly, skimpy dress had no lines to flow. Ignoring Katharine and me she flung herself at Edman. "Oh, you know. I wanted to tell you. He's dead. Dead!"

Edman said, as though to a restive horse, "Steady! Steady!" He heaved the yoke from his shoulders and set the two buckets safely and then he took Dorcas by her narrow waist and, holding her high, twirled around as in a barn-dance jig. Then he tossed her in the air and caught her again while she laughed and made incoherent sounds of childish merriment such as had not been heard at Pargeters since Eli quelled John Adam.

Katharine and I looked at each other and she said,

"They're young." Then Edman proved himself not so young. He set Dorcas down and said, "We know how we *feel*, but the decencies must be observed. Start unloading the cart."

Inside the house no decencies were observed. Marian, making use of what was available had made a cheese cake – a shell of the finest pastry holding a mixture of eggs and grated cheese, and topped by a covering of more cheese, at least an inch thick, brown and crunchy.

She said, "It'd be nice if the Old Master was brought down to share it."

So I fetched him down, and though he seemed more confused than usual and peered from face to face as though desperately seeking one he recognised, he enjoyed the first appetising hot meal he had had since Eli took charge. And then something about the peas made a cog in his mind engage.

"Green," he said. "Green! The most important colour. Any green cures scurvy. Mind you, I never suffered from it myself. My voyages were short, but I've seen ships come in from far places and I've heard sea-faring men talk. They'll eat grass if nothing else offers. And there is some kind of seaweed . . ." He swallowed his peas and lifted his glass of cordial, holding it between him and what remained of the light. "Very good," he said, "very good, but imitation. You can't deceive *me*! No wine that ever came out of Oporto was quite so dark."

We ate strawberries, this evening with cream, a luxury long denied us. Grandfather fell into one of his senile dozes and the rest of us just exchanged casual talk, nothing momentous, simply saying whatever occurred to us without risking a scowl or a rebuke.

Marian said, "You'll be needing a man now Miss Sarah and I happen to know that Jake Adams is free. He's a good man."

Even Harry broke silence. "I remember him. Didn't hit it off with his stepfather and went to sea. Some time back that was."

"As I hear it," Marian said, "he had bad luck. Wrecked or

something and he was fond of his mother so he come home and she's dead. So he'd live in."

"I'll get him in the morning, if he's still free," I said. I thought of the hay still standing, and of the shearing only just begun. I should need more than one man. Katharine should never swing a scythe again, nor would I. If things went well. The dark thought that had come to me as I milked returned, only slightly mitigated by good food, blackberry cordial and common sense.

"Marian, what was in the bag dinners today?"

"Bread and cheese, the same as always."

"And who got it ready?"

"She did."

I knew I was being absurd, building up a mythical case against myself largely because I knew that two lethal pills had been lost. How could a Coroner or even a doctor detect so unusual a poison? Eli had not been sick or, so far as we knew, turned a peculiar colour or been struck stiff. I was being morbid, partly from guilt – I had so often wished him dead; and partly because I recognised that faint resemblance between his death and that of Lady Alice.

Along the table Edman was recounting something he had seen on the Market Place that day, Dorcas was laughing, Katharine was smiling. And Mrs Smith walked in. She had got rid of the head-rag and the whitewashed smock, but she still looked grey and her expression was stricken until it changed to disgust at the sight of the table.

She carried in her hand the strap of keys which I still thought of as Father's. With the undue force that she used towards the most harmless of inanimate things, she clashed them on to the table beside my plate. Then she said, rather like a child repeating a difficult lesson: "I was too late. Liz Cauldwell had sent for the Nettleton minister and the carpenter; everything was arranged." The combination of minister and carpenter meant a funeral, not an inquest and my ridiculous anxiety was relieved. Then I felt another twinge of sympathy for Mrs Smith whom Mrs Cauldwell had forestalled. Eli and his mother had never bickered in public but I knew that Mrs Smith detested the woman and that Eli did not share that feeling. What story, what ancient grudge lay behind the hatred and the tolerance, I did not know; should probably never know. On her way to the door between kitchen and lobby Mrs Smith said, "He'll be buried from Brook. And maybe that is fitting. She was fond of him – once."

In the unaccustomed and extravagant light of three candles, Katharine and I surveyed Eli's hoard.

"Quite unbelievable," she said. "Only just short of a thousand pounds."

I thought of Father who had owned Pargeters, Nine Elms and Brook and left unexpectedly little. Eli had left unexpectedly much. I said, bitterly: "Think of the cost. The lost childhoods of John Adam and Dorcas. Edman old before his time. You and I . . ."

"We shall recover," Katharine said briskly. "And this will help." She indicated the money, gave me a brief, hard hug. "I'm so happy for you, Sarah. You deserve every penny. And the Restoration really can't be far away, now. General Monck is changing sides."

"How can you possibly say that?"

"He's an Army man; but he has reminded the Army pretty sharply that Parliament is the governing body. See? The King could not accept the throne from a gang of rebels, could he? It must be offered – as it will be and in less than a year – by a properly elected Parliament."

We kept a hundred pounds out for immediate expenses and returned the rest to the yawning Trunk. As I did so I had a pang, certainly not grief but just a thought. Eli had been as hard on himself as on us; he'd worked as unsparingly and eaten the same unappetising food, though in larger quantities. Some of this money was undoubtedly his and he would never enjoy spending it. Rather sad, I thought and determined to deal generously with Mrs Smith.

The sad feeling lifted when I returned to the kitchen and found Marian, Old Harry, Edman and Dorcas deeply engaged in a game of Nobbin. Eli loathed playing cards, calling them the Devil's playthings. Marian, too had been reckless with candles and had set three alight, so that outside the window the last of the dusk looked darker than it actually was, so that the sound of a horse coming swiftly from the road to Muchanger, had more urgency than it would have had in broad daylight.

It was only Tom Markham; out of the saddle in a moment, hat in hand.

"I came the minute I heard," he said. And both his breathing and that of his horse gave evidence of hard riding.

"That was kind of you, Tom. Will you come in?"

"Better not. I can't stop. But is there anything, anything at all that I can do?"

"I don't think so, no. Everything is arranged. Even the funeral."

"What about money? I got plenty."

"I have enough. But I'm just as grateful."

"I wondered," he said and he sounded disappointed. I wondered how he knew about Eli. Even had he been to market that day nobody in Baildon knew, not even Edman in the hurly-burly of The Hawk in Hand's yard. But somehow Tom had heard and come, an up-to-date, prosaic version of a knight in ancient times riding to the rescue. I thought hard and said, "There is one thing, Tom . . . Eli did his own shearing. Do you know of a reliable gang not too busy to squeeze in a relatively small job?"

He was as pleased, as justified and fulfilled as though I had asked some great thing of him.

"I can send you three good steady men. Our own. You see, at the Park we run four thousand sheep and it's cheaper to hev shepherds who can shear. They'll be here about midday if I start 'em off early. Well, if you're sure thass all, I'll be going."

I thanked him again, fervently, and in the act of mounting – not, I noticed, the same horse as he had ridden that day at Baildon, but an equally splendid one – he made a sound half amusement, half exasperation. "I nearly forgot. At least I remembered. Back in the old days when you was tired or upset, you liked a little . . ." He pressed into my hands a bottle of brandy, faintly warm from the saddlebag.

In the morning Mrs Smith did not join us at breakfast, which was perhaps just as well, since Marian had fried eggs in butter, a poor makeshift in her view for real bacon fat. A whole side of bacon already figured on Edman's shopping list, a shameless document of greed until one remembered the three shearers now on their way from Flaxham.

On his way to Baildon Edman was to seek out Jake Adams at Muchanger and offer him employment. He must have set off at a run as soon as the words were out of Edman's mouth for within half an hour he was at Pargeters and a few minutes later on his way to the hayfield.

As soon as I had dismissed him I heard sounds of activity in the dairy. Mrs Smith was at work on the interrupted limewashing. I said, "Good morning," I hope not too brightly and she gave one of her grunts. I proceeded to skim yesterday's milk, feeling rather self-conscious about it; as though I were trying to match her in her 'Work Must Go On' behaviour. Presently I heard her step down from the ladder and was aware that she was beside me. She said, harsh and brusque as ever, "I want a word with you."

"I am listening."

"It'll suit me to be here for a day or two more, but I'll earn my keep. Then I'll go."

That statement added lustre to a day already bright, for during the night, sleepless despite good dosages of Tom's brandy, shared by Katharine, I had seen Mrs Smith as a problem, though not as a responsibility. The law, so unfair to women in many respects, struck a kind of balance by limiting their responsibility. I was under no legal obligation to support my mother-in-law. All I knew was that I did not want her at Pargeters where she had bullied us all, but Marian worst of all, and where her presence would be a constant reminder of all I wanted to forget. Another form of THOU GOD SEEST ME, hovering in the background.

Now, in the dairy I wondered briefly why Mrs Cauldwell who had once been fond of Eli and his mother who had adored him, did not set up house together but all I said was:

"But of course, you must do just as you wish. I think you should take your meals apart. I have three shearers and a hired man who'll be here for dinner."

"You see! He was a man in a thousand. Four men it's took to replace him. And you . . . you never realised his worth. To you he was always your father's hired man. You landed him with a load of useless mouths and you never pulled your weight."

She couldn't know, of course, but every word of this tirade was costing her money. Faced with Eli's hoard, part of which she had indisputably earned, I'd thought on extravagant lines, not merely just but generous. Two hundred and fifty pounds, perhaps even three hundred. Now, as she listed my faults my mind conducted its private Dutch Auction where prices ran down from the fantastic to the fairly reasonable and I thought: A hundred pounds and not a penny more; she enjoys being parsimonious, to give her too much would deprive her of some pleasure. "*And* you used to make mock of him behind his back. I seen you and heard you. If you'd been anything like a wife to my boy, Liz Cauldwell would never hev got such a hold . . ." Even in her anger she realised that she was verging on the indiscreet: she snapped off that talk just as it became interesting. And two thoughts came to me simultaneously. My baser nature said fifty pounds! You must think of Dorcas and all you hope to do for her. You are not really rich. Another voice in my mind reminded me that I had no cause now to stand here, like a rabbit before a ferret. I was my own woman again. I owned Pargeters.

I turned and walked away.

The kitchen was empty but there were noises from the dining-parlour. I went in. Since Eli's coming the room had not been used and now and again, amidst a myriad other hurts and therefore almost unnoticed, I'd recognised the fact that disused rooms became desolate. Rooms need people, as people need rooms.

Harry was cleaning the window, Katharine was polishing the table; Marian, just inside the door, was directing Dorcas in replacing the few things I had taken from this mantelshelf in my silly, futile effort to make the kitchen a little less like a kitchen.

"No, no," she said, "the other way round. But how could you know? Poor child, you weren't even born when this room was in its glory."

All values are relative; nothing at Pargeters had ever been glorious, Father was too opposed to ostentation; but perhaps to Marian it had seemed so.

Katharine said, "We wanted to surprise you."

"And surprised me you have. The room looks lovely. I admit I should not have thought of it."

So, in a way, the restoration of Pargeters forestalled by almost a year, the general Restoration for which, it now seemed, everybody in England was eagerly waiting. Even dedicated Puritans had been lulled by King Charles II's promise of freedom of worship; less dedicated ones were disillusioned because the Commonwealth had not proved to be the Heaven on Earth they had expected. The trading and professional classes, while admitting that on the whole the country was prosperous, resented the fact that taxes had kept pace with and often out-stripped profits, and that even for a successful man opportunities for ostentation were few. Fine clothes, the display of jewels, even the building of a new and more imposing house were, if not forbidden by law, out of keeping with the times. As for the labouring class who made up the bulk of the population, they were all for any change. Their wages had risen – but so had the price of bread, and their always dull lives had become duller with the abolition of public holidays, many of which had some connection, no longer remembered, with saints.

The only people who really feared the Restoration were those who had, in this way or that, gained possession of sequestrated property and even for them the new King offered a bit of an olive branch – land claims were to be settled by negotiation with Parliament. Katharine believed, rather naïvely, I felt, that any Parliament which restored the monarchy would be only too ready to restore land to its rightful owners. "You might even get Nine Elms back," she said.

That year I allowed gleaners into my diminished arable fields and gave a modest feast to mark harvest's end and Dorcas's birthday. I did not spend recklessly for I knew that nine hundred and eighty pounds was not a great fortune and that I should never wring the income out of Pargeters that Eli had done. I had abandoned the stall and dispersed the herd, keeping only two cows as in Father's day. The decision had caused me several sleepless nights, but I had good reason for it. I should have been obliged to hire someone to tend the stall, when Edman had gone. Katharine and Mrs Smith would have gone, too, so I should need two dairymaids. And I should still be associated, in the minds of Sir Walter and people like him, with a stall on the Market Place. For myself I no longer minded, but there was Dorcas to consider.

Early in September that year I was forced to consider my daughter in a different context.

Even under Eli's thrifty rule clothes could not be made to last for ever and articles past further repair went into the rag bag which hung on a hook on the kitchen door. I had been into the garden that afternoon helping Harry, and came into the kitchen with a basketful of vegetables and some ripe plums. Marian was polishing my worthless silvered ware and said, "Would you mind, Miss Sarah, finding me a new rag? This is in tatters. A good solid piece if there is one."

I loosened the drawstring of the bag without removing it from the hook. There were few good solid pieces until I touched something crunched into a ball. It was the smock Dorcas had worn on the day of Eli's death. I remembered her discarding it. So swiftly, I thought, that she had left something in one of its pockets. I took it out and stared unbelievingly. The little flask, labelled in faded writing: 'Lethal'.

Unbelievable, yet it must be believed. My daughter – then not ten years old – had killed her father. And I saw and heard myself behaving with the same unnatural calm as she had when she announced his death. Keeping the flask

281

concealed in my right hand, I gave Marian the smock, saying: "It's too large for a polishing rag. But here are the scissors."

Marian shook out the garment and said: "That reminds me. D'you remember Annie?"

"Of course."

"That was a big family," Marian's tone was thoughtful. "And now, I hear, one of the oldest girls is back, a widder, with three. One is just about ready for a place. She wouldn't want no wages at least for a year. Just her keep . . ." It was a question rather than a statement. I gave the hoped-for answer and went away with my secret.

The one thing which no honest-thinking person could overlook was that Dorcas, at a stroke, had set us all free. Pargeters was now an infinitely happier place than it had been four months ago. I owed my liberation, not to King Charles II, still negotiating from Breda, but to my own daughter. Could I without being illogical in the extreme, blame her?

Being raised and having lived all my life as an unbeliever made me muddle-minded now, but a Colonel Titus, urging the assassination of Cromwell, had written a pamphlet, widely circulated, called *Killing No Murder*. Was the killing of a tyrant, far more heavy-handed in his limited sphere than Cromwell had been in a wider one, murder? Should age be taken into consideration? Dorcas was not then ten, and with her sporadic education, did she understand what 'lethal' meant? The answer to that could only be an affirmative, for she was devoted to Edman and as far as was permitted, spent so long in his company that her vocabulary was probably as wide as mine though I had been allowed to read more.

Imagine then that upland, sheep nibbled pasture, Eli, even Eli, perhaps tiring a little and suggesting that the bag dinner be eaten in the shade. The dinners would be in the same bag, the bigger slice for Eli. Dorcas would slip the two pills into his bread or his cheese, both articles hard enough to need vigorous crunching. Then he'd think he was wasting time and jump up, probably before the last mouthful was swallowed; and so died, regretted by no one save his mother and possibly the mysterious Mrs Cauldwell.

I wondered why Dorcas had not thrown the flask away. Probably she was not quite as calm as she had seemed to be. Poor child! And really Eli was himself to blame. So my thoughts went round and round.

I thought of my household, all well fed and well clad and apparently happy, though Katharine and Edman yearned for Brigstowe and were impatient for the Restoration. Marian was gloatingly content and at this moment looking forward to having Mrs Meecham's granddaughter to train. Jake Adams had fitted in well; he milked the one cow which was in milk at the moment, and he churned once a week, though I was quite willing to do so. When he ploughed, either stubble or the ground I was reclaiming for arable, he drove a proper heavy horse, one of the first things I had bought as soon as I had money. Relieved of the work for which they had not been bred, properly fed and well groomed, Sabrina and Bess had recovered their looks and both Katharine and Edman had been teaching Dorcas to ride.

But perhaps the one to benefit most from Eli's demise had been Grandfather for whom I had obtained an attendant from that repository of the unwanted, the workhouse. He was not a boy, or even a stripling but a full-grown sturdy fellow who was regarded as stupid, almost a lunatic, in fact, because he was stone deaf and, never having heard a human voice, could only make animal noises. About a year earlier his mother, who had been devoted to him, had had a small bakehouse and perhaps she had found a way of communicating with him, or perhaps he had merely imitated her – he certainly made good bread. The workhouse authorities had tried to place him in other bakehouses, but nobody had had time or patience to remould him. Even I had doubts, but he did look strong and he regarded me with the wistful look of an ownerless dog. So I agreed to try him for a month. I thought that Grandfather wouldn't mind not being listened to or answered; all he needed was support and more time in the air and sunshine than he had had since I married Eli.

I spent a whole day showing Jamie what was required of him and by the end of it I was exhausted and in sympathy with those who had failed with him. If he happened not to be looking at you, you had to tap him to gain his attention. But I persisted – poor Grandfather must have been taken to the necessary house a dozen times that day. I made Jamie understand that Grandfather was not to go beyond the garden by taking them both to the entries and there going through the actions of a person heading off cattle. But it had been worth it; the two men, neither of them real idiots, very soon established a relationship which had something almost uncanny about it.

So that was my household on the afternoon when I discovered who had made all this happiness possible. How could I reproach her, even in my mind?

Far from it. When she came in – she had been riding with Edman that afternoon – looking so happy and so beautiful, I said, "Tomorrow, darling, we'll go to Nettleton and see if Tom Thoroughgood has a suitable horse for sale."

There was a rather pretty legend about the Thorough-good family and its horses. A Tom Thoroughgood was said to have gone with Richard I on his ill-fated Crusade, and to have somehow become possessed of an Arab horse which, rather than risk to the long sea-voyage home, he had ridden from Syria to Calais. For the short crossing he had refused to consign his precious animal to the hold, but had kept it on deck, holding its bridle and talking soothingly.

What is certain is that Thoroughgoods had been breeding saddle horses of superb quality for at least two hundred years and that none of the present Tom's darlings had gone to the war. Dark stories were told about the marshes beyond Bywater. These were used in summer as cattle pasture, but in winter were deserted. However, even in winter there were small isolated islands on which horses not entirely dependent on pasture could survive. Once the fighting had ceased and horses could no longer be comman-deered, the Nettleton fields were populated again.

The Thoroughgood place was well guarded. There was a fence, calculated to keep even a natural jumper in or out; and there were dogs, very ferocious until quelled by Tom Thoroughgood who recognised me and Bess and regretted that for the present he had only one gelding to offer. "A mite tall for the young lady at the moment," he said, looking at Dorcas as though he contemplated buying her, "but doubtless she'll grow." I shared his certainty. Dorcas was slightly undersized – a fact which she greatly resented – but I had seen workhouse children, or those from poor homes spring up like beanstalks when properly fed.

Thoroughgood horses had never been cheap; Bess had cost twelve pounds, but Jewel – Dorcas named him on the spot – cost forty which even allowing for general inflation seemed a lot. However, as Tom explained, *if* the Restoration came about there'd be a great demand for good horses. I remembered that remark as being the first time I had heard an ordinary person mention the Restoration in connection with business. Somehow it made it seem more certain and imminent.

Riding home I thought about the expression about turning in the grave. How Eli would turn if he could have known that on a single purchase for his unwanted daughter I had just spent forty of his hoarded pounds. And on the very day after I had learned that she had murdered him. I thought: If his Jehovah were as omnipotent and vengeful as he was said to be, down would come the thunderbolt!

And it fell!

Katharine was on the look-out for us. Her hair, usually so neat, was in disarray. She, who never cried, had been crying and was ready to cry again. I could only think that something terrible had happened to Edman. She ran to me and said, "Get down," and as I alighted put her arms around me, holding me close and steady. She said, "Sarah, Eddy is home."

But for her hold I should certainly have fallen. The whole world tilted. My mind went completely blank. I stopped breathing. And I shall be ashamed to my dying day of what I said when things steadied again. At this superb moment, the highlight of my life so far I said the most idiotic thing. "Kat, I can't see him. I'm too ugly."

It was not just the natural damage of the years: it was hardship, hopelessness, privation, it was the sharp answer bitten back, the harmless comment unspoken, the extra effort demanded and met on the brink of exhaustion. All indelibly stamped on in hollows and furrows and wrinkles. And a mouth so compressed as to seem lipless. Poise upon this ravaged face lustreless hair of faded russet with white streaks, and set the whole upon a neck in which every tendon was visible. Ugly was too mild a word.

Katharine laughed and cried, did both together and then, suddenly, solemn and grave, said, "Wait till you see Eddy."

He was unrecognisable and yet, had I met him in the crowded street of an unfamiliar town, I should have known him though the intervening years which had dealt so harshly with me had treated him worse. He wasn't merely hollow-cheeked, his chest appeared to have caved in, pulling his shoulders forward and bowing his back. He was stick thin, like those scarecrows which farmers set up, two cross pieces draped in rags. He was ragged, too. But there was something . . . I have no name for it. It may possibly have been at that moment that I glimpsed the possibility, no more, just the possibility that Father had been wrong in believing that a person consisted of a body and a mind each dependent on the other and nothing else at all. Was there a third element?

I had no time to think more than glancingly because Katharine had opened the door and given me a push, and Eddy stood up from the table, all scattered with dishes, and we met in an embrace which defied the years and all that had happened since we parted. Time was no more.

PART FIVE

That we should be married – and as soon as possible – was such a foregone conclusion that we hardly discussed it at all. Eddy did make one protest, so perfunctory as to mean nothing. "You, darling, are a woman of property. I am a pauper, with nothing to offer. Which seems all wrong. But if you can bear it, I can." Then he laughed. During the time immediately following his home-coming we all laughed so much, at anything, at nothing, that a stranger plunged into our midst might have been forgiven for thinking that we were all mildly inebriated. Pargeters became a merry house, which it had never been before.

Perhaps everybody should once, fairly early in life, experience hardship and misery and then be delivered so that everything thereafter would have a special relish.

I admit that there were occasions when the narrowness of my own escape made me sweat. Imagine Eddy arriving starving and in rags while Eli was still alive. Only four months ago. It was something that didn't bear thinking about, yet I did. And sometimes I was afraid. I'd look at Eddy, eating heartily of the good food which I was now able to provide and which Marian was delighted to prepare and I wished I believed in God – even one as fundamentally disagreeable as Eli's. I needed to give thanks to somebody and there was only Dorcas.

Eddy's way of shuffling off the past puzzled us at first until we understood that it was a deliberate turning away, a denial, or a refusal to remember.

When did I first notice this? I think when Katharine asked a direct question. "Eddy, those provisions that cost me my cosy little niche, did they serve the Cause at all?"

Eddy smiled, but rather grimly. "Not as you intended, Kitty-Kat dear. But we were allowed to take what we could carry, so we ate better than most while awaiting sentence. Does anyone covet this last piece of pie?"

If we had all hungered for a week not one of us would

have grudged it to him. He was so emaciated. And he was my beloved, he was Katharine's dear brother and for Dorcas and Edman he had the charm of one who had come from a far place, with interesting things to tell – if only he would. But he never volunteered more than a bare statement and under direct questioning grew ill-humoured. I thought, perhaps rather fancifully, that he was like Lazarus come back from the dead and saying nothing. Nothing at all. Because he had looked on Hell? From the little bits and pieces which Eddy did tell us, I gathered that he had not only looked on Hell, but lived in it, and for longer than his sentence demanded.

Katharine first noticed the discrepancy in the dates and remarked it. "You say you were indentured for seven years, Eddy. You have been away nearer fifteen."

"Who knew? Or cared? Do you really imagine some official going round and saying: 'Your time is up, my good man.' Near the coast where there is a kind of civilisation that might conceivably happen. Not where we were. Miles inland, the last plantation upriver. No access except by boat. Even the missionaries . . . No, I'll be just. One did venture. But he . . . vanished."

Edman asked, "How?"

"If you must know," Eddy said in an unpleasant way, "our owner shot him and some of the blacks ate him for supper. And why not? They were cannibals in their own country. And meat hungry, poor devils."

Let me remember happier things. Or things which if not positively happy had a lighter side. The business of getting Eddy properly clad. Over the years of what we could now only regard as very mild privation, all that remained of Father's clothing and of John's had been used. Edman had working clothes and one good suit, tailor-made, bought since Eli's death. Since Eddy could not very well go into the one tailor's shop in Baildon wearing his rags, he must borrow Edman's suit and in it he looked comic. I'd often thought that Edman resembled Eddy, and in many ways he did but perhaps he had not reached his full height yet, or would never be so long in leg and arm. With breech buckles above rather than below the kneecap and sleeves ending a good four inches above the wrist, Eddy said: "Well, tailors are said to be suspicious, but I think if I go in like this and say that I need a new suit, I shall be believed."

Outwardly my second wedding was a repetition of my first, inwardly they were so different that no comparison was possible. Nor can the happiness that followed be described; there are simply no words . . .

Around the enchanted isle upon which we lived, great events were taking place: the most important, of course, being the Restoration which took place in May 1660. Katharine was beside herself with joy and said; "Didn't I tell you?" with such smug triumph that one could have imagined that she alone of all the people in England had foreseen, had longed for and now rejoiced in the King coming back to his own. In fact the whole country seemed to go wild with joy. Out came the Maypoles, hidden away for so many years; there were bonfires on every bit of rising ground, firework displays and feasts paid for out of public funds.

Katharine immediately prepared to leave for Brigstowe despite Eddy's attempts to restrain her. "These things take time," he said. "The present owners must be depossessed and they'll put up a fight, you may be sure."

"Ah! There we have been fortunate. Brigstowe was never sold or given away; the Parliamentary forces kept it as headquarters."

"How do you know?"

"I have made contact with one or two of the faithful – ever since I had money for postal dues." Which meant since Eli's death.

The postal service had greatly improved under the Commonwealth. Even in Baildon a coach carrying mail and some passengers lumbered into the centre of the town once a week, and The Hawk in Hand with its famous pliability, had opened a room called the Post Office. There letters could be handed in or collected, and for anybody prepared to pay the price a post boy on quite a reasonable horse would bring your letters to your door. Letters could be prepaid, or handed over upon receipt of a due sum. The truly poor could not communicate with other paupers. Cynthia had been our only correspondent and her letters were always prepaid. When we wrote to her she paid on receipt but she must have written four times to our once, for we had no time and nothing to tell her, and Eli regarded letters as a form of idle chatter. Katharine and I had not bothered to tell him when Mr Clover died, or John Adam went to Cambridge.

I gave Katharine a hundred pounds and Edman a horse. They deserved far more, but I was beginning to be a little careful. Not that I'd ever been spendthrift.

It was when Katharine's departure was certain and the day fixed that we began to have trouble with Dorcas. She must go with them. I blamed myself a little. During Eli's time our affection for each other had been of necessity, furtive. Then had come the brief time when I could show my love and spoil her, when, to be honest, I felt a guilty gratitude; but before our relationship had struck a proper balance, Eddy had come and, I admit, my motherly role slipped away. I could hardly wonder that Dorcas felt rejected and turned to Katharine and Edman.

I did not oppose her whim very strongly. I wanted the best for her and I realised how socially limited our corner of Suffolk was. Katharine had always been most tactful but she'd let slip little things about Brigstowe and the Bowen family before the War. And Katharine herself was in favour of taking the child. "It was the custom, before the war," she said, "for girls about that age to go into other households. I did myself."

Eddy said, "And if my memory serves, you were most unhappy."

"The Duchess was a bitch, but when I had girls, or pages, at Brigstowe my first care was their comfort and happiness. As for Dorcas, Sarah's daughter . . ."

"But you don't know what you are going back to," Eddy argued. "You may have to live in a cottage."

"Or a tent," Katharine interrupted. "I'm fully prepared to do that."

"Very well, a tent. So why not wait to see how things go and invite Dorcas for a visit as soon as you are settled in?"

"Because she wants to come now," Katharine said.

I could not understand Eddy's attitude. Stepfathers and stepmothers were often jealous of – and sometimes unkind to – children of a former marriage, but I couldn't think that of Eddy. Besides they impinged so little on each other, especially as that wonderful summer drew on. Dorcas and Edman were always out; they both loved riding and went far and wide, sometimes just to seek amusement. Once the heavy hand of the killjoy Puritans was lifted any event, even a sheep sale or a hiring fair drew its attendant booths and stalls and individual entertainers.

Afterwards I realised that Eddy, coming new to the scene, was a better judge than either Katharine or I.

So when Katharine rode off early one morning Dorcas went with her, and in a matter of days we received a hastily scribbled letter to say that all was well. She was safely installed in Brigstowe which, since the disbandment of the Parliamentarian forces, had been left in the care of a few old soldiers who had no other homes. "Most of them were glad to remain and work for me, and Lord knows there is work aplenty."

I said to Eddy, "It is exactly as Kat always believed it would be. It rather makes me wonder about Heaven."

"I should think it is an exceptional case. But if such justice is going to be done, perhaps I should encourage my own small private hope."

"Have you one?"

"Hardly worthy of the word, darling. And so far as it exists it centres upon the Queen rather than upon the King. She was the main smuggler and I lost two good ships in her service, I was enslaved, and though never in much of a battle, I shed a certain amount of blood."

And not only from the wound which had brought him into my life. On our wedding night I had been appalled by the state of his back, all ridged and scarred from what must

293

have been savage beatings. At the moment he had said, "Darling, must we talk about that now?" but later on when his reticence eased a little, he had told me that the up-river plantation had been ruled by a negro overseer. "A handy man with a whip. Of course he beat the blacks, too, but he *enjoyed* beating us. Quite understandable. A white man had brought him from overseas. Our owner was white. We four were scapegoats."

Part of Eddy's effort to forget was the deliberate avoidance of names; the plantation was the plantation, its owner, the owner, the overseer, the overseer. And that I partly understood, since I wanted to forget that I had ever been Mrs Smith.

Mrs Smith.

To me Mrs Smith was the disagreeable old woman who had added to life's misery for almost ten years and I hated her. Yet I admired her too. She refused absolutely to take a penny from me.

"I don't want charity."

"You've worked for it," I said.

"Everything I've done in this house I did for Eli's sake. I want nothing from you. I shall find a place in some godly household."

But she was too old, and of too forbidding an aspect to find work where even Katharine and I had failed, so she lived under my ungodly roof for some time longer, earning what she ate, by cleaning windows, after I dispensed with the herd. Marian refused to have her in the kitchen.

I again offered her money and again she refused, even more rudely. "You know as well as I do that you never felt this was Eli's place. That it was yours by rights. And all it earned. Keep it. Much good may it do you! And I'm not without, don't think that. Mr Clover paid me and I saved. God will find the right place for me, never fear."

In a way her faith was justified. A tumbledown old house at Stratton Strawless – a drear and isolated village – fell vacant, and with her savings Mrs Smith rented it and opened a refuge for lunatics. Not mere village idiots, the senile, or the paupers who were classed as demented. Mrs

Smith aimed higher than that. Her prey was the lunatic born into a respectable, well-to-do family; the thing to be ashamed of and put away as far as possible. Rumour – not always reliable – held that her charges were high, in some cases two pounds a week. I reflected that Eli's God had dealt well with Mrs Smith. But what about the poor lunatics?

Now and then I remembered Lady Alice's words: Be brave; much awaits. And I began to interpret them in the most favourable sense; for 1659 had brought back my love and the beginning of a happy marriage, and 1660 enriched me beyond my wildest dreams.

First came a letter from Cynthia. Mr Clover's affairs were now settled and until John Adam was twenty-one she was in charge, and she remembered how I had taken her in and stood by her and she wished to give me Brook. "I had urged James to do that, but you know what a ditherer he was. Now I have about two thousand acres to look after . . ." It was typical of Cynthia not to know the exact extent of Scunthorpe. Always vague. "So please, Sarah dear, take Brook off my hands. I enclose what they call The Deeds . . ."

I had not the slightest hesitation about accepting such a valuable gift; as Cynthia had remembered, I had done my best for her and John Adam. And a house like Brook, attractive to only a certain kind of tenant and in a different county could only be a nuisance to a woman already rich.

Putting the deeds back into the Trunk I said jokingly to Eddy, "Now it only remains for me to get Nine Elms back and it will be as it was in Father's time."

"When I get compensation for my ships I'll buy Nine Elms for you. Probably as a ninetieth birthday present." He also spoke lightly but with a slight sting, for by the winter of 1660 it was becoming evident that the King's restoration had not brought about the instant restoration of sacrificed property of which Katharine had dreamed and which in her case had come true. Few people were so fortunate. It was obvious to all that the King did not wish to start his reign by alienating all those subjects who had bought, or otherwise acquired, forfeited property. The byword was 'compromise', brought about by delays, by commissions, and committees and courts of inquiry. In our little corner, for instance, beautiful Merravay remained in the hands of Phyl Whymark, for Sir Rawley and Lady Alice were both dead, and their heir, Charles, had disappeared, perhaps into some unmarked grave like my brother John; perhaps into servitude such as had engulfed Eddy. Another substantial place, Mortiboys, which had belonged to the Hattons, had a different history. The Hattons had left their house and their acres in charge of an agent, and gone into voluntary exile – not as part of the exiled Court. However, they had been counted as Malignants and their land sold off in four separate lots. Whoever drew up the allotments was careless or inexperienced and had assigned the house to none of the four; so in the kitchen and the former servants' quarters four women lived and squabbled, while the four men quarrelled as to what utilitarian purpose the more splendid rooms could be used. Pigs? Hens? Cattle? Storage?

Moreover, though three of the usurpers had had experience on the land, one had not and there was no spirit of neighbourliness to help him, so he and his family lived in danger of starvation, and since the agent had been negligent even those who knew more did not really prosper. The Hattons had come home rich and it took a comparatively small sum of money and very little persuasion to convince all four owners that they would be better off in a new cottage – built at Mr Hatton's expense – and a small acreage, securely hedged in.

This, like Brigstowe, may have been a rare case. There were other compromises, marriages and betrothals, or an agreement to share.

The King himself set an example of conciliation; of the thousands who had fought against his father the merest handful was punished; just the ten who had signed the death warrant. It was the new Convention Parliament, not the King, who ordered that Cromwell's body be taken out of Westminster Abbey and hung in chains at Tyburn, the place of execution for criminals.

I think that the King, like Eddy, wanted to forget, to turn his back upon the past.

People now came in the evenings to visit Marian, to take a hand at Nobbin, drink ale and eat cake and, of course, to gossip, and it was from Marian that I heard that Jerry Cooper, never happy with Captain Bennett, was now bitterly discontented and looking for a small place to rent. Mrs Cooper had continued with her fowl breeding and had saved a little money. "And she'd do better still if Captain Bennett wasn't so greedy, often wanting two of her best table birds a week. And making it so hard for her to get to market that she hev to pay somebody to take her stuff."

I thought instantly of Brook and arranged for Jerry Cooper to come and see me as soon as possible.

He came, bringing his wife. I had seen them, of course, at the compulsory church services, but not closely enough to mark how they had both aged. They probably thought the same about me! I offered them Brook, asking in return only that Jerry should oversee Pargeters at such times as I should be away. "Jake Adams is an excellent man," I explained, "but he lacks experience." I also spoke of the house, not improving by standing empty since Mrs Cauldwell had departed.

"And the rent, Madam?"

"Just keeping an eye on things here," I said. "And looking after the sheep."

Jerry looked dumbstruck; Mrs Cooper broke into hysterical tears and said; "Now I'm gonna tell her the truth."

"You mustn't. I only told you to keep you from worriting. And you promised."

"Not on oath, I didn't. And why shouldn't Madam know how you've served her all these years?"

She drew a steadying breath and told me. Apparently there was at Nine Elms a point from which some of Pargeters' upper windows were visible, and Tom Markham before he went away had arranged with Marian that if there was anything to report she was to hang a bit of white cloth from her own window, which chanced to be one of those visible. "So every night, fair or foul, out he went. Mostly for nothing; or if there was it was only because the poor old dear wanted a bit of a gossip."

I said, "I am very grateful to you – and to Tom."

"And he didn't want it talked about," Cooper said, with a reproachful look at his wife.

When they had gone I hastened to tell Eddy that as soon as the winter was over we could make the visit to Brigstowe which Katharine had been urging ever since she moved in. I was quite eager to see Brigstowe but even more eager to see Dorcas who was, after all, my only child and likely to remain so, for I was teetering on the verge of the second major change in a female's life. I should dearly have loved to bear Eddy's son and once, after a slight irregularity had led first to hope and then to disappointment, I told Eddy so, adding that I was sorry. He surprised me by saying, "I am not – unless you really crave for another child. I should worry . . . feel responsible . . . wonder what life held for the poor little thing."

I knew of course that under his constant, often almost feverish merriment ran a deep stream of melancholy, something he did his best to overcome just as he did his best to forget the circumstances which had induced it. Sometimes I caught a glimpse of his face when he imagined himself to be unobserved – and when he was sober – and it wrenched my heart. Once I steeled myself and said, "Eddy, wouldn't it be better to talk about what haunts you. Telling me everything might relieve your mind."

"Rubbish, Sweeting. Besides . . . there is nothing to tell."

I knew the sadness was there, but not until Eddy spoke of a child, not yet even conceived, as a 'poor little thing', had I realised how deeply his spirit as well as his body had been damaged.

That Christmas, 1660, was kept merrily and in the midst of it Grandfather died, surely in the way in which had he been allowed choice, he would have chosen. We'd all overeaten and drunk too much and Grandfather had fallen asleep at the table. Jamie had picked him up like a child and carried him to bed. He must have died in his sleep. There was no sign of a struggle; the bedclothes were smooth and tucked in.

I never knew his age, but he had been the father of grown daughters and feeling himself old enough for semi-retirement when he came to Suffolk and built Pargeters. I think that he had enjoyed his early life, his journeys and business dealings and I was glad to think that his last months had been comfortable with plenty of good food and the wine he loved.

I did not send Jamie back to the workhouse; if he could learn one thing he could learn another, so I set him to learn gardening under Old Harry's not-always-too-patient tuition. I also installed another maid, older than Patience Meecham, and who could cook, so Marian's remaining days would be easy. My aim in life had narrowed – no, that is an ill-chosen word, crystallised into a desire to be happy myself and where possible make others happy.

Then one day the following year I received a surprise that made me very happy indeed. Mr Turnbull sent me a prepaid letter by post-boy. It asked me please to state on what day in the following week, and at what time of the day, it would be entirely convenient to receive him and a business colleague. The letter smacked of something hitherto unknown in our few dealings. He'd always been civil and when he warned me against becoming a prostitute even his formal manner could not quite conceal a certain amount of pity. Now he was writing almost in terms of awe.

As well he might, for in some fairy-tale way I was not only a woman of property, I was downright rich!

In that summer of 1642, Father had gone to the plague-infected city of London, sold Grandfather's two ships and whatever else he owned, taken the proceeds along to Lombard Street and found a goldsmith who was not only honest but foresighted, and gifted with the ability to make money grow, as some people can make plants. He'd taken all his own money and all that was entrusted to him and left England a full month before the King raised his standard at

Nottingham and once in Europe he had made the money work.

How it must have worked, all through the Civil War and the eleven years of Parliamentary rule and nearly two years of making certain that the King was firm on his throne again.

Mr Turnbull's colleague had turned out to be an Italian, Signor Bonini, very handsome, young-looking and speaking perfect English but with a lilt, with more gestures of the hands than Englishmen use. He wore tawny velvet, with collar and cuff ruffles of fine lace. He carried a large flat pouch of leather, tooled with gold, and from it he took folded papers to hold before my bewildered eyes the most meticulous, complicated bit of book-keeping ever seen.

"It is completely in order," Mr Turnbull said.

"My father was an honest man," Signor Bonini said.

My mind whirled. I understood a friendly loan, with a gift to show gratitude. Listening to Father and Grandfather in the days when I was very young, I had heard of something called 'interest', a will-o'-the-wisp which had been the undoing of many men, too greedy for gain. "Nothing over five per cent can possibly be safe," Grandfather once said and Father agreed with him.

But Grandfather's original fifteen hundred pounds had been taken and lent out at a rate of as much as a hundred per cent, never less than twenty. And of what it had earned, Signor Bonini had taken half, crediting Grandfather with half. Known names leapt out at me: Amsterdam, Paris, Utrecht and Rome. And I thought of what it had cost me to retain just a fingerhold on Pargeters. And how Eli had tried to put Grandfather into the workhouse; and how often, but for Marian, the poor old man would have gone hungry.

Then to add to my confusion of mind, Signor Bonini proceeded to enlighten me about letters of credit. These did away with the necessity for carrying large sums of money and exposing oneself to danger of robbery. He, for instance had brought none of my fortune with him; instead he handed me a paper which stated that I was in credit with him. If I needed coined money I could apply to Mr Turnbull, who with certain other reliable and well-to-do local people had guaranteed to make themselves responsible. In return for their service and trustworthiness, they received a fee, called a commission. On the money I left in Signor Bonini's care, I should of course continue to receive interest, but at a modest rate.

My first real thought through the haze was: Now I can buy Eddy a ship! It was a delightful thought, for two reasons. It pleased me to be able to give him things, and I hoped that sea air would help to cure his cough. That cough had persisted despite all our efforts – Marian's compound of horehound and honey, and various so-called infallible cures which I had bought from the apothecary, who, since Baildon still had no doctor, regarded himself as one.

Treatment was not made easier by Eddy's refusal to admit that he had a cough at all. Marian and I, he said, were fussing unnecessarily, treating as serious a throat too easily irritated. If a coughing fit overtook him at table, he blamed himself and the food, "I really must remember that salt provokes it." So did pepper and sugar, a mouthful of wine too hastily swallowed, any crumbly food. It was an endless list. Out of doors it could be dust, any form of pollen, even the wind in the wrong direction. Like most coughs it was troublesome at night and excuses were harder to invent. So it must be ignored and this I learned to do, going along with what he wished.

There were days, and nights, when his accusation about fussiness appeared to be justified; the cough would vanish, but only to return – always to my alert ear a trifle deeper and more rending. But apart from the cough and the fact that despite plenty of good food he did not fatten much, he gave no sign of being in other than splendid health. He seemed tireless, particularly in pursuit of pleasure; he enjoyed every bit of our limited social life. The race-course at Newmarket had re-opened and with Chris Hatton, an inveterate gambler, Eddy was often there in good weather. He took great pleasure in steeplechasing which I regarded as a highly dangerous sport and as soon as the now-legal strolling players began their rounds, they must all come to Pargeters and be royally entertained until they had exhausted their repertoire. Our barn, with a stage erected at one end made an excellent theatre.

Until I suddenly became very rich I had occasionally thought that we were living beyond our income, but Eddy's happiness came first with me.

Best of all, however, he liked to get down to Bywater and be amongst ships and the men who sailed them. Possibly some men are born to the sea, as others are to land. Once Eddy said, "If I weren't so happily married, I'd turn pirate. A highly respectable trade now. Prince Rupert, they say, is doing very well at it."

So it was really a highlight of life for me when I could say – after a hasty explanation of the circumstances – "So now, darling, we can have a ship of our very own." I managed to make it sound as though owning a ship was something I'd longed for all my life.

It was then March and the roads were drying out; a good time for travel and Eddy and I had already arranged to visit Brigstowe at the end of the month. Now Eddy seized upon the idea of combining two pleasures – owning a ship and visiting Brigstowe. "We could go by sea," he said, his face aglow.

"Could a new ship be built in three weeks?"

He laughed. "Hardly. But a very nice restoration and conversion job could be done. In fact I know the very craft. Shall we go to Bywater and have a look at her tomorrow?"

"That would be lovely," I said, facing two days of boredom, Bywater being just that much too far distant for a there-and-back-in-a-day trip.

I was, and I remained, totally ignorant about ships and in asking me to go with him, by saying 'we' not 'I', Eddy had merely been courteous, but I knew a little about houses and in the last few months had seen Mortiboys as the multiple owners had left it and then how Mrs Hatton had restored it; when Eddy said that dismal-looking old ship was sound at heart, I took his word for it. I said, "That would be rather a nice name for her, wouldn't it? Sound At Heart."

"Absolutely," Eddy said absently, trying to stab a baulk

of timber with the blade of a pocket knife and looking pleased at meeting resistance. The ship had had a name, *Cromwell's Daughter*. Somebody had obliterated the words with a swipe of limewash, now wearing thin. I seemed to remember Grandfather once saying that to change a ship's name brought ill luck, but I said nothing. Eddy and I could hardly go sailing about in a ship called *Cromwell's Daughter*. Thinking of names, I glanced at the figurehead; a crude thing, far from flattering any living woman, but carved with a certain power which made *Sound At Heart* just right.

The one thing about Bywater which was depressing was the number of seafaring men who had ended on the beach there. Some, through age or infirmity were quite unemployable in any capacity, others were simply unfortunate, victims of a callous system which regarded men as tools to be taken up, used and thrown away the moment they were no longer needed. Governments – even when composed of self-righteous men – were as guilty in this regard as any private employer and amongst the human wreckage on Bywater waterfront were men who had fought for their country. Eddy always came home from Bywater with empty pockets and bitter things to say.

Once, the story ran, a kind-hearted woman had opened a kind of refuge for stranded men, but that was long ago and all that was left of it was the memory and perhaps the name of the inn – Mariners' Rest.

On the day when we went down to inspect *Cromwell's Daughter*, Eddy said to me, "Now that you are so rich darling, can we afford to do a bit of entertaining here?" That was nicely put and plain evidence of our happy attitude towards money. Strictly and legally speaking Eddy owned everything that was mine at the moment of our marriage. But he disapproved of that law and insisted that he was a pauper and would be until he was compensated. At the same time he was not shy or hesitant or self-conscious about borrowing against his expectations as he termed it.

My fortune, coming to me from Grandfather, via Mother, was so guarded by the terms of Grandfather's will that it was mine absolutely.

"We can afford to feed a regiment," I said happily, and leaving Eddy to gather in the hungry, I went to the inn and ordered vast quantities of food to be served in an outhouse, for as the landlady pointed out, the hungry were invariably verminous.

While they feasted Eddy moved quietly among them, selecting two to form his crew and eight others to repair and paint and generally transmogrify *Cromwell's Daughter* who, when I saw her again was quite unrecognisable. And she had a new name.

"Why *Sarah II*?" I asked, looking with gratification at the gilded letters and figures.

"Because the second ship I lost was *Sarah*, of course. You gave me the emerald and the horse. Remember?"

I said, "I'm not superstitious, but some people hold that to change a ship's name brings bad luck."

"Then we'll pretend that we haven't changed it. Cromwell *may* have had a daughter called Sarah."

The voyage, begun on that light-hearted note, was entirely enjoyable. Eddy was truly in his element and coughed less. The weather was kind and we took our time, putting in here and there as the whim took us. I remember Plymouth best, not only for its historical associations – Drake playing bowls when the Armada was sighted and the Pilgrim Fathers embarking on *The Mayflower*, but because of the number and variety of the shops and markets. It really seemed to me that every commodity in the world was on offer here. And I had money to spend.

I had written to Katharine saying that we were travelling by ship and hoped to arrive in the second week in May; we actually moored in an almost stagnant stretch of water at the foot of Brigstowe Castle, late in the afternoon of May 10th. From the small jetty a flight of stone steps led up and up to the grim looking keep, grey against the azure sky.

I was always aware of Eddy's mood and knew that he was remembering the last time he had visited Brigstowe, so I made a great bustle about unloading our gear and who should carry what, but before I had assigned the burdens a bell rang, high in the air, and four men charged down the stairs. They were all small muscular men, with dark eyes and hair. They could have been brothers, and the resemblance was emphasised by the fact that they wore a kind of uniform, tan breeches and fawn-coloured shirts. They were extremely respectful. "Sir and Madam, welcome to Brigstowe."

"I know the way," Eddy said and, placing his hand beneath my elbow, we began to climb. The stairs were very steep in the rise and narrow in the tread and there were no handholds. The steps rose sheer between shoulder-high walls. I said, gasping a little, "I feel that all-comers were not welcome here."

"It was reckoned impregnable from the sea," Eddy said.

In two places the steps widened out into a kind of platform, each wing big enough to take eight or nine archers or swordsmen in the old days, or cannon in more modern times.

Where the stairway stopped Katharine stood waiting. It was two years almost to the very day since we parted and she looked ten years younger, despite the now completely snowy hair. She was wearing silvery grey satin with a good deal of lace about it and the folds so artfully arranged that her crookedness hardly showed. She carried a gold knobbed stick which she dropped in order to embrace us both.

"I cannot tell you, dear Sarah, dear Eddy, how greatly I have looked forward to this moment. All together again, and at Brigstowe! Almost too much happiness . . . I am sorry that Dorcas and Edman are not here, but they had an invitation and the time was uncertain. They will be back for supper."

We passed between the grey bulk of the castle keep and a mass of hawthorn trees, all in bloom, white and red, and there was Brigstowe.

Nothing that Katharine had ever said had prepared me for the sheer size and magnificence of it. The biggest house in our area – beautiful Merravay – was a cottage compared with it; as for Pargeters . . . On our left as we approached the house lay the keep and the ruins of the castle, interspersed with fruit trees, now in bloom. To the left were gardens, not merely a lawn and some flowers but fountains and statuary and topiary work, and a maze. It was more like a palace than a dwelling house. When I thought of Katharine who had lived and been mistress here, working like a labourer and being bullied by the Smiths, I was amused. I was also awed and puzzled. Katharine had been back here for two years but no amount of dedication or money could have given these grounds that mature, untroubled look. I thought of Mortiboys.

"Was no damage done?" I asked.

"None," Katharine said. "I was singularly fortunate. The ordinary soldiers were camped in the park and I think the officers – some men of lowly origin – rather enjoyed living in a degree of grandeur. And of course there was no lack of manpower. Now, come in and welcome again to Brigstowe. Sarah, I so well remember how you made me welcome at Pargeters. I can never, never repay. In fact . . ." She cut that sentence off short and for a moment she looked worried. But the moment passed and the all-is-well-with-the-world expression, which did so much to rejuvenate her, returned.

Then at last Dorcas and Edman arrived. Edman smiled at me, but held back. Dorcas came forward, curtsied and embraced me – or rather allowed me to embrace her. From that first moment of cool greeting I sensed something amiss. I tried not to make too much of it, or to allow it to darken the happiness of the visit. I said to myself: She is shy; the two years at Brigstowe represent a large percentage of her total life, so virtually I am a stranger. I said to myself: I am associated with the old, unhappy times which she, quite rightly, wishes to forget. I must be patient.

I looked back on the two intervening years and wondered what I had done to alienate her. I had written often, sent gifts at Christmas and on her birthday; and at least three times had suggested that it was time she came home. The first time she replied that she was completely happy at Brigstowe; after that she had ignored the subject. I wondered if that could account for her behaviour now. Did she think that I had come to take her away? If so, she was wrong. I should be if not content at least resigned to her remaining here, and in due time marrying Edman. It was obvious to me that a girlish fancy had grown and hardened into love. She betrayed herself in a dozen small ways. She was very young – but Shakespeare's Juliet had been young enough to have a governess still.

Edman's attitude towards her seemed to have changed very little since the Pargeter days – or perhaps his extra years and multiplicity of interests enabled him to disguise his feelings better. And perhaps seeing her every day, several times a day, he was used to her looks which made an instant impact upon others.

She was truly beautiful and the new fashions which the Restoration had brought about could have been designed especially for her. Hair was now worn uncovered indoors, parted in the centre and brushed smooth, then bursting into clusters of curls to frame the face. Dorcas's hair curled naturally, night-black ringlets setting off the pale, petal-smooth skin and the remarkable eyes, truly emerald under narrow, delicately arched brows. She had grown in height but was – I was thankful – less tall than I was, and though slim, not scrawny as I had always been. And she had the quality the lack of which Aunt Lydia had in me deplored – animation. In any gathering she could talk and laugh and provoke laughter; but always, I sensed, with one audience in mind – Edman. See how well I am entertaining this boring old man!

I schemed deliberately to be alone with her. I wanted to talk, and to listen. I was prepared to promise that, subject to Katharine's approval, she could stay on at Brigstowe. If she had taken me into her confidence I would have sympathised with her feeling for Edman, telling her that she was still too young to think about marriage and that Edman was bearing her age in mind when he persisted in holding to his elder-brother attitude. She never gave me a chance; on the few occasions when we found ourselves alone together she kept up a flow of amiable chatter, all about nothing at all, as though we were strangers forced into each other's company for half an hour. I think the only time she spoke to me seriously was when she was explaining her change of name. "As you know, I always hated Dorcas. As for Smith! So I chose Rosalind. And Lacey because it is almost legal. People do take their stepfather's name. You will remember, won't you?"

Of course all my stay at Brigstowe was not spent in brooding over Dorcas. Katharine entertained and was entertained a great deal. There was much to see at Brigstowe itself and Bristol was in easy reach, with shops even more enticing than those of Plymouth. Katharine enjoyed showing me the room she had occupied as housekeeper and matron, the piece of wall which had crippled her where the Roundheads' mine had exploded, the exact point in the long avenue of limes where grateful Puritans had paid their debt on the day that she and Edman had been evicted from their home. And one day when she was reminiscing I ventured to ask her about something which had puzzled me from the moment of our arrival. I could understand now the ease with which she had regained her property, and the splendid condition in which it had been kept; but how did she manage to live in such splendour? When I ventured to ask her the question she looked startled and slightly defensive, as though I had accused her of some crime.

"Splendour? I don't live in splendour."

"No? Only six menservants. In uniform." I had seen two in addition to the four who had welcomed us. "A few maids; a carriage and any number of horses. So much silver." I reached out a finger and touched her stick. "Even this," I said.

"All the men are charity cases. Old soldiers with some disability. Not one of them could do a full day's work. They get bed and board and a shilling when I can spare one. Some of the silver is not mine. I'm keeping it for people who have as yet no place for it. Many houses were burned, you know. All that . . ." – she pointed to a sideboard on which some beautiful things were displayed – "spent the war under-water in the Bristol Channel. This elegant appendage . . ." She waved the stick, "belonged to my grandfather who came here on a visit just after I was married, and died. The estate pays better than it did. Edman's time at Pargeters was not wasted. And our mean elder brother sent me a hundred pounds with a letter pointing out that I could expect no more from that quarter."

I'd heard mention of their elder brother, whom both Katharine and Eddy thoroughly disliked, holding that his only redeeming virtue was that he was a King's man. He had never fought, but he had sold all the family property and gone to the Continent and waited, ready to ease the exile of the Queen and her family. Now he was back and being rewarded by what Katharine said was a very remunerative post.

Eddy and Edman had always got along well together and Edman had remembered what forms of sport Eddy would tolerate and those he would not. He wanted nothing to do with anything which involved the infliction of pain to man or beast, even if the beast were a rat, and hunting he deplored, once almost breaking his rule of silence by saying, "If you've once been on the wrong side of the hounds . . ." But in an area such as that of which Bristol was the centre there was plenty to do and plenty to see. Eddy enjoyed company, which, I discovered anew, I did not. I had no small talk; sit me down at table between two perfect strangers – names imperfectly caught in a hurried introduction – and I was at a loss. Asked a question, I'd answer; I'd venture a question myself, but always testing it first: Is it safe? Is it worth asking? And the silence would grow.

Perhaps because the Puritans had regarded sex as necessary but shameful, after the Restoration the pendulum swung the other way and a kind of sterile flirtatiousness had taken over. Sterile because nothing could ever come of it; the men at any gathering could not possibly be in love with every woman there. It was all a pretty nonsense into which I did not fit. I could not even manage my fan properly. To me a fan was, well, call it a tool, used to cool the air in one's immediate vicinity in an overheated room. Other women, including Katharine and my daughter, used their fans otherwise. Katharine's as a pointer, emphasising a direction, or to administer a tap, sometimes only half-playful to some gentleman who had made a statement with which she did not agree. Rosalind (for as such I must think of her) used her fan as an extension of herself, as one of her many assets. Men were wearing their hair long now, or covering slow-growing hair and baldness with elaborately curled wigs. If a girl had enough audacity she could ply her fan so that the hair, real or false, became disarranged; then she could apologise most prettily and pat it into place. It was one of Rosalind's favourite tricks, but only used when Edman was in the offing.

Naturally, now that we were near a city where there were doctors, I wanted Eddy to seek advice about the cough which the sea voyage had alleviated slightly, but not cured. Perhaps he was correct in blaming some coughing fits on dust or pollen, but the deep, permanent cough persisted. He ridiculed the idea, warned me again about becoming a nagger. Then Katharine tried, and Edman. We were all making a great to-do about nothing. A doctor's job was to tend the sick and he ailed nothing. He would be very much obliged if we would mind our own business.

I had set the duration of our visit at three weeks. I knew that Pargeters and Brook were in good hands, but after the joy of reunion and the pleasure of seeing new places had worn off, I realised that I was homesick. Katharine, of course urged us to stay on; three weeks was so short a time, and we'd hardly ever had a really good talk – which was almost true, there was so much coming and going. But at last there was an evening when she and I were alone in the house. "We'll sit on the terrace," Katharine said. "And shall we drink brandy and pretend that Mrs Smith may pounce at any moment?" I had the queer feeling that her gaiety was slightly forced; and her face wore the troubled look I had noticed several times.

The terraces overlooked the garden and part of the long avenue. The scent of roses and lilies and honeysuckle came up to us.

Katharine said, "I want to make it quite clear that I blame myself for everything. I was blind and entirely lacking in judgment. This difficult situation is entirely of my making. And it is my punishment that I am made to look blackly ungrateful."

I said, "Kat what *are* you talking about?"

"Dorcas. Darling you must take her back with you. Otherwise two – no, three lives will be ruined. And God only knows what scandal . . . Sarah, just before you arrived, on the eighth in fact, there was a ball to celebrate the anniversary of the King's return. Edman danced three times with a girl, Henrietta Talbot, with whom he is in love. Afterwards, when the ladies were donning their cloaks, Dorcas went up to Henrietta and said 'Your hair would look better *so*,' and Sarah, she took a lock and tugged it out *by the roots*. Can you believe? Of course she made some excuse – the hair caught in a bracelet – but those who were near and who saw know that it was deliberate assault. It has made things very . . . difficult. But as I say, I blame myself. I should never have brought her here."

"And I should never have let her come. I'm to blame, too." More to blame in fact, for I knew more about Dorcas. In my mind I could still feel the weight and hardness of the little flask; I knew how headstrong, how singleminded . . .

"But once we were installed," Katharine said, "I should have shoved her into the schoolroom with the strictest old governess I could find. But all her life she'd been over-disciplined, so I wanted her to enjoy herself. And few Royalists were back, or established then, so it was nice, I thought, for Edman and Dorcas to be company for one another. I let her grow up, in fact. Dresses, jewellery, even cosmetics. All far too soon. Even when I realised that a childish fondness had grown and hardened into something more I still tried to persuade myself that she was so young."

"She was never young. But I am her mother. I should have exercised more authority. When she refused my first invitation to come home, I should have come and taken her away."

"It would have required brute force."

311

I said, weakly, "I suppose there is no hope that Edman might change his mind."

"Not a glimmer. I've talked to him. No man likes to be coerced. She's worn away even the tolerance he once had. Besides, look at the age gap."

"I know. I have twice talked to her about coming back with us, I've said how different it is now that we are rich and there is some kind of social life. I might just as well have been a fly buzzing in the window."

So there we sat, two mature women who had had our troubles and survived, fretting ourselves about the problem posed by a girl not yet thirteen.

I talked to Eddy who said, "I know all about it. Edman is most unhappy about it. But we have a plan. Very subtle, though I say so myself."

Next day Edman expressed a great wish to see Pargeters again and an equally urgent wish to go to sea in a real ship, his experience being confined to small boats. Instantly Dorcas was fired by the same desires and her whole attitude changed; she became less guarded with me, even consulting me about what clothes to pack. "Will there really be balls?" she asked, and feeling like the quintessence of Judas, I said, "Of course. We'll give one at Pargeters." There would be balls, but with Edman not there what pleasure could she derive from them? My heart stabbed me again when she said she would not need any winter clothes. For a moment I saw the future through her eyes. The sea trip, the holiday, with no competition, no hated Henrietta Talbot. I'm sure the poor child was certain of a betrothal at least. And all of us conspiring against her. Katharine, suddenly completely light-hearted, promising to send the horses for the return journey.

I remember that happy day. Eddy and Edman like two small boys with a secret and in addition Eddy delighted to be on *Sarah II* again and Edman already savouring his freedom. The two men from Bywater were exuberant at learning that Eddy intended to retain their services. Dorcas jubilant. Even I, apprehensive about the bad time to come, knew a sort of happiness because I was homeward bound, and indulged in false hopes – that Dorcas's extreme youth would ensure swift recovery from the wound; that faced with a *fait accompli* she would accept it.

Having told me what he intended to do, Eddy had withheld further information, saying, "The less you know about how and when, the better." But it seemed to me that on that first day we travelled a long time without covering any great distance; we never caught so much as a glimpse of the wide river but spent the day amongst the creaks which Eddy claimed to know so well and now enjoyed revisiting.

Say the word "creek" to an East Anglian and he visualises the marshes out beyond Bywater; flat dark land threaded by narrow, stagnant streams. The creeks around Brigstowe were utterly different. In places the trees came down to the water's edge; in places houses and a few small fields were visible. Nothing would suit Eddy but that we dine at an inn he remembered – one of his smuggling places. There he was given a great welcome. The splendid meal and the reminiscences consumed three hours. During all that time, Dorcas, doubtless feeling that she had presented *us* with a *fait accompli*, grew bolder and more possessive towards Edman, holding his hand, leaning on his shoulder, touching his hair. He bore it all but did not reciprocate. I thought: Oh, my poor child! Any woman with more experience and a less wilful nature would have sensed the patience and resented the withholding.

Having dined so heartily we needed no supper but were content with wine and cake in the sunset as *Sarah II*, as though having made up her mind at last, headed towards the West and the river. Then Eddy chose an anchorage and suggested that I go to bed. "You, too," he said to Dorcas. She protested. "*I'm* not tired." "I don't care whether you're tired or not. You're sharing a cabin with your mother and I don't want you blundering in and disturbing her." He spoke quite brusquely. Probably her possessive behaviour towards Edman had been irking him all day.

Sarah II had started life as a working vessel with all possible space devoted to cargo; but her interior had been thoroughly stripped and now in her stern there were two spacious, comfortable cabins.

Dorcas came sulkily to bed; angry with me for retiring so early, angry with Eddy for so summarily dismissing her. I guessed that Edman would make his 'escape' some time soon, and my heart ached for her. She was really too young for even a happy love affair; how could she stand the strain of this ill-starred one?

I lay thinking these things and planning to do the only thing possible – give her as much diversion and under-standing as was in my power; and it was some time before I slept. I heard nothing, no untoward sounds in the night and towards morning I slept heavily. I was wakened by loud, wordless cries and knew that the moment I had dreaded was actually upon us. Eddy raised his voice. "Be quiet! Control yourself!" I dragged on my robe and sped on deck, arriving just in time to see Dorcas attack him in a really vicious way. She clawed at his face and pummelled his chest with her tiny, ineffectual hands. "You must turn back. You shall turn back! Give the order! Now! Now!"

He controlled her, imprisoning her hands in one of his and shaking her rather roughly. "You're making things worse. For everybody. And I will not have your mother upset."

I said, "I am all right. What has been happening here?"

"As though you didn't know!" Dorcas flung round on me; but Eddy retained his hold on her wrists. "Liars!" she cried. "Traitors too. All of you. All . . ."

A storm of tears threatened. I waited, hoping that it would break and bring comfort, but hers was not to be the easy way. Trying to pull her hands free, Dorcas said; "I shall never forgive you. Until you turn and take me back to Brigstowe. Mother, please, *make* him turn back."

"Only I give orders aboard this ship, Dorcas," Eddy said. Over her head he shot a significant glance and asked with seeming innocence, "Darling, aren't you even curious to know what all this is about?"

Dear man, he was trying to exonerate me.

"Of course. Exactly what did happen?"

"Just as Edman and I were about to turn in, Katharine's messenger arrived. Something slightly wrong on the estate. She wanted Edman back. Natural enough, surely. So why all this to-do and wild talk about liars and traitors?"

"It was planned. To spite me. We never even said good-bye." That was a desolate statement.

"There was no time. The man had had difficulty in finding us. And Edman was anxious to get back."

"And you knew that if I had known I should have gone too. No matter. Look. There are boats. Stop one and send me back to Brigstowe."

There were boats of all sizes and kinds, for we were now in the open river, with the sun dancing on the water and the gulls wheeling.

Eddy said, "Oh don't make yourself ridiculous."

Without further warning she began to shout and scream, saying, "Help me. Save me. Help!" Voices carry over water and heads began to turn. Men in small boats looked up at us; men in larger vessels came to the rails. There was curiosity and also, since the cries were in a female voice and obviously prompted by distress, a degree of chivalry. Knights errant were popping up.

"This," Eddy said, "is damned embarrassing."

"Hysteria," I said. Eddy caught at the word and roared it out in a voice accustomed to being heard. Then, without ceremony, he hustled Dorcas below and into the smaller cabin. I followed, feeling singularly useless. And slightly puzzled by Eddy's near ferocity.

"That is enough of that nonsense," Eddy said, giving Dorcas a push towards the bed. "Now listen to me . . . You've managed to spoil the first holiday your mother ever had in her life. You've ruined a happy family reunion. And done yourself no good. Would any young man worth his salt look twice at a selfish, mannerless, spoilt brat, however pretty? Of course Edman ran for his life . . ." He went on and on until the effort of handling her and of speaking so violently resulted in a terrible coughing fit that drove him out of my presence.

I half hoped that she would turn to me then but she did

315

not. She just sat, small-faced with misery, and finally I crept away defeated.

"Did you lock the door?" Eddy asked as soon as I appeared on deck. "Then do it, please. We don't want her overboard, do we?"

I told myself that part of Eddy's callousness was due to his having been jerked out of his usual pattern of behaviour.

Up to a point, however, his treatment worked and by the time we reached Bywater Dorcas was subdued, if sullen. He had not hesitated to brandish his authority as her stepfather; if she attempted to leave Pargeters without his consent, he would, he said, raise a hue and cry across half England. Unless she behaved properly he'd take her aboard *Sarah II* and have her confined there. So an uneasy kind of peace set in. And there was haytime and harvest.

It was also the time of much letter writing. Katharine wrote diligently – three letters to my one. Hers always contained undertones of apology: If only things had turned out differently. I feel sad when I look back, knowing how this must end . . . In order to cheer her I lied, saying that Dorcas had settled down well and seemed to be enjoying our modest social life. In truth she despised everything and everybody and was developing a slight permanent sneer which detracted from her beauty.

She wrote to Edman, bulky letters, probably full of derision at what she called our rustic antics. He answered rarely but, poor child, she was making do with crumbs and with hope. And gradually the fact that Edman wrote at all led me to indulge, not in hope exactly – it was too frail for that – but in thoughts which began, What if . . .? What if absence had actually made his heart grow fonder? What if his feelings for Henrietta Talbot had worn off already? What if Dorcas were to win after all? What a desirable culmination! Dorcas was nubile now, in two years would be fully marriageable. And she and Edman would always have something not to be shared with any other people in the world – the memory of privation and hardship

316

sweetened only by little kindnesses and youthful high spir-
its.

Feeling like this, I opened each letter from Katharine with
trepidation, dreading what I might find, and then, not
finding it, wondering whether silence on the subject might
be sinister.

Upon Edman's few letters Dorcas always pounced, to
carry away for private perusal and then to flaunt with
ostentation. You see? He *does* care! Once she left the single
sheet open upon the table and I felt no shame in reading it. It
held no food for a hungry heart. It could have been a letter to
an old school-friend and it concerned itself mainly with the
affairs which here Dorcas derided as rustic.

The blow fell at what was undoubtedly the turn of the year;
the end of August, with a shrewd wind sweeping down
from the North. There would be sunny days in September,
even October, but this was the end of summer. Leaves, still
green but dry as paper, whirled through the air and in the
orchard ripening apples thudded down. "I always hate this
time of year," I said to Eddy. "I don't mind winter when it
comes, I even enjoy it. But this is a menacing time."

"This year," he said, "we'll go to France. Mrs Hatton is
always on about the superiority of everything – including
the weather – in France. But I suppose it would mean
taking Dorcas."

"I'm afraid so." It was an awkward situation. She had
more or less forgiven me for the part I had played in her
abduction but her resentment was still hot against Eddy.
And on *Sarah II* with the limited accommodation . . .

"Well, it can't be helped," Eddy said resignedly. "She'd
be bound to do something silly if we left her alone."

With that, the post-boy arrived, bringing one letter for
me. It was from Brigstowe. I broke the seals with the
familiar feeling of impatience and reluctance and read, in
stark words, the news I dreaded.

"What is wrong, sweetheart?"

"Edman is betrothed to that girl. They plan the wedding
for Michaelmas."

"Here, drink this," Eddy said, proffering brandy. "You gave me quite a turn . . . It's not the end of the world, you know. In fact it is a good thing. We couldn't drift on in the doldrums for ever. Once she knows, she'll accept it and settle down. You'll see."

"And who is going to tell her?"

"If that's all that bothers you, I will." Behind his concern for me, his steady kindness, I detected a lurking amusement.

"Sometimes you amaze me. Making so much of so little, after all you've been through. Ask yourself, darling, how many people marry the first person they take a fancy to? If she'd behaved with a modicum of modesty and discretion she could have carried the secret of unrequited love to her grave – she might even have landed him, given time."

Reasonable talk; possibly true, but with little comfort in it. I said, "Perhaps I had better tell her, Eddy. I mustn't shirk. She is my daughter."

"All the more reason why I should do it. I'm out of favour with her already. She's just unreasonable enough to confuse bad news with the bearer. And we have the future to think of."

Alongside his fundamental lack of sympathy ran a strain of meticulousness. He began to plan a suitable time and place for the breaking of the bad news.

We were due in the next few days to partake of an entertainment which even Dorcas could not decry as rustic. Even our quiet backwater was sharing the rage for play-going which was sweeping the country and not only the plays but the status of the players had vastly improved. There had been plays in the old days – Father had often taken me, somewhat to Mother's disapproval, play-going being regarded as not quite respectable and the strolling players only one notch above rogues and vagabonds. The audience had been easily accommodated in the one public building that Baildon could boast, the old Guildhall. Now something bigger was needed, and beginning next week there was to be a series of plays – the tickets very expensive, the profits to be largely devoted to a Theatre Building Fund.

To put the ultimate touch of respectability upon the enterprise, a small proportion of the money was to be diverted to the old Winter Fund which provided fuel and meat and bread to almshouse dwellers and other indigent people.

Until Katharine's letter arrived I had been looking forward to Tuesday, the day for which Eddy had secured tickets. I enjoyed play-going and I had noticed that it was the one pastime which seemed to take Dorcas out of herself. Now Eddy planned to give her one thoroughly enjoyable afternoon and break the news on the way home.

"I shall ply her well with wine during the intervals," he said, planning almost happily. "And if she behaves as she did on the boat, there'll be nobody to hear or see. Oh, for God's sake, Sarah, don't look so worried. An unpleasant half hour and this whole thing will be over and done with and ordinary living can go on."

"I know. And how glad I shall be."

It had not been a happy summer. Apart from the misery of seeing Dorcas so wretched, and waiting for the blow to fall there'd been the realisation that on the subject of Dorcas Eddy and I were not in our usual full accord. He thought she was wayward and spoilt, and that my attitude towards her was weak and wrong. He had no idea, of course, what we owed her and I could never tell him. Yet I had told Katharine. So what was wrong? Was anything wrong? Was there ever a marriage between two people who saw eye to eye upon every subject? I was asking too much.

That day began with sunshine, though the wind was still chilly. Eddy and Dorcas rode away early, for, determined to make this a proper outing, he had decided that they should dine at The Hawk in Hand which, accommodating as ever, now served an early, play-going dinner on the days when there was a performance. Up to the moment of leaving Dorcas preserved her detached attitude; she did not even bother to say that she hoped my headache – the age-long excuse – would improve during the day. Eddy hugged and kissed me and said; "Now don't fret. Everything will be all right, I promise you."

I busied myself all day, trying to divert my mind from the inevitable home-coming. I wrote to Katharine, sending best wishes to Edman in a rather formal, stilted way and thinking, with some resentment that this unhappy, head-long infatuation had now cast a gloom over a friendship which I valued. Katharine and I would never be fully at ease with one another again. And in future, in Dorcas's presence I must not even mention Brigstowe. In future. I wondered exactly how the future would shape itself. One thing I saw clearly; I must not allow Dorcas and her behaviour to drive a wedge between Eddy and me. I must remain cheerful.

With this in view I prepared to welcome Eddy home. I set a bowl of the year's last flowers and first berries on a chest between the windows and a smaller one on the table. Should supper be set for three, or for two? On the boat Dorcas had eaten nothing for almost three days and I had fussed. I must not make that mistake again.

It would be a good supper; one of Mrs Cooper's pre-Michaelmas geese, apple and quince tart. There would be white wine and red.

I changed into a more becoming gown, arranged my hair, coloured lips and cheeks. Then, with curtains drawn against the gathering twilight and the rising wind, and a good fire going, I sat down to wait.

And waited and waited.

I was not alarmed. Eddy was popular. At the play he could well have fallen in with somebody who had asked him in to drink wine – or even to supper. He might, despite his robust attitude, be willing to fortify himself before telling Dorcas what she must know.

Patience Meecham came in and asked did I wish Marian to hold back supper. "As long as she can without spoiling the meal," I said.

Almost immediately, the commotion began. Marian cried out; the girls exclaimed shrilly, Jake and the boys on a deeper note. Fearful – but of what? – I tore open the door and ran through.

Eddy stood in the yard doorway, just managing to hold himself upright by clutching the doorpost. He looked like a man rescued from death by drowning: his face was blue-white, his teeth chattered so violently that he could not speak, but he looked at me, trying to communicate, to reassure. Jake reached him first and practically carried him to the settle nearest the fire. I went down on my knees beside him, clutching one icy hand.

Marian took charge. One would have imagined that the resuscitation of the half-drowned was a regular feature in her life. She had everyone running; dry clothes, towels, brandy. At first he could not drink; his teeth rattled against the mug, long, violent shudders shook the very centre of his being. Saying, "Try, darling," I held his head steady and, hit or miss, poured some of the liquor in. It occurred to me that there was something here more than a simple dowsing, especially with Eddy, a strong swimmer and a man as much at home on the water as on land. Shock?

His first words were relevant only to me. "Dorcas wasn't there." He spoke slowly and with effort, but with such evident wish to comfort that I said, "I am glad," not knowing what I was glad about.

Marian pushed forward a mug of steaming milk, redolent of spices.

Gradually the rigors ceased; warmth came back into his hands and the blue-whiteness vanished. He spoke again. "And I . . . always thought . . . I was a horseman!" He managed a self-derisory smile. I knew that he was preparing some plausible story; I was equally sure that it was false. I could hardly wait for the moment when we should be alone.

Marian said, "I think bed now," and Jake half carried Eddy upstairs. Somebody had lighted the fire but the room was not yet warm, so we put Eddy to bed in his robe, and heaped on the covers. There were hot bricks already in the bed. Jake stood waiting until I sent him away to tell Marian to dish up. Then I went and sat on the bed.

"Tell me . . ."

"It's bad. She's dead. She drowned herself in Top Pool. All my bloody fault," he said with sudden violence, "taking so much on myself."

"You tried to spare me."

"I tried to save her. I dived again and again."

"Top Pool is said to be bottomless." Black and still, sinister on the sunniest day; long said to be haunted by the ghost of another forsaken girl.

"And I didn't wait," Eddy said defensively, "to tell her when the pool was handy. I told her as soon as we turned into Layer. She said only one thing – that it was all my fault. I thought . . . I thought she'd taken it rather well and then . . . just as we drew level . . . she swerved off . . ." More and more brokenly he tried to tell me until I said, "Darling, don't distress yourself. I can imagine." I realised that had he been a woman, Eddy would have been crying. I slipped my arm under him, lifted his head from the pillow and cradled it on my breast. I stroked his hair and said comforting things as though to a child. And all the time I was thinking about how I had been dreading life *with* Dorcas once she knew the truth. That now seemed an unworthy anxiety but it led me to what I felt to be the truth. "Perhaps for *her*, Eddy, it was the best, the only way. The future held nothing." He then handed back to me what I had so often offered as an excuse for her behaviour: "She was so young."

At that point we were interrupted by the arrival of Patience and her sister with trays and covered plates and a jug of mulled wine. Marian plainly saw no reason why a ducking should preclude enjoyment of a good meal; and it helped, pulling the distorted evening back into shape. Neither of us could make more than a poor pretence at eating, but the wine helped, and Eddy abandoned, I hoped for ever, his attitude of intense self-blame.

"We now have to think what to tell people," he said. I had already seen that problem looming, but had pushed it aside in order to comfort him and restore his self-esteem. Now we faced it together, both anxious to avoid, if possible, all hint of the truth. So many beliefs and patterns of thought had changed or were changing, but the general attitude towards suicide was adamantine and barbaric. I could never see myself why a person in intolerable misery of mind or body who chose to end it all was committing either an offence against God or a crime against the state, yet a suicide was denied Christian burial and must lie in unsanctified soil, alongside common criminals. What seemed even more unkind – for the dead person was beyond feeling anything – was the fact that great disgrace was thrown upon relatives, and even close friends. It was fully as shameful to be associated with a suicide as with a horse-thief or murderer.

This aspect of the affair bothered me very little. I had long since become immune to public disapproval and I could live without people, but Eddy enjoyed company and had even been pleased to be elected to the Board of Guardians. Now he said a cogent thing: "Stepfathers are always suspect. This will reflect badly on me." I thought it over and saw some truth in it. Step-parents had a bad name, not always deserved. Few people would believe that a girl of Dorcas's age had 'died for love'; she was pretty, well provided for, yet obviously unhappy. Something wrong in the family. Blame the stepfather.

I said, "It must be made to seem like an accident. Do you feel well enough to talk about it now or shall we leave it until morning?"

"I shan't sleep until we have settled something. What exactly did I say when I saw you? I had nothing ready. I just wanted you to know that, whatever happens to me – you looked so very stricken, my poor dear."

I told him what he had said and we proceeded in the most cold-blooded manner to plot a story that would account for Dorcas's disappearance. And her re-appearance, in Top Pool.

"How long does it take for a . . . drowned body to surface, Eddy?"

"I don't know. It would depend upon conditions. I'm only familiar with the sea. Men overboard. Men washed up, often miles away, often after many days. I believe deep water has some preservative effect."

"If so, it should help with the timing," I said. And a voice in my mind cried: This is your child, born of your body, the

323

little girl you loved and who loved you. Once. Now it seemed as though Eddy and I had killed her and were planning the disposal of her corpse. The whole thing was too macabre to be real. I could only cling to the certainty that all we had wanted was her ultimate good, and that all this skulduggery was an attempt to shield her name.

Several times as we talked, Eddy raised himself and coughed, holding the bedclothes high and turning away from me. Twice tact drove me out on to the landing to await the passing of the paroxysm. I hoped most ardently that he hadn't taken a chill. From one window Layer Wood was visible, a dark mass against a sky of driven clouds. Somewhere out there, in the dark, the cold, the everlasting night . . . She'd had so little real happiness.

Top Pool in the light of a grey dawn bore signs of the overnight happenings. In several places the fringe of reeds showed a gap, and the smooth green covering of weeds had been disturbed. Nothing stirred. It was still chilly though the wind had gone down, so I rode briskly in various directions, always coming back, dreading, expecting, almost hoping to see some change. All my thoughts were morbid.

I went home to breakfast and tried out one part of our story. Miss Dorcas had been invited by the Hattons who were having a party after the play. To lend verisimilitude to this tale I packed a valise with some of her belongings and said that I should ride over to Mortiboys with it after breakfast and might spend the day. This gave me an excuse for absence and made Eddy more satisfied to stay indoors. He was slightly fevered.

I weighted the bag and threw it into the pool. It sank without trace.

That was the longest day I had known. I'd taken a book, but it failed to hold my attention. Every ten minutes I looked at my watch, every ten minutes I thought it had stopped. I regretted not having brought something to eat and drink. I had little appetite, but it would have been something to do. I took more little rides; I sat in the saddle, and on the ground; I paced around the pool, clockwise and anti-clockwise. I thought of prisoners condemned to years of solitary confinement. I felt the balance of my mind tilting.

There was no danger of being seen: Top Pool did not immediately adjoin the path but lay behind a thin screen of bushes and trees; and in any case these woodland paths were less used than formerly. Farms were more and more tending to become self-contained units, and day-labourers, going where the work was, were fewer. In all that long day I did not hear a human voice. Last evening, facing ostracism I had thought, proudly, that I could do without people. It was not true.

I thought of the past, of course, and something struck me for the first time. Outwardly my life had been hum-drum, but it had, surely more than most, been concerned with secrecy; smuggling money to John; hiding Eddy, smuggling pills to Lady Alice, sharing the secret of Eli's death. Now this. I wondered how many seemingly ordinary lives, if fully exposed would reveal so many hidden places.

At the end of what seemed a year the light began to fade and I rode swiftly home. Despite all my injunctions, Eddy was in the parlour, but in his dressing gown, a shawl over his shoulders and a blanket around his knees. There was a leaping fire and candles and Eddy. It would have been the easiest thing in the world to have gone hysterical with relief; but I maintained control and drank a good deal of brandy.

Eddy said that his story had been accepted easily, even with amusement. Because the stables at Mortiboys were full, he had been bringing Dorcas's mount home, riding carelessly, the rein hooked under a finger. (I had offered Dorcas a new Thoroughgood horse upon our return from Brigstowe, but she had been so obviously unappreciative that I had done nothing about it and she had been riding a quiet, ageing mare.) Something dashed from the underground across the path, Eddy's horse reared and cannoned off the mare who in panic swerved towards Top Pool. There, Eddy, leaning to recover the mare's rein, was thrown. The chief interest evoked by this fabrication was in the identity of the animal which had crossed the path. It was an article of faith amongst local people that there were still wolves in Layer. A fox, Jake held would not have panicked the horses, especially Eddy's which had hunted regularly.

So that corner was rounded. Eddy and I kept vigil for ten days more and Top Pool retained its secret. It was easy to say that from Mortiboys Dorcas had been invited to stay elsewhere and after that was returning to Brigstowe. She had been absent before for two years and since her return had done and said nothing to endear herself to anybody, so it was all very easy.

There followed a blissfully uneventful time. Nothing of much note happened. Marian finally took to her bed and from it maintained control of the kitchen; then, after a few days of lethargy, she died and I arranged for her to be buried as near as possible to our family tomb. I think she had been in love with Grandfather ever since he took her from the workhouse, and I remembered Mother's words about the bones resting where the heart was.

Then there was the flutter of excitement about John Adam's identity. One result of the upsurge of loyalty which accompanied the Restoration was the proliferation of pictures of the King. They varied in merit because not all those given permission to copy the original portrait were equally skilled. The landlord of The Hawk in Hand refused to buy what he called a libellous daub, supposedly showing the King as he was at the moment, and demanded a pleasant picture: "By which I meant, sir and madam, something that wouldn't sour the food on the table." Possibly tongue-in-cheek, on his next round the picture dealer offered the innkeeper a portrait of the King made when he was in Jersey at the beginning of his exile – a boy in his teens.

Never one to miss an opportunity of advertising himself and his establishment, the innkeeper decided to make an occasion of the unveiling of the picture. He offered tickets at twenty-five shillings a head for a meal to be served at five o'clock in the afternoon, just when the play-goers were dispersing. The picture was to be unveiled by the leading lady of the company playing that week. A clever move, obviating all jealousy between local ladies. Eddy was all agog to go and I went, too. I was more at ease in a crowd than in a smaller company where something might be expected of me in the way of sparkling conversation.

The young actress was a pretty girl and she made a pretty speech, though it was apparent that she was not quite clear as to what it was all about. She spoke about this most worthy cause, and had to be prompted to pull the cord. The crimson velvet fell away and I heard myself gasp. There stood John Adam to the life, just a little older than when I saw him last, but quite unmistakable. It was not only the colouring, the dark eyes and hair, the swarthy skin which had once perturbed Cynthia, the likeness lay in the features, in the set of the head, the pose of the shoulders.

The last I had heard of John Adam he was at Cambridge and might still be. The King was often at Newmarket for the races, but he had intellectual interests too and sometimes visited Cambridge. Imagine them coming face to face in the street.

Eddy and I started for home cheerfully enough, with me going into more detail about Cynthia than I had hitherto done and joking about having had a royal cuckoo in my nest and Eddy saying that by this reckoning, and always supposing it could be proved, John Adam was born before Lucy Walters' son, the first of the King's acknowledged bastards, and the apple of his eye.

Abruptly my mood changed and I was face to face again with the one unsatisfactory aspect of my marriage. I should so dearly have loved to bear Eddy a son and the hope dwindled as time went on. I was not yet so old – thirty-six – and had proved myself capable of bearing, though my mother-in-law had thrown the word 'barren' at me. Lately however, my link with the moon had wavered, there were days of hope, paid for by searing disappointment.

I suppose believers in Eli's spiteful old Jehovah would say that now I was being punished for my behaviour when first pregnant with Dorcas. "He that would not when he may, when he will he shall have nay." But in no way were the two things comparable. I was now wealthy and leisured, and I wanted a boy who would resemble Eddy.

Eddy professed not to care. Young children, he said, were uninteresting and older ones a responsibility. "We can face responsibility," I said.

"I mean in the wider sense," said Eddy. "Once you bring a human being into the world you are responsible for what happens to it, and its children, its children's children, for ever. It's a dangerous old world, sweetheart."

I knew what he was thinking: Look what happened to me!

In the main we avoided the subject and made the most of what we had, which was, I admit, more than our share.

Eddy was always happiest and I thought healthiest, when aboard *Sarah II* and we used her a good deal in the year following Dorcas's death. We even went, as he had promised, to France, to Calais and Boulogne where he looked up some of the merchants who had supplied him with arms in his smuggling days. They, of course, had been doing nothing illegal, simply plying their trade so they had no reason to remember those transactions so many years ago. Yet Eddy seemed annoyed not to be recognised instantly. "God! Have I changed so much?" he demanded. I said, "Grown older," and felt a pang, for I had grown accustomed to his altered looks and now only thought of his health when his cough was unusually severe. The truth is one ceases to notice what is under one's nose every day. And Eddy's attitude almost forbade one to notice.

However, thus sharply reminded, I took stock and found no immediate cause for alarm. I had feared a chill after his plunging into Top Pool, and it had come, but it was slight. He seemed no worse afterwards. He still consumed quantities of food without gaining flesh and he still coughed; but he was lively and active and resolutely cheerful and, towards the end of the fourth year of our marriage, delighted to be twice recognised as a solid citizen. He was asked to be a member of a committee in charge of the building of the Assembly Rooms at Baildon; and elected as magistrate in the place of Sir Walter Fennel, whom gout had finally incapacitated. The latter office he refused. "It may sound ridiculous, Sarah but when you've once been on the wrong side of the law – as I was – impartial judgment is impossible."

In the early summer of 1664 the Assembly Rooms project received unexpected encouragement in the form of a bequest of a thousand pounds, a sum it would have taken years to accumulate little by little, and which caught the members of the Committee largely unprepared, since they had not even decided upon a site. Some favoured the centre of the town, on the far edge of the Market Place where some near derelict houses stood, others deemed this site insalubrious and noisy. There were several rather acrimonious meetings about this but the Market Square faction won; the site was cleared and an architect chosen. He was to submit his preliminary plans to the Committee at five o'clock on the third Wednesday of June.

"I shan't be late," Eddy said, preparing to leave immediately after dinner with a list of things to be bought, "but don't wait up. And I shan't want supper." I knew that, for there were always refreshments at such meetings, the members taking it in turns to provide them and vying with one another.

"Have you got your candy?" I asked. Eddy scowled as he always did when reminded of his cough. For him the one drawback of men's gatherings was that almost every man smoked, and the fumes provoked his cough. The candy was one of Marian's palliatives, sugar, honey, horehound and a little laudanum, bound with white of egg and baked into a meringue-like consistency.

The afternoon was hot and I attributed my lack of energy to this fact. Or getting old? my mind asked relentlessly. I had almost to force myself into the garden where the lavender was ripe for cutting and the roses just in the condition for the making of pot-pourri. In Marian's day I should have taken everything into the kitchen and we should have worked on the scented things together. As it was I put everything on the table in the hall. I missed Marian, I realised. I was, in fact, being thoroughly morbid that day – such a beautiful day, too, with the late cuckoos calling and the doves. Layer Pool; Top Pool; Dorcas . . .

Such melancholy, useless thoughts stemmed, I told myself, from too much of my own company. At first I had been pleased that Eddy should find interests outside Pargeters, but lately I had become conscious of loneliness. Well, the remedy was in my own hands; I must make more effort to be sociable, entertain more, and more willingly, accept every invitation, defy my innate shyness.

As I made these pious resolutions, I heard a horse, ridden hard and abruptly checked. I went to the door and there was one of the post-boys, leaning from the saddle to tug the bell. He was out of breath.

"Mrs Lacey?"

"Yes."

"Can you come? There's been an accident."

"What sort of accident?"

"Don't know. I just happened to be handy . . ."

Just inside the inn yard stood six other members of the Assembly Rooms Committee. Their stance and expressions told me all I needed to know. One of them broke away and as I dismounted, returned with Mrs Fiske, the landlord's wife who with a mixture of good-will and diffidence took my arm and said; "I am so sorry. We are all so sorry," and led me towards the rear of the house to a small room where, on a table Eddy lay, covered by a sheet.

I stood there, looking down. I could not cry or speak. I could see, and there was no sign of the fatal haemorrhage which I had feared for so long and so often, dreading it every time a coughing fit was unduly severe or over-prolonged. By the light of the one candle on a stand, Eddy's dead face looked calm. He could have been asleep.

Mrs Fiske, not designed by nature for anything but cheerful roles, said, "It was very quick. He didn't suffer."

I wanted to ask, "What happened?" but could only mouth the words. In the little dark room there was the smell of burning and here and there on the floor were bits of charred paper.

I was there; I could observe; but thought and feeling as well as speech were suspended. I was stunned.

Everybody was kind, expressing sympathy and telling me not to worry about anything. All would be seen to. Mrs Fiske took me upstairs at last and put me to bed, giving me brandy and a dose of some dark, bitter-flavoured sedative. When I woke Eddy's body had been coffined and placed in a newly-washed wagon in a cart-shed well away from the main building. Innkeepers were as reluctant to house a corpse as sailors were to ship one.

I had recovered my speech, though my voice seemed to come slowly and from a distance. Mrs Fiske was concerned about my solitariness. Had I no friend, was there no member of my household who could be fetched? I said, No; there was nobody; I should be all right. Finally she made a great effort and offered to accompany me herself. I thanked her and said it would be unnecessary. She was anxious for me to break my fast – but food seemed unnecessary, too.

I mustered enough force to ask what exactly had happened. Not that it mattered. However, whyever Eddy had died, he was dead. And when men were dead they were dead.

"I don't know exactly. I wasn't there. It seems some papers caught fire and blazed until beaten out. Nothing really, but the smoke was thick." Thick enough to suffocate a man whose lungs were diseased.

A man drove the wagon from the yard and the landlord himself came up with my horse. "You must let me know what I owe you," I said. He made a deprecatory gesture and began, "Thass all right, Mrs Lacey . . ." then remembered himself and said, "There was the carpenter. Night work, too."

Outside the inn I overtook the wagon. I said to the driver, "Do you know the way to Pargeters? It is just off the crossroads, by Minsham church."

"Born at Muchanger," he said.

"Then I'll go by the wood," I said and rode on.

I should really have been going through the village, rousing the Reverend Althorpe, telling him what I knew of

Eddy's end and letting him decide whether we needed the Coroner and his jury to say that the death was accidental. Then I should go home, tell everybody, find a black dress, cut flowers, gather candles, prepare for Eddy to lie in the hall, as Father had done, and Mother, and Grandfather and Marian.

But I did none of these things because at the sight of Eddy, lying dead, I'd died too, and dead women have no duties or obligations. No memories either. Nothing to regret and nothing to gloat over. I had done with it all. And never, since I was very young, had I felt so carefree, so completely unencumbered as I did that morning.

I dismounted, patted my horse's neck, then tapped her rump. I said, "Honey, go home. Home." She trotted off and I turned aside.

Top Pool. Black under its weedy green, bottomless, secretive, the gateway to oblivion, that most desirable of states.

Fool! To think of escape. Not to realise that a life sentence must be served to the end.

I was actually parting the reeds when something kicked me, not from without, from within. Only a woman who has borne a really lusty baby knows how one can kick. I clapped my hands to my side and waited. It came again and I knew. I stood there, counting back. Months of irregularity, of avoiding the forbidden subject, of take-no-notice, you ate something that disagreed, you overtired yourself, you are ageing and all middle-aged women are inclined to bulge. And all the time, ignored, un-rejoiced-over, the hidden life going on, awaiting this moment.

Slowly, I backed away from the reeds, found a fallen tree and sat down. Thoughts ran helter-skelter through my mind. Perhaps the bitterest of all was that Eddy would never know. Yet how could I be so sure? I had only Father's word for the assumption that when a man died he was dead and all that that implied, the universe a haphazard arrangement of material, man a mere plaything of chance. Because Father was so fundamentally good and honest, and because I had loved him, I had accepted his negative beliefs as unquestioningly as I accepted his knowledge of good farming. Now I could see that life had warped him. And Eddy, the other main influence in my life, had been warped, too. It was unfortunate that the only experience I had with believers had been with the Smiths, themselves twisted in another fashion. There was Katharine, of course, so quietly pious, so steadfast and so brave. Why hadn't I heeded her more?

Thinking, I realised at last, altered nothing. Facts must be faced. I could not condemn an unborn child to death; therefore I must live, bereft and lonely, simply managing as best I could, day by day.

I stood up, re-shouldered the burden of living and stepped out, quite briskly, towards Pargeters.